A Secret Life

Lee Carver

Published by Prism Book Group
ISBN- 9781940099736
Published in the United States of America
Contact info: contact@prismbookgroup.com
http://www.prismbookgroup.com

ENDORSEMENTS

"Through research and experience, Lee Carver knew the historical details and significance of her story. That made the read even more enjoyable. I love books that are authentic to the time period, and *A Secret Life* definitely is. Carver gave the story a unique twist I haven't read before in this time period. Some sections were hard to read, but we need to know the truth about what happened, so we won't forget and allow the same mistakes to be made. She created fictional characters who grabbed my heart and drew me into their lives. And they didn't let go until the very last page. The strength of the characters and story still haunt my thoughts. This is a book that shouldn't be missed by any reader of historical fiction." Lena Nelson Dooley, multiple award-winning author of *Maggie's Journey, Mary's Blessing,* and *Catherine's Pursuit*

"Lee Carver weaves a masterful story about staying true to one's core beliefs when the risks may result in loss of identity and death. *A Secret Life* explores duplicity as a way both to serve and to survive during World War II and its aftermath. A good read all around." Robin Sink McClelland, Unit Historian and Editor of the *Five-O-Sink*, newsletter of the 506th Parachute Infantry Regiment commanded in WWII by her father, Col. Robert F. Sink

"Lee Carver skillfully weaves history with fiction to create a smart, compassionate, and compelling family saga. Richly layered, complex characters make readers view World War II from balanced and rarely revealed perspectives. A Secret Life provides hours of entertainment." Bonnie Bartel Latino, former columnist for Stars and Stripes newspaper in Europe and co-author of the award-winning military love story, *Your Gift to Me*.

DEDICATION

To my husband Darrel, without whose vast knowledge of World War II I could not have written this book. All my research falls short of his profound understanding of the history, the people, the countries, the geography, and the vehicles and weapons of war.

More important to this novel, Darrel showed me that the love of a faithful man is a gift of God. Grace comes in many forms.

And to his father, Royce B. Carver, who penetrated the Siegfried Line at Aachen and marched through Germany until meeting the Russians at the Mulde River on May 3, 1945, two days before Darrel's birth. Thank God he lived to rear his son and daughter.

ACKNOWLEDGEMENTS

In 2010, my husband and I, with a few close friends, took a private tour organized by Keith and Robin Sink McClelland. The daughter of Col. Robert Sink, Regimental Commander of the 506th Parachute Infantry Regiment, Robin traced the path of her father's campaign from their parachute drop behind the lines at Normandy until the end of the war in Europe.

Royce Carver fought through much of the same countryside with the Timberwolf Division, the 401st Infantry, which made the tour personal. Never a student of history, I came to understand the European theater of World War II as never before. I am indebted to the McClellands for this world-expanding experience, and to my husband for insisting that I accompany him.

My gratitude also goes to Prism Book Group, its noble leader Joan Bauer Alley, and editor Susan Baganz. Thank you for bringing this drama to light.

To American Christian Fiction Writers and its ACFW-DFW Chapter known as Ready Writers, thank you for your support, education, and social networking. Every writer needs what you offer.

This love story is completely fictional against the reality of the war. The critique group that meets in the home of Lena Nelson Dooley, our teacher and mentor, soldiered with me in the writing of

A Secret Life. We slogged through the trenches together, supporting one another in our separate battles to represent truth in fiction.

AUTHOR'S NOTE:

While every attempt has been made to maintain an authentic link to events and dates of World War II in Europe, certain artistic license has been taken concerning prison activity in Dachau, Germany.

CHAPTER ONE

September, 1942
Munich, Germany

KARL KNEW BETTER than to raise his voice to Father, but his anger boiled within like steam under pressure. "Why did you leave Mother in danger? And Marta, too?" He paced the width of Father's study. "We're the same bloodline—"

"That's enough! How dare you question my care of the family?" Father stood from his desk, went to the dark velvet curtains, and yanked them closed. Little good that would do now.

Father's face flushed, creating headlights of his blue eyes. "Your mother and I have always been careful to maintain her dual citizenship and an active church membership. They have no reason to come after us."

With a huff, Karl dropped into the burgundy leather armchair and rubbed the back of his neck. He had said enough to get Father furious, yet he pressed further. "They could still book passage to the

United States. Or somewhere in the opposite direction. Brazil. Lots of people go to Brazil."

"That's ridiculous." Father slapped a dark green folder on his desk, probably the Swiss account. "Portugal, maybe." He muttered, slipping a hand over his retreating blond hair. "I've heard talk about Lisbon..."

So he had considered escape.

"But I can't leave the business here in Munich." Father's chest strained the worsted three-piece suit. "If I abandoned my responsibilities, the economy of the Fatherland and all our clients—some of them life-long friends—would suffer an unthinkable blow."

Only his father's hands touched their firm's securities and investments of the Reichland. No one else—*no one*—knew how much or where they were. Certainly not himself, as a junior officer of the firm. Father would be arrested and shot as a traitor if he tried to leave Germany now.

Karl shuddered. Since university graduation, he had little excuse for not serving in the Army. Worse, his native country had the power and the will to drag him into a labor camp. "But what about Mother and Marta? They don't have to stay. I could continue in the firm with you. Keep hoping they honor my deferment. With the British bombing farther south all the time, it just makes sense for them to leave."

His father paced the study, pausing before the medieval tapestry. He might be seeing its idyllic forest and mountain nymphs, or simply be using the weaving to ignore Karl's plea. "Your mother says she doesn't want to leave me. Our home." His voice became a rumble. "She's comfortable here. If the Allies lose the war, she will continue to be safe."

"And if they win?"

"She's an American citizen. Yourself and Marta too. She'd be the salvation of us all."

"But when both nations are at war, we have to choose. Especially me."

A rap from the hall cut them off. "Dinner's ready."

Karl opened the study's door to his mother's troubled face. Not wanting her to realize their closed-door conference concerned family safety, he forced a smile. "Come, Father. That account will wait until we've taken care of this beef roast."

EVEN WITH A satisfying meal and a bit of schnapps, sleep eluded Karl. War consumed the world. Internal conflict tore the fabric of the nation. Years ago, when the Nuremberg Laws first required Jews to wear bright yellow Stars of David stitched on black armbands, Mother just went inside and pretended she had nothing in common with those people. She had never attended a synagogue in Germany, never spoken Yiddish to a shopkeeper, never worn religious jewelry other than the elaborate gold cross his father gave her when they married. Maybe she would be safe.

And his sister? No young, beautiful woman remained secure where battle raged. Karl tossed in bed to throw off horrible images. Though her hair darkened with maturity, her laughter drew suitors like butterflies to an apple tree.

Ah, Marta, what will happen to you?

May, 1943
Munich, Germany

KARL EMERGED FROM the kitchen, buttered bread in hand. Four o'clock on a Saturday afternoon, and his father remained at the firm.

A knock came from the front door, as strong as if a bear demanded entry. "Herr von Steuben, *öfnen-sie.* Hauptmann Schmidt, SS, *hier.*"

His mother gasped, her eyes wide. Motioning for the housemaid to come, she clutched Karl by the shoulder and shoved. "Go upstairs."

"Why?" He spoke around the crunchy *brotchen.* "Who is Captain Schmidt?"

"The SS. Do as I say. Quickly." She jabbed the air toward the stairs.

The pounding came again.

His mother removed her shoes and ran up the steps behind Karl. "Where's your sister?"

"In her room, reading." She spent her days sprawled on her bed with a book. Her velvet prison allowed little else.

Karl listened from the upper hallway. The front door unlocked. The maid spoke a greeting. A growl responded. Heel-clicks of men entering their home echoed off the hardwood floor.

"What do they want, Mother?" he whispered close to her ear.

She put a finger across her lips and shook her head. Her trembling hands and the look of terror ignited his own fear.

He reached an arm around her shoulders, the instinct strong to protect her from a common enemy. His pulse pounded, banishing any thought of enjoying the bread and jam he still carried. His service to the nation through the investment company was arguable, making deferment of military inscription shakier every day the war continued. Father had all the power and held all the secrets.

The maid's footsteps sounded on the stairs. She appeared, one hand on the bannister and the other bunching her apron. "Frau von

Steuben, I told them your husband isn't here. They insist on speaking with you. What should I do?"

"I'll go. It's probably nothing." His mother's worried face belied her words. She pushed Karl toward the deep linen closet.

Heavy moments dragged by like the gigantic feet of monsters. He shoved the last bite into his mouth, now too dry to swallow. The crust scratched down his throat. He dared not cough. His imagination rampaged through dark corridors searching the rooms of his mind but found nothing to grab. He feared American bombs, yes, but also the German military. Munich had no secure corners.

Waiting in the closet, unable to tell what transpired below, he squeezed out prayer-thoughts. *Please don't let them take her. Don't let them come upstairs.* He still obeyed his mother. He hoped that meant hiding in a closet at her command wasn't cowardice.

He wanted to cruise down the stairway and confidently bluff his right to be here. The cost would be too great if he lost that gamble.

The heavy front door slammed, and her delicate steps on the old boards signaled her approach. She opened the closet, relief obvious in the slump of her shoulders.

"What was it, Mother? What did they want?" He emerged, squinting against the late sunlight piercing through lace curtains at the end of the hall.

"They wanted your father." She always reverted to English when frightened. "I don't know why they thought he would be taking Saturday off. I reminded them that he serves the war effort by keeping the firm going."

"What did they say about that?" he replied in English, but whispered. Normally, she had him speak German even at home, suppressing his mother-tongue.

"They laughed. Snarled, really. But don't worry. They won't draft him."

"Isn't he too old anyway?" Fifty-two candles on the cake lit his face three weeks ago. "They might be coming for me."

She sighed, the frown returning to her brow. "So many soldiers have died. Older men than your father and younger than you are pulled off the streets to fight."

They drifted toward his room, his haven. "Why didn't we leave when the war started? I don't understand why Father didn't move us before the passenger ships stopped."

She lifted her shoulders in a futile shrug, her eyelids squeezing tears onto her cheeks. Nothing hurt more than to see his mother in pain. She didn't deserve to be caught between two nations at war. His throat burned and the hard roll churned in his stomach.

"If Father left, the firm would collapse." Karl flopped at the simple study desk and propped sideways on its straight chair. The room had changed little during high school and university. Except for the briefcase on a side table, a twelve year old might still live here.

She sat on the foot of his bed, fumbling with a lace-edged handkerchief. "You must understand. Your father is accustomed to responsibility. And wealth. He couldn't imagine giving this up and starting over in America." She worked the muscles of her hands in a tense massage. "And then, well, there's the loyalty. He is German to the core, you know."

"But you and Marta could have moved to Grandma and Grandpa's house in Atlanta, couldn't you?" His mind conjured the cozy home, the hugs of welcome against Grandma's bosom, the Passover they celebrated there his twelfth year. He chose to overlook how they ranted because Mother and he had become Christian.

Her face clouded like a storm in the Black Forest. "The house has been sold since they died. We don't have a place to go anymore."

"But Mother…"

She shook her head. As she drew up her posture, he watched doors slam closed in her mind. "Don't question your father. He did what he thought best."

She rose from the bed then crossed to the doorway. With a half turn, she paused and looked back at him. "He is working on a plan. Transferring our funds. Trying to ensure that even if Germany falls, we won't lose everything."

Hope filled Karl's chest like a cool pool in summer. Father worked out plans, as expected of a shrewd investment counselor, but he shared few of those ideas with Karl. Ironic that he might have to be a full partner in the firm to discover his own family's funds. He nodded to his mother with the glimmer of a smile.

Strains of Viennese waltzes provided background music for Karl and Marta to arrange the blackout curtains that evening. Bombing raids, though infrequent, ranged this far south, so they performed the nightly ritual without question. Marta twirled from one window to the next, adding a strange dimension to a somber task.

Their father arrived after nine, not unusual lately. The family had waited for him, despite the allure of roasting meat and buttered carrots drifting from the kitchen.

A serious mood prevailed at dinner. Mother sat at the corner near his father, rather than at the far end of the long mahogany table. Eating by candlelight and Wagner, they spoke little except in appreciation of their greens, carrots, and potatoes.

"Father, Mother told you about the SS men who came this morning?" A lame way to open the conversation, but he needed a toe-hold.

"Of course, son." His father sawed a bite off the tough beef roast. They were fortunate to have meat at all.

"What did they want?" Father didn't make this easy.

"Don't worry about it. They needed to talk to me." His gaze fixed on the silver candlestick centered on hand-worked lace halfway down the table.

Karl leaned forward, unwilling to be brushed off. "Excuse me, sir, but I do need to know what's going on."

His father paused chewing to level a warning glare at Karl.

"Father, is it me? Were they coming to draft me?" His voice scratched around the lump in his throat.

His father sipped from a cut crystal wine glass and inhaled deeply as he relaxed against the carved chair back. "No, son. It isn't you, though if you don't stay out of the public eye, they might grab you."

"Then…why did they come?" He treaded touchy ground here. Improper questions wouldn't be tolerated. "Please don't keep me in the dark. I'm an adult professional. I should be aware of any threats to the family."

Karl expected rebuke. A storm of emotions played on Father's face, and then his stern expression melted.

"Son, they came to *request* that I *accept* civil patrol duties in our neighborhood." He paused for another taste of wine. "They reminded me your mother is American, and my loyalty to the homeland must never be in question." He reached for his wife's hand, and his eyes captured hers for a charged moment.

She looked down, but held on tightly.

"Do they know...uh...about her parents' religion?" This last he whispered, as if the walls hadn't already heard the secrets they enclosed.

His bushy eyebrows gathered in a severe line. "No. And they must not know."

May, 1943
Atlanta, Georgia

GRACE SHORE FILED into the memorial service with Matthew's parents. At the front of the sanctuary, where a casket might have been, an American flag hung from a pole topped by a decorative golden eagle. The absence of Matthew's body made the scene surreal. The sole evidences of his death were the words of two uniformed men in an olive drab car and General Eisenhower's letter of condolence they left with the Grangers.

No one prayed harder. Surely God understood the Grangers needed their only son, and she needed the man she had loved since tenth grade. She dug for another tissue but had saturated them all.

She tried to shut out the organ's gentle hymns and the tenor's solo. Intended for comfort, instead they rent her heart.

The pastor's homily began with Matthew's birth and a kindergarten incident that indicated his brilliance...

She would never bear his children. Never be Grace Granger. The life she dreamed of dissipated like the fragrance of a magnolia bloom browning in the Georgia sun. They would meet again in heaven, little consolation for a woman planning a wedding.

She must sit up straight. Consider the loss to his parents. Her crying made the service even harder for them. Her thoughts meandered to what might come next. Not working would kill her.

She had to return to nursing duties and stay involved with her patients.

Her eyes fell to her clasped hands and her mocking bare ring finger. Money for Matt's medical school took a higher priority than an engagement diamond. She missed her chance. She would never love again like she had loved him.

So close to marriage and family, she longed for independence. To do things the way she wanted. Gain freedom from her parents' watchful eyes, their well-intentioned rules.

"Matthew Granger served admirably to save us all from the world domination of an evil tyrant." Words of the sermon sometimes connected with her pounding head. Something about Rommel's Afrika Korps. Matt's death in a scorching, dry land made no sense to her in springtime Atlanta. Did he die thirsty? With his last breath, did he call for a cup of water?

"God mourns with us," the pastor said.

Then He should stop this madness. How many men would fall before good triumphed? Where was the God of mercy now?

CHAPTER TWO

May, 1944
Munich, Germany

THE ANGUISHED VOICE of Helga, the cook, reached Karl as he read the financial pages in the living room. She argued with Mother. Unimaginable. He folded the newspaper and sauntered, curious and hungry, to the cold kitchen. By now, he expected a fragrant goulash simmering on the stove, or a chicken baking in the oven. Instead, angry words and yesterday's bread met him.

Helga threw a fistful of Deutsche Marks onto the weathered work table. "They're worthless. There's nothing to buy." She wiped her reddened face with a coarse cloth, her swollen eyes squeezed tight. "People stand in the lines, some of them shouting and shaking their fists. Children hungry, begging even. For hours I can get nothing, and then maybe…nothing is left."

His mother's hands, propped on her slender hips, slid from their insistent posture to hang limp at her sides.

Karl's glance passed over wood cabinets polished by thousands of washings for four generations. They bore neither a carrot nor a crumb.

Saturday, his day off from the family firm, he caught up on the financial pages of the *Munchener Merkur*. The crucial need for food now took a higher priority. "I'll go, Mother. Give me the money. I'll find something."

The cook whipped around to him with a frying glare. "You think you can do better? You think your nice clothes will get you closer in the line? Humpf. What do you know about buying food?"

"I'll buy whatever I find."

"There's nothing to buy, I tell you. This city is starving." Helga again wiped sweat and tears. "I've decided. I'm going to my brother's farm in the country." Her voice softened to a murmur. "He will have something. It's spring. Soon the garden will be making." She paused and rocked her weight sideways, eyes downcast. "You want to come with?"

Mother's eyes filled with tears. "No. Thank you for offering." Always the lady, her manners impeccable. "We'll stay in town. I'm sure my husband will devise a plan."

The plan was to leave. Karl had seen the leather suitcases brought out of the attic. They should have left years ago. Father's reasoning wore thin that Mother's lineage could not be traced. He said that what people didn't know couldn't be used against them. As if immune to this stupid anti-Semitism, he thought he could protect Mother.

Karl gathered the coins and crumpled bills. "Don't worry, Mother. I can go farther and return with a heavy market bag. Walking is too hard for Helga."

"I should go, dear." Her lips quivered and she pulled an embroidered handkerchief from her pocket. "It's dangerous for you to leave the house."

"More so than for you?" He didn't think his mother "looked Jewish," whatever that meant, but suspicious townspeople turned in their neighbors every day. For that matter, she had given him and Marta her brown eyes and thick hair, dominating Father's elite, blond features.

"Yes, much more dangerous for you. Since that awful carnage at Normandy, the Army is conscripting every man they can snatch."

"They won't draft me. My deferment, remember?"

She touched his shoulder and searched his face. "You're not safe. I can't let you take the risk." He had seen that look often as the grip of the SS tightened. "Besides, your father is still out with the car. You'd have to walk."

"You know he'll stay in his office until dark. He prefers to handle certain portfolios when no one else is in the building. I can walk."

He hadn't convinced Mother. Before she could kiss his cheek, he grabbed the bag and dashed out the side door.

KARL STRUCK OUT for yet another green grocer or meat market. So the cook was correct about all the nearby ones. There used to be a fresh market a kilometer away. Probably down Kugelstrasse. He turned right and picked up his pace.

Shopkeepers told him the way, begrudging more than volunteering information. Queuing on the cobblestone sidewalk, he realized how much his awareness of Germany's condition had changed this morning. Instead of the deference he had come to expect, citizens who didn't want to share the food remaining in the city growled at him. His family's money and profession mattered little to those who had no money, no provisions, and certainly no investments.

The roar of two German Army trucks startled Karl from his thoughts. They pulled in front of the store, bracing the customers right and left. Soldiers waved their Mauser 98 rifles and dismounted from the cabs and canvas-covered backs before the tires stopped rolling.

There goes the food. He stepped out of line, the urgency to escape spiking his heart rate. These men were dangerous.

"*Halt!* Get back here. Where do you think you're going?"

A soldier with several stripes on his uniform grabbed Karl's shoulder and shoved him toward the end of one of the trucks.

"Show me your *Ausweispapier.*"

Karl handed over his ID paper. The fellow glanced once and slammed it on the clipboard of the other soldier. That man copied the details then pushed Karl against the truck.

Stumbling, he braced on the high floor and found men staring out from benches along the inside walls. The reality of forced conscription stabbed his lungs. They would take him away without a word to his family and send him off to die in a war against his mother's people and his father's politics.

"Wait. I have a deferment. Von Steuben Investments manages Reichland funds—"

The kick half-missed its target as Karl turned to explain, to beg, whatever necessary to return home with or without food. His rear end throbbed with pain.

The soldier's laugh broke from a crack in hell. "Yeah, and my son's a lawyer but he's serving. Get in. Now."

An arm jerked him upward off the street, yanking his shoulder joint hard. Dangling, he scrambled for a foothold, scraping his shins on a metal edge, until he fell into the truck on his stomach at the boots of another soldier. His rifle barrel motioned for Karl to sit with the others. Its bore, aimed at his head, killed any idea of escape.

A man, fifty or sixty years old, climbed up at gunpoint.

"That's all. Let's go." The soldiers with the uniform stripes swung into the truck as it lurched.

Shadowed occupants around Karl had to be too young, too old, or too sickly to fight, while his own prime condition made him a sure target. But nabbing him off the street was wrong, just plain wrong.

The older man stared out the back with haunted eyes, his mouth open as if in a silent scream. He slapped a hand over his heart, showing a thin wedding band. A family man. With him gone, they might not have food either.

A boy too young to shave sobbed, tears and slobber running down his face.

Karl held back the sting in his eyes, blinking hard.

I. Will. Not. Cry.

He gripped the bare wooden bench as the streets of Munich passed beyond the truck's open back. Bumping over the rough cobblestones, his bruised rear took further beating. Three times the truck stopped to nab more men and boys. Three times his heart pounded with the challenge to make a dash for it, but the guard assumed a strong stance with his Mauser assault rifle at the ready and a dare in his eye.

Would they tell his family? Could his father find out where they took him and appeal his abduction? Most of all, he hurt for Mother, who would wring her hands and walk the floor crying. He had thought himself impervious to conscription.

Hours later, the captive recruits passed through a security checkpoint and into a barebones camp. Was this a prison camp? Had they found out about Mother?

Shouting orders and waving rifles, soldiers shaped the men into lines and marched them into wooden rooms where others took their information.

"Name?"

"Karl von Steuben." He wanted to say he was a financial advisor, something to indicate his importance, but that might be dangerous. Already conspicuous in this ragged crowd, flaunting his status held no advantage. They would find out soon enough, and feathers would fly. They were going to be in so much trouble.

At the bottom of the "application," a line required Karl's signature affirming he had volunteered to serve in the Army.

"But I do not wish to volunteer in this manner. My service is needed in Munich as a—"

From his side came a fist across his mouth, knocking his head so hard his neck popped. "Sign it." The soldier, twice Karl's size, glared at him with a hand cocked for another blow.

Karl touched his split lip and diverted his eyes. He knew better than to look directly at a mad dog. He signed the page and was shoved toward an open room with rows of showers streaming from the ceiling.

"Strip and walk through the shower. Soap's gone."

Raucous, naked men whooped and hollered under the frigid water, running and slipping on the concrete floor. Karl laughed despite himself and ducked under the icy spray. Tenderly rinsing his bloody mouth, he crossed the space without falling and reached for a towel. Wet. Used by other men. Never in his life had he been forced to dry off after someone else. His muscles convulsed in the cold.

Two soldiers stacked pants, shirts, and underwear on a rough counter.

"Grab a uniform. Smallest are on the far end. Shoes and socks in the next room."

He wasn't going to get back his own handmade shoes? They were the finest leather. He paid a lot for them. He willed his tone not to show his annoyance and caught the eye of the soldier. "May I please have my shoes back? They fit me well, and I'd like to—"

"Keep moving. They're already gone."

The other soldier sneered. "If they're any good at all, the sergeant's got them."

Karl pulled over his goose-bumped body a washed but stained uniform, pants and sleeves long enough for his height. With foreboding he noticed a patched hole over the shirt's left chest.

Sure enough, he saw no footwear of decent quality in the open racks. Recruits sat on every bench trying on different types and sizes. Karl spotted a large pair. He stood in them, wriggled his toes, and took a few steps. These would do. He smiled, imagining the disdain of Herr Lange, the shoemaker.

A whistle pierced the commotion. "Hurry up. Line up outside. *Schnell-schnell-schnell!*" The fellow might be a junior officer, but Karl didn't know. With no military background in his family, he couldn't even read the stripes on a soldier's arm.

He copied the posture of others at attention in the yard, waiting for more to join them.

Rigid, moving nothing but the cogwheels of his mind, he had a few moments to review his personal insertion into history. Even in a country ravaged by the Great War, Karl knew war not as a military experience but as an economic concept. His father and grandfather taught him how to survive financially, guard and hide funds, and how to invest so as to profit during a war.

Karl shot well enough on a hunt. He had participated in the damage a gun inflicted on a deer or fox, but could not imagine hunting down and killing a human. His father simply had to stop this madness before it went any further.

When about fifty men were assembled, an officer gave a congratulatory speech. His words would have been more appropriate for zealous military graduates who had been selected from among thousands for the honor of serving in the German Army. At the conclusion, they recited a commissioning pledge and raised a straight-armed salute with the joint cheer, *"Heil, Hitler."*

Karl had sworn loyalty and obedience to the man who sought to eradicate his mother's—in fact, his own—race. Furthermore, he had invalidated his dual citizenship and now became guilty of desertion if he escaped. He was a liar, a deceiver, and a coward for not standing forth and declaring himself an American citizen and sympathizer.

And a Jew.

May, 1944
Atlanta, Georgia

HER MOTHER'S INSISTENT pounding on her bedroom door startled Grace. "Yes?" Her groggy word triggered a cough.

Her mother peeked in. "Are you all right?"

"Sure. I just fell asleep. Didn't mean to. Wanted to rest a minute until dinner." She gave an exaggerated stretch, hoping Mom wouldn't act so worried.

"I knocked and knocked—"

"Sorry. The sound got mixed in with my dream about bombs."

"Bombs?"

"In Tunisia." The recurring dream of Matthew's death.

The pain transferred to her mother's eyes. "The pastor's wife is on the phone. She asked to speak to you."

"What does Sally Ann want?" She knew, though. She dragged herself off the bed and reached for her brush. "Can't you tell her I'm too tired to help with that Friday night meeting after a hard week at the hospital?"

"She needs you, honey, and I think you ought to be with other young people."

Grace stopped brushing her hair and leveled a flat glare at her mother. "There aren't that many men who come, and I'm not interested in any of them. Please stop…trying to marry me off to whoever didn't get killed yet."

Her mother might have gotten angry at her disrespect, but instead tears glistened behind her bifocals.

"I'm sorry, Mom. Usually only about three fellows are there, and the girls smother them with attention. Hank is recovering from battle wounds and the other two are 4-F. For lots of reasons." She rolled her eyes.

"Now who's considering their eligibility as husbands?" She gave a teasing smile. "Some who aren't physically fit for battle would still make good family men."

She hated arguing with her mother, especially when Mom was right.

"Sally Ann's waiting, hon."

The sincere request for more help in the kitchen drew Grace back to the church. Her agreement had nothing to do with Sally Ann's inside information that a returning soldier named Johnny Johnson would be there.

With women at the event hanging on his every word, Grace didn't meet Johnny until she dished up spaghetti on his plate. By that time, she had clothed herself in a better mood as an act of will.

Sally Ann pushed her out of the kitchen as the singing began. "Get out there. We'll wash up. You need some social time."

Johnny sang poorly or didn't even try. He did look her way sometimes with a nice smile, but Grace didn't care to compete with his adoring lovlies.

To her surprise, he broke loose after the closing prayer and followed her to the kitchen. "Say, are you free tomorrow night? There's a new Bing Crosby movie out."

"*Going My Way?*" She hadn't had a date since Matthew left and responded out of pure-dee selfishness. "Yes, I'd like to see it."

BING CROSBY AS an Irish priest with problems in his congregation took her mind off the reality of war. Johnny even bought popcorn. But when he tried to corner her into a kiss later on the front steps of her home, she backed into the door and ducked her head.

"Whatsa matter? Didn't you have a good time?"

"Yes, of course. I enjoyed the evening. I just don't kiss on the first date."

"Why not? If we like each other, I mean, and want to go out again…"

Not sure she would ever agree to another date with Johnny, she had nothing to lose by pushing him away. She had let him hold her hand by the end of the movie, but she felt crowded like a puppy in too small a cage. He never missed a chance to touch her arm, her shoulder, once even her thigh.

His major fault was not being Matthew.

CHAPTER THREE

May, 1944
North German Countryside

TRANSPORTED IN TRUCKS to various camps, Karl dozed when he could. Sometimes he and the other new privates marched overland. Scrambled like tiles of a board game, in fatigue and confusion, he hardly knew his current location and didn't know where he'd been. His father would never be able to find him.

On the edge of sleep on yet another canvas cot, Karl understood. He would not be rescued. His eyes sprang open in the night. A roar came to his ears and pressure mounted in his skull. If he had been standing, he'd have fainted. Father wasn't coming.

Karl prayed more fervently, more sincerely than ever before in his life. *Father God, when I die, I will be with You. I fear pain and battle, but I do not fear death. Take me if You will, for I do not wish to fight against the Americans.*

When that prayer met deafening silence, depression overwhelmed him blacker than death.

If he protested, he would be called before the troops and summarily shot. He rationalized he held greater value for the Jewish people from within the German Army than as a martyr. But he didn't know if God answered the pleas of a liar.

Only mind-numbing training cleared the dark clouds in his head. He became inured to the rigors of marching uncounted kilometers carrying heavy equipment. He learned hand-to-hand combat, to disassemble and clean his rifle and to shoot blanks.

Soon it would be his turn to go to the front lines. His unit moved to a farm close to the village of Alsfeld, northeast of Frankfurt, called Schultz Post. Not far from areas the British bombed nightly, he might die at any moment.

His company marched back to the stone farmhouse, barn, and outlying buildings. Cots for a hundred men spread in every available area, including those previously inhabited by sheep and cattle. The few remaining animals seemed indignant at being pushed out. He imagined the owners' reaction to having their property taken over. No Schultzes remained at Schultz Post.

Army vehicles hid under shelters and camouflage, obscured from the cameras of enemy scout planes. Senior officers and sergeants lived and had their offices in the main house, and a smaller dwelling nearby held the kitchen and dining area.

Bone-tired, wet from a cold drizzle, Karl trudged in boots heavy with mud. His sergeant called the company to attention, berated them for being born, and dismissed them for lunch. His hunger gnawed so hard the smell of meager bean soup rations lured him to the dining house. As he bent to scrape his shoes, someone called his name.

He stood and whipped around toward the sound. "Private von Steuben here, sir."

"Report to the Commandant's office."

Ice ran down his backbone. He had been careful to obey every order and tried to keep up with the best of these farm boys until faint with fatigue. *Has Father found me? Or do they know about Mother?*

He scraped his combat boots and trod to the main house, praying all the way.

Saluting, he repeated his rate and name.

A slender, dark-haired officer waited in the front room with papers in hand. His patch read *Müller*. Karl thought he was a major, but still needed that lesson. "Private von Steuben, the induction forms you filled out indicate that your mother is American."

The blood in his head drained to his dirty feet. "Dual citizenship, sir. She was born in Atlanta, but has lived in Munich since before my birth." He had to appear calm. He inhaled and held his breath to stay at attention like an inflated balloon.

"Do you speak English?"

"Yes, sir."

"Can you read English, too?"

"Yes, sir." This sounded less threatening. He dared to breathe.

"What does this say?" The officer handed over wrinkled papers with rain-smeared ink.

Karl accepted the pages with shaking hands. He moved under the ceiling light. "It's a letter, sir. Something personal. From some guy...named Joe...to his girlfriend, or wife."

The sergeant nodded. "Major Müller and I assumed it's supposed to look like normal correspondence, but it could be coded or disguised. See there on the second page he writes something about *Feldmarschall* Göring? What's that part?"

Karl flipped the page, scanning the scratchy handwriting for the words "Field Marshal Goering," as a Brit or Yankee would write it. "Here it is, sir: 'I shot down one of Goering's planes last week. That will teach them to mess with us.' Nothing specific, sir. Nothing good for intelligence."

"Do you type, private?"

"Not well, sir. But yes, sir, I can type." Enough to do endless financial studies and term papers in the university.

"Have a seat here." Müller motioned to a chair before a simple desk dominated by a black, heavy-looking typewriter. "Translate the letter to your best ability, and watch out for double meanings and code phrases."

Although relieved not to be shot or sent to a Jewish labor camp, it troubled him to be thrust into a position of aiding the German war effort. Pulling out the chair, he paused to consider the actual paper and form of the letter. "May I ask, sir, how this was obtained?"

The officer's brow gathered in a scowl. "None of your business. Just do the job."

"Yes, sir. But it might help in the translation if I knew what this purports to be." Karl sat with his most business-like manner, hoping his obedience wouldn't be questioned.

"We got it off the body of an English pilot, not that it matters to you." The officer stepped to an adjoining room.

Karl rolled a blank paper into the typewriter and spread the first page of the letter to his right. The soldier's message to his "sweetheart" hinted at the importance and success of his bombing runs, but gave away no useful information.

He finished in less than ten minutes, despite jamming keys and tedious erasure of typos. He had not used a typewriter since graduating two years ago. Even as an assistant in his father's firm, he relied on a corps of pretty, young typists. Karl smiled at the memory as he pulled the finished product from the roller.

WHY ARE SMELLS more intense in the dark? Karl's dirty sheets had absorbed the mustiness and mold of a century of cattle in the barn. Soldiers swept the floor every day, but never created the fragrance of wax on hardwood. If he lived, his highest hope was to return to a normal life in a clean and comfortable place.

In the brief moments before sleep overtook him, his gut reaction to the translating job condensed to a solid reality: he had aided the enemy. His homeland, Germany, had strained his sympathies to the breaking point. He no longer doubted the rumors that Jews were being systematically isolated, starved, imprisoned, and killed. The Fatherland would do the same to him if his secret were known.

THE COMMAND TO translate letters or odd bits of paper occurred frequently over the following weeks. Once he had to wait for another enlisted man to finish at the typewriter, and then the major handed him the page to render into German. His lieutenant checked one against the other. He may have even arranged the accidental overlap as a warning—translate correctly or else.

Karl had seen enough to understand what would happen. A "volunteer" like himself, a soldier named Hans had been jerked out of the line and taken for questioning. Whatever he had done or not done, he suffered for it. Hans was kept in a room reserved for interrogation day and night until the troops heard his moans escape through its walls.

Soldiers dragged the barest semblance of the man before the whole company standing at attention on the farm road beside the main house. Held up by men on each side, he slobbered and cried.

Karl's pulse jumped until pain built at his temple. He didn't want to see this. He didn't want to know what was going to happen to Hans. Impending horror churned his stomach and caused his breath to come in shallow jerks.

The strong voice of the major pierced the cold, gray morning. "The Fatherland deserves absolute honesty and loyalty. Nothing else is acceptable. Is there anyone here who doubts the truth of this requirement?"

A company of men had never been so silent.

Hans's two bracing soldiers left him to stand alone. The major pulled his sidearm and shot Hans through the temple. "*Heil* Hitler!"

"*Heil* Hitler" came the company's instant reply. Somewhere in the ranks a couple of men wretched into the mud.

"Dismissed."

His old university psychology prof could have made a field study of nervous reactions from this unit. They walked on shaky legs, pretending to be tough, but they exhibited every expression of discomfort from silly laughter to silent tears. Karl's eyes met those of a friend of Hans, and he attempted to flash an unspoken message of sympathy. The fellow turned away, white-faced and trembling.

CHAPTER FOUR

May, 1944
Munich, Germany

DIETRICH VON STEUBEN parked his car in the garage, still preoccupied with the concerns of his private investment clients. The enormous aggregate of funds he managed for the Reich troubled him most of all. Should he hedge by moving some to Argentina? Argentina's president, Juan Peron, sympathized with Hitler and supported the Axis Powers by exporting raw materials to Germany. Switzerland, the historical safe haven for money and securities, had the advantage of geographical proximity.

Better to leave the funds in Switzerland and Portugal for now.

He closed the double doors, smiling at the squeaky hinges that would alert the dog to his coming. Karl and Marta had long matured past the point of running to meet him after a day's work, but Tilli rushed him at the front door.

He entered, put down his leather satchel, and received his pet's enthusiastic affection. He scratched the shepherd behind the ears and smoothed her thick fur. When he saw Anna's face, puffed and red from crying, he pushed Tilli aside and went to his wife, extending his arms wide.

"*Meine liebchen*, my sweetheart, what's wrong? What has happened?"

She buried her head against him and sobbed. "Karl. He didn't come back."

"What? Didn't come back from where?" Karl remained inside nowadays either at the firm or home. His friends being in the Army or, sadly, in their graves, he had no more Saturdays playing soccer nor weekend parties and pub nights.

Marta descended the stairway sniffling, her dark eyes sunken and puffy. "Thank heaven you're home, Papa. What are you going to do?"

Anna pulled away, her lips contorted in grief. "He went to find food. I told him not to go, but we had nothing in the house for supper. And he never came back. Oh, Dietrich, have we lost our son?" Her moan ripped his presence of mind to shreds.

The breath left him, and his heart turned to ice. His son. Their only son. "Where did he go?"

"I don't know. To buy food. Anything. I've called everyone with a phone. No one has seen him." The two of them held each other. When he became aware of Marta standing close, he tucked her under his arm.

But maybe the women's fears were needless. Karl had deferment papers which he kept with his ID at all times. "Come, Anna, let's get in the car and search for him. He probably got tired carrying home the food and stopped at Ernst's house—"

"Ernst was sent to Italy, remember?" His wool suit coat muffled Marta's voice.

"Then at Johan's—"

Anna pulled a breath across her sobs. "How could you forget? He was the first friend Karl lost."

"Never mind. Marta, stay with Helga—"

"But Papa, Helga left. She quit today. Please let me go with you. I don't want to remain here by myself." Marta clutched his arm, imploring him not to leave her.

"Okay, but keep low in the back seat." Nothing good happened to women in wartime.

Together they cruised the streets without headlights. Anna directed him to all the grocers and small markets, closed now as darkness settled over the city. He strained his eyes until they hurt with dryness, but no one walked the cobblestones at this hour.

The last possibility, a greengrocery kilometers away on Kugelstrasse, had a faint light behind the black curtains above the store. Dietrich climbed the stairs to the side of the building and knocked on the door, hoping the grocer lived there.

He waited. Quiet inside. Too quiet. He pounded hard, taking out his frustration on the weathered wood.

He heard shuffling steps. A man grumbled from inside. "Who is there?"

"Dietrich von Steuben." Not that his name would mean anything to a grocer. "I've come to ask you something. Please, just speak with me."

"I cannot give you anything. I have nothing more to sell." But he didn't walk away, either.

"Have you seen my son? He came today searching for food to buy, and he didn't come home."

The door creaked a slit apart, then a bit wider, revealing a few centimeters of the whiskered face of a tired, old man. "They took some men. One too old, one too young, and another, a young man in good clothes."

"Who? Who took my son?" Dietrich's voice broke, desperation scratching his throat and eyes.

"The Army. They had guns, uniforms, two canvas-covered trucks." He opened the space between them another few centimeters. "It's the next layer of draftees. Didn't you read in the paper? Since the invasion at Normandy, they need more men on the front."

The grocer seemed to move and blur through Dietrich's tears, shades of gray and shadow becoming indistinct. "Yes, I read about it, but...I didn't think they'd take...my son. Where did they take him?"

The man shook his head. "I know nothing more. My sons, they're already in the Army. I don't know where the draftee processing center is."

The two fathers stood for a moment, communicating their immense sadness without words. United by fear, they could not speak of so great a loss.

Dietrich nodded. "Thanks." He plodded down the steps to his waiting wife and daughter, who looked expectantly to him.

"The Army took him. There's nothing more I can do tonight."

"But Papa—"

"We must return home. If bombers came tonight, we would be...it would be very bad."

June, 1944
Schultz Post

KARL STARED AT the blank page of lined paper. "Dear Mother, Father, and Marta..." He couldn't tell them his location. He couldn't tell them his company had orders to move out to an active war zone. And he didn't want to indicate what he did for the enemy.

At significant crossroads in his life, he had made decisions by listing attributes in left and right columns of a page. Like when he decided whether he was being pushed into his family's business or actually wanted that career, and to which university he intended to apply.

What he needed to determine now couldn't be written down because any quandary would get him shot. Or worse. So he worked the process in his mind.

What did he really know of America? He had been to Atlanta as a baby and again as a twelve year old, at his American grandparents' insistence. The birthday which would have been his bar mitzvah year, they grilled him about his beliefs.

The family religious conflict had been hard on his mother. She cried a lot. Everyone talked too much and waved their hands in the air as if stirring up reasons for their theologies as connected yet diverse as co-joined twins. He remembered most the drama and emotional pain. Until then, he had wondered if Mother had only adopted Christianity to please Father. But it was real. She believed in Jesus with such a strength and conviction that her relationship with God intensified after the trip. He saw his mother's life more clearly as a journey of faith.

Eight-year-old Marta followed them to her own confirmation. They had united as a Christian family.

Okay, back to the list. America allows religious freedom. His Jewish grandparents had been respected and successful, the owners of a shoe store well patronized by Atlantans.

America fosters economic and educational choice to a degree not available in Europe. College was available to anyone, Mother said. Men didn't have to follow their father's tracks, whether in farming or business.

Leaving Germany meant walking away from economic security and a ready-made career, assuming the possibility still existed after the war. He had decided long ago he earnestly wanted to pick up the reins of his father, grandfather, and great-grandfather. The rare combination of academics and risk, financial counseling and management enervated him. He woke up every day ready to go to work.

Beyond the matters of wealth, prestige, and professional education and position lay the one true reason to be American. Himself, here and now. Because loyalty to Germany equaled loyalty to Hitler, a megalomaniac who wanted him dead. Who would starve, torture, and kill his family for being Jews, and put Father in a labor camp as Jewish sympathizer. At stake were his own life and death.

But even if he had a chance to desert, how could he leave Mother and Marta?

Late July, 1944
Schultz Post near Alsfeld

"WAKE UP, KARL. Now. Come quick." The sergeant shook Karl's shoulder and spoke with an urgent whisper.

Karl's heartbeat fired up from resting to racing. Snatched from his dream, already bad enough, he woke to a flashlight in his eyes and some unknown emergency.

He recognized his sergeant, threw back the sand-paper-wool blanket, and rolled off his sagging cot.

"We need you to translate something. Just pull on your pants. Major Müller says get over there now."

Report to the major without brushing his hair or his teeth? In the middle of the night? He dared not imagine why. He stumbled over his tall, hob-nailed boots, then he slipped them on and grabbed his coat.

"Run. Now."

Karl followed the man out of the barn, across the gravel road to the Major's office. The sergeant opened the door without knocking. Karl tripped over the facing and stumbled into the room. Hunched over a large VHF radio on the desk were Major Müller, a captain, and another fellow who did some translating like himself. The major motioned hard, as if he could pull him through the clouds of smoke.

"What are they saying?"

Only silence came from the machine no matter how he stared at it. "Who is it, sir?" He whispered to keep from missing anything coming off the radio.

"Pilots. British, probably. Americans bomb in the daytime. They've gone silent again." The major hushed his reply. "For a moment they were talking, but he couldn't understand." He motioned to the other enlisted translator, name-tagged Richter.

"British. Lots of jargon. Maybe code words, I don't know." The red-faced fellow sweated in the cool room. "Then someone said, 'Shut up, you idiot. Maintain radio silence.' No one has spoken since."

[33]

Karl nodded, trying to show partnership with the guy under pressure, having experienced the same thing. "Where are they?"

"Within a hundred and sixty kilometers." The captain stubbed out his cigarette and reached for another. "That's the maximum range of VHF."

Words burst from the radio. Karl and Richter grabbed pencils and leaned close. "I'm hit!"

Easy to understand. Both scribbled on their notepads. They waited with shallow breaths though the VHF came through clear, static free.

"Did you get the target markers down?" A different voice, raw with urgency.

"American, not British." Karl whispered, not wanting to embarrass Richter, who blushed and nodded.

"Dog One, did you mark the target?" Louder, tense as a tow rope.

"Kausuntris. Nothing but Kausuntris."

Karl wrote what he thought he heard, and waved his arm toward the officers. "Give me a map. Where's this town?"

The sergeant rushed to a wooden cabinet of shallow drawers and rifled through maps until he pulled out a large sheet and crumpled it onto the little space left on the desk. "Light. We need that lamp." The major jerked out its cord and replanted it over the map.

The two translators knocked heads as their fingers searched over the features in many colors. "Kühlungsborn…Lützow…"

"Those aren't significant targets." The major huffed and bent over the map. "The bombers come in straight lines from England. The leader drops a marker bomb, and the planes behind navigate from there and spread out to their assigned targets. We have to know the focal point."

Richter muttered names and searched, his little brown eyes bugging and then blinking. "Klötze? Kalbe?"

"Too far south. I don't see anything like Kausunt..."

Karl looked away. "Kausuntris, nothing but Kausuntris." The heat of a blush rose to his cheeks. He ducked his head.

"What's the matter, private?" The major had caught his reaction.

"Not Kausuntris, sir. 'Cows and trees, nothing but cows and trees.' *Kühe und Baumen*. The flight leader didn't drop his marker bomb on the target city. He was hit and went down bombing nothing but cows and trees."

The hardened eyes of the major squinted. Karl didn't breathe. No one so much as drew on his cigarette.

The captain broke into laughter first, then the room rocked with belly laughs. Richter blushed and laughed with the others.

The airwaves went silent again, no matter how they searched the frequencies for more chatter. As dawn broke, Major Müller ended the session with a suggestion that they all go for breakfast. "Von Steuben, Richter, grab a bite and then sleep it off. Meet us back here tonight at sixteen hundred hours. You have a new job."

Conflicting emotions hit Karl at the same instant. Relief that he didn't have to march for hours under a heavy pack, and shame for using his mother tongue to aid the Fatherland.

June, 1944
Atlanta, Georgia

GRACE BORE ANOTHER soldier's memorial service only by achieving a detached mental state. If this were not the brother of her sister-in-law, she would never have come. Killed in the D Day invasion on the beaches of Normandy, he deserved every accolade, every praise for his bravery. How could thousands of young men charge as German guns raked the sand and the best and finest fell?

Paul's homily filled the air around her but did not touch her lest it scorch and render her useless to heal those in her care.

When the news came of Paul's death, she argued with Daddy about going to England to work in a military hospital. A chance to see the world, to serve in the battle.

"A chance to die crossing the ocean, that's what you're considering." He flushed so red she worried about his blood pressure.

She tired of double days, working weekends, and broken bodies. The dream of marriage and children receded like distant mountains hidden by haze. The inkling of indomitable spirit nudging from behind her lungs urged her to find a new dream. Finish a B.S. in nursing, become a head nurse, and move into her own apartment. Live alone, but live.

CHAPTER FIVE

July, 1944
Munich, Germany

ANNA HEARD HER daughter shove the heavy front door closed then hurry on the entry flooring.

"Mother! It's a letter!" Marta shouted through the house. "A letter from Karl."

Anna rose from her bed, gathered her robe about her, and came to the upstairs bannister. Below, Marta waved an envelope high, her pretty face the image of delight.

Anna flew down the stairs, her toes kissing each smooth surface for an instant. "Oh, thank you, God, thank you." She plucked the message from Marta's outstretched hand and tore its flap, her fingers uncoordinated and jerky. After mumbling over the words, she held the page close, savoring the proof that her son was alive.

"What does it say?" Marta angled beside her, trying to read Karl's strong cursive.

Dear Mother, Father, and Marta,

I've been recruited into the Army. My company is in training, preparing to defend our homeland against the savage Russians as well as the British and Americans. Every day we march with heavy packs, do target practice, and learn the care of our guns. I want you to know I am healthy, and miss you very much.

With all my love,

Karl

Anna barely breathed. She extended the page toward Marta so she could read it better. The two stood silently, Marta's arm around her waist, heads together, gazing at the words as if trying to decipher the mystery behind them.

"It sounds like someone else wrote with Karl's handwriting." Marta expressed the strangeness Anna felt.

Certain Karl had not volunteered for service the afternoon he left to buy groceries, she expected some information about how he was forcibly inducted. Nothing. Not a hint. But she knew his handwriting.

In training. He didn't—no doubt couldn't—say where. Not yet fighting. Well, that was something. But Hitler threw men and boys at the Allies like rag dolls. Fodder for cannons, targets to be shot at.

And if he had to fight, would Karl kill or be killed by an American?

She folded the letter with trembling hands, reinserted it into the envelope, and put this evidence of her son in the pocket of her robe. Near her womb, safe and warm.

She and Marta clutched each other and cried, not speaking for a long while. She took Marta's hand and pulled her toward the living room, where they kneeled against the oversized leather footrest. They remained that way, whispering prayers, until their sobs dried up and their knees hurt.

She had maintained the illusion of protecting him since he wore diapers until he left for university. Only God could protect him now. And hadn't that always been true?

August, 1944
Schultz Post, Alsfeld, NE of Frankfurt

KARL AND SERGEANT Meyer rocked and bumped along in a staff car on a dirt road about ten kilometers from the camp. Any rougher and he would bounce out. The crude, open-top vehicle offered no creature comforts. This one didn't even have a spare tire mounted on its front housing.

"Why haven't they paved this? The wear on Kübelwagens must be costly."

"Ha!" Sarge stubbed his cigarette and threw it into the wind. "You're still living in your city world, my boy. We're fighting in Russia and all over Europe. Land, sea, and air. This stupid lane has a priority of minus ten."

"Yeah, I guess you're right," Karl shouted over the Kübelwagen's noise.

"Of course I'm right. Besides, if the road got paved, it would point enemy bombers straight to our camp."

"Like this hard-packed single lane doesn't? Granted, the Brits can't see it at night, but the Americans wouldn't miss it."

Speculation condensed into fear as an organized pattern of black dots appeared in the sky. Enemy fighters routinely returned from bombing runs strafing anything that moved or looked like it might house Germans. Trucks, houses, bridges, large buildings all existed as national support to some degree or other, and therefore were targets.

Screaming across the heavens at four hundred eighty kilometers per hour, the dots became P-47's within a few seconds.

Meyer scanned the waving fields of grass for cover and cursed. Nothing. They were out in the open.

He raced the vehicle up a slight rise, went airborne on the other side, and came down hard. Still nowhere to hide. Some tall weeds and scrubby bushes. He jerked the vehicle to a skidding halt.

"Run. Get away from the car."

The sergeant leapt out to the left. Karl ran to the right and dove beneath the nearest sapling. To his horror, a fighter broke from its formation and swooped low. In a burst of fifty caliber rounds, the guns strafed the car and chewed up the gravel path. As the roar subsided, the ringing in his ears became Meyer's screams.

"I'm hit." Blasphemy spewed from his mouth like a ruptured puss pocket. "They got me, man. Help me."

Karl checked the sky, sprinted for the first aid kit in the car, and found the sergeant on the ground, holding his leg and bleeding bad. A large piece of bloody metal lay a meter away.

"You're gonna be okay, Sarge. Not a direct hit or you'd be in pieces. Let's see, we got a...We got some gauze...alcohol..." He tore the pants leg from the wound point on the thigh, used scissors from the kit to cut strips, and tied a tourniquet above the injury.

The sergeant reached for the tin box. "Is there any morphine? Man, it hurts bad." He dumped the collection in the grass and rifled through the contents. His hands shook so much they were useless. "Some idiot took it. Some fatherless addict…"

Sweat dripped into Karl's eyes. "Sarge, I don't think these kits have morphine. The hard drugs are all at the front. Just lie back for a minute." He pushed on the man's chest, making a bloody handprint on his uniform.

Panicky and white-faced, Meyer twisted to see. "Do you know what you're doing? Where did you learn how to do this?"

"My mother's a nurse. She taught me stuff. Now relax. Chew on a nail or something." Karl lifted the thigh and wound the strips tightly. Looked like the piece of metal had cut the deep gash. The tourniquet might cause the sergeant to lose his leg to gangrene if they couldn't get back to the base fast enough.

Meyer groaned and spit out expletives in rare combinations, clenching and unclenching his fists. "You're killing me."

"I'm saving your life. Now just wait here for a minute. Let's find out if this bag of bolts still runs."

Karl dashed to the shot-up car and inspected the damage. Despite its torn metal and strewn contents, the left rear seemed to be the only hit. He sent up a prayer, turned the switch, and got a start-up as if nothing had happened. He shifted. Fearing he might be blown up by a gas leak, he gripped the steering wheel and eased toward the sergeant, a few meters of tall grass away.

Meyer struggled to get off the ground. Karl hopped out, and together they loaded him into the front passenger seat. Every rock and rabbit hole must have jabbed daggers of pain into the leg. Meyer reused his darkest vocabulary as Karl crested the hill in the damaged vehicle and headed back to the base.

Soon the sergeant got too quiet. Unconscious or nearly so, he needed warm blankets to ward off shock. Karl barreled down the gravel road as fast as he dared.

Breaking into the hollow that held the camp, Karl surveyed the damage to tents, vehicles, and men, unable to exhale for long, frozen seconds. The bombers had hit the station hard. People shouted, the major barked orders, and any remaining strong soldiers carried the wounded toward the large mess hall tent.

Karl slid the vehicle to a stop and commandeered helpers to get his patient inside. "We're here, Sarge. We made it." He commandeered assistance getting Sarge to the triage tent.

"Thanks." The crusty sergeant's tears ran through dust and blood onto his collar.

Karl wandered, dazed, into the pandemonium. Where to start?

He helped load bodies in a personnel carrier. A lone priest moved about the corpses, pronouncing holy words for souls already departed.

AS SOON AS the dead and wounded were transported out, Karl resumed his long hours in the major's office with ears bent toward the radios. On the desk before him spread maps of Germany, France, Belgium, and Holland. The additional HF radio, rattling with static, had a reliable range of several hundred kilometers. He might get more or different air traffic communication, but so far they hadn't learned much.

Working alone now, he looked for the opportunity to assist the American cause with a translation, or mistranslation. To that end, he spent hours studying the radio manuals, English grammar, and making notes of where Major Müller said battles were occurring. His mind's eye roamed the land while his fingers twiddled the dials and searched for sounds.

By pretending not to notice anything the officers uttered in the command post, he learned a lot. Mainly, that the war went badly for

Germany, and the major had plans to send his company into the fray this week. Maybe tomorrow.

He wished for a way to transmit German intel to Allied Forces, but he'd never had voice contact with them. The idea alone jangled his nerves. He knew the punishment if he were caught. Traitors died hard deaths. Given the opportunity, did he have the courage?

The Major escorted a captain from his private office to the front door. As he returned, he paused at Karl's desk. "Anything happening?"

"Not much, sir. Haven't heard a word for a couple of hours." He changed the frequency, trying to look busy. "Where's Richtner, sir?"

"Who?"

"The other private who used to work with me."

"Oh. He got hit when the fighters flew over. Didn't make it." The major delivered the information with no more chagrin than if he were saying the newspaper didn't come today.

That's what war did to people. With death everywhere, soldiers avoided personal attachments.

"Take a break. Let's get some breakfast."

Karl thought he had misunderstood. Eat with the major? That didn't happen. Something was up.

A LUXURY FOR him as a mere private, the eggs, warm toast with jam, and two cups of fake coffee went down well. Sitting in the back corner of the officers' dining room before their empty plates, Karl's gaze followed the lazy curl of the major's cigarette smoke.

Müller rang the table bell for an orderly. "Come take these dishes. You expect me to watch the yolks dry?"

A limping teenager in a private's uniform scurried through the double door and picked up the major's dish.

"His, too. And bring some hot coffee."

Three cups? Or maybe he was expected to offer to leave.

The major pulled another cigarette. "Would you like one?"

"No thank you, sir. Not a habit I've acquired." He abhorred the smoke, and even more the officious posing and pointing as if with a prop in a stage play. He kept his expression calm, wondering from what script his senior officer read.

Müller retrieved a silver lighter from his pocket and made a production of igniting the tobacco and taking a deep draw. "Your father handles investments, right?"

"Yes, sir. My great-grandfather started the business."

"And you expected to inherit the firm someday?"

Karl had an urge to deny it, but why? So he wouldn't be seen as a rich kid, a spoiled fellow with an easy entry into the family enterprise? But he did have that expectation, and wanted more than anything to return to predictable days with pleasant people living planned lives. He wanted to forget fighting, find a good woman, and establish a family who looked up to him the same way he respected Father.

"I studied economics, graduated from Ludwig Maximilian University in Munich just as the war was declared. Went to work with my father's firm."

The orderly brought in fresh coffee, poured for the major, and waited for indication of whether to serve Karl. A pointed flick of the wrist gave him the command. After sloshing and wiping up, the server couldn't leave fast enough.

The major shook his head and pressed his mouth together as if tired of dealing with incompetents. "Maximilian. The oldest and best. Not surprised. Were you in the White Rose group?"

"Anti-Nazis?" Now Karl wished he did have a cigarette with which to stall. He could answer honestly only because he studied too hard to get involved in politics. "No, sir. I knew some of them in my classes. Most disappeared after I left." He tried not to sound accusing, but not unaware either.

"You weren't a member?" The major pinned him with a squint.

Karl didn't blink. "Sir, would I admit it if I were?"

Müller cracked a sardonic smile. "So what did you do for your father's investment firm? Did they let you handle clients?"

"As an intern, I assisted the partners of the company. Sometimes they included me in client conferences, but I didn't have my own accounts." He sipped the strong, dark brew. "My father's business isn't with ordinary street traffic, you know."

"Ha. I can imagine. I heard he handles funds of the Reich."

One doesn't ask a woman's age, or a man how much he's worth. What was he getting at? Not a snowball's chance this was aimless chatter. "Yes, sir, I heard the same rumor. Not something I discussed with Father."

The major laughed, rocking back in the flimsy chair. "So did you count money, stack up gold coins in neat little rows?"

"No, sir, never. We dealt mainly in securities transactions and transfers. Maintained custody accounts. We don't handle much currency in a business like that." He knew the major had no idea what those words meant. Just as well.

"Hmm. Pity."

"Went to Zurich sometimes. Took suitcases of bearer securities on the train. Had a good night in a hotel, some excellent *raclette*, and got back the next afternoon." The memory of fine, melted cheese on a plate of pickles and breads caused a sudden sting inside his jaw.

"Courier, huh? Your father must have trusted you."

Karl straightened up in his chair. "Sir, of course he did. He reared me."

"*Ja*. Well, let's get back to the office. Sergeant Meyer's injury is inconvenient. Hard to find a replacement sergeant at this stage in the war. I'm transferring you to my command." The major stood and reached for his hat.

Karl did the same.

"You'll work days in the outer room, and nights, too, as things come over the radio. Officially, you're an office boy. Unofficially, you're a translator and the eyes in the back of my head. Dismissed."

So the interview ended abruptly without a single question about Karl's confused loyalties. Not that any doubt of his fidelity to the Fatherland could be tolerated. He stood at attention and saluted.

The night passed badly, the drone of bombers sending them hiding under the bottom bunks or in the shower room. As if fluff and splinters blocked bullets and bombs.

Returning fire from the ground brought cheers from all but Karl.

"They hit one. Look, it's in flames." A soldier at the barn window was smothered by the crowd. The bomber shook the hills, hitting a few kilometers away. Its flame threw an eerie glow to the horizon beyond the ridge to the west.

"Did anybody get out? Do you see any parachutes?" Spectators of a deadly game pushed for space at the window. With the barn's ancient stone wall their only security, they eventually tired and bedded down again.

"Von Steuben, wake up."

Karl jerked up when the hand shook his shoulder. "Huh? Radios?"

"No. We got a live one." The messenger's teeth were visible through his triumphant smile. "Come quick. Müller wants you to debrief him."

He threw on clothes, ran to the latrine, and rinsed his mouth.

"Right now. Major's going to have my rear end if you don't put some speed on."

Karl took off toward the post headquarters.

"No. He's with the medics. He's in bad shape." They reversed directions and headed for the mess hall building with one room converted for medical treatment. A couple of candles led them to the captured airman bleeding on a stretcher.

The major stood against the door facing. "Talk to him. Find out their target, how many planes, what kind. Here's his dog tag."

Dark blood spread from his middle.

Karl pulled up a rickety wooden chair, taking time to swallow hard against everything that wanted to come up. He held the tag close to a candle to read the man's name, rank, and serial number. American, by his uniform. *About my age, and he won't get any older.* He decided to take a calm approach.

"James Fuller, I would like to speak with you in English." That sounded dumb. What was he supposed to say? "You are seriously wounded. Care for some water?"

Fuller's eyes registered he understood. He nodded almost imperceptibly.

Karl called for a glass and helped the man lift his head to drink.

"The pain. Can you give me something for the pain?"

"We have no hard drugs, and the doctor is just a medic. I do not think we can adequately treat you here."

"What was their mission?" The Major's impatience flared. "Ask him quickly. We need to radio their target."

"Fuller, what were your orders? Where were you going?"

The airman closed his eyes and shook his head. Müller pulled his side arm and aimed at the man's knee, spitting demands in German.

"Major, please allow me to talk to him. He's barely conscious. If you shoot him, he'll just pass out."

The Major held the shaking gun and cursed profoundly. His rage smoldered like a forest about to explode in flames.

"Give me a moment, sir. Let me win his confidence. Sir, could I be alone with him? I think I can get him to come around."

Müller maintained the position for an awful space of time. Then he re-holstered the gun, spun on his heel, and exited the room, slamming the door on the way out.

Karl released his breath. "Okay. He's gone. You've got to give me something to pass on, or I won't be able to protect you."

"You're American?" The captive's face twisted with the question. His eyes scanned Karl's uniform.

"German."

"But you sound so—"

"My mother is American." Common knowledge, but he said it quietly. Like a mouse on a wheel, his mind whirled with how to say what he needed to without giving himself away. The Major might have his ear to the door, and Karl had no idea whether he understood English.

"Tell me something I can give to the Major." His expression locked Fuller's with urgency. He mouthed but did not speak, *True or not.* "Understand?"

He nodded. "We flew south from a base in England. No one knows the target until...ah... we're airborne. I'm just a gunner. Sometimes I don't know until we get back."

Karl made a gimme-more hand motion.

"Okay, we were doing air support for Normandy. Continuing the advance."

Karl shook his head. "You're too far off course."

"Yeah, the pilot got lost."

Karl shook again. "Not good enough. Your uniform has pin holes for a pilot's wings, and your dog tag says you're a lieutenant. Gunners are enlisted. You have to do better or they crucify us both."

Fuller groaned and his lids drooped like he might pass out. "All right, so I'm a pilot. But honest—and this is true—we never know the target. We follow the lead. When he drops a marker, we have assigned instructions to go off at an angle from there."

That didn't ring true, either. The navigator would have maps on board with high priority points indicated. "Were you going or coming?"

After a pause, he admitted he was en route to the destination.

"You hadn't released any bombs yet?"

"No. They went down with the plane. Look. What time is it?" Fuller tried to raise his arm, but groaned and dropped the effort. His watch was missing anyway.

"Four a.m." Karl lost his fine Swiss timepiece at his forced induction, but a cheap electric clock hung on the wall.

"Then it doesn't matter. My plane went down at 1:17 a.m. Wherever we were supposed to hit, we either did by now or won't. It's over." Fuller closed his eyes, jaw clenched. "Can I see the medic?"

"He's not capable of treating anything worse than a boot blister. If you're a praying man, this would be a good time." Karl opened the man's shirt and almost threw up. The skin, torn across his abdomen, crusted with blood. At least the body cavity looked closed. The pilot might live, but it wouldn't be easy.

He offered a handshake. After hesitating, Fuller accepted. Karl wished they'd met a different time and place. He called the medic.

Fuller left on the back of a troop truck the next day, a long, rough trip. Karl wondered where he was being taken, and if his international Prisoner of War rights were respected. Probably not. Karl would most likely never find out whether he lived.

CHAPTER SIX

September, 1944
Munich, Germany

ANNA PULLED THE newspaper out of the mailbox and unrolled it in the bright morning sun. A horrid photo slapped her in the face. The bodies of people accused of attempting to assassinate Hitler hung on meat hooks, displayed for all to scorn. Authorities even suspected *Fieldmarshall* Rommel, wounded last June by a strafing fighter in France.

She shivered despite the sun's warmth on her light sweater and turned her back on the world to retreat to her comfortable home. A shuffle of activity at the gate caused her to glance toward the cobblestone street, where two black Mercedes had parked. That awful Captain Schmidt had returned with several other men in uniform.

"Good morning, Frau von Steuben. May I come in?" Without hesitation, he lifted the lock and entered.

Anna looked to the front door, left ajar, where Tilli barked a warning.

"Put away the dog. We have business with your family."

No choice existed. Tilli might protect them from a thief in the night, but these soldiers would shoot their pet without a second thought. Anna entered, took the leash from the peg, and led Tilli, much against her will, to the back garden. She smoothed the Shepherd's fur and tried to calm her with baby talk, but had to loop the leash around the post of a heavy dining chair on the patio.

When Anna returned, Hauptmann Schmidt stood, chest puffed out, in the middle of her living room as if he were buying it. The other four leered at the art and furniture. Until Marta stepped to the upstairs landing. Mesmerized by her beauty, they might have been drawn to a statue of Venus on a museum pedestal.

Anna recognized the danger and motioned her to go away, but the eighteen year old had no intention of retreating.

"Please do not wake my father. He isn't well. We've called the doctor, but he can't come until later."

Captain Schmidt pulled papers from an inside pocket and shook them open with a rattle. The trance broken, his men closed their mouths and swiveled toward their leader.

"Your father's health is not our concern." He turned to Anna. "We've come to search the house for documents. Take us to his office." With several doors from the living area, Schmidt started toward the dining room.

Anna motioned past the stairs. "It's over there. But he doesn't keep business papers at home. You must go to the office if you want—"

"Another search party took that assignment. And I seriously doubt he would leave incriminating documents where an assistant might stumble over them."

With Karl in the Army, only the judge's son remained at that level. The other two partners of his firm did not have access to his files. "Incriminating? My husband is an honest financial advisor. He even manages some of the funds of the Reich."

"Exactly. We have information that he embezzled funds, sent them to hidden accounts in Switzerland and Portugal—"

"To protect them and invest at a good rate." Dietrich's voice, lacking its usual boom of authority, came from the upper rail. He stood, pale and weak, in his nightshirt and robe. "I've hidden nothing. Every *pfennig* is accounted for."

Dietrich did not stand in his usual erect posture, but rather slumped. He massaged his upper left arm. Anna couldn't remember his hurting it. Then her old nursing experience came to mind. She rushed to the stairs.

"Go see what they're hiding in the bedrooms." The captain's growl sent two soldiers that way.

One of the young men passed her at the landing, pushing her to the wall.

"No, we're hiding nothing, I tell you." Dietrich began the descent toward her but crumpled against the railing. He fell the last two steps as she attempted to catch him.

She encircled his head, holding it to her bosom as they tumbled to the midpoint.

"Anna." Dietrich gasped. *"Ich liebe dich."* After he declared his love, his eyes locked into a fixed stare and did not move.

"Dietrich, Dietrich, I love you, too. Don't leave me." Her words broke in a sob. "God in heaven, help us." Hungrily her fingers searched for a pulse but did not find any sign of life. She held him close and rocked back and forth, wetting his face in her grief.

Marta shouted from the upper floor, pushed against the clutches of the soldier, and flew to her father. They embraced Dietrich and each other and wailed.

When it seemed that nothing else could matter ever again, Hauptmann Schmidt stood over her and grasped her shoulder. "What's the combination?"

She looked up toward his hard voice, her tears obscuring her vision. "Combination?"

"There's a big safe in the office. What's the combination?"

"I don't know. Really. I've never known. He only keeps a little household cash there."

Marta's fearful eyes were trying to tell her something.

Anna's arms ached from the strain of holding her husband's body. She straightened her legs farther down the stairs from the landing, hoping her ankle hadn't broken. "Marta dear, please call the doctor. Tell him…"

Marta squeezed her close and then stood. "Yes, Mother." No one prevented her.

The soldiers broke from their searching and offered to carry Dietrich downstairs, where they laid him on a sheet and folded the sides over his body. This last kindness they performed with all respect. Then they returned to ransacking his personal space, the room that even Anna rarely entered.

Eventually, the ambulance's loud two-tone alarm approached. *Why use the siren at this point?* The men in starched, white cotton uniforms came in the gaping front door and asked their questions.

She uncovered his face and brushed his cooling lips with a kiss, and they took away her Dietrich.

Marta and she started toward her bedroom, but the captain insisted that they remain in the living room. Sitting close on the sofa, they held hands.

"I should have realized. His face was so white and clammy." Her whisper broke into another jerk of breath.

"Shh, Mommy. You could do nothing. Even if the doctor had come, it wouldn't have made any difference."

"Maybe if he had stayed in bed though. If this..." She nodded toward Dietrich's office. "...hadn't happened..."

Another officer walked right in and interrupted their private mourning. He introduced himself to the captain as the *geldschrankknacker*.

The word didn't register with Anna. She looked to Marta, brows indicating her question.

"Safe cracker." Again, fear played on her face.

Upstairs, furniture scraped across the floor. Occasional thumps and clinks sounded like the soldiers were ransacking the bedrooms.

"Is the new maid in the kitchen?" Marta glanced in that direction.

Anna shook her head. "She left by the side door when they came in the front." She rolled her lips inward, making a tight grimace, and squeezed her eyes closed. "Who do you think raised suspicion against us?"

Anna had never liked the maid, but Dietrich insisted they give her a job because her family went to their church. Had she reported them for something? Or since the search concerned business, perhaps a secretary or the judge's son at the firm triggered this invasion. "I've been wondering the same thing. Why are they searching here?"

Laughter and congratulations came from the office. They must have opened the safe.

Anna took Marta's hand again and leaned close. "What are you afraid of?" She couldn't imagine her daughter knew more than she about the contents.

"The jewelry." Marta mouthed the word as she touched the simple gold cross around her neck. "Father once showed me…"

"So?"

Upstairs, one of the men strode from Anna and Dietrich's bedroom holding high her mother's menorah, a gleam on his face. The Jewish candelabra had been in her family for many generations. Unable to part with it, she had hidden the memento deep in a closet of seldom used linens. Anna's heart stopped.

Upon that discovery came another. Hauptmann Schmidt marched from the office holding a delicate silver filigree box, the red velvet-faced lid open. He lifted the gold Star of David necklace she had worn in the United States before her conversion, and life as she had known it ended.

Humiliation did not begin to describe Anna's experience. After Dietrich's death and the ransacking of their home, she and Marta were hauled like cattle in the back of a truck to a detention center.

A female guard shaved them bald and ordered them to strip for the shower. Clothes here, shoes there, jewelry and personal effects into a metal bucket.

The woman pointed to Anna's right hand. "Wedding ring, too. Naked as you were born."

Anna had never undressed in front of her daughter, nor had she seen Marta nude since her childhood. She balked.

The surly amazon pulled a whip from her belt, raised it to strike Marta, and repeated the command.

A ploy, Anna thought, a technique that probably worked every time. Her cheeks burned and tears flowed. The unbearable had to be borne. "God help me." Her whispers must have reached the ears of the Almighty, because she was able to do as instructed.

Marta sobbed, her fingers unwilling to remove her own clothing.

Turning the whip to Anna, the guard spoke to Marta. "Do you want to see your mother beaten?"

"No, no! Don't hit her." She removed her clothes and ran into the showers, followed by her mother.

"Why don't you tell them, Mother?" Marta scrubbed the shaven hair off her head and shoulders, covering her words from their tormenter.

Anna moved close to speak. "That we're Christian? I yelled that all the way into the truck. They didn't care."

"Citizenship. Tell them."

"Not sure what would happen. Better or worse." She ran a sliver of soap over her goose bumps. She had the skin of a freshly plucked chicken. "Whom should I tell? They might shoot us, you know."

"Could it be any worse?"

15 October, 1944
Schultz Post, NE of Frankfurt

KARL RATIONALIZED THE absence of mail from home as normal for a country at war. Connected by radio and the office news he pretended not to listen to, he was aware the Reich struggled. Hitler's insistence on control resulted in worsening strategy.

Three months after Allied troops fought their way ashore at Normandy, American soldiers had reached the western frontier, the Siegfried Line. German soldiers scratched and clawed the Dutch city Arnhem back from American grasp. Many perished on both sides.

The Schultz Post trainees shipped out to the front with raucous false cheer. They weren't ready. They couldn't shoot, they were untrained in how to wage war, and they didn't possess clothing warm enough for winter's approach. Karl realized that his translation job spared his life.

With the camp empty, the major relaxed with a little midafternoon schnapps. He sent a runner for a thermos of hot coffee and put his feet up. "What's on your mind, private? Something bothering you?"

"Oh, it's nothing. Since it got quiet, I've been thinking about my family."

The runner returned not only with the coffee, but also hot raisin bread, its plaited ropes glistening with butter. Karl's eyes lit up and his mouth watered.

"Hand me my field knife, private. I'll cut you a piece, too."

Sergeant Weber, replacement for the wounded Sergeant Meyer, roused from his desk and produced some plates from a closet. "My wife used to make bread like this, sometimes with cardamom and candied fruits."

The major laughed. "My wife isn't much of a cook, but there's this bakery in the same block where we live. She saves money by making soup instead of *saurbraten* and then runs down there for fresh bread. Mmm, I've missed that bakery almost as much as her fat bottom." He made squeezing motions with his free hand.

Karl laughed with the others, thinking that the major had never mentioned having a wife before. Did he have children then? The real major hid behind Karl's two-dimensional, cardboard cutout image of him.

After they demolished the bread and drank all the coffee, the schnapps came out again. Karl accepted a shot in order to remain in the major's office for a better look at the map spread on a side table. Might he even ask questions concerning the progress of the war?

"You're not married, are you, private?" The major definitely had loosened up.

"No, sir. Mother, father, sister. No wife."

"So what are you worried about?"

"Not exactly worried, sir, just haven't received a letter for a couple of weeks now." He tipped back in the straight chair. "My mother and sister usually write every week."

"You have a phone number?"

"Yes, sir." He had never had an opportunity to call home. Not once.

Major Müller motioned to the sergeant. "Take his number. See what you can find out."

"Really?" Karl's delight at this prospect lifted his spirit more than the raisin bread. "That would be fantastic, sir." Might he even speak to Mother or Father?

Two days later, while the post still awaited green recruits, Karl directed a phone call to the Sergeant in his small side room. Weber's unintelligible grumble vibrated through the walls. He left his office, knocked at the major's door, and was admitted. They spoke softly, and Karl wondered about activity on the front lines.

Weber came to Karl's desk. "Leave it for a minute. Major wants to talk to you."

Anything out of the ordinary forced Karl's pulse to pound in his ears. He rose and entered the major's office.

"Take a seat, private. I have some bad news."

Karl took the hard chair. This wasn't about the war. This was personal.

"Sarge couldn't reach your home, but he got a call through to the other number you gave... " Müller consulted a note. "...von Steuben Investments. He spoke to an officer there, Herr Olson. Your father's had a heart attack."

"My father? But he's not very old. Is he in the hospital?"

"Sorry. He died straightaway, at home. Wednesday of last week."

Karl's ears rang. He felt light-headed. This couldn't happen. The pillar of the family, the captain of a major firm. Father. Dead.

"Take the afternoon off. I'll send a runner if I need you."

Karl stood on unwilling legs, gave a wilted "Heil, Hitler" salute, and shuffled outside. Where to go? How to spend an afternoon alone in a place he didn't want to be?

He made it up to a slight hill overlooking the camp before breaking down. He cried out his pain to his Heavenly Father. "Tell him I...respect him a lot, God." Probably theological nonsense. "I...lo...love him." He rarely thought of love in relation to his father. Respect, definitely. Tremendous respect for his professional knowledge, too. So much more Karl had hoped to learn about the business.

Father died last Wednesday. The funeral would have been held right away. Without him.

And where were Mother and Marta now? He should be there to protect them. Would the Army give him a release—or at least temporary leave—to go help them?

Darkness came to Karl's hillside. He would be a sitting duck if enemy fighters flew over. But they hadn't. Unfortunately, he had to continue living.

He stirred from his rock and descended to the command post. Weber manned the front desk. "Sergeant, may I speak to the major a moment?"

The major's door stood ajar. "Come on in, private."

After saluting, Karl posed his question. "Sir, would it be possible for me to get a few days' home leave?"

The major dropped his pen and gave a vacant gaze toward the darkening window. Slumping backwards in his squeaky roller chair, he released a long sigh. "I'd like to give you some time off, but I can't spare you right now. Or a car. Transportation is a mess, and rails and bridges are being bombed every day. Sorry."

"Yes, sir. I understand." He raised his arm to salute, but the major didn't seem to be finished.

"Wait. There's something..." He rested his cigarette on the ashtray and then crossed to the open maps on a side table. "You're from Munich, right?" He spoke with his back turned to Karl.

"Yes, sir."

"Hmm. The Dachau Camp is about sixteen kilometers away." Drawing imaginary lines with his fingers, comparing that map to another one, he then faced Karl. "I've been tasked with picking up...*confiscated items* from some of the nearby labor camps and taking them to the south. Sort of concentrating materials away from the battle areas. Come look at this." He bent over the maps as Karl joined him.

The major touched a pencil eraser to several dots northwest of their base. "Tomorrow you and Sarge will go to four camps to pick up...*items* held by each command post. They're supposed to have logged everything by the time you arrive. Just pick up the packages and return here. I'll review what has been delegated to me then send you south to Dachau."

The map Karl had been conniving to glimpse lay bare its mysteries. Not far from Aachen, on Germany's western border with Belgium and the southern finger of The Netherlands, someone had scribbled *US 1*. The United States First Army had advanced that near? Their own camp could be overrun in the coming weeks. Karl's American heart beat furiously inside his German uniform.

He noticed the dots the captain pointed out. "So many." The words escaped against Karl's will.

"Pardon?"

Karl cleared his throat and bought a few seconds to recover. "So many labor camps. I mean, everyone knows they've been established, but I wasn't aware there were this many near Frankfurt."

On marches and patrols, he had seen emaciated workers with the gold Star of David on their sleeves. Hired out by farmers and housewives for day labor, the Jews wore striped prisoner uniforms and torn-up shoes.

"Yeah, tens of thousands in Germany, more in Poland and Czechoslovakia. POW's, Jews, political enemies of the Reich... We're trying to get them moved to Auschwitz. Several big camps in Poland. But the war effort must come first. Priorities, you know."

Yes, and priorities in distribution of food and warm clothing. Karl wondered whether any of his acquaintances suffered in a prison like this. Probably not, if only because Mother had kept him and Marta out of synagogue and removed from close friendships with German Jews. They were all fools for not leaving when the Nuremberg Laws went into effect. Yes, his own family too. Stupid.

"As soon as you and the sergeant gather up the packages, deliver them to Colonel Weiter, Commandant at Dachau. Weber's from some farm village on the Isar. After you drop off the goods you can take off for the night. Spend one day and two nights with your family. Work out the details with him. Report back here the second day."

With difficulty, Karl pulled his gaze from the map when the major backed off for his cigarette. "Report to me at daybreak. Your orders will be ready."

"Yes, sir." Karl saluted, trying to act as calm as if he were sent to fetch a keg of beer.

"Don't worry. You should be safe."

CHAPTER SEVEN

15 October, 1944
Schultz Post, NE of Frankfurt

AWARE THAT MAJOR Müller was briefing Sergeant Weber in the command office, Karl tuned his ears more to their conversation than to his radios. A five centimeter opening of the old farmhouse's solid wooden door gave the advantage he needed. The major reviewed the maps in detail, listing several labor camps which would turn over goods to them.

"Sir, may I be frank for a moment?" Weber spoke in hushed tones. "The kid...shouldn't I run this operation with someone more battle-ready? Higher than a private?"

"Sarge, 'the kid' has experience with transporting valuables. Besides, he's from a rich family. He's not going to be impressed with gold jewelry. He's used to seeing it all the time."

So the packages were personal effects of the prisoners. Worth less to them now than a bowl of porridge. They did hard farm work all day for a meal.

"I hadn't thought of it that way." Sarge too-readily agreed with the major.

Müller folded the maps. "He's the kind of guy who grew up with a code of honor. I picked him out of everyone left here in the camp, and I don't think I'm wrong."

Pleased he had the major's respect, Karl hoped his eventual defection would be possible. If he could figure out how.

He had become so perverse.

KARL AND SERGEANT Weber met Müller in his office at daybreak. The major appeared unkempt, like he had rolled out of bed five minutes ago. Easy enough with his room on the second floor of the farmhouse. Majors didn't sleep on cots in a cold, drafty barn.

"Here's a map of the four camps. Show your ID and orders, receive the goods and inventories, and drive hard. These aren't places where you want to have to spend the night. Bring the packages to me—no one else."

"Heil, Hitler." The two men saluted in unison.

"Heil, Hitler," returned the major. "Good luck and Godspeed."

What did God have to do with any of this? Karl picked up food for breakfast and lunch, a thermos of grain-based "coffee," and a jug of water.

Weber pulled an open-sided, canvas-topped Kübelwagen around to the mess house.

Karl shuddered with bad memories from the day planes strafed Sergeant Meyer. He swung the food and water behind the front seat, hopped in despite his unease, and poured each of them coffee. Within two revolutions of the wheels, they dodged the slosh.

Weber slowed, slugged down the hot drink, and asked for a *brotchen*.

Karl reached in the bag for the crusty bread roll, one of the few things a field kitchen got right.

"And put on butter and marmalade, will you?"

"Sure. Just pull over at the next farmhouse and I'll ask for some." He hadn't had butter or jam on his bread for weeks.

Dawn broke so clear and beautiful Karl wanted to yell out, "Stop the car. Let me out. Let's quit fighting. This is stupid and I want to go home."

But of course he said nothing. Red clouds streaked the sky until the sun popped up and brought tears to his eyes. When they passed the place where Meyer was wounded, he shouted out the story against the Kübelwagen's noise. Weber slowed around the pockmarks still in the dirt road.

Their first destination lay a half hour from Schultz Post. Karl had no idea what to expect, but not this.

Weber pulled up to the narrow front of a long, unpainted wood building. Off one side stretched a two meter high wire fence, supported at intervals by concrete posts, around a bare dirt enclosure. The top, strung with barbed wire, angled inward. Inside the yard, hollow-eyed, rail-thin men wandered listlessly. Seeing the car, a few dirty, ragged prisoners migrated to the fence at a dismal pace and watched with hands hung on its strands. An armed guard lifted his rifle toward them.

"Come on, private. Let's get this done." Weber's words broke his trance.

Together they entered the only door. In the rickety, bare-bones office they approached the man at the desk. Karl stood back of Weber, saluted, and each one pulled out his ID and orders.

"We've come for the box." Weber's cryptic message prompted a haggard major to check their documents and produce a release form. "Sign this." From an even smaller cubicle, he lifted a sturdy wooden ammunition box fitted with a padlock.

Weber accepted the key and an envelope marked "Inventory" and motioned Karl to carry the load out to the car.

After placing the heavy container on the back floorboard, Karl took his place and Weber scratched off toward the second labor camp.

Inside razor wire fences, women and children sat in the sun. The few little ones who came to the fence were soon clutched back by shaggy females with fearful eyes.

Eerie silence followed the men into the front office. The exchange of documents produced another heavy box, this one of bent and scratched metal but also fitted with a padlock.

Weber and Karl reached the third camp with their stomachs rumbling. The desire for food died instantly, though, killed by the stench of the inmates. Something was wrong here, something more wrong than in the first two camps.

A few prisoners dug holes, perhaps graves, in the dirt yard. Three scrawny bodies lay in the sun. A digger paused, appearing too weak to continue. A grimacing guard beat his boney back.

Karl wanted to yell at the guard. To rush to the man's aid. Adrenaline pumped through his limbs, urging him to action.

"Let it go, private. None of our business. They're just Jews and gypsies." Weber continued to the room with an outside door. Together they entered, saluted, and presented their papers.

Karl's legs trembled. He needed to vomit. With his handkerchief over his mouth and nose, he stifled a gag.

The soldier dragged a gun box from beneath a skirted desk. "Dysentery. The whole camp has it. They're dying like poisoned roaches. Take their filthy gold and get away. Sorry I can't offer you fellows something to eat, but believe me, you don't want to eat here."

"Right. We'll just be on our way." Weber spoke as if he were trying not to inhale.

The Kübelwagen jostled them toward their final pick-up. A narrow, clear stream coursed alongside the gravel path. "Let's pull over for a few minutes." Weber set the brake and reached for their lunch of bread and cheese. Across the stream stood an orchard of picked-over apple trees.

They busied themselves hunting for discarded fruit without a worm hole, reaping a few decent bites.

"On a day like this, if we had a picnic basket and a blanket—" began Weber.

Karl lifted his eyes from the waving autumn grasses of yellow and red to the clear, blue sky. A cool day, crispness that in normal times stimulated the senses and encouraged outdoor sports. But today his heart burned like a stinking garbage dump because of what he had seen.

"—and a couple of lovely *frauleins* and a bottle of *apfelwein*..." continued Weber.

"Yeah, with women and wine you could almost forget about the war." Yet in that car waited three boxes of valuables. Karl couldn't rest. "Aw, we'd better keep driving before we either get robbed or strafed."

At the last camp, a lieutenant seemed reluctant to give them the locked box. "What are you going to do with the goods?"

"Deliver them to Major Müller," Weber answered with a testy edge to his voice.

"What happens then? Where do they go?"

"I hear they support the war effort, but I don't know. Sir, is the list of goods ready? We have to return before dark."

"Everything's itemized, down to the last coin and wedding ring. Sign here." The lieutenant kept eyeing the container and glaring at Weber and Karl.

Weber held out his hand. "The key. Or do you want the major to use a crowbar?"

The lieutenant handed him the key like a petulant child forced to obey.

Karl and Weber saluted and left before he changed his mind.

Sarge shifted the Kübelwagen and sent gravel flying. He sped like a horse racing back to the barn.

"The lieutenant at the last camp acted like he didn't want to give us the goods," Karl shouted over the road noise. This vehicle discouraged conversation.

"Yeah, I think he wanted to keep the box for himself." Sarge laughed. "I wonder what's in it. Anything more valuable than the other pick-ups?"

"Don't know. Like you said, it's none of our business."

Weber took his eyes off the road for one hairy moment, almost sending them into the ditch. "What's the matter? Does it bother you, taking their jewelry and stuff?"

Karl had participated in stealing the most precious things the prisoners had. His soul, pushed in like a dead soccer ball, creased with the heavy weight of compassion. "Yeah, it bothers me. A lot." Black clouds condensed over his head.

"Well, don't let it. Those poor wretches don't need gold where they're going."

"Where's that?"

"Didn't you know? All these camps are being torn down and the inmates are shipped to Auschwitz, the extermination camp in Poland."

The car hit a hole. Weber's jerk to the left almost threw Karl out. He grabbed the support of the canvas top and held on. Had he understood the Sarge correctly?

"Extermination?" Horror rose with burning bile in Karl's throat. "Like bugs?"

Weber laughed. "Yeah, like bugs. Worthless pieces of dung. These camps are part of the 'final solution.' Get rid of all our national problems. Start over after the war with a pure race."

"Look, Sarge, I'm getting carsick. This road is terrible. Can you stop a minute?"

Weber skidded to a halt. Karl bolted from his open side and vomited into the ditch. He returned shaking and wiping his mouth on a handkerchief. Bending his head low to quell the nausea, he braced his elbows against his knees.

"Maybe I was driving too rough, kid. Just breathe deep and you'll feel better." Weber shifted to neutral, but didn't kill the engine. "Say, I think we ought to check those boxes and see what we're carrying. I mean, we're out here risking our lives. We could get strafed or bombed, and what for?"

Karl didn't want to see their cargo. Today he had witnessed evil beyond his ability to imagine. He shook his head. *No* wasn't strong enough word.

"Well, I'm going to. You can just take a rest." He stood out of the car and pulled keys from his pocket. "Hmm, this opens the first one..."

The lock rattled and hinge creaked. Weber let out a stream of profanities in a voice of pure awe. "Mother of—would you look at this. Gold, man. Rings, necklaces, tooth fillings... A wooden box of gold. And some silver. Diamonds and rubies... Those worthless vermin wore jewels when honest working people didn't have enough to live on."

Karl turned in his seat and considered the cache. Amazing, but not in the sense Weber thought. So many wedding bands. He stretched backwards, picked one up, and read inside, "10 February, 1917." A memory. Two lives. A generation. He replaced the band onto the pile with reverence.

Weber dug his fingers into the box. "My wife never had a gold ring. I had to buy her silver. She deserves better."

Karl fixed on the road ahead. "Let's get back, Sarge. If anyone came up on us right now, we'd be robbed and left dead."

To say Karl had a headache when they returned would be a phenomenal understatement. His skull wanted to explode, his eyes burned like coals, and his neck and back strained against tight ropes of muscle. But he hauled half the loot into Major Müller's office and dropped into his chair at the table of radios and maps.

Since the door stood open a few centimeters, he saw Sergeant Weber lift each lid. The jewelry gave a light tinkle as their hands raked the jewelry.

"This stuff stinks." The major let rings trickle through his fingers.

"Yeah, their filthy smell is still on it." Sarge stacked the four inventory folders on the desk. "But if the Army melts it down to bullion, that'll burn the stink off."

"How did the trip go? Did you see any action?"

"No. Real calm." Sarge leaned closer. "You were right about the kid."

In the adjoining room, Karl made out his raspy words.

"Right about what?" Müller closed a lid.

"He wouldn't steal any of this stuff. Wasn't even interested."

"Good. Take the half-ton truck tomorrow early. You and Private von Steuben deliver all this to Colonel Weiter at the prison camp in Dachau. Travel with your rifles and a couple of armed guards. They are not to know what they're guarding. Understand?"

"Absolutely, sir. But…wouldn't the train be safer?"

"Not since the bombing in Frankfurt in March. The rails got destroyed. You have to drive as far as Würzburg to go by train, so you may as well go the rest of the way and use the truck. And Sarge?" The major rubbed his whiskers with a frown.

"Yes, sir?"

"Bring it back. A truck that runs is becoming a rare commodity." Then he brightened. "You can pull a day's leave and return the following day."

"Yes, sir. Thank you, sir." Sarge looked out of the office, toward Karl.

He dropped his head close to the radio, as if he hadn't been listening to their conversation.

"What is it, Sarge?" Müller sounded impatient.

"I was wondering, sir…"

"Yes?"

"The wife never had a proper wedding ring. Is there any chance—"

"I don't want to know about it." The major turned his back to the cache and stepped to the map table.

Sarge dipped his hand into the box. Judging by his grin when he left, his wife finally got a gold band.

What could be more personal and sacred? Karl simmered with rage.

CHAPTER EIGHT

17 October, 1944
Schultz Post, NE of Frankfurt

KARL REVIEWED THE road map over bread and coffee. "South to Würzberg. After that we find better roads. It'll take us most of the morning just to reach Nuremberg."

Weber's finger traced the line southwest. "Two hundred kilometers, maybe two fifty, even if we stay east of Frankfurt, and I think that's safer. Yeah, we should be able to pull into Dachau before dark."

Cook came out with a large basket. "You got your sausage, cheese, bread, a couple of apples apiece. Enough for four men for two days. Not gourmet, but it doesn't have to be chilled. And water for the road." His aproned belly jiggled with laughter. "You boys will be drinking beer once you get to Bavaria."

The small amount of salary in Karl's pocket screamed for a nice wiener schnitzel and potatoes. Remembering he had left home for groceries, he cooked up an idea. What if he walked in the front door with a big satchel full of meat and vegetables?

Energized with the thought of being with Mother and Marta for two nights and a day, Karl hopped in the truck. The guards climbed into the back, where they protected, as far as they knew, a couple of heavy, padlocked munitions boxes. Weber would drive while Karl tried to keep them on the right road.

Once past the neighboring village of Alsfeld, its sheep and farms, Sergeant Weber became more cheerful and talkative. "So, kid, you have a girlfriend down in Munich?"

"No." He hoped Sarge wouldn't be distracted by conversation as if they were old comrades. The way he weaved around the horse-drawn wagons endangered the other traffic. He competed for rights on the narrow road.

"Why not? A young man like you, educated and a good family, you ought to be married by now. How old are you?"

"Twenty-four."

"Why don't you have a girlfriend already?"

"Well, I kind of liked one, but she didn't like me. Wanted the blond, Arian type. Gee, thanks, Mr. Hitler."

"*Ja*, I know what you mean."

Karl shrugged. "I had something going with another girl, but her family left when the war heated up."

"Is that so? Where'd they go?"

He laughed at the sergeant. "People who run away from their homeland during a war don't leave a forwarding address. I don't know. Switzerland, maybe."

"Probably. Look, kid, I've got this beautiful daughter. She's seventeen, cooks good—"

"Sarge, come on, man. You're not going to try to match me up with your daughter, are you?" Wouldn't that be something, having Sarge as a father-in-law? Of course, he wouldn't be offering her if he knew Karl's lineage.

"Why not? She could do a lot worse. And the way this war's going... I'd hate for her to be an old maid."

Such normal emotions. Sarge, a husband and father looking forward to being with the family. And hating Jews and gypsies enough to laugh at taking their valuables and starving them to death. How was that possible?

Karl willed his thoughts not to show his own growing hatred. He summoned the discipline to stay in the conversation. "Too true. Lots of women won't have a chance to be married. I wonder about my sister. She's kind of delicate. Stays inside, doesn't go to parties much. When there used to be parties."

"Is she pretty?"

Karl brought Marta to mind, trying to answer the question objectively. "Yes, when she dresses up. Lipstick and hairdo and all." In truth, Mother had kept her inside so much she hadn't developed a sparkling personality. "She's nice. She goes with my mother to hold babies in the orphanage. They play with them, give them baths, and change their diapers."

"Your mother works for an orphanage?" Incredulity spread from his words to his face.

"Not for pay. She volunteers in one. She's a nurse. My father doesn't—didn't—want her to work. I don't think she has even kept up her license to practice, but she does things for the babies. My sister, too. Mother shows Marta what to do. Can't just let them die."

He checked the map again. "Uh, Sarge, we're getting close to Würzberg. We'll be coming down to the east, and catch the road to Nuremberg." The map's line veered away from the River Main, so the town must be near. "I didn't expect all the slow carts. Hard to get around them on narrow roads."

Weber nodded. "Anyone with a wagon and horse has loaded up and headed away from the action."

"As for the cars, the new highway to Switzerland doesn't help over here," Karl grumbled. "So much for Hitler's grand plan for a network of autobahns."

"There's a roadside restaurant. Let's park and eat lunch. I can't shift and manage a bratwurst at the same time. Besides…" He rolled his shoulders and popped his neck. "I need a break."

They were a kilometer beyond the town when three P-47's came screaming over, spitting death and destruction from their fifty caliber guns.

With a burst of profanity, Sarge gunned the truck straight into a farmyard and through an open barn door, scattering chickens and goats in a wild panic. "Where did those planes come from? I never heard a thing until they hit that water tower."

"Yeah. At six hundred k's an hour, you don't know they're coming until they're there." Karl shook so hard his canteen sloshed. All the bad memories of his experience with Sergeant Meyer hit him full force. "Meyer and I saw black dots on the horizon, and then they were strafing us. They're fast, man."

The farmer banged with his fists on the driver door, pushing their jagged nerves a level higher.

"What do you think you're doing?" The man's mouth twisted with rage. "You hit my goat. My best milk goat."

Weber cut the engine and wiped sweat off his face with his sleeve.

The guards ran from the back of the truck, guns at the ready. "Everyone okay up here?"

"Yeah, we're fine, soon as I change my pants." Sarge killed the engine. "Let's remain under cover until we're sure they're gone."

The farmer went back to his bellowing goat. Karl got out of the cab to check how much damage they had done. The poor animal's hindquarters were crushed. She fought wild-eyed against the pain.

With a swift and strong slash, the farmer cut her throat and then cried as her blood ran into the dirt.

A young girl appeared at the back door. "Papa, papa, what happened? What's wrong with Mitzi?" She ran to her father and the goat. "Why is she bleeding?"

The farmer turned his daughter toward the house, opened the door, and sent her inside.

"Okay, guys." Weber called to the guards. "Move the goat out of my way and give me some direction so I don't run over a stupid chicken or something."

Karl wished he could give the farmer money to reimburse him. All they had was a load of gold which had to be kept secret even from its guards. The owner, now standing with arms crossed, stared him down as Weber backed out.

DARKNESS SETTLED EARLY on the autumn afternoon as the truck pulled up to the white, plaster-walled front of Dachau. The building straddled a walkway to its center. Karl sighed his relief at having the tedious journey over.

Weber set the brake and climbed down. They both entered the deep central passageway which led to an iron gate enclosing a huge open space. Karl estimated at least five hectares. Iron scrolling over the gate proclaimed its motto, *"Arbeit Macht Frei,"* promising the inmates that if they worked hard they would be set free. Emaciated prisoners with gold stars on their sleeves did all manner of meaningless tasks in the bare, sandy yard. Breaking rocks, carrying loads, digging ditches, and filling holes. None of this, Karl knew, would ever win them release.

The major's Army map had shown about a hundred and fifty camps. How many people?

Behind them advanced fierce guards with machine guns leveled at their chests. "Turn around. Raise your hands."

With slow and careful motions, they complied.

"I'm here to deliver material to the commanding officer." Weber dropped his normal superior demeanor. "I have two armed soldiers in the back of my truck. Request permission to present my orders to the commandant of this post."

A door opened in the passageway. "I'm Post Commandant Weiter."

Karl and the others snapped a salute.

Weiter responded with his own. "Tell your men to come down without their guns."

Weber motioned to Karl, who returned and called to the soldiers. They left their rifles and handguns and jumped off the truck.

By the time Karl escorted them to the entryway, the Dachau guards had dropped their machine guns to a more hospitable level. Weiter studied Weber's documents. "All is in order. Bring the material into my office." He indicated the door from which he had come.

Karl, Weber, and their guards hauled two heavy, wooden munitions boxes off the truck. Together, they strained muscles to carry them to the darkening passageway and into the Commandant's office, where he indicated they were to put them on a desk.

Accepting the padlock keys from Weber, he creaked open a lid. A gleam lit his eyes. "Ah, yes. And the inventory inside. All is good."

The commandant turned to the four men from Schultz Post. "I see you have a day's leave. The truck remains here."

The men sucked air in unison. Weber regained his voice first. "Sir, we have specific instructions to return with it."

"*Ja, ja,* my driver will take you to your homes, Munich, wherever you wish. You don't want to visit relatives in the half-ton, right? Think of the gas required. You return by daybreak Friday."

That solved a problem for Karl. He'd wondered how he would travel home from Dachau as night came on. Mother and Marta didn't expect him and couldn't come for him anyway. Father's car might still be in the garage, but everyone had to stay in with lights off.

"Go now, or you must wait until morning." Weiter dismissed them with a wave, then he spoke to his assistant. "Corporal, fetch a driver from the pool."

Two cars and drivers arrived immediately. One dropped the guards off at the barracks and took Weber home.

As Karl mounted the other, his idea blossomed. "Say, do you think we could find a market open at this hour? I'd love to walk in the front door with an armload of groceries."

"Yeah, there's one on the outskirts of town. The owner lives in the back. Maybe he'll open it up for us if we ask nicely." The driver grinned and patted his revolver.

"I hope it won't come to that." Karl didn't like bullies.

They pulled up in front of the market, now dark. The driver beeped the horn and called out.

"We're closed. Can't you see?" A thin, white-haired man in work clothes shouted from behind the building.

Karl hopped out and approached him, not giving the driver opportunity to imply any forceful action. "Sir, I'd like to buy some food for my family. I'll take anything you have. Cabbage, turnips, beets. I want to go home with a basket in my hands."

The old man studied him and his uniform. "Meet me at the front. I'll find something."

He loaded up a basket of greens, potatoes, and various root vegetables and seemed surprised when Karl paid for them.

"My wife makes brown bread. We have one loaf remaining in the back. Would you like it?"

Delighted, Karl added the homemade loaf atop the vegetables and shelled out more bills. They parted on good terms.

Karl and the driver strained their eyes, continuing home in the dark along abandoned streets. They stopped every few minutes, first listening for airplanes and then turning on the headlights for a quick glimpse. Bombed church spires hung over the city. The rail system and most sizeable buildings were destroyed, perhaps suspected of being munitions factories. Rarely did they see a man on the stony sidewalks, too drunk or too stupid to stay inside.

Karl ached for his city, this beautiful repository of the arts, home of the finest classical musicians. The streets on which he had ridden his bicycle in short pants, the squares where he and friends had kicked soccer balls, cowered in darkness. Nearer the house, his private school bore a bomb crater in the playground.

His home loomed in the dark, clustered with trees. No lights were visible. No surprise.

Karl appreciated the risk taken by the driver. "Would you like to come in?"

"Thanks, but I can't. It took longer than I thought to get here. Better head back to the post."

Karl reached to shake his hand, but the fellow gave him the *Heil, Hitler* salute.

He returned the salute. "Thanks for the ride." Grabbing his overnight satchel and the basket of vegetables, he turned to the gate.

Should he knock at his own front door? Yes, he wouldn't want to frighten Mother and Marta. He put down the food basket and knocked.

Waited.

Knocked again. "It's me, Karl. Mother?" He thumbed the bronze handle and pushed open the heavy, wooden door.

Darkness. Silence. "Mother? Marta?" His voice echoed and the barest visible outlines didn't seem right.

He brought in the food, slung his bag to the floor, and reached inside for a flashlight.

The beam stunned him by what it did not show. A barren, cavernous room, disgraced by dust and shoeprints, violated, raped of all art and decoration, remained of his family home. Breath caught in his throat like when he skied on an icy slope. He was unable to cry out. Afraid to cry out.

CHAPTER NINE

17 October, 1944
von Steuben Home, Munich

ON RUBBERY LEGS Karl ran upstairs, the narrow, yellow light bouncing in front. First to his parents' bedroom, now devoid of their heirloom furniture. Their balcony doors were ajar, and rain damage marred the parquet floor.

He dashed, not caring how much noise he made, to Marta's room and his own. Both bare, both violated of their privacy and robbed of possessions.

Could they be hiding in the closet? He shouted until panic pinched his voice like a little lost boy. Not in the big linen closet, now containing the oldest sheets and tattered tablecloths.

He took the stairs by twos, rushing down to the pantry, to the laundry room, outside to the garden. Nothing but dirt and desolation, weeds and broken pots in the dark.

Might they be in the attic? With a sudden burst of hope, he retraced his path upstairs to the end of the back hallway and pulled on the rope to let down the ladder. He called out again. He flashed the beam as he ascended, finding the trunks opened and clothes strewn about, but no Mother nor Marta.

Gently he sat on his German Oma's rocker with stuffing breaking out of its cushion. Karl turned off the light, put his head in his hands, and sobbed. He cried until he couldn't inhale over the spasms and gasps. He rested back on the chair's tired spindles, rocking and moaning.

Wailing to God from the depths of his despair, he begged to know what had happened to them.

The slightest glimmer of hope dawned. Maybe they had chosen to leave and the home had been ransacked by vandals. Everyone tried to find something to sell or barter for food and necessities. Perhaps Mother and Marta had escaped to Switzerland after Father died. They might be safe and living in comfort there.

Hunger stirred him from the attic. With nothing of Cook's packed lunch left in his bag and no electricity or gas in the kitchen, he remembered the guesthouse a couple of blocks away. They served dinner. As he reached the street, though, air raid sirens pierced the night with their warning.

He returned to the house and slid the front door's bolt. Finding that the house still had running water, he busied himself washing and scraping carrots. Raw potatoes and greens held no interest for him. Thank heaven for the bread. He sat on the floor and ate in the dark. Bombs rumbled in the distance, compressing the air with unholy vibrations.

Gathering unclaimed linens, he made a place to lie down in his old bedroom. One pathetic pillow left in a guest room gave its comfort. He curled up and prayed for sleep.

The gray of pre-dawn granted permission to stretch his cold-cramped legs and rise from the tangle of his makeshift bed. Cold water ran from the spigot. He shivered through a basic cleanup and brushed the sweaters off his teeth.

A day and night in Munich. He resolved to learn as much as possible about his family in the next few hours. A bakery nearby served fresh breads and *ersatz* coffee, the wartime substitute. Such a place spread neighborhood gossip like warm butter.

"*Gröss Gott.*" He greeted the *fraulein* in the typical Bavarian expression as he entered the warmth and fragrance of the shop. "Olga, is that you?" He recognized her from elementary school.

"*Ja.*" She did a second glance. "Karl? I didn't know you in the uniform." Her bright smile dimmed. "I'm so sorry about your father. Did you come home to visit…no, I guess not."

Olga's mother peeped from behind the gingham curtain to the kitchen. "Ah, bless me, it's Karl von Steuben." She stepped out and offered her floury hand to shake, pumping with vigor. "How have you been? In the Army now, are you? You look so fine."

He didn't, having slept in his clothes, but returned her greeting with kind words. "Frau Keller, I just arrived at the house last night after dark. It's…abandoned. What happened to Mother and Marta?"

Frau Keller flushed strawberry red and turned her face. After looking about, she motioned for Karl to follow her into the kitchen. "Sit here. I'll get you some breakfast." She pointed to the small family table in a windowed alcove.

Returning with a cup and breads, both crunchy *brotchen* and sweet raisin bread, she flustered about and then plopped into a well-worn chair.

He took a sip of the most marvelous, hot, fragrant coffee he had ever tasted.

"I don't understand, dear Karl." She leaned close and whispered. "They said your mother, God rest her soul, was Jewish. We knew she was American, but..."

Karl's heart pounded. His cup rattled, and he steadied it with the other hand as Frau Keller reached to save it.

"Is it true? She was Jewish?"

"You said, 'God rest her soul.' Did they...kill Mother? And Marta?"

"The SS took them away. What they used to do was put the women to work in munitions factories around Dachau. We hear that all the Jews they take now go straight to Auschwitz in Poland."

"Auschwitz? The extermination camp?" The vice on Karl's temple squeezed tighter.

"Surely not. I don't believe that. The Reichland would never..." She flushed and bent her head.

Karl projected from her embarrassment that the heap of deceptions had begun to crumble under its own weight. How did anyone subscribe to such a hate and not lift a hand against it?

But his own family had hidden from the pogrom rather than fight it. Was ignoring anti-Semitism as great a guilt as participating in the resulting evils? The mice in his mind ran through their mazes until Frau Keller's nervous patting on the table brought him back.

"We heard the trucks coming down the street." She looked through the window at their side. "I was taking breads to the guesthouse that morning. The SS pulled your mother and sister to their truck, holding guns on them. She yelled, 'We're Christian. We're Christian.' They didn't even pay attention."

Frau Keller mopped her brow with a once-white handkerchief. "It was later we learned about your father."

"About his heart attack?" Karl needed to know, though knowing hurt more.

"At the same time. He collapsed on the stairs in your mother's arms while the SS searched the house. The Gruber boy witnessed it all."

The teenager next door, the one who had such a crush on Marta, became the conduit of bad news. If he found him home today, several questions might be answered.

"Your father gave us the loan to start the bakery." She swept an arm wide within her toasty domain. "I bless his name for his kindness. Here, eat all you wish, and I'll prepare bread and cold cuts for you to take with." Her face clouded in something like pain, and embarrassment still colored her fat cheeks. "If you don't mind, slip out the back door when you leave. Everyone has eyes now. People tattle on each other."

"I understand. How much do I owe you for the food?"

"No, no, nothing. May your sainted father look down and smile."

Karl had never thought of his father as a saint, but he had helped any number of people on loans with generous terms. On this day, the Kellers paid in full.

He pulled coffee through the bites of bread. Otherwise, his mouth would have been too dry to swallow.

Karl returned to his home, so empty that wall scratches where furniture had stood cried and pointed out their losses. With the mystery of darkness removed, the timbers lay devoid of soul.

Last night, he had not gone into his father's office other than to call for Mother and Marta. Strange that with Father dead and the house raided, he still opened the door with a certain awe.

The desk, chairs, and tables had been taken. Papers and files occupied every available surface of built-in cabinets and windowsill. He scooped up a pile. Notes on properties long paid off, yellowed receipts strewn about, were all either garbage or indecipherable treasures. He scanned pages knowing the SS wouldn't have left anything meaningful.

Books raked from their library shelving and the wooden wall paneling punctured in several places indicated the SS had searched for hidden compartments. What a ludicrous quest. All the valuable documents stayed at the office. Mother only let him smoke cigars in his domain and on the back patio. A glorified retreat, nothing more.

He picked up his satchel and left the house, closing the front door with reverence.

Either the Grubers weren't home, or they didn't open up to him. He couldn't blame them. Jewish sympathizers reaped the same punishment as Jews. The Grubers dared not risk being seen talking to him.

How long would an Army uniform protect him? Considering the German penchant for record keeping, how long before the Army became aware of his Jewish heritage? If he had gone through anything like a normal induction, they'd have discovered his secret. He owed his life to the breakdown of army infrastructure and blown-up bases.

Father's car and its spare can of gasoline had been taken from the garage. No surprise there. Despite having money in his pocket, he chose to walk three kilometers to Father's office. Such a stroll didn't compare with marching all day under a loaded pack.

Walking did wonders for his mind, though he'd rather have run the distance. No need to attract anyone's attention. The first kilometer, he thought about the past. The second kilometer, he thought about the present. And the third, about the future.

Annoyed the Grubers hadn't answered the door though the house looked occupied, Karl had endured further embarrassment when Frau Keller asked him to leave out the back. Even after admitting his "sainted" father had financed their bakery. They had lived together in this neighborhood all his life, and now they were ashamed to be seen with him because Mother was Jewish. Christian, American, but Jewish. Well, Mother was a finer gentlewoman than any of them. She had taught him Jews are God's chosen people. Heavens, Jesus Christ was a Jew. How on earth did German Christians harbor prejudice against Jews? Totally illogical.

What if the Grubers reported to the Gestapo or SS that he had returned to Munich? The SS would snatch him up, rip him out of uniform, and throw him into a camp like those he had seen. Or send him straight for extermination. Rumors circulated of torture at Dachau. He tried to deny he had heard human screams when they approached the gate, before the commandant appeared. He considered those news films showing medical experiments done on volunteer prisoners. Did they have a choice?

Approaching the firm from its western wall, he noticed bomb damage near the back corner. The explosion had torn a gaping hole in the top of its three floors and destroyed half of the block behind. This brick structure meant more to him than most churches, and bore the same kind of reverence in his heart.

Karl halted and brought a diagram to mind. That area would hold archives. No telling what had been lost.

He veered toward a coffee house a few meters away.

Through the smoke and cinnamon ambience the proprietor greeted him, directed more at his uniform than his face. "*Gröss Gott.* Coffee?"

"Thank you. And an apple roll." He didn't need it, wasn't hungry, but longed for the familiarity of his all-time favorite treat at mid-morning. He took a round table for two at the window.

Warming his throat down to his center, the dark, steamy fake coffee charged him in a way that had nothing to do with caffeine. Normal. A piece of life as it used to be and should be. Karl longed for a future as he had expected, in the manner he would have designed. Himself in a decade or two, with a growing family and at the helm of a humming business.

A black Mercedes-Benz pulled up in front of the firm, and a man went inside. He wore the black uniform with skull and crossbones on his cap and red armband with a black swastika. With SS controlling an investigation, absolutely anything was possible. Except good. The SS did not have to answer to any other agency or court of authority, not even the Gestapo.

Boxes were hauled out. Hard to be sure from this distance, but their bearers appeared to be clerks who had worked for the company while he was there. Karl wondered if Herr Olson continued as senior investment advisor. A good man, he loomed in Karl's affection as a mentor, like an uncle, and a person in whom Father placed great trust.

Karl relinquished his intention to enter the firm. He would wait for the cover of darkness and try to speak to Herr Olson at his home. Meanwhile, what? Stroll the public parks? The ancient Marienplatz at noon? Someone might recognize him and turn him in. An evil spirit dominated his country which encouraged treachery against friends and family. As much as he wanted to visit his church and pray in its comforting arms, fear prevented him.

The Old City and its magnificent cathedral had been laid waste, as well as huge portions of the business area. Any attempt at sightseeing or simple reminiscing dripped with danger.

Escape. The plan began as a pinpoint of light and bloomed into a full sunburst. Escape to Switzerland. He knew the train system, had been to Zurich many times for Father. Yes, the railway network had been bombed. Karl didn't know how much remained of the magnificent transportation plan of Munich, but some streetcars and buses still operated. Asking questions about the existing routes to anywhere in Switzerland sounded foolish. Simple observation with lots of trial and error might get him to the southern reaches of the city.

He could walk. A hundred fifty kilometers in a week or so. Food available from farmers along the route, as he did have a little money... He began to plot, to visualize the kind of trek necessary.

His American passport—could it still be at home? Doubtful. Some clothing remained in his wardrobe. He needed other shoes, not Army issue. Heavy underwear, because he couldn't count on a place to sleep at night.

Karl signaled the waitress for his check.

She studied his face too long, like a student unsure of a date on a history test. Maybe she remembered him from his frequent breaks there before his life flipped on edge. "Visiting the old neighborhood?"

His body said run. His mind argued for calm. "Yes, lots of damage done." He pulled out a bill, noting the high inflation since he left home.

"Too bad you had to leave the business." She nodded toward von Steuben Investments. "On the other hand, just as well you're not there right now."

"I kept walking when I noticed the commotion. No point wasting my day off answering questions." He smiled a confidence that conflicted with his fears. "Father ran an honest firm. Let them dig. They won't find anything amiss."

"I'm sure. Did you read the newspaper today? They're trying to replace the men lost in Normandy and Aachen."

"No. What's happening?"

She fetched a much-read copy of the *Muenchener Merkur* and dropped it before him. "All males from age sixteen to sixty have to report for duty."

The newspaper headlines screamed Hitler's announcement. He scraped the bottom of the barrel. Germany was being poured out like sacrificial wine to the vanity of the Führer.

"The Little Corporal's going to kill us all." Horror slapped her face as soon as she uttered the words, and she covered her mouth. "I'm so sorry. I didn't mean any disrespect. Honest, I don't know why I said—"

"Don't worry about it. It goes no further than this table. But tell me…" He nodded toward his father's firm. "…how long has this been going on?"

She pulled out a chair and sat down. "Let's see. This is Wednesday? I think they started Monday morning." Her eyes searched his face, his private's uniform.

"Ah, yes. The company managed some holdings for the Reichland. They would store everything in a safe place." He smiled as if taking the boxes was normal. "Good sense, really."

Another document box was loaded on the truck.

"When did the damage happen?"

"Wednesday night of last week. People who came in here said no one was hurt. Just lots of papers in an upstairs storeroom."

The coffee house owner, with gathered brow and hard voice, called his daughter to clear tables.

She stood and took Karl's payment, counting change from the pocket of her apron. "Sorry, I have to get to work. Will you be here long?"

He did not want to tell anyone anything but also did not want to appear rude. "I doubt it."

He'd like to ask about the rails. Even a few hours on a train would save days of walking. He had better get back to the house, gather things, change to civilian clothes, and hope against all reason that his passport remained in Father's office.

Then it hit him. Every stranger would know he was between the ages of sixteen and sixty. If not in uniform, he was a deserter. Even the crippled and wounded had to serve.

A couple of blocks from home, a Kübelwagen passed him and skidded to a stop. The driver turned in the seat. "Private von Steuben? I've been looking for you. Hop in."

The charge to flee coursed through Karl's legs and his white-shocked mind.

Run! Run to Switzerland. Go now or you miss your chance.

Go now and he pulls a gun or chases you down with the car.

The driver backed up the vehicle and stared at Karl's name patch. "What's the matter? Get in, von Steuben. Colonel Weiter needs you back now."

Reason won out. Karl approached the passenger side. "We were supposed to have the day and tonight off." He pulled out his leave orders.

"Weiter has a job for you to do before you return north, and your major says you have to be back tomorrow. A colonel trumps a major."

"Let me get my satchel from the house." He stalled while he considered this unexpected twist. Karl's escape possibilities drained down a pipe with no bottom, pulling away his innards.

He opened his empty home, gathered his razor and things back into the satchel, and looked down at the basket of vegetables left in the entry. He snatched them up and put them in the car.

"What's the matter? Your family didn't want cabbage?" The driver sneered and shifted.

"Let's return this way. We can catch an intersection with a major street." In anguish, Karl passed the houses too quickly. Memories billowed from each one and rolled together into a cloud—his first little girlfriend here, the guy who collected insects on pins through their middles

in the next house, the neighborhood grouch in another. Would he ever see these houses again?

"Hey, stop a minute, will you? I need to leave these vegetables with the old lady."

"At the bakery? We don't have time." But he stomped the brake and slid on damp cobblestones.

Karl jumped out, grabbed the goods, and ran to the front. He couldn't go around back with the driver watching.

Olga Keller opened the door with a stunned expression, her eyes darting between him and the Army vehicle. Cinnamon and butter fragrance enveloped her and tumbled down to Karl on the second step.

"Take these, won't you? I brought them home, but, you know, no one's there." He lifted the gift to her arms.

"Wait." She put the load inside and dashed to the glass case of breads and sweets. She folded four thin slices of *apfel kuchen* into two paper napkins and returned smiling her gratitude.

He accepted without protest, bid her good-bye, and backtracked to the car.

"Some little old lady." But the driver didn't argue when Karl offered him half of the sweets. He took a bite, balanced the rest on his lap, and scratched off like a racer.

"She has a daughter." His mouth watered so much that he pointed directions and neither man spoke again until they had savored the last crumb.

Umm. Frau Keller makes the best pastry in the world.

His mood darkened as he observed bomb craters, rubble, and confusion everywhere. Women under a cold, gray sky gathered construction material around a gaping hole in a church wall. The driver dodged street damage and, once, a fallen tree. The city's grandeur had been blasted away.

He considered the enormous losses Germany had taken in recent months. Low on men, materials, and munitions, Hitler's personal pride obscured the obvious mounting defeats. Karl's thin chance to escape to Switzerland had evaporated.

Forget it. With my German passport, I would have been deserter. With my American passport, I would have been shot as the enemy. With both, I would have been shot as a spy. He slumped in the seat and watched the passing, as if by gray-and-white newsreel, of the landscape and pitted city.

What did Colonel Weiter want him to do? Or would this messenger take him to his death?

CHAPTER TEN

ARRIVING AT THE office block of the Dachau labor camp, Karl spotted Sergeant Weber and the two guards who came with them from Post Schultz. Weber gave a shrug as if he didn't know why they'd been called back either. The four shuffled into Colonel Weiter's office resembling school children sent to the principal.

When Weiter entered, Karl clicked his heels and saluted in unison with the others.

"At ease. The truck from Major Müller's post has been refueled. You must report to a women's satellite labor camp about twenty kilometers from here and bring back more boxes like these. Do not leave there until the inventories have been completed. Three of my men will accompany you for security. They have the map. My assistant has prepared your orders. That is all."

Karl saluted to his retreating back, accepted his written orders, and the four met the other three on the gravel road out front.

One of Weiter's men motioned. "Let's get some lunch before we head out."

He started off walking west and they caught up. The size of the post surprised him. How did the charming village of Dachau tolerate such a huge place of torment? Didn't the bright flowers in the town's hundreds of window boxes wilt with the stench?

The smell of human filth took away Karl's hunger. He wasn't sure if it came from the prisoners pounding rocks in the courtyard or from the stream which ran beneath the road to the entry. Howls from inside the walls did nothing to calm his stomach. A heavy pressure hung over the camp, evidenced by the sunken eyes and beaten-dog semblance of the soldiers.

Following the men to a mess hall near the guards' barracks, he accepted a bowl of hot stew and took a place along a benched table. The steaming vegetable broth with bits of meat stimulated a growl of hunger. He lifted his spoon and ate.

His head snapped up when he heard the crack of a whip and a cry outside.

"Ignore it if you can. That goes on day and night. Poor beasts. The lucky ones get shipped out tomorrow."

"Shipped out?" Weber tore a piece of bread and dropped it in his soup. "Where to?"

"Auschwitz. Box cars of them."

"Poland? Why?" Weber gave his busy spoon a moment's rest.

"Extermination. Those who don't die here, if they survive the trip to Poland..."

Weber shot an I-told-you-so look to Karl.

"But why?" Karl asked on impulse.

The man shrugged. "They're Jews. A few gypsies. Political dissenters, Poles, some French." As if that were reason enough.

Karl forced himself to finish his meal. If he protested, they might just throw him in with the prisoners. He needed to eat. His uniform hung loose on his frame, now sculpted by Army training and poor meals.

"Haul yourselves out of here. We need to be back by dark." The soldier took his empty bowl to a side table, grabbed another roll, and stuffed it in his pocket. "For later."

Four guards mounted the rear flatbed covered with canvas. Weber drove, and Karl and the guard with the map, Jung, rode up front. The rutted, country road bounced the men until they all groused.

At the satellite camp, guards checked their ID's and orders and directed Weber where to park. They waited for the seven to dismount and follow them to post headquarters.

The commandant slumped in his crisp uniform. Lines crossed his forehead, and bags hung under his eyes. "The inventory of the last container hasn't been finished. It could take another couple of hours. I need two men to work with my security guards to complete it. Give me one from Colonel Weiter and one from the other camp. You, private." He pointed to Karl.

He followed the Commandant and Corporal Jung into a room to the left. A stunning amount of gold gleamed from a mess hall table where the local guards scribbled on long pages.

"Give them paper and pen and show them how you are organizing the stuff. We have to send this with them as quickly as possible."

"Okay, all the gold fillings we separate into small, medium, and large. We count them and put them in those." The guard indicated ordinary canvas draw-string bags of about a liter size. "Simple wedding bands go here, and rings with stones we write some kind of description on the list. Same with necklaces. If there's any engraving, put that down." The two men moved over on the bench to share the work space.

Aghast, Karl sat down hard. Before him lay the net worth and marital aspirations of thousands of people.

"Just dig in. We've got to get this done." Jung's voice did not indicate even a drop of pleasure in the task.

Close to the end of the job, Karl and Jung scooped handfuls of necklaces at the same time, tangling their strands. As they separated the pieces, a familiar form became distinguished from the others in Karl's palm. It looked like...so similar to... He turned it over and found the inscription on the back of the ornately scrolled gold cross. "Dietrich to Anna" vertically, "5 May" on the left arm, and "1917" on the right.

He froze. Spots swirled in his vision where the beautiful cross lay in his hand.

"What's the matter?" Jung's pen paused over the page of detailed notes.

What could he say? He held the warm and heavy gold of his mother's necklace, minus its chain. The one Father gave her the day they married. "It's a cross. This isn't Jewish."

"Probably a dissenter. Maybe French."

Karl knocked some of the jewelry to the floor as if by accident. He took the chance since others had also dropped items in their haste to catalog and bag them.

"*Ach du!*" His exclamation surprised no one. He bent under the table, stuffed the cross in the top of his high boot, and then sat up with the rest in hand.

Men had been killed for such stupidity.

Karl struggled to control the tremble of his hands as they sorted the once-precious items, now mere gold for the continuance of an evil regime. Evidence of his mother's death left him unable to think clearly.

If Mother and Marta were still here, he might break through the gate with a machine gun and spray the guards with bullets, shoot Weiter in the heart and pull his family to safety.

In my dreams. The camp guards would rivet him before he breached the courtyard.

Maybe he could learn more. He endeavored to make his voice sound as off-handed and casual as possible. "So are these the last group taken from Dachau?"

One of the local guys looked up from his list. "No, these were collected weeks ago. We didn't get orders right away on where to send them. The camp was short-handed. They were just stashed until now."

Karl picked up the last ring, a wide gold band with a woven strand design. "Do you ever wonder about the person who wore this?" He read from the inside. "HMP. A man, from the size and style."

"Don't do that. Don't think of them as...people." The Dachau guard delivered this order. "If you do...you cannot...Just don't."

Karl nodded. He couldn't have spoken around the lump in his throat. *I will think about her tomorrow.*

He rose from the bench and carried the gold to the truck, twisting his foot to let the cross fall deeper into his boot. Though uncomfortable walking with the large, ornate piece concealed, he tried not to limp or favor that side in any way.

The ride back to Dachau was the longest fifteen kilometers he had ever traveled. Visions of his mother crowded his mind. Her kindness, her gentleness, her mercy to the poor, the orphans...every thought an ache deeper than hell.

I will not cry. I will not cry. The mantra in his brain attempted to postpone the grief, which, if obvious to Weber, could end his life.

He lowered his window a couple of centimeters to let the chilled air dry his eyes. The cold created an excuse for them to be watering. He faked sneezes. He pretended to sleep.

Weber kept looking at him. "What's the matter, kid? You taking this kind of hard?"

"Aw, man, I'm so sleepy I can't sit up straight. I feel awful."

"Big night in Munich? Lots of beer and women?"

"Yeah, got to bed late." Let Weber believe that and he wouldn't look for any other reason.

Upon their return to Dachau, Weiter had yet another surprise for them. "You'll be delivering certain packages to Heilbronn on the way north. My men will accompany the truck that far. Then you will continue to your post."

Karl cut his eyes sideways to Weber.

"Sir, is Major Müller aware we will be delayed?" Weber spoke carefully. Getting Colonel Weiter angry had negative results.

"Phone lines are down. We're sending word by shortwave. You'll bunk here this evening and start to Heilbronn at daylight."

Karl and Weber bunked with the platoon. They had a hot but humble supper served with a lot of rye bread and butter. The local men kept quiet, not at all welcoming. Not surprising, considering their duties at Dachau.

Karl decided to open up some conversation and see what he could learn. "So what's in Heilbronn besides salt mines?"

One soldier laughed. The others nearby exchanged glances as if checking on the wisdom of speaking.

Weber leaned closer. "There's rumors that all kinds of valuable stuff is hidden in the salt caves. Protected from bombs, you know."

"Not just rumors." A gruff voice emanated from a soldier soaking up the last of the pot liquor with his bread. "They got art from museums and rich Jews' homes in those mines. Caves go for kilometers, some of them really deep. You fellows taking things up there tomorrow?"

"Suppose so. With guards from here." Karl used the back of his spoon to smooth butter on his bread. *If Mother saw me do this...* He stopped that thought. "Then we continue north to our post."

"Dangerous territory." A sandy-haired soldier stood from the bench and picked up his bowl. "You know the Americans took Aachen, don't you?"

"Yeah, only two hundred kilometers due west of our post." Karl followed him with his own bowl. "Most of our troops have already moved toward the lines."

"So where did they go?"

"Don't know. It's not like they tell us anything." Karl wouldn't have passed on information, but he was always ready to listen.

They ambled outside as the sun dropped from view, leaving the sky in glowing reds and oranges. The contrast of God's glory and the enemy's evil rendered Karl speechless. He vowed again to get on the right side of this conflict and make his life count for good.

He turned up his collar and drew the wool coat close. Another early evening with lights out. He prayed for sleep. At least the screams had stopped. The masochists tired of their malevolence.

Morning came clear and brisk. As he stretched in the crisp air before mounting the truck, he noticed smoke rising from inside the walls. The breeze carried a horrible smell.

A local soldier nearby must have seen his alarm. "Just cleaning up the night soil in the camp. Dozens die over there every night. Can't bury them all."

Karl nodded, hoping his mother's imprisonment had been brief. And Marta's. The thought of what might have happened to his sister caused a shiver.

A soldier caught the motion and did a double take on Karl. He buttoned his jacket and rubbed his upper arms in a pantomime of being cold. Weber came out with the guards, and Karl climbed into the cab.

His mother's cross slipped lower in his boot and scraped against his ankle. All night inside his sock, it reminded him of the suffering of his mother and sister. The gold dug into his flesh as he walked. The discomfort represented a small share of their pain.

"Let's go, guys. Vacation's over." Weber and one of the Dachau soldiers, Sergeant Neumann, rode up front with Karl, and the others went in the rear with Weber's two men. Cold in the cab and colder in the back.

Neumann directed Weber to a country road northwest over rolling hills and along autumn fields.

Open spaces relieved the anxiety of the war-torn city. Squeezed between the two soldiers, unable to study the map in the jostling truck, Karl had too much time to think.

The dead space in Karl's chest grew larger. Its frigid edge crowded his lungs against his ribs, not allowing more than the shallowest of breaths. There he put his grief, pity for the prisoners, and his loneliness.

By isolating the pain, he hoped to be able to function without breaking down in the ice of reality. Loss of that aspect of humanity was the price paid for his sanity. Somewhere along the way, he decided to live, or die trying. Germany would not extinguish the memory of his family without a fight.

Weber glanced toward Neumann. "How far is it to Heilbronn?"

"About a hundred kilometers. Hope we don't have to back up and go around any bombed bridges. I made this run three weeks ago, and it wasn't too bad."

After a half hour's bumpy ride, Karl had an *oh-no* sensation. "Did one of you get the inventory?"

"Inventory?" Neumann looked blank. "I got the papers the Colonel sent with the gold." He patted a slender black folder wedged against the door.

"So the jewelry we picked up yesterday is going to the mines for safe-keeping?" Karl wished the Colonel had been more explicit about their mission.

"No, not until the stones are removed and the gold is melted down into ingots. There's a regular cottage industry in one of the satellite camps to do that."

"We're taking ingots, then?"

"And stones. A little bag of them. But I'm not supposed to know." He grinned. "Neither are you."

"Don't know a thing." Weber made a click with his tongue.

In Augsburg, Weber detoured around a damaged bridge, but soon crossed the countryside toward Stuttgart. Finding the rail system there bent, burned, and broken, he picked his way through town and continued to the north.

With fewer hills here, this segment of the new autobahn, on another day, would be a fine adventure. Karl sat forward and stretched to see the Neckar River wriggle toward its union with the Enz. He imagined a long summer bicycle ride which ended with a swim.

Sarge had no part in this dream. Worry lines stacked up on his forehead. "The truck's running mighty rough." He shouted a decibel above the road noise.

Karl laughed. "How can you tell?" Even on better highway, this ride ranked with the most rugged of his privileged life.

Neumann, jostled by Karl's shoulders as well as the road, guffawed until he snorted, which kept Karl's chuckles coming.

"It's balky." The angrier Weber got, the harder they laughed.

Like a rebellious mule, the truck seized up with the horrible rattle of metal on metal. Viewed in the rear-view mirror, black smoke poured from the exhaust. "Uh-oh. Ride's over."

The soldiers in the back pounded on the cab.

Weber hopped down and slammed the door, lifted the hood and told the engine in precise terms what he thought of its condition.

Seven men stood around the smoking motor. "Must have blown a piston," said one.

Another hopped onto the front bumper. "Maybe just a ring. I could fix it if I had the right tools."

"And a couple of days in a garage," commented the first.

Karl only knew how to give it a loan or manage its investments, so he stayed out of the offering of free opinions.

On the roadside opposite the river lay a pretty cemetery under bare trees, bordered by a low, natural-stone wall. Some fifty meters farther, recessed from the thoroughfare, an old church perched on its stone foundation.

"Great place for a picnic. Get out the sandwiches and beer, men." Sergeant Neumann spoke as if he were assuming command.

"Now hold on a minute." Sarge Weber backed away and crossed his arms. "First we call Heilbronn and tell them what's happened."

Neumann got the map out of the cab. "Not so sure, Weber. We're close to enemy lines. We can't radio that we're sitting on the side of the road with a truck load of gold."

CHAPTER ELEVEN

THE TWO SOLDIERS from Schultz Post gasped. The two from Dachau nodded. They must have already known they guarded pure gold.

"I'm not stupid enough to broadcast what we're transporting." Weber's face appeared under so much pressure it might just explode off his neck. "They know we're coming, and I've got a call sign for Heilbronn. I'll tell them we're having trouble with the truck, and they'll have to come for us and the cargo."

"Okay, and meanwhile we'll lay out the food." Neumann jerked his head toward his men, and they circled to the back. All the others followed except Weber.

Karl picked a bun from the bag, broke it open, and inserted cheese and a slice of sausage so thin it was almost transparent. The crust crunched as he sank his teeth in, and the chilled cheese released its rubbery goodness. He'd sure like to have a hot drink right now, but he thanked God he had food at all.

Every meal brought the memory of grace being said at the family table. His throat tightened around the bread, and he had to take a swig from his canteen before swallowing the bite.

Sergeant Weber shouted into the radio, his volume rising with anger.

"What do you mean, tomorrow? Do you want this load or not?" Weber stomped in the dust.

The handset jerked as he yelled and tramped dying grass on the side of the autobahn. "What do you expect me to do in the meantime?"

Sarge ended the call and marched across the road where the guys lounged with their lunch. He drained a beer from the supplies, then took the last bread, cheese, and sausage.

Karl sat on the stone wall and avoided eye contact. *Let him settle down. He'll be okay.*

When he had finished eating and chugged another beer, Weber called them together. "Look, guys, it's going to be a while before they procure a vehicle and pick us up. They said tomorrow, but I told them what I thought of that idea. Von Steuben, go see if we can get into the church over there. Got to be warmer than waiting out here."

Karl jogged up the road to the quaint building. A stable testimony to perfectly balanced architecture, the ancient stone structure represented peace in a cyclone of strife. He found the solid wood door unlocked. Passing the basin of holy water, he advanced to the altar while calling for the priest. No one answered. He listened for indication of anyone else then opened the vestry door. Empty. In the cabinet hung one worn robe, so the church still held services.

He trotted back to Weber and the others, relishing the warm-up. "Looks good, Sarge. It's open, and no one's there."

"Okay, men, here's what I want you to do. We can't leave our cargo unguarded. Everybody take a load with you. Divide the contents of the boxes if you have to, because each bar weighs fifteen kilos."

Karl looked from the half-ton to the chapel, wondering how many trips they would have to make. He did a pushup onto the flatbed and joined the soldiers reverently lifting solid gold bricks from the two wood boxes labeled as munitions.

The guards opened the wool felt wrappings to view their cargo. The crude, gleaming blocks bore no foundry imprint.

Karl had never heard of a world standard bar of fifteen kilograms. In his hands, he held the product of the cottage-industry melt-down of Jewish gold.

He knew well the value of investment property and did a quick calculation. If each bar was fifteen kilos, fifteen thousand grams, and the price of gold ran about twelve Marks per gram when he got drafted… Even given that the gold wasn't 99.999% pure, each bar equaled a fortune. Ten per box.

He picked up two and joined the line to the church.

As they entered, the Catholics among them put their loads down long enough to dip into the holy water and kneel. The irony hit Karl with a sucker punch to the gut.

When all the bars arrived, the soldiers took advantage of shelter from the freezing wind to stretch out. Felt-covered bricks spread on the middle pews, with the men scattered at ease nearby. Except for Sarge, who wandered the beautiful house of worship, examining the two side chapels and their carved wooden embellishments. He stepped up to the main altar and raised its linen covering. Then he lifted a trap door behind the altar and went below.

Sarge re-emerged, woke the snoring beauties, and regrouped them and those on guard out front. "It's going to be dark in another hour. We need to hide this gold in case…things don't work out. There's a crypt with some old stone tombs beneath here. Pick up the bars and follow me."

Each soldier carried a brick or two until all were at the top of the ladder leading into the dank, musky darkness. Weber had a flashlight, in bad need of new batteries, to guide the relay of gold to the basement.

In the crypt, Neumann ran his hand over the tomb of a long-dead priest which lay under a century of dust. He waved to the two Dachau guards to come. "Let's try to slide this lid aside."

With the three straining together, the cover moved the barest amount. "Weber, can you give us a hand?"

All seven men pushed in unison until the marble top balanced on the rim. The yellow beam of Weber's weak flashlight revealed a skeleton in the black vestments of a priest a century ago. Dried, browned, leather-like skin stretched over his boney face. A square-bottomed black cap with three points sat upon white hair which extended to the shoulders, appearing brittle as a spider web.

"Put the gold inside. On the sides, at the feet, wherever there's room." The gruff sergeant's voice wobbled. One of the Shultz Post guards broke away, shinnied up the ladder like a chipmunk escaping a hawk, and tromped the church boards toward the door.

Weber laughed. "No second sandwich for him."

Weber went to the far side of the casket, lifted the dried skirt of the garment, and nestled the last two blocks beneath. Then he pulled the small draw-stringed pouch of gems from his pocket. With a sardonic smile, he placed it under the skeleton's hands folded in pious repose upon his chest.

When the storage had been completed and the lid repositioned, Karl itched to leave. Upstairs might be breezier, but he wouldn't be spending the night down here. The men retrieved their bags from the truck and settled on the pews.

The long, icy hours passed on a hardwood pew too narrow for him to lie on his back. A single strip of carpet ran down the center aisle of the sanctuary and proved to be the best place to rest. He rolled from side...to side...to back. Hunger gnawed at his middle. A gray dawn showed through the stained glass windows. He quit trying to sleep.

His mouth tasted as though something had crawled inside and died. Forcing himself to brave the sub-freezing morning, he padded over soft, new snow in the churchyard and scooped enough into his canteen to drink and shave.

Back in the church, Weber's voice rasped into the radio and static answered. "Okay, men, they'll be here in an hour. I told them to bring some coffee and breakfast."

A hurrah rang throughout the sanctuary, and men began to come alive.

Sergeant Neumann leaned on a pillar while Karl shaved in the vestibule. "Mind if I use your razor? I hear the Heilbronn colonel is rigid about personal appearance, and we can't iron our uniforms."

"Don't mind at all. Just put it in this duffle when you finish."

The razor got passed from man to man, most not bothering to ask permission. *Pity the scraped face of the last one in line.*

A two-ton truck growled up the road. Filing out into the snow, the soldiers walked double-time, huddled against the wind. Karl joined the gang, fueled by his expectation of coffee and bread.

Sitting with the others on the flatbed, Karl savored his bread and cheese with coffee and remembered Frau Keller.

Embellishing the bakery story to the guys, he left out the part about learning his mother and sister were captured as his father died, or that he had to leave the Kellers' by the back door after eating. Instead, he told that he had been warmly welcomed and fed at the family table until he wanted no more, and Olga gave him and the driver *apfel kuchen* to take back.

A burly mechanic, stained and smeared with engine grease, revived the motor by mid-morning. Karl returned to the sanctuary to get his razor. The familiar rumble of bombers filled the sky. He rushed outside and closed the door as a long whine sang above the noise.

The air raid siren from a nearby village squealed its alarm and five-hundred-pound bombs dropped from the sky.

A deafening blast rocked the stone church and knocked Karl off his feet. Ears ringing, he struggled up and steadied himself by gripping the door's massive iron handle. Two more conjoined explosions occurred.

White blotches swam in his vision, and his ears were muffled and aching. His heart jumped against his shirt. Where the two trucks had been, a crater smoldered with strewn truck parts burning.

The men. They had been in the vehicles or gathered near them. He raced to the area, hoping to find his sergeant and Dachau's Sergeant Neumann, the secret enemies he hardly knew who suddenly seemed friends he didn't want to lose.

The intense heat of the fire pushed him back. He found no one to rescue. Only body parts, blood, and metal. Farther away lay someone in the snow. Karl ran to help him. Jung's broken limbs spread in ways arms and legs don't go. Snowflakes fell in his open eyes.

Nearby a donkey, still bearing his pack, brayed weakly. A dead man, woman, and girl were arrayed on frozen ground. The bomb killed indiscriminately.

Karl, with ears ringing, wandered in a daze back toward the road. The solid church, witness to all this grief, withstood no apparent damage. He sat on the stone wall where the crumbling stopped. Too stunned to emote, he watched travelers approach the disaster and motion to each other, explaining what they had seen.

A bomb fell from the sky. What needed to be explained? Allied bombers returning from a run south of here, discharging unused bombs on any rampart, road, or rail. It happened every day.

But never before to Karl. What should he do?

He circled the crater in the range of the melted snow. He walked in ever-widening circles, looking for life or perhaps for some task, something he could do about this catastrophe. His hearing began to return, though the piercing tweedle continued.

An Army motorcycle with a sidecar chugged from the south. As it pulled up to the damaged road, Karl pushed off the wall and approached the driver, a lieutenant.

Karl saluted. "Just happened, sir. A few minutes ago. Killed my unit of seven and a couple of mechanics from Heilbronn. Our truck broke down, and they came to assist." Out of caution, he didn't mention the gold. "Two trucks, a half-ton and a two-ton, bombed and burned."

"Terrible waste."

The men or the trucks?

The lieutenant shook his head. "I don't have a radio." He twisted back toward Stuttgart and then in his onward direction. "We're about fifteen kilometers from Heilbronn. Were you headed there?"

"Yes, sir."

"Hop in the sidecar. I'll take you to the base commandant and you can report the damage to him."

The lieutenant veered around the edge of the charred area, working his way past carts and wagons going south, away from the battle zones. "I don't suppose there's anything to guard here. Nothing to loot."

The cogs of Karl's mind ground against each other as he thought of the enormous fortune hidden in the church. Conflicted, he played out several scenarios while bouncing in the sidecar. He should assume the Heilbronn commandant expected the shipment. If interrogated later, he could say he intended to keep the gold safe by telling no one about its existence, and certainly not its hiding place.

On second thought, he decided to pretend he didn't know what they carried. After all, the guards from the northern post hadn't known until Weber let the info slip. Germany's disarray and poor communication worked to his advantage.

God had taken back what Nazis had stolen from his chosen people.

If he could escape Germany without giving up the location of the gold, it might not be found for centuries. If he got caught in the deception, he was worse than dead. His escape had a new urgency.

The shambles of Heilbronn stunned him. He had visited the lovely town in the curved embrace of a gentle river. An involuntary *unh* sound escaped his chest, and the lieutenant looked around at him.

"Yeah, it's bad." He shouted over the motor. "The enemy has been bombing for four years. Americans during the day, and British at night. They got the airfields and military targets first. The rails are destroyed. Now the houses and roads. Anything they can hit."

Karl couldn't comprehend such devastation. Everywhere he looked, steeples had tumbled, holes were blown out of the walls of tall, proud buildings, and bomb craters pocked the landscape. The city, snuggled in a bend of the Neckar River and renowned for its sport clubs, suffered worse than he had seen anywhere.

The lieutenant drove with caution down the damaged streets to the entry of the Army post. "Think I'll go in as well. Might be easier if I tell them what happened."

Karl's needless unrest about facing the senior officer became a mere battle report to a colonel. He wrote the names, rates, and post assignments of the dead insofar as possible.

The colonel groaned over the loss of the trucks and two of his best mechanics. "What was the purpose of your unit? Why were you coming to Heilbronn?"

"I wasn't told, sir. Just following orders. We were on the way back to Schultz Post northeast of Frankfurt, sir. Our commandant, Major Müller, ordered us to return with the truck as soon as possible."

"Right. Well, I've got your details. Lieutenant, deliver the private to the enlisted barracks and show him the mess hall."

Upon the mention of food, Karl's stomach growled. His face burned with embarrassment, but the officers laughed.

"You've had a bad day, private. Requisition a new uniform, get fed and rested. I'll see you here at eight hundred hours tomorrow."

Some dead stranger's bunk became Karl's best friend. After a hot stew, bread, and a shower, he slept as if his brain had turned off.

Over coffee the next morning, he considered his possibilities. If he had any kind of vehicle—anything at all—he'd try to escape south to Switzerland. How long would it take him to walk a hundred kilometers? Could he buy or find food? Assuming he bought civilian clothing, how would he get across the border without a passport?

Zurich being a short distance from the border, he might find the bank with which his father had dealt, the one to which he had traveled several times.

But with every man between sixteen and sixty conscripted, the Army would shoot him for sport like wild game.

He reported to the post commandant's office.

"Wait there, private." The sergeant working the reception desk pointed to a hard bench. "The colonel's busy."

Insignificance washed over Karl. Pushed aside by the urgencies of a losing war and amid the swirling confusion of the army post headquarters, he mused on how he got to this point. Thinking on anything except the loss of his family, he asked God to take control and determine his next move.

"Private." The sergeant's bark snapped him to attention. "What do you do, Private?"

"What do I do?" Strangely, his mind's first response was investment management.

"You a driver? Work dispensary?" The sergeant growled like a bulldog.

"Radios, translations, that sort of thing." Karl turned his hat in a circle around its band.

"You ride a motorbike?" The question challenged his manhood. All men rode motorcycles.

"I've driven one a couple of times." Not a lie. A friend had owned one when they were in a private high school. The friend let him drive, and Karl nearly killed them both.

"The phone lines are down. We need a message taken to the front. Think you can do it?"

Before he spit out a qualified answer, the colonel stepped into the room from his office.

Karl clicked his heels and saluted.

"Private von Steuben, this way." He stood, not closing the door or offering Karl a seat. "I confirmed that your post northeast of here has moved out. You're to be reassigned. Collect a motorcycle and return for a message and map. You'll go to the front near Alsace to deliver a message and return with the response."

"Yes, sir."

"I assume you can drive?"

"A car, yes, sir. A motorcycle, more or less."

The colonel paused, eyes squinted. "Good enough." He stepped behind his desk, looking aside and rubbing his face. "And private…"

"Yes, sir?"

"Be careful. This is not a safe assignment." The colonel's brow shadowed his sharp eyes.

"There aren't any, sir." Karl firmed his expression to avoid smiling.

The colonel could kiss his cycle good-bye.

CHAPTER TWELVE

KARL ADMIRED THE low, flat-gray motorcycle with the BMW circle mounted on its side. After slipping on the leather helmet, goggles, and gloves as if he did this every day, he spent a few minutes cruising around the post. He knew little about the machine or how to pilot one, except turns required a certain angle of leaning, and gravel could be deadly. When he cut the engine to pick up the message and map, the thought occurred that he may not be able to restart. The timing and force of the kick seemed important.

Upon return for his assignment, he didn't have to wait. Waving him inside, the colonel delivered a stern commission. "Soldier, you are to protect this message with your life. You will not open the bag. You are not to read the message. Do not delay for any reason. Request a response and return immediately. Do you understand?"

"Yes, sir."

The colonel unfolded a worn map. "From Heilbronn, swing west along this route to Saarbrücken, avoiding the more difficult hills. About a hundred kilometers. Aachen has fallen, just to the north. The Allies entered the Fatherland at that point. We must contain them in the Ardennes, in Belgium south of there. I tell you this to underscore the importance and the danger of your mission. Should you be forced off the route, do not go north."

"Yes, sir."

Karl rocked the motorbike off its stand and kick-started a new phase of his military service. The colonel didn't realize he'd pounce like a tiger on any opportunity to give his secrets to the Allies. He hoped to use this cycle to run as far away from Germany as he could get. Somehow, the vehicle made possible his escape.

Traveling south on the autobahn, he soon passed the quaint church pregnant with solid gold. No activity showed. Hopefully, no one knew about its treasure yet. Already a path circumvented the yawning bomb crater, stained with blood and dark burns but cleared of body parts. The Neckar River drifted along, unmindful of being crowded by the rubble.

Karl's route took him a park's width from the border with France, a line guarded by troops, tanks, and heavy artillery. German military vehicles ground over the hills and roads, churning grass into mud and puffing clouds of diesel fumes into the air. The vibration of the earth triggered a gut reaction to get out of there.

He had heard of violent atrocities against French resistance. Apparently, his escape did not lie in that direction.

Karl stopped and pulled the rain gear from a side satchel. Though a favorable temperature for fall, the wind chilled him until he shook. The high school friend had sold his motorcycle in the winter. No wonder.

All manner of traffic fleeing the battle lines opposed him. He dodged cars, carts, and cows. Quick reflexes developed long ago for tennis became survival skills. Muscle fatigue set in. He loosened his shoulders, hunched against the cold, and pushed on.

Checking the map for the last detail, he located his destination, the farm adopted by the military unit. After parking his cycle and scraping his feet, he entered the front door of the home as another soldier exited. His numbed hands still vibrated when he held out the message pouch to the major. He waited at attention.

The major scowled like a brewing storm. "He wants a reply. Tell him they're throwing everything they've got at me. I need men. I need tanks." His tirade increased in volume with every protest.

"Sir, please put that in writing and seal the pouch, sir."

Karl's body begged for food. He hoped he didn't have to make the return trip without lunch.

"I'll prepare a written answer by the time you're ready." He grumbled at his sergeant. "Point Private von Steuben to our enlisted facilities. Get him something to eat."

Following directions, Karl went to the closed tent behind the house for lunch. About fifteen dirty, wrinkled soldiers, bent over their bowls and bread, paid him no mind. Finished eating, one focused on Karl's riding gear and asked what unit he was with.

He considered the simplest answer. "I'm temporarily attached to Heilbronn."

The tall guy leaned back from his lunch. "Pretty little town. Hear they're using the salt mines for art storage."

Rumor said slave labor enlarged the mines. Karl nursed a hot cup of fake coffee. "That's what they say. I haven't seen them."

"So are you returning today, or be for a while in camp?"

"My orders are to return. Tell me, how safe is it here?"

The whole group laughed. A wiry fellow quipped, "If the bombs don't get you, fatherless Americans up in Aachen just broke through with their tanks. I guess it's as safe as anywhere else on the western front."

Maybe these guys had current information. "So is the American First Army coming this way?" He primed the pump with a detail from Major Müller's map.

The tall one lit a cigarette and took a long draw, squinting against the smoke. "Probably not. So far, looks like we're holding them."

Karl picked at his food and their minds with patience, but he got nothing in the way of military secrets. The danger of an officer overhearing kept them wary. No one should be talking about positions and strategy.

He entered the post headquarters which stirred with grumbles and an air of frustration.

The colonel called him in. "Private, does your unit have a translator?"

"Yes, sir. What can I help you with?"

"My sergeant will copy a message we intercepted and send it back with you for translation. And if the land lines aren't reconnected, you must return with the answer."

"Sir, I'm a translator. I worked on the radios with a unit north of Frankfurt before this assignment."

The colonel couldn't have been more surprised if he'd kissed him. His head popped back and brow appeared startled. "You? Are you sure? I mean, that's too good to be true."

"I graduated from Ludwig Maximilian University, sir. I can translate." No point telling him Mother was American.

"Take a look at this. Here—Sarge, show him what you've got."

Karl entered the side room where the sergeant had scattered maps and scraps of paper on a rough table.

A lieutenant stood near, pulling on his ear. "Honestly, this is only bits and pieces. I studied a little English in public high school. I looked up words, but I'm not getting meanings. Maybe it's in code."

The two men showed Karl the message.

"May I ask where this came from? You see how the letters are made. This wasn't written by an American."

"No, I wrote that. The original is—Sarge, do you have it? We took it off a casualty when our tank hit his Jeep in France, the Ardennes."

The sergeant pulled a bloodied page from beneath a dual language dictionary.

Karl studied the folded paper. Handwritten. "We're contained in the...Battle of the Bulge? Capitalized like a name. English doesn't capitalize all nouns like German. What bulge? Are they surrounded on a hill?"

Silently, the three men bent over the map again. The Ardennes had hills, but no actual mountains.

He looked back to the message. "Need supplies, warmer clothing." Nothing top secret here. But what bulge was it talking about? He found no geographical answer to the puzzle. "Sorry, Sarge. That's the translation, but the meaning isn't clear."

With beans in his belly and petrol in the cycle's tank, Karl accepted the reply and checked his map. Not that he doubted the route back to Heilbronn, but he doubted whether he would return. A conservative nature and preference for security had gotten him exactly nowhere so far. His family was dead, his fortune looted, his home ravaged. He vowed to do nothing more, now or ever, to facilitate this evil regime.

Karl set his face toward Aachen.

The distance was about the same as the return to Heilbronn. He could reach the front lines there before he would be missed in Heilbronn, unless battle damage slowed him.

He drove himself into the jaws of death. What kind of fool had he become? Colder with every kilometer, he bent into the wind, ducking as much as possible behind the inadequate shield. His shoulders cramped more with each revolution of the question, *Why am I doing this?*

Answers began to come. Because his country was wrong. Because its generals would torture, starve, and kill him if they knew of his Jewish blood line. Because they killed his mother and sister and precipitated Father's heart attack.

Those answers sufficed for the first twenty-five kilometers. Then another level of reasoning slipped in. Because he was Christian and worshipped only the Triune God. Every time he clicked his heels and saluted *Heil, Hitler*, bile rose in his throat. He thought of the Old Testament stories of Daniel and Shadrach, Meshach, and Abednego. *Thou shalt have no other gods before me.* No other gods. No man, not even the angel Gabriel, was to be worshipped.

Heil, Deutschland would be appropriate, especially in the Army. He had always been a loyal German, proud of its beauty and work ethic. But not *Heil, Hitler*.

Confusion settled in. Somewhere in Corinthians, Paul wrote about obeying the king. Hitler, in this case. But if the king erred, like Daniel's king, he had to put God first, right?

He pulled off the road, allowing Army trucks to pass around a bomb crater. He took the moment to clean his goggles and readjust his rain gear, and he recognized the tremble of his hands as fatigue and fear. He rolled his tense shoulders and pulled the canteen from its straps.

[121]

People fled the area, no doubt leaving homes and animals to the chances of war. Did they fear the Americans? Should he?

Karl needed a plan. Assuming he got to the lines, he couldn't walk over to American troops and say, *Hey, guys, I don't want to be German anymore.* They would shoot him before he could speak.

The traffic had passed. Still he stood beside his cycle, frozen with indecision. Too late to go back. He had already burned his bridges. No, he would never again serve the enemy.

His eyes focused on a Catholic church up the road, and he went to it. He thought of taking the message inside and locking the bike, but it would be stolen faster than thunder follows lightning. He sat on the stone steps, leaned his head into his hands, and cried out to God.

What must I do? What can I do? Is it too late to ask for your direction? For your providence?

The next level of reasoning came over him. *Use me. You gave me talents, intelligence. I want to use them for Your people. Christians, Jews, Your people.*

A priest came from inside. "Can I help you, my son?"

Karl twisted to look up. Their eyes locked, and he found kindness.

The priest stepped down to his level and sat beside him. A kindred spirit surrounded them for precious moments of silence.

Karl dared not share his agony with anyone, not even a priest bound to respect secrecy. He wiped his eyes and blew his nose. "No, Father. I think I have my answer. Thank you."

"These are hard times."

"Yes, Father. They are indeed." Many people had lost much, but he had lost everything.

"You're going toward the battle?" The priest's calm, patient voice gave solace.

"Yes, sir." Ironically, his escape from conflict took him into the hottest point of the war. Around him, the earth split and trees leaned sideways in eerie testimony. And he hadn't approached the front lines yet.

"Do you wish to confess and receive absolution?"

Karl did not want to die with unresolved sins, but he couldn't confess to being a traitor, a deserter. "Thank you, Father, but I'm not Catholic. I can pray directly to God. He will forgive me."

The priest's gentle expression did not change. "Are you sure?"

An immense resolve, an unreasonable peace beyond understanding blanketed Karl. "Yes, I'm sure." He stood to go.

"You don't have to leave. We can hide your motorcycle in the shed behind the church for a while, and you can come inside."

"Thank you. I appreciate the offer, but I must push on." He removed his glove and offered the priest his hand, unsure of the exact protocol with a priest. They shook, sharing a brotherhood beyond this time and space.

Karl stomped the kick starter, bringing the engine to life, and continued toward Aachen. Seeing a family walking in his direction with loaded backs, he stopped short and drank from his canteen while they approached.

He tried to appear non-threatening. "Good afternoon."

The man paused. Their caution was evident as the man, woman, two girls, and a young boy watched him, the boy's eyes more on the motorcycle.

"I see you're leaving. How far has the enemy advanced?" Nothing suspicious about asking what he might run into down the road.

The man glanced backwards and shifted his load to the ground, silent permission for his wife and children to do the same.

"They've taken Aachen. The Siegfried Line will hold them for a while. Our army retreated inside the border to Stolberg."

Karl had visited the concrete row of dragon's teeth across the countryside when his family went to the Three Corners area, where Germany, Belgium, and Holland came together. A happy excursion in a different lifetime.

"Are you from this area, sir?" Again, Karl contrived to be just a tired soldier sharing a dangerous path. He hoped they overlooked the protrusion of his revolver beneath the rain cover.

"A small farm west of the Roer River. With all the action near there, I thought I should move the family out." He nodded toward his girls, in the shadow of their mother.

This poor farmer displayed better judgment than Karl's "sainted" father. But then, the farmer had less to lose by leaving.

The man rubbed his neck and shoulder. "So how much farther must you go?"

"As far as I can. I'll be searching for an officer to give him a message. Are they still firing at Aachen?"

"The guns fire all day and night. Tanks running around, soldiers everywhere. A bad place to be."

"*Ja,* I guess I'm going the wrong direction." What lay ahead, and how could he get from the German line to the Americans?

"If you don't find your man in Stolberg, there's a rumor we're setting up fortifications in Duren. On the other side of the river." He pointed off toward the east. "Just a rumor, you know, but it makes sense. Nothing else of any size around here." He bent and lifted his load, jerked his head to his family. "Come, let's go."

With grunts and huffs, they hoisted the bags onto their backs and shoulders.

"I wish you a safe journey, sir."

"*Ja,* thank God it isn't snowing."

They parted then, and Karl advanced several kilometers toward Duren until a soldier ordered him to halt, his growl menacing as a Rottweiler.

CHAPTER THIRTEEN

KARL APPROACHED THE last meters slowly, nodding to indicate compliance.

The first test.

His heart rose in his throat.

The soldier swung his Mauser 98 without pointing the rifle directly at Karl. "State your business and your destination, private."

He swallowed hard before trusting his voice. "I have a top secret message to deliver to the front, and I must bring back a reply to Colonel Weiter."

"Who is your message for?"

Karl stalled by removing his goggles and brushing dust off his rain cover, still insulating him from the worst of the cold wind. He turned off the burbling engine. "That depends on who is in command of the retreat—*reorganization*. Have our forces pulled back to Stolberg? With the phone lines cut and radios silenced, the Colonel's information is sketchy."

"The phones are working again. Our men ran new lines. Got them completed this morning. You may as well turn around."

Distant rifle pops echoed over the flat land. Artillery booms rolled through the hills. Karl looked across the fields toward the sound. "Wish I could. But the last thing I need right now is a court martial, you know what I mean?" He gave a sarcastic laugh, remounted, and started his cycle.

"Carry on."

Karl's head floated with relief. He had to come up with ready answers. He needed a plan.

Once out of the soldier's sight, he stopped to consult his map. After Duren, two villages lay between there and Aachen. Maybe he'd better avoid Duren if forces were building up there. Not everyone could be put off like that last guy. Should he take the motorcycle off the road, head out cross country?

He considered the field beyond the ditch. No, this land looked boggy. Hard slogging in that grassy stubble.

Karl continued, hoping for a side lane. He rounded a bend. Too late. The street led him right through the middle of Duren. Chugging along, giving no one opportunity to catch his eye, he had driven a couple of blocks when two soldiers jumped into the street waving their arms.

"Your motorcycle. Give us your motorcycle."

If he plowed through them, someone would be injured. Probably himself.

One of them pulled his sidearm but pointed it up, more like a warning. "Halt. We need your cycle."

Another grabbed the handlebar as Karl slowed. "Get off. Give it to me."

"I can't give you my cycle. If I don't return with this thing, my colonel is going to kill me." He dramatized desperation to project the lie.

The men glanced at one another. "Who's your colonel?" The speaker seemed less sure than when he forced Karl to stop.

"Colonel Weiter, of Dachau. I'm his messenger."

"Dachau? Oh." A slight shake of the head from the soldier with the gun. "I thought you were from our unit." They stepped aside, disappointment showing like being shooed away from a banquet.

Karl gunned the engine on the slippery stones, almost throwing himself off. Wobbling, he regained his balance at the last second and dodged a one-ton Army truck. At an intersection he spotted a bridge over the Roer, a small tributary to the Rhine, only a few meters wide at this point.

He swung toward the river and crossed into the village of Eschweiler. Artillery shook the ground, both from nearby German guns and Americans returning fire. What if he ditched the motorcycle, bought or talked someone out of some civilian clothing, and walked across the marshy land toward Aachen?

No one could be trusted not to turn him in. He would be gunned down as soon as he took off his uniform.

After passing through the village to the countryside, he mounted a slight hill. An advancing roar vibrated in Karl's bones. The world came alive with explosions from Allied airplanes racing above the land. Artillery rumbled, chewing up the hills from the east, answered by the sharp sounds of high-velocity tank guns to the west. Hand grenades from the German line gave their distinctive dull reports, and machine guns chattered their response.

The screaming dive of a fighter-bomber iced his veins. Karl skidded, dropped the cycle in the road, and jumped into the ditch. He covered his head and prayed. Bombs fell on the fields, throwing mud on his rain suit. When the air cleared and he dared to look, his vehicle lay in several twisted heaps of metal on the pitted road, burning in a fire of the precious little petrol remaining.

That settled it. On foot the rest of the way. He stood over the destroyed motorcycle with a ridiculous need to say a few words of obituary. The faithful steed had served him well.

A couple of meters from the fire, his satchel lay split. Bread and cheese, his last meal as a German soldier, tumbled out. Covering his face from the flame, he retrieved the food, map, leather message bag, and his orders.

Karl spotted the gray concrete dragon's teeth drawing their angry line across the land. With whispered prayers, he turned into the marsh rather than pass through villages where the German Army regrouped.

Very few trees, all small, graced the field. With every step, his mother's cross pendant rubbed against his foot until it wore a raw place. While not given to masochism, something about the pain filled a gnawing emptiness. He hurt because he was alive, and she wasn't.

Alongside the field ran a natural stone wall, most likely built centuries ago by farmers who cleared the land. Perhaps the earth would be more solid there. He used the boundary as cover, crouching to crest the next rise.

Lying on relatively dry grass in the darkening afternoon, he scanned the landscape for guns. A German tank clanked kilometers away to the east. If he could make that next ridge, he would crawl forward, keeping his white handkerchief at the ready.

His view flipped past a dark clump, then darted back. Not a bush. It didn't move, but it emitted mechanical sounds. Maybe voices, as through a radio. Karl lay low and watched for a long time, preferring to take in the glory of a red sunset. By that time, he had decided the dark lump was a dead soldier.

He threw a rock near the spot. No motion at all. He tossed more, becoming braver against the deceased.

The sky's embers burned low, and guns on both sides settled into occasional protests. Karl squirmed across the frozen land toward the soldier. In the fading light, he reached an American corporal, strapped with a field radio. Cool, but not as cold as the ground. Dead a short while. Under the back edge of his helmet, his neck, torn open by some projectile, bled into the earth.

A quick death. Probably never felt the pain.

He searched the man's pockets and found nothing but a folding knife. The dog tag gave basic information: Viertel, Henry, U.S. Army, Protestant, A Pos.

Hmm. A German surname on an American soldier?

A plan formed. If he approached the American side in their uniform, they wouldn't shoot before he had a chance to declare his defection.

And if he left his uniform and ID on this man, the Germans would record him killed in action. They might wonder why he was so far north, but they wouldn't come looking for him. A definite advantage.

In the dark, Karl removed his rain gear and clothing, shivering with cold and fear. He exchanged his pants, shoes and socks with the soldier, piece by piece, dressing the American in his German uniform. Not a perfect fit, but adequate for an hour. Last, he transferred his mother's necklace into his sock. He took Henry's turtle-shell headgear and staged his motorcycle leather helmet with Henry's blood as if it had been blown off.

When every item had been exchanged, the new Henry Viertel closed the eyes of the deceased Karl von Steuben. He slung the radio over his shoulder, and moved in a cautious crawl toward the Siegfried Line.

In deepest darkness, Karl inched forward to the gray fortifications jutting from the earth. Along that line, German soldiers in bunkers shot at western invaders. The precise location and number of such protected areas he didn't know.

This area seemed to have only the "dragon's teeth" to prevent the entry of tanks. Crumbled, some destroyed, they offered little defense. Good. They hadn't held up well against the Americans. So much for German propaganda, and the thousands of lives—mostly young boys and slave labor—eaten up to build the line.

He rested a moment, commanding his pulse to settle. If soldiers guarded the border through the night, they would find him by his heavy breathing alone.

The true no-man's-land stretched between here and his goal, Aachen, held by Americans. Fighters hadn't hit the hills behind him tonight. He dared to trust luck.

The radio squawked, triggering a frantic jerk to turn it off. He searched for the knob in the dark.

"Report your position."

He couldn't say *Siegfriedstellung*. What was the English? Siegfried Wall? Hoarsely, he whispered, "Siegfried."

No question came back. He left the radio on, even while wondering if its noise had caused the death of...who? Henry Viertel. Better remember his name.

He went to his hands and knees, then slithered down the hill of wet grass toward a copse of trees. *Take your time. Your life depends on it.*

So close to relative safety of the woods, guns opened up behind him. Answering volley came from the forest. Caught in the space between, he pressed flat against the earth and shifted the helmet.

Another rifle crack from behind registered in his mind as searing pain tore his back and head.

URGENT VOICES WHISPERED nearby. Someone grasped his arms and dragged him on his belly over the ground. Dirt in his mouth and something salty with a sharp taste. Blood.

"One, two, three..." Men grunted, lifted him roughly, and bore him on a stretcher.

He tried to open his eyes, but the left one seemed stuck closed. Trees whizzed by overhead. Dizzy, sick to his stomach, he relinquished his consciousness to the jiggling and bouncing.

Awake in a tent with the barest light, he groaned against the cold sting of alcohol. Prostrate on a hard table, he lay in a pool of blood and saliva. A bag of clear liquid dripped into his arm.

Around him but not within line of sight, people spoke in English. He twisted to look, but it hurt too much.

"Easy there, Henry. We've got you. This is a field aid station. You're going to be okay."

He didn't feel okay.

An indeterminate time later, two soldiers placed him on a rack in some sort of vehicle. Still night, men worked with flashlights. With his good eye, he saw a tier of stretchers on the opposite wall and at least one man above him. Various ones moaned, others lay deathly quiet.

Cold. The word formed in his mind but could not reach his lips. He shivered in pantomime, stretching to catch the attention of his caretaker.

"Yes, I know." The soldier with the flashlight tucked the blanket closer about him. "We're taking you to a field hospital. The aid station gave you a good triage number. You're going to make it." The light wobbled as he stood to check the stretcher above. "Not sure about this one." The vehicle roared and jerked along.

Blood dripped on him as the truck swung around a corner. The medic braced himself and swore. "These meat wagons aren't made for comfort. You okay, Henry?"

The medic had spoken to him. He didn't feel like a Henry. They used the same name back at the aid station. If not Henry, then who? No answer came. He slept again.

The back door opened wide with the light of dawn behind two men in white. Angels coming to get him. At the far wall vapor curled from the mouth of a patient. His eyes were open, unblinking.

He wanted to cry for this stranger. His throat hurt with the emotional response, but nothing came out.

His turn to be carried out. Except for gritted teeth, he tried to just relax and let it happen. *Oh, my head.* Not only the wound, but inside. The pressure threatened to burst his skull like a rotten melon.

On the table, English surrounded him. He couldn't understand why that seemed strange.

"I'm Dr. Small. We're going to take a look at your injuries and do a little repair. He lifted the dog tag. "Henry Viertel. Henry, what's your blood type?"

He didn't know. What's more, he seemed unable to tell them he didn't know. Frustrated, he worked until he made a noise, but no words came.

The doctor leaned closer. "Henry, can you hear me? Bat your eyes if you can hear me."

Who is Henry? But the guy looked straight at him. Hear him? Barely, through cotton wadding and an impossibly loud squeal in his ears. He batted his good eye.

"Are you Henry Viertel?"

That's what they said at the aid station, and he didn't have any better idea. He batted his eye again. How many times should he blink to say a line of pain ran up from his back and exploded his head?

"Okay, Henry, we're going to give you some Novocain and stitch you up. First, this pretty nurse has to clean your wounds." A sweet, round face came into view. Calling her pretty stretched the imagination.

Aside to the woman, the doctor said, "Penicillin in the line. Call me when he's ready. He's shocky. Keep him warm."

"Blood, Doctor?"

"Supply's short. But yes, do a cross match and start a liter. Dog tag says he's Type A positive. Better check that."

Her treatment was tender torture. She began with the head wound, which bled again as she dissolved the crust. Then stitching the area with a hypodermic, she spoke gently. "Novocain always makes it bleed more, but you won't hurt when he closes the wound. Now let's roll you over so I can get to your back."

She removed bandages and began the stinging Novocain injections. He drifted into some existence less than consciousness while the doctor sewed skin together with countless stitches.

When she pulled off his muddy combat boots and socks, something fell on the floor. She picked it up and brought it to his view. An intricate cross, about three centimeters tall, with the appearance of time-burnished gold.

"Is this yours?" She turned it over and read the inscription. "Dietrich to Anna, 5 May, 1917."

Familiar. Something he should remember.

"It cut into your foot." She stung the raw flesh with alcohol. "Hmm. May be infected. Here. Put this in your pocket." She handed him the cross.

Transferred later to a clean, dry bed, Henry found himself in a large ward of patients with all manner of bandages and IV bags. Despite being surrounded by activity, he succumbed to sleep.

"Henry, I'm here to give you a bath."

He climbed through layers of gray cotton to get to the voice, which emanated from a square-built, brunette nurse. In complete lack of privacy, she proceeded to wash off mud and blood, then gave him the soapy cloth to clean his private parts while she busied herself with not looking.

Chilled to the bone, he pulled fresh sheets and the wool blanket over his hospital gown and bunched up into a shivering ball. She draped an additional blanket over him. After adjusting his IV and placing an enameled bedpan nearby, she gathered his clothing and turned to leave.

The cross. In his pocket. Waving wildly, he made a guttural sound.

She paused. "What do you want?"

He pointed to the pants and motioned for her to give them to him. Finding the pendant, he showed her the prize.

She opened the small drawer of a metal bedside table. "Want to put it in here?"

With some reluctance, he dropped the treasure into the drawer and watched her close it.

Smiling, she left him in peace.

Chicken soup at lunchtime brought the first warm calm inside his body. Real coffee afterwards sharpened his senses and extended warmth to his icy feet.

Tall, thin Dr. Small approached, stethoscope around his neck and clipboard in hand. "Good afternoon, Henry. Do you remember me?"

He nodded.

"Say the word. I want to hear you say something." Lines of worry stacked above his piercing eyes.

He made noises. Words didn't happen. They were in there somewhere, unconnected to his mouth. Finally, he shrugged and shook his head, spilling tears of frustration.

"Okay, don't worry. It may take a couple of days."

A lieutenant visited a patient on the ward the following afternoon. The injured man gave a tour of his wounds and told details of his evacuation. More serious talk ensued about the progress of battle and number of men wounded and killed. He envied the patient, wishing he had someone to drop by and chat.

To his surprise, the lieutenant said good-bye to the fellow and came straight to his own bed.

"Good afternoon, Henry. Glad to see you made it." The sandy-haired officer smiled through a certain look of uncertainty.

He shrugged and touched his lips, trying to convey the inability to speak.

The man nodded. "Dr. Small told me you're having trouble talking." He shoved his hands in his pockets then rocked on his toes. "The squad is pulling for you. They risked their lives to get you out of the woods."

He nodded, trying to remember anything about where and how he had been hit. Everything seemed to start with the field aid station and then transfer and treatment here.

The lieutenant chuckled. "They kept your radio, though. One of the newer ones." His gaze clouded. "Henry, Doc wants to know if the injury affected your memory." He motioned to the bandages. "Do you remember me?"

Embarrassed, he shook his head.

"Honestly, I thought I remembered you, but I guess not." The officer fiddled with something in his pocket, looking mystified. "I mean, replacements come in every few days. It's hard to remember everyone. But we had this conversation when I noticed your German surname, and you told me about being from settlers in Texas, and how your family still speaks some German."

At last, an explanation of why so many words circling in his brain weren't English. He let his attention wander for a moment, trying to reach through the fuzz.

The lieutenant propped a foot on the bottom rail of his bed. "I just thought, I mean, I sort of remembered you as blond with blue eyes, but you're not." He laughed. "Never mind. I'm glad you're still with us. Get yourself together. You might be able to help us finish this war."

He saluted with a smile.

Henry returned the salute from his reclining position. His legs stiffened reflexively, and even his feet jerked to attention. He felt silly and the officer laughed as he turned away. Lost in this new world as a mute, wounded, and weak soldier, he opened the small drawer by his bed and reached for the gold cross. Whoever Dietrich and Anna were, they comforted him.

CHAPTER FOURTEEN

HENRY SLEPT WITH the pendant clutched in his hand. The nurse joked that he kept a death grip on it. She returned later with a shoestring and helped him tie the cross around his neck without hurting the bandaged areas.

When asked about his hearing, the best he could do was sort of waffle his hands over both ears. He heard, but not clearly.

"How's your vision?"

To that question he nodded as much as the tape allowed and attempted a smile.

"And your memory?"

Confusion reigned in his mind, pushed aside by the headache that nothing stopped. He shrugged.

Moved to a smaller ward of recovering patients, boredom settled in. He passed the hours by handing things to less mobile patients, helping in any way possible.

The doctor still came by twice a day. He didn't do well on his writing test. When told to write his name, he wrote Henry Wirtell, trying to sound out what he had been told. The doctor frowned, then told him to write anything he wanted to.

Dexterity wasn't the problem. He wrote, "cold always, need books."

Dr. Small smiled at the note. "We have a library for ambulatory patients. Reading might help you get your words back."

So for about three days, Henry read. Magazines, comics, poetry by Robert Burns, classic novels—whatever drew his attention in the paltry offerings of the library. The visits gave him an excuse to wander the halls.

As silly as it seemed, he sometimes grabbed a moment of privacy to practice making sounds like the guttural *uh-huh, yeah,* and *unh-unh* used by people around him. When those worked, he graduated to *no* and finally *yesss.*

Bored and wishing for a *Münchener Merkur* or any financial newspaper, he pulled a dusty economics text off the shelf. Might be interesting, or might help him go to sleep tonight.

A patient wheeled into the room, straining as if rolling the chair were a hard mountain to climb. Yet he smiled at Henry and read aloud the title of the book he'd chosen. "Man, you're getting desperate, aren't you?"

Henry shrugged, wishing to say he couldn't speak.

"Hi, I'm Jim Fuller. Been here for a long time. I'm going stir crazy."

Henry nodded. He hadn't associated with other patients because of the speech problem, but the man seemed familiar. Henry pointed to his head bandage and then pulled out his dog tag, careful to keep the gold cross inside his pajamas and robe.

"Henry Viertel? Don't think you were in my squadron, but I don't know. So many guys passed through. Army Air Corps. You?"

Henry shook his head, waved good-bye, and left. Not talking was awkward enough, but the patient, for all his friendliness, gave him a distinct unease. As if he had something against the stranger, or vice versa.

After he had healed well and was walking about with coordination and strength, Henry received Dr. Small's permission to eat at a table in the dining area. "I'm not sure what we're going to do with you. Look good for a discharge, but you're safer here right now than crossing the English Channel."

Sitting alone long after the lunch crowd had cleared, he busied himself arranging the elements of a fine sandwich to go with his hot soup. When he looked up again, the square-shouldered nurse stood at his table with her food tray.

"May I join you?" She put down her lunch.

He sprang up to assist with her chair. That triggered a flash of head pain, which he tried to mask.

"My goodness. You're such a gentleman. I didn't expect that." She flushed and flipped a strand of short, dark hair behind her ear. "You're Henry, right?"

Nodding, he fervently desired the ability to speak.

"My name's Sarah. Sarah Pickett." She pointed to her surname tag. Her eyes traced the long line of the bandage on his forehead. "I'm kind of surprised you're still here. I expected you'd be medevaced to London to a neurologist at the big Army hospital there. You know how it is. We had a guy last week with a bullet lodged in his frontal lobe. I think he got your place on the plane."

Henry's skin crawled. He could have been that guy.

"Dr. Small is really good." The nurse kept up the one-sided conversation. "He has to be, considering all the different injuries we get here."

Henry dipped into his bowl and savored the chicken bits and juices.

"What are you eating? Chicken noodle?"

"Sssoup." He did it. He connected a word. He grinned like a schoolboy who proudly surprised the teacher with the right answer.

"You said it! That's great, Henry. Is this your first time to speak?" Her eyes shone in delight.

"Fffirst…time."

She reached as if to pat him on the shoulder, but he pulled away because his back wound still hurt. Instead, she squeezed his upper arm. Looking around the room, she called to someone filling his cup at the massive steel percolator. "Hey, Bill. C'mere."

A solid, muscular first lieutenant approached with a pleasant, interested expression.

"Bill, this is Henry. Henry, Lieutenant Bill Hanson."

Henry stood, knowing he shouldn't salute out of uniform but feeling awkward anyway.

To Bill, she continued talking. "I told you about him last week, remember? He just said his first words since his injury."

Bill put down his tray and gave Henry a firm handshake. His hazel eyes and fine, light brown hair framed a warm smile. "Congratulations. I reckon you're on your way back to the land of the living."

If he didn't die of boredom, and the headaches eased up. Henry liked this man's optimism. He smiled and nodded.

Sarah set down her coffee as if drawing a nonverbal exclamation point. "Yeah, but if you want to stay alive, you'd better get your dog tag changed. You're not Type A. You're B. If we hadn't taken time to do a routine cross-match, you might not be sitting here today." Her big, brown eyes sent a warning.

Blood types were a mystery to Henry. He had barely been aware of some flurry of activity the night they brought him to the hospital.

Bill peppered his roast beef. "What did you do?"

"Rrradios." He didn't remember, but the other lieutenant told him and he wanted to speak, say anything, so badly.

"Henry was a forward scout. He got hit this side of the Siegfried Line. He was lucky. The bullet grazed his back, ripped under his helmet, and came across his forehead. Almost dug in. A quarter inch closer and he'd be dead."

Nurse Sarah knew more about his injury than he did. But when she said "Siegfried Line," he had a sudden picture of the concrete emplacements growing from the earth, leaning toward the west.

"*Siegfriedstellung.*" He spoke the word just above a whisper.

"Oh, and Henry speaks German, too." Sarah smiled at her prize patient.

Bill's eyebrows shot up. "You do?"

Nodding, Henry struggled to organize thoughts into words.

He needn't bother. Nurse Sarah jumped into the space. "He's from Texas. His lieutenant looked up his records, and told me he's a second generation Texan, and his family still speaks German."

Henry needed those records. Why had Sarah been given information he himself didn't have?

"Radios and German fluency. A valuable combination." Bill gave the mashed potatoes a rest and buttered his roll. "We could use you here. While you're recuperating, I mean. We've got some POW's being treated in a separate wing of the hospital, and we interrogate them. Humanely, of course. But you'd have to be able to speak."

"Yes. Speak. To them." Henry recognized an honorable way out of his boredom. A purpose to support the Americans.

A strange thought, as if he were not American.

POW's? A picture flashed of ragged, starving men with haunting eyes. "Not torture."

Sarah and Bill laughed out loud.

Bill slapped him on his sore back. "No, we won't let you put these guys on the rack. Most of them are pretty badly shot up. Hope you can take a little blood and guts."

He spoke as if Henry were joking, but he wasn't. He would not inflict pain during interrogation. A memory flitted through like a ghost. A captured man and an angry officer who threatened to shoot him in the knee for information. The captive spoke English, the officer German. It made no sense. Henry chased the vision, which blew away like smoke.

Sarah and Bill tossed around ideas about how long Henry might be confined to the hospital, while his mind raced along a maze. A job. He could do something useful. He needed this.

Bill checked his watch. "Well, I've got to go. Good to meet you, Henry. I'll talk to some people and try to get you helping in the POW area, at least as a volunteer." Then he turned to Sarah. "Coming to the flick tonight?"

She batted her eyes with a shy smile. "Maybe. If I get off on time."

Bill left, delivering his tray with a certain bounce.

Henry grabbed her attention back with a touch to her arm. "Need to see…" What did she call them? "…records."

Her blush this time seemed to be less cheerful, more like an embarrassment. "I'm sorry. I just remembered something. I don't think I was supposed to tell you."

"Why?"

"The doctor said he wanted to see how much you remember on your own. If we show you your file, we won't know if you're actually remembering."

That made sense, considering Henry already adopted information he had no memory of, but couldn't they understand his agony? He needed to know his identity.

Sarah gathered her tray items and stood to go, but Henry reached for her wrist. "Dietrich and Anna. Who?"

"Excuse me?" She lowered the tray to the table. "What are you asking?" Her intense focus assured him she cared.

Did he dare show her the cross? Would it be taken from him if he did? He scanned the almost-bare cafeteria. Pulling the shoestring from his hospital gown and robe, he held her eyes to express his trust.

"Oh, Henry. It's beautiful." She slipped her fingers around the pendant and bent to look closely. "Where did you get… Is this from your family?" Turning it over, she read the inscription. "Dietrich to Anna… That's what you wanted to know?"

He nodded three times. "My parents?"

"I don't know, but I'll try to find out." She placed the treasure in his palm, and left with a smile.

Hope blossomed as he sat alone, draining his coffee. Maybe this would be a crack in the door to his identity. Until then, answering to the name of Henry, which he considered a nickname, became a simple convenience.

The medical staff had instructed him to be aware of his accidental thoughts and dreams. Starving people with gold stars on their sleeves? He reasoned that they were Jews, but didn't know why he thought so. And what did they have to do with a soldier from Texas?

CHAPTER FIFTEEN

"HEY, HENRY. THROW on some pants and come with me. We're going to the POW building."

Henry, languishing in bed, sloshed coffee on the dog-eared *Saturday Evening Post* he was reading. "Pants? No pants."

"Figured as much. I brought some of my fatigues."

Sarah bounced down the corridor, her smile beaming good news. "You're checked out to Bill for today. First, make me an honest woman. I told Doc you were talking now. So tell me 'Good morning.'"

Henry's smile went shaky, but he responded, "Good m-morning, na-Nurse Sarah." Heat rose in his cheeks when he realized he'd called an officer by her first name. "L-L-Lieutenant Pickett." At least he knew better than to salute from the bed in his pajamas. Where had the urge to click his heels come from, anyway? He'd become proficient at copying what he observed, and the Americans didn't do that.

Nurse Sarah radiated joy. "Great job, Henry. Y'all have fun."

Bill had thought of everything. Henry pulled on the fatigues and boots. Real clothes. With his solid gold cross hanging on a shoestring underneath.

Lt. Bill explained his expectations for Henry as they went out the side door of the hospital and hurried through light snow to a well-guarded, prison-like building. "The POW's are treated here. Most of them are in pretty bad shape, and they may not have any knowledge that would help us. They're just line soldiers. But General Allen thought if we could chat with them, sort of soften them up, we might get something."

"How…they come here?" Henry wanted more than anything to speak well enough to be useful to the war effort.

"In the capture of Aachen, most of them. Some shot up too bad to retreat. We picked them up when we purged the town." Lt. Bill scrubbed his feet on the doormat. "After the locals re-entered town from the refugee camps, we acquired a few more. We don't have anything but names and ranks unless they had documents on them, and most didn't."

Henry's language confusion had become familiar, similar to the ringing in his ears. If he didn't listen to it, it didn't bother him. The same attitude might help him through the scramble of words. But if they expected him to participate in physical force against captives, he could hide behind his injury and be unable to assist.

The lieutenant pulled open the heavy door and motioned Henry ahead of himself. "I suggest we simply act friendly. Show sympathy and develop rapport."

Sounded reasonable. Henry could go along with that.

They saluted the armed guard, and Lt. Hanson explained he had brought a translator, motioning to Henry, for informal interrogations of the prisoners. Passed to the Officer of the Day, he introduced Henry as the bilingual patient he had told them about. They were given free access to the wards, and the lieutenant ambled toward a particular bed.

Blood and a clear bag dripped into the soldier from a pole at his head, and a tube snaked from under the sheets at his side. As they approached, he seemed semi-conscious but with a deep grimace.

Lt. Hanson checked the folder in its holder attached to the foot of the bed. "Lieutenant Hans Leiter. This is Henry Viertel." He waved a hand to Henry, omitting his rate.

Henry pronounced the standard greeting in German.

The patient's eyes widened. His glance took in the American fatigues, and his brow lifted in question. "American?"

"*Ja*, but...speak German." Henry continued in the patient's language, pointing to his own bandage. "Wounded." Leiter stared at Henry's wrappings.

"Where?"

"*Siegfriedstellung*." Henry glanced at Lt. Bill, not sure what he could tell the prisoner.

The patient nodded.

"And you?" Henry waved toward the man's leg, wrapped in a complicated contraption.

"Aachen. Where am I now?"

"He wants to know where he is," Henry said to Lt. Hanson. "Can I say?"

"Tell him he's in an American field hospital, and we're taking care of him."

Henry repeated the assurance and asked where the soldier came from.

The wounded man paused before answering. Every question between them merited evaluation first. "Near Frankfurt. You?"

The back part of Henry's mind echoed *Munich*, but he knew he was from Texas. He gave the correct response, then motioned to the man's wedding band. "Family at home?"

Leiter blinked, and his eyes filled. "Wife and a boy. But I think they left. I hope they're safe."

Henry nodded. "I hope so, too. They say Frankfurt is badly bombed." Words seemed to be coming without such a struggle. Maybe he had turned a corner in his healing.

Leiter began to fidget. His eyes dashed about and he picked at the sheet. "Are you my interrogator? I don't know anything, honest." His expression pled for belief.

A slow smile came to Karl's face. "Not an interrogator. Just…a translator. You have a message? For your wife?"

The patient's eyebrows rose in question. "A translator?"

"I'm a patient, too. Lieutenant Hanson said German patients need translation. You want to say something?"

"No." He looked as confused as a puppy searching for his mother.

An American whom Henry assumed to be a doctor came to the bedside. He checked the blood pressure and dripping bags, making notes in a file. "Y'all talking to this guy?"

Lt. Bill nodded. "This is Corporal Viertel. He speaks some German."

"Yeah? Tell Leiter I'm a medic, and ask him how he's doing, especially his leg. I mean, I know it hurts, but we need to know if it's infected inside the cast."

The medic's distorted English carried a familiar twang. Henry addressed his questions to Leiter and responded to the medic.

"Getting better. He keeps it on the, ah, the pillow." Henry pointed to the pillow in case he hadn't used the right word.

Leiter motioned to his middle. "Ask him what they did inside."

The medic checked the file. "They repaired shrapnel damage to the stomach and liver. He was lucky the intestines didn't get torn. He should be out in a few more days."

Upon translation, Leiter's eyes saucered. "Where will I go then?"

Henry got the answer. He would be in a POW camp, or possibly traded to the Germans for wounded American POW's. The man's frame relaxed as if a gun has been moved from his head.

Having passed this first test, and with his speech increasingly available, Henry followed the lieutenant around the POW unit and assisted with several mundane translations. The civility of the setup calmed his unease. He wouldn't be expected to shoot a prisoner in the kneecap to get information.

Where had that image come from, anyway?

After lunch in a mess hall away from the POW area, Henry sipped another coffee. "Lieutenant, there's something I..." He had difficulty expressing his doubts.

"What's up?"

"It's just that... I don't feel like a Henry. Like it's not my name. I don't know. It's strange."

Lt. Bill stirred in more sugar, squinting and glancing about. "Well, we're just going by your dog tag and your unit lieutenant's identification."

"But he didn't remember me, not really."

"Maybe you're used to being called by a nickname, like 'Bud' or 'Junior.' Don't worry about it. It'll come to you." Lt. Bill's attention escaped to something else. "'Scuse me. I've got to catch the Major before he leaves. See you tomorrow morning?" He rose and picked up his tray.

"Sure. At the hospital or POW building?"

"POW. I'll have a uniform delivered for you."

[149]

HENRY BROKE THE starch on his new pants and shirt and checked the alignment in the sink mirror. His newly issued corporal's uniform with the nametag "Viertel" looked good. Funny how everyone pronounced his surname. From the spelling, he would have said something like "Feertel." Didn't matter. He was an American soldier, striving to walk and talk like other American soldiers, especially Lt. Bill Hanson.

On the day of his release from the hospital, Lt. Bill arrived with a new set of orders. "You're reassigned to me for POW interrogation. You'll bunk in the enlisted quarters. I've got you a good room assignment with just one other guy, Corporal Chase. You'll like him. Come on. I'll help you move your stuff over."

"Nothing much to move. The hospital gown stays here. The boots are a size too small. The books belong to the library." His fingers went to the gold cross under his shirt. Nothing else had any value.

Lt. Hanson chuckled. "You're talking better every day." He led out through the wide hospital corridor and down a hallway branched with other wards. "Say, how's your reading and writing?"

"Reading is similar to working a puzzle. Not writing anything." They approached the library, a jumbled modified storeroom near the hospital entrance. "Wait. Here I leave the books."

Continuing to the enlisted quarters, the men buttoned their jackets and pushed into the cold.

"Haven't you written your family in Texas?"

Henry ducked his head and took a moment to answer. "What do I say? I don't even remember my parents."

"Have you gotten a letter from them since you've been here?"

Was Lt. Bill asking because he knew, or because he didn't know? Between the doctor who wouldn't show him his own file and Nurse Sarah who was so proud when he remembered something, he doubted himself and his best friends.

"No. Maybe I write if they write."

The possibility became a reality when Henry received three letters from home, bound in a rubber band, a few days later. He went to his room, expecting his roommate to be out for several hours. He sat at the metal desk staring at them, building up the courage to open one.

Viertel Family, New Braunfels, Texas. Postmarked October 10, 17, and 24. Like a parent who methodically writes on the same day of the week. A precisely spaced script in pencil covered the front of a red and blue-hashed V-mail envelope. "V" for victory. He smiled at the not-so-subtle propaganda. Gently, he lifted the flap, and it gave way with little persuasion as if eager to deliver news of a family he didn't remember.

In English but with frequent German words and phrases, this woman, his mother, told of the Oktoberfest in their community, of fields dotted with bright pumpkins, and illness of their pastor. A heavy scrawl at the bottom, from "Papi," said he prayed for Henry every day.

Henry's eyes stung with the threat of tears. Resting the thin paper on his open hand, he gazed toward the window's wintery gray light. Somewhere, far away in Texas, these people prayed and waited. But not even reading their words brought a vision of their faces. He had no image of them bent or strong, white-haired or in the prime of middle age.

After folding the letter along the original lines, he put it away and opened the second. The newspapers all said the Allied victory was certain, and everyone expected the war to soon be over. Margaret asked about him every Sunday, and wished he would write her. His father worked too hard in the fields harvesting and preparing the herd for winter.

A herd. Herd of what? Cattle? Goats? He put the message aside and reached for the last with a hunger for belonging.

The same penciled script told of canning jars and jars of his favorite marmalade. What kind was that? He favored apple butter, didn't he? But hadn't had any since…?

The letter went on about people he didn't recognize, places he didn't remember, and the farm setting which might have been someone else's life. None of it—*nothing*—bore any familiarity.

In a fit of frustration, he left the letters on the desk and stormed outside. He walked until the cold doused his internal fires and darkness came on the hospital compound. On the fourth or fifth pass around, a guard challenged him.

"Soldier, state your purpose and destination."

Henry halted. "Only walking. Letters from home…"

The guard's face relaxed. "Yeah, I know what you mean. Better go inside. Always the possibility of snipers, and you're unarmed."

Unarmed, and in shirtsleeves. He must appear foolish. "Right. Time for grub anyway."

He sat alone in the noisy mess hall until his new roommate spotted him and came over with his tray. "Join you? Or were you expecting a hot babe?"

When Henry laughed, the smile lines cracked his frozen, somber face. "Hi, Walt. Have a seat. Looks like she's not coming."

"I noticed you got some mail." Walt Chase buttered bread as if storing up food for a famine. "You're lucky. Not even my girlfriend writes me."

"At least you have a girlfriend." Henry gulped ice tea and gave the mysterious pat of meat and gravy a poke with his fork. "Your letters are probably held up somewhere. I got a batch of three today."

"Say, that's great. From your family?"

"Yeah. Thought I'd remember them when I read their letters. Can't even remember what they look like."

Walt chewed, his mouth too full. His manners were no worse than most of the enlisted men. Henry chose to overlook mealtime faults in his hunger for friends.

"Say, yeah, well, I guess that'll pass. Have you written them yet, I mean, about your injury?"

"No, suppose I'd better, but what do I say? 'Sorry, Mother, I don't remember you?'"

"Well, maybe I can help. Let's pick up some stationary at the Red Cross room on the way back, and we'll get a letter out. They need to hear something. Who knows? Maybe it'll help you, too."

Henry addressed the envelope first, copying the information from their letters to him. Then he stared at the flimsy airmail paper.

"Okay, it's to your mother. Anyone else?" Chase coached from his position on the side of his bunk.

Henry reviewed the endings of his three letters. "'Mutti und Papi.' She mentions other people, but the names mean nothing."

"So let's keep it simple. Start with 'Dear...' whatever you said. Mom and Dad."

Together they worked out a brief message and read the finished product before he sealed and posted it in the drop box.

Dear Mutti und Papi,

Thank you for your three letters which I received today. I should tell you that I am in a field hospital with head wounds. I do not remember my home and family. Do not worry. This may pass in a few more days. Please keep writing. Your letters might help get my memory back.

[153]

Your son,
Henry

Henry dreamed that night of a grand home with ornate wood embellishments and a family who spoke German. The father wore three-piece wool suits and the mother's dresses floated in layers of filmy, delicate fabric. He had a sister who sprawled on her bed upstairs and read books all day long.

Henry awoke more confused than ever.

He puzzled this out while shaving, until Lt. Hanson burst into the latrine. "Henry. Get over to Intelligence. They brought in a whole bunch of Germans last night and they need you."

CHAPTER SIXTEEN

7 November, 1944

U.S. Field Hospital in France

THE HOSPITAL COMPOUND churned with activity such as Henry had never seen in his several weeks there. While crossing into the guarded German prisoner area, he and Lt. Hanson waited for ambulances and heavy trucks to pass, stirring melted snow into mud slush.

"We're fighting in Metz. Wounded have been coming in all night, both ours and theirs. We need their field positions, tank strengths, anything we can get." Lt. Hanson bounded to the top step of the Intelligence Unit and turned to Henry. "This matters, Henry. Lives are at stake."

That much of a commissioning ceremony charged Henry with enough adrenaline to burn his brain. "I'm ready. Let's go."

After the security check, they hurried down the labyrinth of hallways and guarded doors to the tight, bare interrogation rooms. The shouting had already started. Henry had observed the techniques used to get information. Hunger, sleep deprivation, verbal attack, and a lot of pounding on the table broke down most prisoners. Since they only got wounded prisoners at this hospital compound, the added pain of battle injury worked in their favor.

Henry and Lt. Bill found a colonel in the hallway giving directions like a traffic policeman. Hasty introductions identified him as Col. Strang, head of this interrogations unit. "Take Corporal Viertel into room four. He'll work with Captain Knox. He's got a German lieutenant in there."

Lt. Bill opened the door and nodded to Capt. Knox, who had the reputation of the meanest fox in these woods. Knox came out, where Lt. Bill made introductions and left. Henry entered the cage-like space. The remainder of the prisoner's bloody arm lay extended on the table.

Henry's empty stomach knotted when he saw the stump wrapped below the elbow. The German, pale, weak, and shaky, must have lost a lot of blood.

"I've got his name, rank, and serial number. Keeps saying them over and over. Nothing else." Capt. Knox wiped his shiny scalp with a handkerchief. In the chilled room, the captain had worked up a sweat. Knox left for a moment, returning with Col. Strang, who stood against the gray plaster wall.

Captain Knox continued his tirade. "Tell him this: We've already taken Aachen, and now we're taking Metz. The war's over, and you've lost. There's no point in holding out. How many more men will Germany throw at a losing battle?"

Henry took a different approach from his usual mild-mannered coaxing. He swaggered and yelled like the captain, throwing in a few slang expressions.

"You're German?" The weary prisoner's face twisted with his question. Doubt flickered in his eyes, and maybe a gram of fear.

"I am American, and proud to be from the land of the free. And you? You disgraced your country by following a madman. He uses you and your men like mindless slaves to prop up his ego. Where is he this morning? Huh? Sipping wine with his woman in the clear air of Austria?" Henry slammed his palm on the table and barked words at the suffering man.

"You marched for him in Hitler's Youth." He continued full force with unfounded assumptions. "You turned in Jews to their death by starvation and torture, and what for? Because he told you to. Did it ever occur to you that he was destroying the Fatherland?"

Capt. Knox's controlled surprise registered with Henry, but he didn't stop the onslaught. The colonel stood like an olive green shadow on the wall.

Henry caught the prisoner's motion to his pocket, and told Capt. Knox, "He wants a cigarette."

"Good. He's not getting one until he talks."

"Tell us your troop numbers and tank positions." Henry motioned toward the handless arm. "We'll bring in a doctor to treat you. There's no need to die of gangrene."

The prisoner stirred. "You are German. You have a Munich accent. How could you be a traitor?"

Because my mother was Jewish. The phrase hit Henry's mind with staggering force. What on earth? Was this a ploy his subconscious suggested, an argument he might use? He rejected the idea.

"I am American, and you are the traitor. You put that vain 'little corporal' before God and country." Henry softened his voice now, making the words drip with sadness. "You risk the lives of your family to pursue his glory."

The lieutenant's head dropped with a sob. His shoulders shook.

Henry glanced toward Capt. Knox, who twirled a forefinger in a "keep going" motion.

"Your family will be respected. Help us end this terrible war." He noticed the man's wedding band. "Let's go home to our wives and parents. There's no point in dying to the last man. How many Panzers do you have at Metz?"

"Only a few left from Panzer-Brigade 106." The prisoner's hoarse whisper escaped through tears. "From nearly fifty down to twenty."

Henry reached for the pad and pencil and started scribbling notes.

The prisoner drew a rattling breath. "Then Panzer-Brigade 112. Running around, separate lines west and east... They didn't know what they were doing. The bombers... The Fuhrer told us to hold Metz. We waited every day for his command to withdraw."

"No help came. They left you stranded." Henry leaned close. "How many remain?"

"The French are killing tanks with machine guns mounted on Jeeps." Anguish and humiliation twisted his face. "We have no air support. What are we supposed to do?"

"Give me a number."

"Twenty tanks, jockeyed by frightened boys. They don't have a chance."

Henry showed Capt. Knox his notes, translating both the facts and comments. "Can we get him a doctor now?"

"Yeah, go—never mind, you stay with the prisoner and keep him talking. I'll find a medic."

Henry asked about troop numbers, supply movements, anything he thought would be helpful. Sometimes the prisoner spoke, sometimes he shrugged, but he was broken. He hung over the table and met no one's eyes.

Animation perked when the medic arrived. He asked for morphine.

The medic examined the arm with a gentle touch and nodded. "I'll be back in a moment."

"Don't you want him moved to the hospital?" Henry had never been briefed concerning the procedure for a prisoner giving information.

"No." Col. Strang, still standing against the wall like a green ghost, gave the order. "He stays here for a while. Keep talking to him. Ask for the bunker positions scattered out there on the hills."

An infantry officer in a Panzer brigade, the German expected to be protected by the mighty armament. Through disorganization and inadequate training, the roaring lions of the German army were crippled and silenced. If he had a map of the outlying defensive bunkers, he might have given it to them. Mere tidbits of information came forth now.

The medic returned with materials to clean the German's splintered limb and asked if he were diabetic or had ever been addicted to morphine. He gave him an injection—"Just enough to control the pain so I can work on him."—and teased off the gummed-up bandage.

Henry went out to the hall, sure now he would be sick.

The silent colonel followed him with raised a brow.

"Sorry, sir. I never had breakfast. This is nauseating on an empty stomach."

"Worse on a full stomach." He lit a cigarette. "You did a good job, Corporal. I think we've gotten about all we can from this one. I'll take it from here."

"Do you speak German, sir?"

"Enough."

Henry looked back at the prisoner, now with his head resting on the good arm, his face going slack. "What will you do with him?" Maybe he didn't want to know.

"He needs surgery, then he'll be in the prison wing until he's ready to transport to a POW camp."

Henry nodded, trying not to show his relief.

"Go get some lunch, corporal. See you back here in half an hour."

Henry pulled on a jacket with trembling hands and crossed the muddy yard, glad to breathe fresh air. A caldron boiled in his mind filled with horror, sympathy for the man he had grilled, and a sadistic power over the prisoner. Many men performed acts they despised to win this war. He had joined them.

He rolled his shoulders, pondering the past few hours. The colonel and captain said the Americans took reasonable care of the enemy POW's. He didn't think the Germans so generous, and the Russians had the reputation of being barbarians. *If this is where I'm needed, I can do this.*

Going up the stairs to the mess hall, he adjusted his posture and saluted an officer. As he twisted the knob to enter, his thoughts darted in a different direction. *The man said I have a Munich accent. What do Texans sound like?*

Nurse Pickett called to him as he reached the enlisted mess. "Henry, wait up. I've got the information you wanted." She approached, digging in her pockets. She offered him a scrap of paper and a beaming smile.

Henry read the scribble. "Johann and Inga?"

"Your parents' names. You asked me to find out, remember?"

"Of course. Thank you very much. It's just…"

"What?" Her glow faded with his reserved reaction.

"Nothing. I thought they would sound…familiar. Johann and Inga." He met her eyes. "I appreciate this."

He chewed his hamburger to the rhythm of their names. Johann and Inga. Johann and Inga. Still didn't seem right, but he would get used to it.

As he sauntered to the intelligence unit after lunch, Col. Strang met him, his stern brow raised to one bushy line. While Henry had relaxed over supper, the lines on the Colonel's face had doubled. "Quick. Room ten. We've got an enlisted guy in there spilling his guts." His hand on Henry's back propelled him to the end of the narrow hallway. "We're trying to get it on tape, but he's talking so fast no one can understand him."

The scrawny kid, showing more terror than a damsel tied to a train track, looked up as Henry entered. "Honest, that's all I know."

Col. Strang leaned toward Henry. "He thinks we're going to string him up by his thumbs. Let it work for us. Don't tell him otherwise." The colonel motioned Henry to a hard chair at the metal table.

He nodded and sat down before the paper pad and pen bearing someone else's scribbles. Name, rank, and serial number of the prisoner were at the top, then "supply," "Lorraine and Alsace," and "Col. Sekendorf." The unit already heard that Col. Sekendorf had died in battle.

"Okay, let's start from the beginning."

Henry wrote hard for an hour. Most of the useless rambling wasn't worth the pencil lead to write it down, but occasional nuggets came forth like beautiful gems in a tumbling stream.

Combined with information from other prisoners, details of a clearer battle picture emerged.

At the end of the day, Col. Strang debriefed Henry. Piecing together his frantic handwriting, impressions, and general observations, they recorded what they knew, thought they knew, and didn't know. Therein lay the plan for future interrogations.

"You've done well today, corporal. You have all the skills we're looking for in this unit. Personable enough to get them to open up to you, and good enough translator to understand what they say when they do. I'll see you back here in the morning."

"Yes, sir. Thank you, sir." He wanted to say something like, *It's a pleasure doing business with you, sir,* and shake the colonel's hand. Confused by the errant urge, he just saluted and departed.

The headaches continued. Henry had done nothing but sit and talk in a small room, yet exhaustion saturated his neck and shoulder muscles. Asleep at last, nightmares raged. He went from interrogator to being interrogated. He dreamed a bloody American pilot rose off a bed and shot him through the kneecaps. He thrashed and snorted himself awake.

His eyes wide open against complete darkness, he threw back the covers and sat up until his sweat evaporated and left him chilled. Clutching the gold cross, he prayed for peace, both personal and national.

Even the cross troubled him. If Johann and Inga were his parents, who were Dietrich and Anna?

"Whatsa matter, man?" Chase mumbled from his bunk.

"Nothing. Sorry I woke you. Having a bad dream."

"S'okay. Almost time for reveille. Wanna turn on the light?"

Henry didn't want to be awake at all, but he obliged.

Chase rolled off the top bunk. "Think I'll hit the shower before everyone else gets up." He grabbed his towel and plodded down the hall.

Wisps of the dream tore like gauze and drifted away, but he caught the last bit. That soldier in the hospital library. He was the wounded pilot. One version of the dream had him shaking Henry's hand and saying, "Thanks."

Thanks for what? Something about not using torture.

Henry arrived early at the Interrogation Unit where Col. Strang already paced and flipped through charts. The colonel pointed him into a room and discussed specific goals for the day's questions. He proposed an intelligent, organized approach rather than picking blackberries wherever they found them hiding in the forest.

"You're an excellent translator, corporal. Keep riding your intuition on these interrogations. Go where your perceptions lead you."

BY THE END of November, General Patton had captured Metz and the Americans had a strong footprint in Germany. Proud to be a part of the victory, Henry celebrated with all the guys in the enlisted mess hall until far into the night. Enormously relieved, he relaxed more than had been possible for months.

Finally, whistling a German folk song on his way back to the barracks, he ran into Lt. Bill Hanson. "Sir, good evening, sir."

"Are you drunk, Henry?"

"No, sir. I'm happy. While doctors and nurses and medics are patching up Germans tomorrow, I won't have anyone to interrogate about Metz."

"Right, but we've only won the battle. Not the war. The next area is already hot. There'll be plenty of people to grill in the morning." He leaned close to Henry's ear. "They're calling it 'the Battle of the Bulge.'"

"Bulge?" Henry swept his hand down in an arc as if describing the shape of a pregnant woman. "What bulge? There aren't any mountains here, are there?" He had heard the term used by some of the soldiers and felt dumb asking.

"The Alsace. German divisions pushing west around our men through the Ardennes." Hanson used both hands, starting low and drawing a pouch. "They try to contain us, we push out against them. On the map, it looks kind of like a bulge. The worst, coldest fighting anywhere." Lt. Bill glanced both ways and whispered. "We can't let them get to Antwerp. They'd have a good harbor, transportation for supplies."

Henry confirmed this with the colonel the next morning, and fixed the intelligence targets for the next battle. Positioned between the colonel, whose dignity he admired, and Capt. Knox, who looked meaner than a guard dog, he began to develop new interrogation techniques.

In his off hours, he practiced them on himself. Teasing out facts, following elusive clues, his slow revelations frightened him.

Then the big packet of photos and letters came from Texas. Pictures of his parents, an older brother, and his family, a sister about to get married. A gray-toned snapshot of the brick and stone home, dog on the stoop and black Ford in the yard. He didn't know these people. He wasn't their son.

The mornings his head didn't hurt, he felt like he stood on a green hill and breathed fresh air and the world went on forever. And he knew he was German.

How did this happen? He could not tell the colonel or Lt. Bill. He visualized Nurse Sarah's bright smile. No, he could never tell these, his best friends and co-workers, that he was their enemy.

Hadn't he proved he wasn't? Hadn't he earned the right to be American?

Henry—or whoever—strode back to work determined to be the best American soldier in the Interrogation Unit. Let no one doubt his loyalty.

CHAPTER SEVENTEEN

Early December, 1944
U.S. Army Field Hospital

A FRESH WAVE of Allied and Axis wounded arrived at the field hospital as the battle for Bastogne intensified. Deepening cold and inadequate clothing for the soldiers caused rampant frostbite casualties. Not that adequate clothing existed for soldiers who dug into frozen ground for weeks.

Henry's repertoire of shouting and cajoling worked well for him on most interrogations. He produced even better results when he teamed up with Capt. Knox. The captain did the tough-guy threats, and then Henry came in and chatted in German. His recitation of the idiocy of this war and the people's blind faith in Hitler brought many men to tears. How sad to put everything on the line for a leader who placed himself at the center of the universe.

As if in a parallel world, every day Henry wore a U.S. Army uniform on a German body and used someone else's name. Did he need to cover his tracks? Who might show up in the American scene and recognize him? Hadn't God Himself engineered this situation when the fallen soldier available at the Siegfried Line was of German descent and language? Therefore he operated under God's permissive will.

So why the guilt?

Colonel Strang, with eagle eye and dagger mind, had the resources to investigate if he ever suspected duplicity. Gradually, the colonel took the roles of mentor and father figure. Henry enjoyed working in his unit, yet feared the possibility of discovery. In this hall of mirrors, the most frightening apparition was himself.

Despite the division between enlisted and officer, Lt. Bill Hanson stood out as a friend. After that early attempt to tell Bill he wasn't a Henry, what would Bill do if he said he thought he was German? Without proof or any details, he might give the same brush-off as before.

Hanson spent hours off with Lt. James Fuller, the downed pilot who seemed so familiar. When Lt. Fuller hung around, Henry found somewhere else he had to be.

Needing Lt. Bill after a long, late interrogation, Capt. Knox sent Henry to the Officers' Quarters with a sealed message. Henry located him playing cards in a lounge area with Fuller and a couple of others.

Lt. Bill waved him over. "Hey, Henry, want us to deal you in?"

"Thanks, sir, but my rank isn't high enough to sit at this table. Neither is my base pay."

The men laughed, and Henry handed him the envelope.

Lt. Fuller squinted and gripped his jawline, then he slapped down his cards. "I've got it. You look like the German who interrogated me when my plane was shot down. Not quite the same. I think he was a little heavier, maybe darker complexion. But that's who I've been trying to remember ever since the first time I met you in the hospital."

Henry went spit-less. He forgot to breathe. "Where was that, sir?"

"Somewhere in Germany. I don't know where I was. Thought I was dying. And I would have, if it had been up to the other guy. He wanted to shoot me to make me talk. But this von Something-or-other fellow, I think he had American sympathies." Fuller stretched into full story-telling fashion now. Henry backed away from the table, feeling naked in public.

"He spoke good English. Oh, yeah, he said his mother was American, or maybe his father. I don't know. I was barely conscious by then, I'd lost so much blood."

Hanson wrote something on the delivered message and handed it back to Henry, who saluted and left the room.

The last words he heard were Fuller's continuation of the tale. "That guy saved my life. I didn't give him any information they didn't already know, but..."

Light-headed, Henry stumbled on the first step and caught the railing. It was true, then. Henry had done interrogation before. For the other side.

Col. Strang took the response from Hanson. "Got the shakes, corporal? Better go get some supper. It's been a hard day."

"Yes, sir." Henry re-buttoned his coat and pulled the watch cap low. In the icy early evening, he glanced twice at every shadow. How long could he pull this off? What if a German who knew him well from before became a prisoner here, and he walked into the interrogation cage and—

As he entered the cafeteria, Walt Chase called him over to his table. "Hey, Henry, you look like you saw a ghost. What's up?"

Henry faked a chuckle and shucked his winter gear. "Just cold, man. As soon as I down this coffee, I'm going to find a heater to prop my feet on." Diversion and distraction became his favored tactics.

Fortunately, he had a mouth full of hamburger when one of the men at Walt's table stood and shouted at a new soldier. "Carl. Come here. I been waitin' for you, man."

Henry's head jerked up and he would have answered if he could. Karl. Von..Something-or-other. Karl what?

"Guys, this is Carl Smith, the new orderly. Carl, that's Walt, Henry..."

Henry begged out of the casual group as soon as possible, claiming fatigue.

"Hey, you don't need to go. We're gonna play a little gin rummy." Chase spent a lot of nights playing cards.

"No. I wouldn't be any fun." He slapped the new man on the back. "Good to have you here. See you around."

Alone in his room, he slid facts and suppositions against a hazy background. *Karl von What?* Pulling the gold cross up on its shoestring, he fingered its magnificent lines and read its inscription again. *Dietrich Who? Anna Who?* If they married in 1917... He did the subtraction on a scrap of paper. Twenty-seven years ago. I'm twenty-two. No, I'm not. Henry's twenty-two. I'm twenty-four.

Gradually, the details came to him. Not all at once, but as individual revelations. Interrogating himself, checking his facts, reaching deeper into the past, he recalled his home in Munich and the last time he saw it. Father had died, Mother and Marta were captured and carted off to Auschwitz.

He gripped the gold cross in his palm until the edges hurt. Mother's cross, the one she had worn all his life.

Karl grieved again, muffling his anguish in a pillow. By the time Walt stumbled in, about three a.m., Karl von Steuben had cried out his pain. Curled in the dark, he made a decision to be Henry Viertel for the foreseeable future. Finding no merit in being arrested and sent to a POW camp, he dedicated himself to earning his American citizenship back.

No one would believe him if he told the truth now.

17 January, 1945
U.S . Field Hospital in France

THREE WEEKS AFTER the most dismal Christmas of Henry's life, The Battle of the Bulge, or the Ardennes-Alsace Campaign, was won by the Allies. The longest and bloodiest battle of the war came to an end when the weather lifted and air support made possible the linking of the First and Third Armies. The Americans, who suffered over 19,000 deaths, exacted a higher toll on the German Army. Henry speculated the war might be over by spring.

Or maybe summer.

The Interrogation Unit had worked around the clock for longer than Henry could recall. Now he planned to share in the joy and pride of a job well done.

Col. Strang caught his attention and pointed to his office.

Not another offensive already, Henry hoped. They all needed a breather, but his work was a lot easier than that of the soldiers who had slogged through recent history's coldest winter with no shelter. He wanted to think he had shortened that time by working from the inside.

"Henry, I've got good news for you." The colonel's slow smile, a rare sight in the Interrogation Unit, indicated possible glad tidings. "You're going home."

Henry felt slapped in the face with a wet towel. Stunned, his mouth seemed to be missing a screw. "But...Sir, we still have work to do here."

The colonel's eyebrows shot up. "Well, yes, we'll always have work to do. But you've been in a war zone for two years. It's time for you to go back."

Two years. He didn't even know that. "Sir, with all respect, I don't want to leave." Henry fumbled with words about making a meaningful contribution to the war effort.

Colonel Strang picked up a discharge paper and frowned. "Dr. Small is concerned about your amnesia. He's checked various references and talked to a specialist in brain trauma in London. They think if you don't recover soon, you may never recover."

"Would that be so bad, sir? I mean, I can function, work every day..."

"What about your people in Texas? They're waiting for you. Go back to them, Henry, and fit into your family."

He should stop this sham, tell the colonel right now, *I'm not Henry Viertel. I'm a German who loves America.* He would be arrested, shamed in front of the friends he had deceived. Hauled off to POW camp, where he might die in disgrace.

"Not yet, sir. Let me work until the end of the war. I'm not finished here."

Strang sat at his desk. "I can't believe you, corporal. Ninety-nine percent of the guys out there"—he waved an arm—"would give anything for a Purple Heart and a ticket home."

The burn rose to Henry's cheeks. Now or never. But could he ever live again in Munich, where his lifelong neighbors had turned in his mother and sister and let them be imprisoned and exterminated like vermin? The firm—his expected professional future—had been bombed and its files carted off by the SS. If he never saw Munich again, it would be too soon.

"You'll cross the Channel overnight and take a troop ship to New York." The colonel assumed his usual business-like manner. "Here are your discharge papers, a copy of my Purple Heart commendation for you, and your pay draft. I realize most of your salary goes to your parents, but you'll need some travel money. I advise you to use this for yourself."

"Yes, sir." He accepted the papers.

"There will be a farewell tonight in the enlisted mess hall at eighteen hundred hours. Be there."

"Yes, sir."

"Take the day off. Organize, pack, whatever."

"Sir, it doesn't take long to return a library book. I'd like to continue the interrogation I started yesterday, sir."

Henry waited with frozen posture while several emotions played over his senior officer's face. "Granted. Dismissed."

Henry spun into action. He accelerated a plan begun weeks before. Diverting questions toward facts learned during his months as a German solider, he led prisoners to tell about the atrocities against the Jews, the labor camps, theft of valuables—everything he wanted the Americans to know but couldn't reveal himself. He put words in their mouths and pressed them to sign statements.

Today, even that didn't move fast enough. Knox and Strang let him interrogate independently, so he tried a new tactic on a wounded line officer. "We know the Führer is on a long campaign to annihilate the Jews in camps like Auschwitz in Poland and Dachau in Germany. What other camps exist?" He pushed a detailed map of Northern Europe across to the wounded prisoner. "Show me. Are there other major camps? Satellite camps?"

"I don't know. I've heard about others, but I've never seen them." The prisoner, too weak to sit up straight, seemed befuddled. He let the pencil drop onto the table.

"Pick it up. Mark the camps. You know there are some here, here, here, and here." He pointed to the four labor camps he himself had visited with Sergeant Weber to pick up jewelry and dental gold. "Mark them."

The man put X's on the map exactly where Henry pointed. "It's all hearsay. I know nothing."

The one secret Henry never exposed related to the cottage munitions factories around Dachau and other major camps, because the slave labor of Jewish prisoners ran them. To pinpoint those would insure bomb drops on the very people he wanted most to save.

When he had dismissed the prisoner to the POW hospital, Henry requested to work with a particular belligerent officer Knox had questioned that morning. "Let me have him for a few hours alone. I think I can play him with the casual routine."

Henry sauntered into what he thought of as the gray cage and began with an informal chat.

The sullen, curled lip of this guy made him angry. He would have to control his own emotions to get to the man beneath. "Sounds like you're from Berlin, am I right?"

Surprised, the prisoner hesitated before nodding. "And you're from...Munich?"

Henry worked the bait and switch method. "How's the fair city of Berlin? How do you like having the Führer holed up there with Eva Braun while you're fighting his war for him?"

"You're wrong. He's in the south, at his Eagle's Nest."

"Ah, yes, the emperor's teahouse on the mountaintop, safe inside Bavaria for when Germany is overrun. And it will be, quite soon. But it's you who are mistaken. He and his mistress have gone to Berlin. He leaves you on the battlefield in the snow, to die to the last man holding Metz—"

The officer slumped. "I came after that."

Henry never let up. "—then to attempt to march past Patton's armies and break through to Antwerp. How cold was Bastogne? I hear a lot of our men lost their feet and hands to frostbite. The medic tells me you're in danger of gangrene yourself. A bad way to die. Worse than a bullet. Fever, vomiting, you watch the purple lines come up your leg…"

The prisoner propped his head on a fist and squeezed his eyes shut.

"You need treatment, man. Lucky for you, we treat POW's better than you treat ours. The camps are even heated." He spread a map on the table. "Show me the setup at Oppenheim, here at the Rhine. You know you can't stop us."

When the prisoner broke, Henry rushed the fresh information to Col. Strang.

The Colonel's eyes bugged out behind his military-issue glass frames. "You just got this?"

"Right now, sir. It's current information."

Strang slapped Karl on his sore shoulder, spun and ran for the secure lines, leaving a stream of congratulations down the hallway.

Karl remained in the passage. His head pounded to the explosion point, a carryover from the wound. Rather than hide in a dark room until the farewell, he retrieved an officer he'd interrogated a couple of days before.

Starting with the usual preamble, he meandered to the knowledge of valuables hidden in the salt mines of Heilbronn, the name of the commandant and size of the base.

The surprised prisoner skipped the denial phase and went straight to, "Who told you that?"

"Everybody knows it. We've known it for a long time. Art, precious metals, everything confiscated from, shall we say, uncooperative citizens."

The curl of the man's lip and nod, indicating agreement, angered Karl. Drawing a hasty map, he marked the location of the mines from his own memory and conned the confused prisoner into signing the bottom.

After dismissing the man, he scribbled notes all over the page. The commandant's name, details of the post, even the use of slave labor to enhance storage area of the caves. There. That justified his cowardice and compliance during his months as a German soldier. But he wrote nothing about the twenty gold bricks guarded by the skeleton of a certain priest.

Henry pushed and pulled all afternoon, checking his watch to be sure he didn't miss his farewell party. Like a dog that wouldn't let go of a bone, he gnawed slivers of information from an injured officer. Finally, he called in a medic and went to take a shower. He had done his best to leave the unit with a treasure chest to be examined by others.

Decisions crowded his brain. Major issues, like where to live and how to support himself in America.

It wouldn't be on a farm in Texas.

CHAPTER EIGHTEEN

September, 1944
von Steuben Home, Munich, Germany

HAUPTMANN SCHMIDT MARCHED from Dietrich's office holding a delicate silver filigree box, the red velvet-faced lid open. He lifted the gold Star of David necklace Anna had worn every day before her conversion, and life as she had known it ended.

Her heart stopped. She had forgotten about this piece of jewelry. At her side on the sofa, Marta gasped.

The SS captain met with the soldier descending the stairs holding high the menorah, found in the back of the linen closet. "Jews. Living right here in a neighborhood of respectable citizens. Where's your armband? You know the law."

"We're Christians. All of us." She almost added *and Americans,* but this evil man might kill them on the spot. The SS didn't have to answer to any other power. Why, oh, why hadn't they left years ago?

Hauptmann Schmidt motioned to two of his underlings. "Load them in the truck. Take them to Dachau, where they belong."

One man grabbed Anna by the forearm and shoved her forward. She turned to see Marta receive the same treatment. He slapped a stinging blow across her face.

"But we're Christians. Look." She held out to him the beautiful gold cross necklace which she always wore, Dietrich's gift to her on their wedding day. "See hers? Marta, show him your cross."

Marta retrieved the pendant from below the high neckline of her blouse. She glared at her captor. "I'm Christian, baptized at birth."

"Tell them at the induction center. It won't do any good. If your mother's Jewish, you're Jewish."

He didn't say "either parent." He said "your mother." They had inside information before they burst into her home. Someone reported them. Probably that maid.

At the truck, Anna and Marta tried to climb into the back. The soldiers pushed them on their bottoms, causing them to fall on their faces. The indignity of such handling caused her to burn with shame.

The men vaulted onto the truck bed and tied their hands and feet with abrasive ropes. Then one stayed to guard them while the other drove.

They bounced on the rough streets, unrepaired since the war's beginning. Rocked from side to side, they were unable to brace themselves. She feared the soldier's gun might go off and kill them until she realized sudden death would be so much better than labor camp.

What about Dietrich's funeral? Such a prominent citizen deserved a proper burial. Who would pay the undertaker, and who would order his flowers?

The truck paused for a moment. Marta bent her head to Anna's shoulder. "Mother, I love you. I'm proud to be your daughter."

No sweeter child existed. "Let's pray, *liebchin,* my dear one." Together they called on the name of Jesus, over and over. Down cobblestone streets, looping through the quaint, pretty town of Dachau with its flowerboxes at the windows, twisting over its hills until they arrived at the gates of a large installation at its outskirts. Parked near the front gate, the driver approached and knocked on the door of the guardhouse. Behind him, over the wide entry, they read the words in wrought iron, "*Arbeit Macht Frei.*" Feeding on the national propaganda that lazy Jews created Germany's downfall, the camp promised if they worked, they would be freed. How could anyone believe such nonsense?

The driver came back and shouted to their guard. "They don't want them here. We've got to deliver them to one of the satellite camps for women."

The guard cursed. "Which one? How far?"

"Just a few kilometers away. Won't take long."

At their apparent destination, they were untied and shoved to the door of what appeared to be an industrial building.

The driver brought with him an envelope. Onto the desk he dumped both German and American passports for Anna, Marta, and Karl, and the German passport of Dietrich.

Anna caught the glance of Marta before closing her eyes in a silent prayer.

"Her husband." The soldier pointed to Dietrich's document. "He died at the house today. Heart attack or something."

"Von Steuben. Was he Jewish too?" The soldier receiving the documents caught a shrug from the driver and then looked at Anna.

"No, he wasn't. The von Steuben family have been prominent—"

"Shut up, woman. When I want to know something, I'll ask you." He did ask all the basic questions, then checked the answers against their passports.

He opened another passport. "Who is this Karl von Steuben?"

"Our son."

The soldiers exchanged glances and the room went still. "At the same address?"

"No. He left. I don't even know where he is." For the first time, relief came as she said the words. If they couldn't find him, they wouldn't imprison him.

Anna and Marta had not eaten since breakfast, which contributed to the ache threatening to pinch her head from her shoulders and block her vision. She heard blows and loud crying from inside, and realized no relief would come.

After their driver and guard saluted and left, the man at the desk ordered them to go to the showers, pointing toward a door.

There a woman, dressed in a drab shift like a prisoner herself, told Anna to sit on a bench. With the largest shears Anna had ever seen, she cut hanks of hair from her head and lay them aside in careful rows. To be used somehow?

A coarse woman with an evil eye and foul mouth told them to remove all their clothing. When they did not respond immediately, she pulled a bullwhip from a loop on her belt and threatened each of them with the beating of the other. It worked.

Anna prided herself on her modesty and the correct upbringing of her daughter. Nothing had prepared her for standing naked, shivering though her face burned hot as coals, before Marta and these strangers.

"The jewelry. Wedding ring, earrings, everything." Her tormentor pointed to a wooden bowl already containing a few items, most of them costume pieces.

Anna worked off her diamond-embellished wedding bands with difficulty, fearing the crude woman might cut off her finger if she couldn't. The rings had only been off her hand during her late pregnancies, when her fingers swelled. Living without them was unimaginable.

The woman stared at her necklace, whether in admiration or greed.

Warmed by her heart for twenty-seven years, this talisman of Dietrich's love and her faith in Jesus lived on her neck day and night. She often fingered the pendant as she read her Bible and prayed. Though ornate and heavy, she had become so accustomed to its weight that she only sensed it when it wasn't there.

She would rather tear flesh from her bones than give the cross to these evil heathens. She kissed the inscription of their names and wedding date and placed her most precious possession in the bowl.

The woman cinched up her whip with a sneer, and Anna was sure she would never see her cross again.

Satan's handmaiden dumped a dishpan of water over Anna's head. "Sit down and be still." She nodded to the one who had cut batches of her hair. This person shaved her butchered hair and pointed her to the shower, where she rinsed the clippings from her body.

She bore the frigid flow from a bare pipe in the wall until Marta came to the position beside her. "My sweet child, I'm so sorry."

The whip slipped into the hand of their tormentor and cracked in the air, reverberating in the concrete block shower room. "No talking."

At the other end, they attempted to dry on damp towels and got doused with a white powder. The gummy coating stood up on their chill bumps.

To her surprise, Marta began to laugh and point at her. "Mother, you look like..." She bent over, unable to speak for laughing.

Puzzled, Anna turned in wonder to her daughter, pasty white all over, bald, crossing lean hands over her groin. In hysterics, obviously, her reaction was infectious nonetheless. "What? What's so funny?" She whispered, though the guards had given their attention to the next victims.

"...like a skinny Christmas goose."

Anna and Marta covered their mouths to muffle their hilarity. They turned to each other, though Anna refrained from embracing her daughter. Quickly, she snatched up underwear and pulled on one of the plain, shapeless shifts.

When Marta had done the same, Anna put her hand on her daughter's thin shoulders and looked into her beautiful, brown eyes. "We'll get through this. By God's grace, we can endure anything."

Anna and her daughter were directed into a high-ceilinged factory of some sort. Warmer here due to the busy action of many machines, the noisy space contained rows of women at work on metallic objects. The hiss of escaping air pressure and the loud clank along the lines made the building sound like a place for men's work.

A touch on her shoulder surprised her. Standing close, an older woman shouted in her ear. "We're building parts for tanks. This will go into the engine. The tracks are assembled over there." She pointed to their far right. "That takes less mechanical experience. I think we'll start you on that job." Marta followed her mother.

"I'm no good at this kind of thing. I can hardly use a screwdriver." She called for help if she so much as needed a light bulb replaced. She knew nothing about heavy machinery.

"Don't worry. You'll observe for a while, and someone will teach you what to do." The kind woman shouted to a tall, strong-looking younger woman, Petra, and left them with her.

Along the worktable were arranged small stacks of metal pieces. "You take this wide piece, drop the bolts in these holes, nuts on this side, tighten them down…" Petra went through the process twice, her scraped and scabbed hands moving quickly with the greasy parts. Then she told Anna to construct one of the units.

"I don't have any mechanical skills—"

"You didn't yesterday. Today you can build army tanks. Believe me, it's not bad duty." Petra eyed Marta and spoke into Anna's ear. "Is the girl with you?"

"Yes, she's my daughter."

"Make sure she leaves grease under her fingernails. A little on her face wouldn't hurt. If one of the overseers comes around, tell her to look away and stay hidden behind the machinery."

Anna's empty gut wrenched. Her mouth went slack at the horror of Petra's implications. This pure child had spent her life in protection. Always chaperoned, Marta had never dated or partied alone.

Dear God, she is in your hands. Only You can stand guard over her now.

"Wilma—the line supervisor who brought you over here—she tries to cover for the young girls. Unless she'd prefer the easy life of an officer's woman?"

"No. Absolutely not." She made this decision for her daughter without asking. As much as she wanted Marta to live, she feared spiritual death more than death of the body. She would coach Marta on remaining inconspicuous when they had time to talk.

Work in the factory continued all day until they were faint with hunger and exertion. Being late fall, darkness came early. The cacophony broke down as separate sections of the huge space stopped production. They followed the stream of bent, plodding women funneled into a weathered wood room crowded with narrow tables and benches. They filed past someone scooping watery soup from a pot, and took seats with Petra.

She wanted to put the bowl to her lips and drink it all, but then it would be gone. Refills probably didn't happen. Straightening her spine in good table etiquette, she spoke to Petra, as much to prolong supper as to gain information. "How long have you been here?"

Petra shook her head sharply and lifted a finger. Without even whispering, she mouthed the words, "No talking."

In the bunkhouse, Petra showed her the hay-filled, thin mattresses. "We pull one on the floor, anywhere really, then stack them back in the morning. Bathroom's over there. We take turns cleaning it, but we don't have supplies. Only rags and cold water, sometimes soap."

Anna and Marta added their mattresses to the general organization of rows and columns. Anna dropped onto hers and bonked her bottom on the floor. No different from reclining directly on the planks except for the scratchy hay. She ached all over. Her body remained stiff against the pain. With her eyes closed, she reached to delicately rub an itch.

"Sorry about the fleas."

Surprised by the voice, Anna peeked. The kindly, older woman, Wilma the line supervisor, stood beside her. "Nothing can be done about them. At least you won't have lice as long as you're bald." She said this with a sad smile.

Marta stirred. "Is it true if we work hard, we'll be freed?"

"Humpf." Wilma shook her head. "You work hard, you starve, you die, and then you're free."

Her daughter's face twisted in anguish. "That's not fair. We've done nothing to be treated this way."

"There is no crime for which this is just punishment." Wilma's ready answer indicated she had heard this protest before. "Are you part of the political resistance?"

"Heavens, no." Marta had never joined a political group. Not even Hitler's Youth.

"Then why are you here?"

Anna sat up and lifted her chin. "I'm Jewish, but I'm American." She almost said *married to a German.* Only this morning he died in her arms? She didn't want to tell these women of her grief. They already suffered so much that her own loss of Dietrich might not be, well, appreciated. Having his death slighted would be unbearable.

"American? That must be why they didn't lock you up in Dachau. Or send you straight to Auschwitz. This camp is for female POW's and dissenters. And Jewish sympathizers, if you'll pardon me."

"No offense taken, I assure—"

The weak lights flipped off without warning, an event noted by curses that should never curl the tongue of a lady.

"No talking after lights out," Wilma whispered as she fumbled to her mattress.

Anna reached for her daughter's hand the few centimeters between their mats. Silent tears coursed down their cheeks until exhaustion carried them into the arms of sleep.

CHAPTER NINETEEN

28 September, 1944
A Labor Camp near Dachau, Germany

ANNA HAD HER eye on the pregnant prisoner. The baby had dropped days ago, and now she stopped several times to bend over her work table, clutching the rough boards to stand.

Anna watched her, red-faced and trembling, suffering labor on her feet. Finally, Anna could bear it no longer. "Cover for me, Marta. She needs help."

"No, Mother, they might beat you."

She left her position anyway and went to the mother, putting her arm around her shoulders. "I'm a nurse. Let me assist you."

The woman pushed up from the table, looked both ways, and nodded. Marta had left her tasks also and helped brace her as another contraction overtook her body.

"What's your name?"

"Marie. Do you speak French?"

"A little." Years had passed since Anna had conversed with a friend in French.

Marta's French was fresher. "Lie down."

With nothing to pad her and no insulation from the dirty floor, Anna feared the worst for this delivery. The baby had already crowned. She would keep her own unclean hands away from the area as much as possible and catch the newborn as it emerged. "The baby is already presenting. Push. Curl up and push hard."

In a few seconds, the tiny child slipped into her palms. Thin, not reacting well, but alive. She cleared his mouth and nose. After he took a first breath, she passed the unwashed newborn to his mother's outstretched arms.

Marta found a sharp metal band among their work supplies.

Anna clamped off the umbilical cord and then cut it.

A stained, ragged cloth was thrust before her, and Anna looked up to see Wilma. Not smiling now, her frown indicated that the baby's arrival created a problem.

Anna took the cloth and used it to wipe the child's face and nose. She squeezed open his mouth and checked for any obstruction to his breathing. When she had cleared the mucus, he inhaled and cried.

"Shhh. Keep him quiet. Quick, give him the breast. He must not cry."

Anna swaddled him and told the mother to hold him close and offer him her breast. Showing more than explaining, Anna taught the new mother how to hold the baby and squeeze out the first drops of mother's milk.

Wilma returned with other rags, bits of towels, and a clean shift, which she held out to the mother. "Change clothes right here, right now. Take this long piece of cloth and tie him under your dress."

She glanced toward the entrance and handed some rags to Anna. "Wipe up the mess and throw it in the trash barrel. I'll make sure it gets burned today."

Anna kneeled to clean the floor and wrapped the placenta in the foul scraps of towel.

"Quick. Back to work as if nothing happened. The inspector's in the kitchen."

Moments after giving birth, the mother had to stand and at least pretend to build components of an army tank. Anna assumed from Wilma's response that the baby would be taken if he were discovered. She returned to her position at the table without asking, quite sure she didn't want to know what would happen to the newborn if the inspector knew.

SERIOUS ILLNESS HIT the labor camp. Victims of diarrhea and vomiting were isolated to one side of the sleeping room, near the toilets. Unable to stand, they could not work. Left alone all day, they would die without care.

Wilma came to Anna during the evening meal, a bowl of watery oatmeal. She took a seat on the rough bench between Marta and Anna. "You're nurses, aren't you? What can be done for the sick ones?"

Anna let her assume Marta was also a nurse. In many ways, she was in training. "They need medicines to help control the symptoms, and they must replace the fluids with water and clear fruit juices."

"We have no medicines, nor can we give them fruit juice." Wilma's rounded back and downcast face spoke volumes about their chance of survival.

She made one suggestion after racking her brain for ways to help without the most basic of aids. "Can we give them boiled water with a little sugar and salt added? Or the liquid of a vegetable soup? We had that for supper last night."

Propped on an elbow, Wilma gave a small nod. "That's possible, I suppose. I'll find out what the cook has on hand."

"And showers. Cleanliness is very important. If we don't wash the women, the disease will spread through the camp. Especially if it's typhus. We could all die within the week."

Wilma jerked her head up and scanned the women slurping their porridge. "All of them?"

"All of us."

She stared, mouth hanging open. She propped again, this time with her hand over her mouth.

Anna scanned the room. "How many women are sick now?"

"Seven are on their pallets. A few more with symptoms."

"Let me talk to them, explain the need to keep drinking water and bathing. Then I must have help carrying them to the bathroom and getting them to wash. It makes more sense for those assisting to be people already infected. Let the healthy ones stay clear."

"Yourself?"

"No, I'll care for them."

"But why? You can give orders from a distance."

Anna sighed and examined her heart. "I'm a nurse. It's what I do." She had bathed and fed infants in the orphanage for years, often at risk to herself. Sometimes she did get sick handling the babies. The home in which she volunteered had healthier children than most. Her care was part of the reason. She blessed and prayed over them every day, and many went to good homes. These thoughts brought a smile to her face and her mind.

Wilma glanced at Marta and then leaned close, gathering mother and daughter with an arm around each. "Young women have been requested to come out of the labor camp to...*serve*...the officers. It's a choice Marta might want to consider, especially in light of this epidemic."

"No." Marta's emphatic reply came before Anna answered for her. "I'd rather die here than be used as their prostitute."

Her response stunned Anna, who thought her daughter wouldn't understand the proposal. She must have been reading more profound works than Anna suspected.

The rattle of dishes and scraping of benches filled the seconds while Wilma held the women. "If you're absolutely sure..."

"I'm sure."

"If you change your mind, let me know." She stood and spoke over the noise, organizing the prisoners to hear Anna's instructions for care of the sick.

ANNA'S AWARENESS OF Marta grew during the night. She had been up twice or more. Anna reached over and touched Marta's cheek. Hot. Definitely fever.

Marta took her mother's hand. Anna whispered a prayer. "Dear Heavenly Father, please don't let this happen. Please heal my precious daughter." Her throat closed up, and she couldn't speak anymore.

Marta retched, her stomach already empty of the measly broth and bread they had for supper. She stirred and went again to the bathroom.

Finding her still gone when she woke again, Anna went to find her. She whispered into the dark. "Marta? Are you in here?"

"Here, Mother. The third toilet." As morning light crept through the high windows and across the concrete floor, Anna stayed with her sweet child, praying for her and bathing her forehead.

From the dining room she brought a cup of boiled water, but could not beg even a spoonful of sugar. She dissolved a piece of her bread, knowing some nourishment was essential for life. Marta lay, weak and feverish, on a straw pad near the other patients. "Drink this little by little."

"I can't. It will only come up again, Mother."

"You have to keep drinking fluids. Just a sip at the time." She lifted Marta's head and held the water to her lips.

"I have to go now, sweetheart. Wilma won't let me stay with you. I begged her, but…"

"I understand, Mother. There's nothing you can do here anyway."

A sob caught in Anna's throat as she stood to go.

"I love you, Mother. Don't worry."

Anna prayed in whispers at her work station, fluctuating between intense sorrow for Marta's suffering and Dietrich's death. As much as she loved him, anger overwhelmed her that he had convinced her to stay in Germany, saying Americans didn't have to wear the Star of David on their sleeves. He believed being Christian and American exempted her from the Jewish pogroms. Well, she hoped he could see her and their daughter now in this cesspool.

Background sounds of the workshop shifted. Anna scanned the area. Wilma and two SS officers strode straight to her.

"This is where she usually works, sir." Wilma indicated the space to Anna's right. "She's too sick to even stand up." Her gaze avoided Anna. "As I said, she has the fever. I'm sure you don't want a woman with typhus."

The man swore. "Show me where she is, then. I have to report I've at least seen her." Assembly racket covered the click of their boots to the exit.

Anna trembled with fear and cried out to heaven. *Don't let them take her. She's yours, Lord. Don't let her be defiled by these agents of Satan.*

Hours later, she took water and her own soup broth to Marta, who raised on an elbow to sip.

"Some soldiers came to the factory for you today, sweetheart."

"I know. Wilma was with them. I played dead until she pointed me out and told them I had the fever. Then I gave them the benefit of an extra heave." She smiled weakly. "They didn't want me."

Comfort came over Anna for the first time that day.

Marta reached a shaky hand toward the bowl of broth. "I'll take another sip, if you don't mind. I'm better than I was this morning."

Tipping the bowl to Marta's lips, she sensed the presence of God in their hellhole.

CHAPTER TWENTY

14 October, 1944
Prison Camp near Dachau, Germany

ANNA AND MARTA trudged through the snow to the factory, glad it would be a few degrees warmer there. Sleep had been difficult on the cold floor. They curled together on one hay mattress and covered themselves with the other. At least the morning porridge had been hot.

By midmorning, Anna's mind churned on its customary devices to ignore gnawing hunger and stiff, sore muscles and joints. She dipped again at the well of happy thoughts, snippets of memory from when the children were young and Dietrich's business boomed. He left home for work each day so handsome, the fragrance of his shaving lotion on her cheek after a farewell kiss.

By her side, Marta fitted nuts and bolts into the tank track segments. Her returning strength evidenced the power and protection of Almighty God.

The tromp of boots and voices of men broke into their world. Oh, no. Had they come back for Marta? She kept her head down as the steps advanced toward them. Marta reached up to scramble her hair and swipe grease on her face.

The men went to the metal stairway at the far corner, rattling each step in their climb. They must have come to inspect damage from the last bombing. The back wall of the factory, constructed of old brick, developed long cracks and swayed like a pregnant woman with a backache. Climbing the stairs attached to that wall seemed unwise.

A loud rattle presaged the clank of the metal steps, and stones rained from the sky. Anna and the others darted to the other side of the factory with arms over their heads.

One of the SS officers cried out in pure agony. He had fallen most of the way down, where his leg caught in the structure. The other man lay spread out on the floor, limp and unmoving.

All the machines in the shop stopped, leaving an eerie silence. Panic whispers rasped against the walls.

Anna advanced with caution to the accident, drawn to the man's groans. Suspended by the trapped leg, he pulled on the side rail to release the pressure. His pants had torn, revealing the stark white shin bone sticking through the skin. Both of the lower bones had broken, bent at a grotesque angle.

Anna motioned to Marta. "Let's help him."

Without question, Marta joined her. "I'll get under his torso and try to lift. We have to get the weight off." She waved for more help from the women. Only two responded. Remaining on the floor, they lifted his head and back to release pressure from the leg.

Anna reached through the uprights of the railing and grasped the foot hanging behind the stairs. Hesitating a moment, she eyeballed the man. "This is going to hurt. Hold on."

His eyes were wide, his teeth clenched.

With slow and careful movements, she lifted the leg from in front and pushed the foot from behind the step.

He screamed to God and cursed him in the same breath.

"Don't move. Let me do the work." To Marta, she said, "Back up a bit and lower him to the floor. I've got his legs. You—" She nodded to a stronger-looking worker. "—help her." Changing her position to the front of the steps, Anna carried his legs along.

When the man lay moaning on the floor, Anna knelt to determine how to treat the injury. "Someone get me some clean cloth. A towel or something large enough to wrap the leg."

Wilma left at a trot.

Anna looked to Marta. "How's the other man?"

Marta turned to the unconscious one. "He's still out." She placed her fingers at his neck. "He has a pulse." She felt under his head and came up with blood. "Head injury." Running her hands along his legs and arms, she found no obvious breaks.

His eyelids fluttered, and he frowned and squinted. He rolled his head with a look of confusion.

Wilma returned with two towels and a glass bottle of rubbing alcohol.

Anna twisted toward Frau Wilma. "Can you get this man an ice pack?"

Wilma huffed. "Am I a magician?"

"Then please…send someone for a big handful of snow."

Her patient stared at Anna with wide eyes.

"The snow will help control the bleeding and swelling. Lie still. Do you hurt anywhere else?"

"No. I don't think so." He patted his chest. "Are you a nurse?"

"I'm the closest thing to a nurse in this building right now. Here, I'll make you a pillow of snow."

The officer curled to sit up.

"Lie still." She still remembered how to rebuke an uncooperative patient.

He lay back, shock playing on his face.

"I'm going to help the other man."

Anna returned to the first patient, checked for bleeding, and found the situation better than expected. "I don't think the bone cut through an artery." She reached to take the SS dagger from a scabbard at his waist, but he grabbed her hand with a fierce grip. "I need to cut your trousers to get at the bone. You have a compound fracture."

Studying her face as if to determine whether he could trust her, he relaxed his hold. She took the knife and sliced down the front of his pants leg. Marta stood ready for instructions.

"Get me a stick or a narrow board or something to use for a splint." Anna waited, considering how normally she would say comforting words to a patient, maybe hold his hand. Never before had she treated an enemy.

The man studied her face. "Why are you doing this?"

"I'm a nurse."

His eyes traveled over the women gathered in clumps nearby. "Are you one of the prisoners?"

"Yes."

"Then..." Lines stacked on his brow and around his eyes. "Why are you helping me?"

Anna did not look at his face at all, but concentrated on the wound. "It's what I do."

Marta brought back a piece of wooden siding with white paint scaling off. "Will this work?"

"Sure. Put it under the leg. Now we'll rinse the area with this alcohol—hold on, it's going to sting."

The patient inhaled in a long hiss between his teeth. The leg jerked, which must have been excruciating. He gripped his thigh.

"Now Marta, you're going to have to pull the leg straight while I try to work the bone down."

"I don't know if I can do that, Mother." Marta's face paled.

Anna pointed ever so slightly toward the SS emblem on the man's sleeve, and Marta's eyes followed to the skull and crossbones there. "I'm sure you can."

With a smooth, concerted motion against the background of moans from the patient, they repositioned the bones with the skin covering the ragged edge.

As they completed splinting, four more soldiers rushed into the building carrying canvas stretchers rolled on their poles. "Where are they?"

Wilma pointed to the injured men and then to the stairway, dangling from attachments above. Explaining about the previous bomb damage and how the accident happened, she concluded with praises for the nurses. "These two women treated them. This officer would still be hanging upside down with his bones sticking out if not for them."

Anna averted her eyes, knowing attention in a prison was not a good thing.

The soldiers opened the stretchers and lifted their patients onto them. As they started to carry the men out, the one with the broken leg called out. "Wait. Bring the nurses. I want them to come with us."

Anna and Marta pulled together, seized by fear of the officer's intentions.

"Come along, then." Not having a spare hand to pull his gun, the porter jerked his head toward the door.

The women glanced at Wilma, questioning with their expressions.

She gave them a kind smile like the one which first greeted them to the factory. "Go along. It's okay."

No one knew if that were true.

ANNA AND MARTA held onto the bench edge in the back of the ambulance. Built like a tall, boxy truck, it had racks on the sides for stretchers, where their two patients now lay. Though short on sympathy for her captors, Anna knew the bumpy ride caused a lot of pain for the man with the broken leg.

Two soldiers rode in the cab and the other two in the back. These identified themselves as medics and asked more detailed questions about the accident.

"So why are you in the POW labor camp?" The younger one studied them too closely.

"We're Americans, with dual citizenship." Anna didn't see the need to mention the racial problem.

Her leg patient stirred. "Americans? Why didn't you go home before the war began?"

Her answer led to telling about her husband, his business, and the family dilemma.

"Your husband was a von Steuben? I've heard the name. Surprised you didn't buy your way out of labor camp."

"Frankly, it never occurred to me." He could find out more about their arrest if he tried. The SS had unlimited resources and powers. She wouldn't make it easy for him, nor would she apologize to anyone for being born Jewish.

The vehicle hit a bump so hard they all bounced. The wounded men shouted and the medics pounded on the front panel.

When he could speak again, the SS officer reopened the question of why she had treated him.

"I am a nurse. That is my calling in life. I do not ask what religion or nationality the patient is."

"The army hospitals need nurses." He propped up, keeping a hand on his knee. "Would the two of you work in one?"

"Would we be respected as professionals?"

"Of course. You'll be fed, given a place to live at the hospital... I can't promise you a salary, maybe a little pin money, but it's better than where you've been."

She read a guarded acceptance in Marta's slight nod. "Then we will serve together as nurses."

"Go into the hospital with me. I'll introduce you to the doctor. Explain about the accident, and what you and your daughter did for us. I think he'll want to keep you."

MEAGER CHRISTMAS DECORATIONS appeared in the wards, and Anna thought of the cold labor camp. How many had died since they left? When they were there, several worked with pneumonia. The rattle of their coughs at night told of their doom. They had no chance with poor food, inadequate clothing, and almost no heat.

She paused by a radiator and held out her hands. Marta would be dispensing the medications in a moment. Their paths crossed several times during the day, and they shared a miniature dorm room, dubbed the "mouse cage," at night.

Here she comes. She looks so much older in a nurse's uniform and cap. And pretty. She got all the best attributes of Dietrich's family and mine.

Marta smiled when she noticed her mother. "Nurse Anna. How goes it with you?"

"Very well, Nurse Marta." Then she spoke more confidentially. "Watch out for the fellow in bed thirty-five. He's proposing to everyone today."

Marta winked. "I turned him down yesterday. Told him my boyfriend would hurt him even worse."

"Must be time for him to be discharged. Home for Christmas."

Marta flicked a sad, bent-up little bell hanging on a string at the door to the ward. "Wish we could…"

"Don't even think of it, dear. We're fortunate to be here."

"How can you say that, Mother? We're on our feet twelve hours a day—"

"Yes, and it would be much more difficult to do this if I hadn't gained stamina at the factory." She dipped her voice low. "If we had been forced to come here from our comfortable home, it would be horrible duty. But coming from the camp, it's like God's Christmas gift especially for—"

"Ladies, ladies. We can't stand about chatting all day. Patients to bathe, sheets to change."

"Yes, Head Nurse Hedda," they chanted in unison. Nights were their time to talk, and then they were too tired.

On this night, however, Marta found her mother propped up in her narrow bed, re-knitting yarn raveled from old sweaters. She sat close as Anna moved her knees aside. "I've been thinking."

In the dim light, Anna's eyes tired easily. She brushed her fingertips over them, careful not to let the needles drop a stitch. "What have you been thinking?"

"We have a lot of freedom. No one guards us to keep us here. Especially overnight."

"Those are dangerous thoughts, my dear." She eyed Marta over her knitting.

"We're somewhere close to Munich, with a little money for transportation."

Anna relaxed her hands into her lap while holding the threads in place. "We couldn't go home. You realize that. If our neighbors turned us in before, they would do it again."

Marta's lips puckered into a pout, and tears came to her eyes. "It isn't fair. They have no right to imprison us."

Reaching to gently massage her daughter's back, she searched for words which not only kept her own bitterness at bay but also gave comfort. "No, it isn't fair. But we have food and a place to sleep, and even blankets. As for our hard work, we have an opportunity to aid in the healing of wounded soldiers."

A defiant glare shot from Marta, and she inhaled, no doubt to argue.

Anna didn't want her to express rebellious thoughts. "These are young men forced to serve in the army, like your brother. They had no choice. Now they're hurting. Some are amputees. Others will die or suffer for the rest of their lives."

She leaned back and put her needlework on the cardboard box which served as a bed table. "I search for Karl every day. Hoping to see him, dreading I will." She sighed, her lips trembling at the threat of tears. "When I care for these men, I pray for Karl. And if he's wounded, I pray he will be so well cared for as we do for them. I'm reminded of the scripture about..." Tears dropped, and her words wobbled with emotion. "...whatever you do for the least of these, you do for me. But instead of Jesus, I'm thinking of Karl."

DRAWING CLOSER TO the holidays, Anna sensed a prevailing cheerfulness, however strained. Colored lights drooped over the hospital's front door, a rumpled red bow hung above the nurses' desk. Taped on the wall, a Bavarian card had little windows to open, revealing pictures of cheerful children, as one counted down to Christmas Day.

While Marta assisted her with taking temperatures and checking glucose drips, Anna commented on the increase in the number of visitors in the hospital.

"Yes, a lot more family members have been coming lately. Christmas spirit, I suppose."

Then she helped Marta pull medications, which gave them an hour out of the hall traffic. Marta glanced both ways before whispering. "How easy would it be to hitch a ride into Munich with a visitor, pretending we have the afternoon off?"

Anna's heart rate picked up. The dangerous dare tested her nerve. "We know nothing about the security around the hospital. What if a guard stops the visitor's car and demands some paper?"

"I suppose you're right. But most of the patients here don't know we're from the prison camp, do they? They think we're ordinary nurses. They probably think we come to work, and we can go home on our day off."

"Which we haven't had since we arrived." She finished the tray for that wing and turned to her daughter, clasping both her shoulders firmly. "Marta, promise me you won't do something foolish. I couldn't bear it if they sent you back to prison camp. Or shot you for trying to escape. Promise me."

"Yes, Mother."

"Yes, what?" She re-enacted the scene of a mother demanding obedience of a young child.

"I promise I won't try to escape. Without you." She grinned enough to show her dimples, pecked her mother on the cheek, and left with the medicines.

As Anna exited the pill room, the elderly surgeon came toward her down the hall. "What's the matter, Nurse Anna?"

She hadn't realized she wore trouble on her face. "Oh, nothing, doctor. I just…well, it's nearly Christmas, and I think always of my son." The half-lie became a plan. "I'm not home to get any phone calls or letters, so I don't know how he is, or even where."

"Aren't you having your mail sent here?"

"Is that possible?" Noticing they were alone in the hall, she stepped closer. "You're aware Marta and I serve as nurses rather than be prisoners in the labor camp?"

"Yes, I'm quite aware. I had to agree to the arrangement."

"The POW's don't get mail." She allowed tears to pool in her eyes. "Sir, would it be possible to make one phone call to a friend in Munich to ask about my son?"

The doctor shoved both hands in the pockets of his white coat. His wild, hairy brow came together as he studied her face, then he relaxed with the kindness of an indulgent father. "I don't see why not. Especially if you don't mind my remaining with you while you make the call."

"I don't mind at all. When can this be?"

"Meet me at my office at one o'clock. First floor, the wing on the right."

Anna counted the minutes, fearful Head Nurse Hedda would prevent her leaving the wing. When the time came, though, Hedda said the doctor had already informed her.

Anna decided to call Herr Olson, Dietrich's partner in the firm. She trusted him completely. The doctor gave the operator the company's number, confirmed the connection, and passed the receiver to her.

She didn't recognize the voice of the man who answered. "This is Anna von Steuben, the widow of Herr Dietrich von Steuben. May I please speak to Herr Olson?"

The fellow clunked the phone down and left her waiting.

"Frau Anna? Is it really you?"

Aware of what the call might be costing, she quickly told him she and Marta were nurses at an army hospital near Munich.

"Rumors passed that you were…imprisoned at Auschwitz. Never mind. Are you well?"

"Well enough, and Marta also. Tell me, have you heard anything about Karl? He wrote that he served in the Army north of Frankfurt." She shouldn't have said that. The doctor probably knew she was Jewish. She glanced at the surgeon, whose kind expression had not changed.

The pause went on too long. Anna sucked in a breath.

"I'm so sorry, Frau Anna. The letters came here. That is, I had all your mail forwarded to the office."

"Wonderful. Please, open his letters and tell me how he is."

"Frau Anna, how can I say this? The message came from the Army. I recognized what it was, and you were…gone, so I opened it to confirm."

She heard the scrape of a chair and imagined him sitting down.

"Dear lady, your son was killed in action. He was buried with military honors."

"No, please God, no. When? Where?"

"In late October, I think. They didn't give any other information."

Anna fell against the bookcase, wracked with grief. The phone dropped to the floor as the dear old surgeon guided her to his chair.

[203]

CHAPTER TWENTY-ONE

23 December, 1944
German Army Hospital near Munich

ANNA AND MARTA met in the medications room, where they could talk without being overheard. Paranoia reigned in their own bedroom, though it made little sense anyone would care to eavesdrop.

Marta dropped aspirins into individual patients' pill cups. "Tomorrow's Sunday. Christmas Eve. Few of the doctors come in."

"Nor the head nurse."

Anna lifted a brow. "We should take a day off."

Anna's pulse pounded in her temple. "How can we leave the hospital compound? The guardhouse stands off the west wing."

"We need a pass. I have an idea." Marta kept her head down.

"What? What are you planning?"

"If it works, I'll let you know. I won't leave without you, Mother. I promised."

Anna passed the day on edge, nervous as a snowbird. She had seen Marta exiting an empty patient room smoothing down her white uniform and straightening her cap. Moments later, a dumpy, middle-age doctor emerged, a sneer twisting his chubby face. What was that girl up to?

The hospital lay under winter's blanket Saturday evening. Their patients dosed and drowsy, Anna and Marta ended their long day with a hot stew and bread in the employee's dining hall.

Dr. Huber winked at Marta, and she batted her eyelashes and pretended shyness.

"What are you doing?" Anna did not mistake the flirtation. "You know he's married. How could you be interested in him, anyway? He's so—"

"Shhh. Play along. Here he comes."

"May I sit at table with you ladies?" Dr. Huber didn't wait for an answer, but put his tray down and pulled out a chair with a noisy scrape.

"Doctor, I'm sure you've met my mother, Anna von Steuben."

They nodded at each other, though Anna regarded him with suspicion.

"Mother, Dr. Huber offered to take us for a ride tomorrow afternoon. Isn't that marvelous?"

The doctor cleared his throat loudly over Marta's words. "Well, I'm not sure if I can—"

"Of course you can, Herr Doctor. No one in this hospital has the authority to prevent us. The surgical wing couldn't function without you." Marta's flattery blossomed.

"Ha ha. My dear, I'm subject to ranking officers and hospital administrators like everyone else."

Marta touched his hand with the tip of her forefinger. "But you promised." Drawing her face into a pout, she drew tears on command.

Anna couldn't believe her daughter's display, nor how well she toyed with the man's vulnerabilities.

"It's almost Christmas," Marta purred. "Going for a drive would be such a sweet gift. Please say you'll meet me as we planned. Just for an hour."

Anna raised her eyebrows in question and nodded ever so slightly sideways, indicating *shall I leave?*

Marta nodded *yes.*

"Please excuse me, Herr Doctor. I'm so weary."

"Of course, Nurse Anna. If you don't mind, I'll remain and have an evening coffee with your daughter."

Anna waited in their room, dozing with the light on.

Marta eased in late and shot her a triumphant gleam. With a pencil and scrap of paper, she wrote, "After lunch trays are collected tomorrow."

Sleep eluded them both until the wee hours.

Dressing for work, Marta and Anna slipped their small amounts of money in their pockets. They had nothing else to take from this room except a change of underwear. At the door, they both paused and looked back without regrets.

Anna worked energetically, steamed by hope. Trying to appear normal, she progressed through the duties of the day. Her emotions soared and plunged countless times. She feared disappointment if their plans went awry. Then, seeing Dr. Huber on rounds flirting like a young sport with Marta, her pulse quickened. The insect dallied near, oblivious to their web.

When Anna entered a room to deep-clean after the death of a patient, she walked in on the doctor clutching her daughter in a frenzy. "Oh. I beg your pardon." Stunned, she remained stuck to the floor.

The doctor's face flashed three shades of red. He straightened and tugged his coat back in place.

Marta giggled and touched his lips with a forefinger. "See you later, Herr Doctor." She scooted out before Anna, who found her feet but not any appropriate words.

Anna followed Marta into the supply room. "What are you—"

"Don't say anything, Mother. I'm doing this for both of us."

Tears came to her eyes. What sacrifice would her daughter make for their freedom? "Please be careful, dear. You are so precious—"

"Don't worry. Just pray and prepare a syringe of anesthetic. Enough to put a heavy man to sleep, but not enough to kill him."

When the lunch trays had been collected and the hospital settled into an afternoon lull, Anna and Marta each slipped down to the emergency room door. Dr. Huber made eye contact then left. Shivering against the December snowfall, they followed him to his car, parked at the side.

"Marta, please sit up front with me." He opened the door for her and then the back door for Anna. "Don't you ladies have overcoats?"

"No, Herr Doctor. People never allowed to go outside don't need overcoats." Anna trembled as she slipped onto the cold seat. "Thank you for allowing us to see a bit of the world this afternoon."

"My pleasure, Frau von Steuben." He cranked the car on the third try and drove toward the main gate and guardhouse which blocked their freedom. He rolled down the icy window enough for the soldier to recognize him. A sharp salute bid them good-bye.

The women pointed and gasped at bombed churches and factories, holes blown in the road, and tumbled walls.

"I'm afraid it will take years to repair all this once the war has ended. Our city has suffered terribly. Such a blight." The doctor worked his way toward town, which required frequent deviations.

"Where is your house, Dr. Huber? Would you like to show us where you live?" Marta flirted with skill.

"Oh, no, I don't think we should go there. No, that wouldn't be a good idea at all."

Anna visualized his wife's reaction and choked back a laugh. "Then let us show you where we live, or lived before…we came to work at the hospital. We could go inside and relax for a moment. My husband had some fine French cognac. I wonder if it's still there."

Wandering about aimlessly changed to driving with a purpose as Marta directed him along the route. They waited at a rail crossing, counting the precious minutes. "The trains are working. I would've expected them to be torn up."

"Some are, but this line still runs into town. They do what they can to repair the transportation. So few people own cars." The doctor's voice droned on about damage in the city. Finally, they crept across the rails.

She became more excited with each kilometer, pointing out the landmarks of their neighborhood until they pulled up on the cobblestones in front of her house. Snow piled over the walkway and small garden, on every window ledge and bush.

"How shall we get in, Mother? We don't have a key."

"I used to keep one in the shed." Anna started around the house, but Marta tried the front door, which opened.

A wide-eyed glance passed between them. The women entered and Dr. Huber trailed behind.

Marta made a guttural noise. Anna stopped, stunned to see her home emptied, covered in dust. No one spoke. They wandered through the bottom floor. Only a broken chair remained in the living room. Papers littered Dietrich's study. The sound of scurrying little feet came from behind kitchen cabinets.

Dr. Huber chuckled. "I suppose the cognac's gone."

Anna turned to him, dumbfounded he could joke at such a time. Nevertheless, she led to the kitchen, opened the pantry door, and showed him its raided shelves.

"Let's go, ladies. We'll find a nice place for a dinner of *wiener schnitzel* and then make our way back."

Anna slipped her hand into her pocket and nodded to Marta, who batted her lashes at the doctor and sashayed toward the door. He quickened his step, leaving Anna behind him. With trembling fingers, she popped the cover off the syringe.

His overcoat left no bare skin except hands and head. Cold fear set her insides quivering. She had never deliberately hurt a patient before.

She raised her arm high, stabbed Dr. Huber in the side of his neck, and pushed the plunger hard. He turned, his mouth agape. She twisted and held the hypodermic, which broke off as he swatted her hand away. Too late, the anesthetic glazed his eyes and his face went slack. Anna and Marta braced against his weight. He toppled into them, but they protected his head from cracking on the kitchen tile.

Anna pulled the needle out. Unable to sterilize the site, she pressed hard with his own clean handkerchief. The horror of her action shook her body.

Marta felt for his pulse.

They waited.

He breathed again.

They had done it.

"Now what?" Spots swam before Anna's eyes. She could not think past this terrifying moment.

Marta dropped his wrist. "Now we scram."

"And leave him here? On the floor? He might contract pneumonia."

"How long will he be out?"

Full of remorse, Anna checked his pupils. "Probably a few hours. Maybe three or four. I don't know."

"Leave him. His coat will keep him warm."

"Search for any of our clothes upstairs. We must change out of these white uniforms, and we need coats or at least sweaters."

Breathless, Marta brought down old coats, wool skirts, and sweaters from the attic, all with moth holes and faded colors. "Everything else has been stolen. I guess the poor didn't want these things."

"They're fine. Let's dress and go."

They kept their nurses' dresses to discard elsewhere. The less evidence they left, the better. Marta dug in Dr. Huber's pocket for his car key and they scurried outside and closed the door.

"Mother, can you drive this car?"

"Of course. I think. I haven't driven much in years, but I used to." She slid under the wheel and studied the display. With a foot on the clutch, she moved the gear stick through its pattern, illustrated on the knob. Easy, so long as she never had to back up. She always had difficulty finding reverse.

She inserted the key. "Please, God in heaven..." She started the motor, and jerked down the street.

Marta laughed, no doubt hysterical, but it distracted Anna. She had to think. "Stop that cackling. Where are we going?" She eased around a corner, careful not to skid on the icy cobblestones.

Marta looked like a grade school child trying to guess an answer in a spelling bee. "Aunt Berta's?"

Anna shook her head harder than necessary. "No, they'd look for us there first, or at the firm or anyone attached to the company. We've got to hide out somewhere, and we don't have much money."

"Church? A friend's house? Someone who wouldn't turn us in?" Marta stacked ideas like a house of cards to be blown down.

"And who might that be?" Anna began to tremble with fear. Being caught now meant certain, torturous death. "I have one idea. Helga went to live with her brother on his farm. Remember, she asked if we wanted to go with her? Said he had plenty of food?"

"Yes, but that was before everything happened. Father was alive. She knew we wouldn't come."

"She worked for us over ten years. I trusted her completely. Do you have a better idea?"

"Do you know where the farm is?"

"Remember the summer I took you and Karl because you'd never seen a cow milked? We drove out there for the day."

Marta nodded, but tentatively. "Let's not drive the doctor's car to their farm. We'd get caught, and Helga's family would suffer. Let's go north, ditch our uniforms, leave the car, and take the train into town and then east. Even if the lines aren't all working, we'll be away from the house and the car. We'll think of something."

So they parked in a churchyard a couple of blocks from the northern rails, and backtracked into the city center. Passengers to the east could travel only a short way because of rail damage, and then they caught a bus.

The bus driver stopped within the hour and turned in his seat. "We can't go any farther in this snow storm. We have to stop here."

Fatigue weighed on Anna. A day's work, a night's evil deed, and now a foiled escape. She wiped fog off the window.

The driver motioned for them to exit. "There's a guesthouse here. Maybe you can stay for the night. The cook's good."

Snow driven by the needles of wind numbed her face, hands, and legs. They slipped their way up the steps and out of the bitter cold. In the dark entrance, Marta pulled money from her pocket and counted it.

"Where did you get that?" Surprise marked Anna's whisper.

"The same place I got the car keys."

Lord, forgive us. Their sins compounded. Or was it sinful to escape the enemy? Anna shoved her guilt in a mental box and slammed the lid.

A succulent goulash dinner later, they climbed the narrow stairs to a warm, cozy bedroom. Though humble by previous standards, its feather bed reached around them with arms of blessing.

Enjoying the morning's breakfast of crisp *brotchen* and perfect soft-boiled egg—the first since they left home—they pretended normalcy. By the second cup of ersatz coffee, they felt like royalty.

Marta set her cup down, her satisfied smile changing to something more serious. "Okay, how do we get the rest of the way?"

"As soon as the bus can make the trip, we'll continue to her village. Then I hope someone will be able to take us to the farm. I doubt she has a phone."

They touched hands, bowed, and prayed, a common display of faith through their tribulation.

A slow, skidding and sliding journey later, they descended from the bus in the village nearest Helga's farm. First they warmed inside over a bowl of soup at the guesthouse there. The manager, a kindly, graying woman, seemed approachable and, Anna hoped, trustworthy.

"Can someone deliver us to the home of a friend? We are able to pay a reasonable fee."

"How far would that be?"

"Only a kilometer or so, I believe."

The lady checked the hour on the polished wooden cuckoo clock above her desk, one of the few decorative objects in the reception area. "Perhaps my husband can take you, if you don't mind waiting a while."

Their nerves rattled about and threatened to upset their stomachs. Did they wait for a ride to Helga's or to prison? When the tired, apron-stained hostess indicated that her husband was ready to take them, hope surmounted their fears. They bundled up and thanked her graciously.

Transportation in an open, horse-drawn carriage anchored them squarely in the last century. Wrapped in quilts from the guesthouse, they bumped and jiggled along the dirt road. Fortunately, the gentleman knew Helga Fischer and her brother's family and took them without mistake to the farm. Blanketed in snow, with all identifying markers concealed, the route would've been impossible for Anna to find.

A stocky man opened the door as they reached the front porch. He bore neither a smile nor a gun.

"Good afternoon." Anna's chin jerked against her greeting. "We're looking for Frau Helga. Is she here?"

Sizing them up with a glance at their poor clothing and no purses or luggage, he permitted them to enter. He showed them to the kitchen, the one area kept warm in a farmhouse.

At the black iron, wood-burning stove, a woman stirred a pot. She looked up, worry on her wide, weathered forehead. Not Helga. Perhaps her sister-in-law?

"Sofie, the ladies ask for Helga."

"I sent yesterday for the doctor. Are you his nurse?" Concern clouded her face.

"I am a nurse, though I came as a friend. Is Helga sick?"

"Oh, sick unto death, dear lady. I've done all I can, but it isn't enough. The compresses haven't worked." She wiped shaking hands on her worn apron. "Please, come. I'll take you to her."

Upstairs, ensconced in a bed under piles of quilts, lay a red-faced Helga. Body smells assaulted their noses. Helga inhaled to speak and coughed instead, rattling from the depths of her lungs.

"Helga, it's Frau von Steuben…Anna and Marta." Before she continued, Helga sat up, astonished as a child given a toy when it wasn't even her birthday.

"My dear God, have I died already and gone to heaven? Frau von Steuben and Marta." She coughed hard and spit into a rag. "You've found me on my last day on earth. Oh, sweet Marta, precious child. You look like an angel." Hacking racked her body.

Anna approached the bed and touched Helga's hot forehead.

"You mustn't touch me. You'll get the fever, too." And yet Helga's eyes pleaded for compassion.

Anna had no medicines or treatments to apply other than common sense and the experience of caring for patients with the barest provisions. She took layers of quilts off the woman's laboring chest and spoon-fed her nutritious broth. Under a tent of tea towels, a steaming menthol inhalant helped her breathe.

Through it all, Anna and Marta sat with her day and night, prayed, and read psalms from the Bible and bits of poetry from an ancient book.

Helga stirred on the fifth morning, her eyes less rheumy and breath not so labored. Sipping hot tea with honey, she seemed more aware. "Frau von Steuben, how did you know…? What brought you here?"

Anna tensed, fearing this moment of truth. "We've come to ask for refuge, Helga. We've run away from the city."

Helga's face took on an expression of relief, colored with awe. "Dear lady, you saved my life. God in heaven sent you, and here you must stay."

CHAPTER TWENTY-TWO

15 December, 1944
Military Hospital, England

JERKED FROM THE field hospital in France and shipped overnight to England, Henry Viertel felt fate had torn a huge hole in his chest and ripped out his life's purpose. A few hours after his farewell party, mainly silly jokes with friends in the Enlisted Mess Hall, he stood on the dark deck of a troop transporter crossing the English Channel.

Lt. Bill Hanson and Col. Strang had come to the party for departing soldiers, most of whom were wounded, either continuing treatment in England or going on the next ship from England to the United States. Henry's destination remained undetermined. His entire future hung on how well he convinced himself and all his examiners he was the real Henry. The prize, life in America, lay ahead.

The pre-dawn offloading in England was conducted under a surreal fog due to fatigue, the sudden change of every familiar aspect of his surroundings, and the danger of enemy submarines or airborne bombs. How ironic if he died as Henry going home to Texas.

Therein lay another quandary. He could never go home. Not to Texas, and not to Munich. When he landed in New York City, where would he go? The only city he knew in America was Atlanta, where his mother had grown up. Her parents had passed away years ago. If he avoided his aunt, her husband and two children, they would never know he existed.

Trucks, ambulances, and jeeps met the ship. Henry assisted however possible with stretchers and wheelchairs, then accepted a ride to the hospital. At the bottom of the triage list, he pulled a bed in a ward by mid-morning.

An orderly pushed him there in a wheelchair, against his protests.

"Sorry, corporal, those are my orders." He gave Henry a gown and robe. "Put this on, open in the back, and hop in bed."

"But I don't need to go to bed. I'm not sick. Just hungry."

A doctor attending a nearby patient entered the discussion. "You will put on the gown, go to bed, and not eat anything until we have time to determine what tests we need to give you. You are subject to disciplinary action if you disobey."

"Yes, sir." They obviously ran a much tighter organization than the field hospital.

Questions and exams over three days produced nothing but a clean bill of health, except for his feigned amnesia. The neurologist and psychologist conducted their final evaluation.

"Coordination, speaking, reading comprehension, mathematical ability—all functions have returned satisfactorily."

The lean, sharp-nosed neurologist flipped through pages in a folder, reciting results of all his tests.

"You see, corporal, we find no reason for the continued amnesia." The psychologist, a paunchy and balding colonel, stammered his conclusions. "That is to say, the initial injury being healed, the ability to speak having returned, there is no guarantee that memory of your former life will ever be regained."

Unspoken communication passed between the expressions of the two professionals.

Henry feared they had found him out and were about to call the MP's. Did they have a photo of him in the file? Why didn't he think of that before? The over-heated room closed in on him. He began to perspire. In a rigid oak chair, he tried to appear concerned about the prognosis while a hammer pounded at his temple.

The neurologist nodded to the psychologist.

If they arrested him, he planned, as they used to say in the Interrogation Unit, to spill his guts. He'd tell all, from the beginning. The room, overcrowded by three men and a desk, began to swim. He stared at the diplomas on the wall as a fixed a point of reference. He would not run. He would not panic. Telling the truth would come as a relief, even if he had to go to a POW camp.

The psychologist slumped forward, looking at the floor as he began to speak. "Now corporal, don't take this as a criticism, but some amnesia patients, shall we say, *choose* not to remember." He looked up at Henry. "It's as if the trauma is too painful, don't you see?"

Henry nodded, afraid to say anything. Choose not to remember? Indeed, he worked hard at not remembering.

"One finds it, I suppose, *safer* to retreat from memory of the injury and the particular event which caused it. In these cases, there is nothing medical science can do, or perhaps should do, to remedy the situation."

He pulled a cold pipe from his pocket and gave a ceremonial draw. Then holding it by the bowl, he pointed toward Henry's file in the neurologist's hands. "So what we propose, Henry, is that you return to your family and normal life. In a safe environment, your memories may all come back. And if not, well..." He raised his shoulders in an exaggerated shrug. "...you'll have to start over and pick up life from that point."

Henry exhaled, unaware of how long he had held his breath. No MP's, no jail. Unfortunately perhaps, no confession. He was still Henry.

"There's a troop ship leaving in a few days. Won't arrive in time for Christmas, but no doubt the family will celebrate when you get to Texas." The neurologist's mouth turned up a twitch. "Take this medical statement to the hospital administration office. They'll get you space on the ship and prepare your honorable discharge."

Henry thanked them for their efforts and left on shaky knees.

During the Atlantic crossing, Henry stifled his gregarious nature. His greatest fear, being recognized by a soldier as German, would destroy his new life. He filled the days making himself available to assist with the severely wounded. The less conscious his acquaintances, the better.

After an uneventful trip, the hospital ship came into port in New York. Carrying a duffle of little more than discharge papers, a shaving kit, and spare underwear, and with his mother's precious gold cross still on a shoestring around his neck, he boarded a train for Atlanta.

At his roll-out in England, he had received a tidy sum of back pay which had to last until he got set up somewhere and found a job.

He marveled that the train tracks hadn't been bombed and cars had gasoline. A strong spirit of optimism prevailed. Based on public chatter on the train, rationing seemed a challenge and almost a privilege rather than a tribulation. Compared to Germany, food flowed in abundance.

Excitement swirled about him. Americans anticipated imminent victory. Germany's depression due to living among bombed churches, pitted roads, and empty markets faded in his mind. In total contrast, America suffered no bombs and its citizens wore warm clothing and ate in countless restaurants.

He had been fed far better as an American soldier than... He remembered when he went to find food in Munich and was forcibly conscripted instead. If he only had his family here, now, in this land of abundance.

His delight with his new home country wilted over the weeks. He had never been so alone. Even in army barracks people surrounded him, talked to him as if they had a lot in common. Here, isolated amidst thousands, he passed his days inside his own thoughts.

Henry bounced around in Atlanta. Miserably cold in its humidity, he slept once in a cheap hotel. During the noisy nights with thin walls, people came and went at all hours. He searched for a clean, better-run weekly rental the next morning.

With money dribbling away and nothing coming in, he found and rented a furnished, one-room apartment near the center of town, utilities included. Dropping his duffle on the creaky wood floor, he tested the countertop gas burner and opened the toy-sized refrigerator. The two windows looked out on other buildings. This would do for now.

The job search took longer. He couldn't walk into an investment bank and ask for a position. He had a college degree and the German equivalent of a CPA, but not in Henry's name. In fact, he didn't even have a copy of Henry's high school diploma. He needed documentation.

Meanwhile, he scanned the want ads, including work as dishwasher, janitor, the sort of job which didn't require proof of graduation. Those also wouldn't support him well enough. He had to stop the bleeding with minimal income while hunting for something better.

Backing up a step, he prepared to face the cold to purchase basic requirements. The landlady said to ask her anything. He knocked on her door.

"Ma'am, where can I buy some sheets and a pillow?"

Even such a simple question—and then her answer—had to be repeated. She drawled worse than his Atlanta grandmother had.

"Woolworth? What kind of store is that?" He struggled with two W's in one word.

She looked at him as if he were an idiot, and kept repeating the store name. "They have everything, and for the best price. It's only a few blocks from here. You can't miss it."

He could and he did, because he couldn't fathom how to spell or pronounce the name. After stopping strangers twice, he spotted it on a huge horizontal strip high above the front doors. "Woolworth" in gold paint on a black background. A marvelous, enormous store, Woolworth really did have everything. even hot beef stew. He sat on a bar stool at the long, shiny counter and watched himself in the five-meter mirror.

Warmed and filled, he hauled the necessities of life up three flights of stairs to his new home.

In the envelope he received from the Army, besides the DD 214 Honorable Discharge form, the real Henry's hand-printed Army induction form gave the facts of his life. He needed a letter from the

New Braunfels High School verifying his graduation. He wrote the request before going to bed but feared the school office might give his current address to Henry's family. Better not send it.

The next day he returned to Woolworth, the store whose name he pronounced with difficulty, and applied for a job.

"What position are you applying for?" The dumpy woman buttoned her cheap sweater over an ample bosom.

"Ma'am, I've just been honorably discharged from the U.S. Army." He smiled at the lady, trying to break through her disinterest. "I've been fighting in France and Germany. I'm strong and able. I'll do any job you have."

"We get applications every day. But I guess for a veteran... Fill out this application and we'll see."

Within a few days, he secured simple stock boy work.

Henry picked up a discarded newspaper during morning break in late January and learned the Russians had liberated Auschwitz death camp in Poland. Sitting on the nearest storeroom box, the wind knocked out of him, he stared at the photo of emaciated prisoners and piles of bodies. Could Mother and Marta still be alive? Of the skeletal inmates, he recognized no one. Most were men. He would almost rather his loved ones be dead than to have suffered such an experience. Almost.

Dennis, a young coworker of limited intelligence, found him with tears streaming. "Whatsa matter, Henry? You sick?"

He pulled out his handkerchief. "No, not sick. Just...looking at these poor people." He explained the news article, and Dennis sat on a box beside him and cried, too.

Henry's fifteen minute break ended. "I guess we'd better get back to work. It won't help these miserable people if we lose our jobs."

"Can't lose my job." Dennis appeared startled, maybe afraid. "Too hard to get another one." He wiped his face and nose.

Henry folded the page and put it in his pocket. If he could only be in Poland for a few days.

Studying newspapers daily, he questioned what proportion was pure propaganda. They claimed Germany was under attack from the air and from all sides on the ground, and would be defeated. And then what? Could he ever go back?

Soon after the last winter storm, spring burst upon Atlanta. The city moved from ice to sprigs of green. Hundreds of peach trees came into full bloom and dogwood blossoms showed their brilliant white faces.

Henry boarded a city bus one Sunday in March simply to ride around and discover the area. He hopped off and walked in the sun through a gracious neighborhood north of the center and was captivated by a magnificent, regal church.

Though nothing like the church he had been reared in, its dignity and beauty called to him. As he stood on the sidewalk looking up to the portal, a spiritual hunger overwhelmed him, an emptiness created by his months out of the practice of worship with other believers.

His anger at God had cooled. The free will of sinful, prideful people had caused the persecution of Jews. The whole war, for that matter. But he also thought the all-powerful God of the universe should have intervened. He had nursed a recalcitrant attitude about worship. The time had come to accept the truth and heal.

Dressed in casual slacks and shirt with a cardigan sweater, he observed the clothing of others entering the church and decided to go in. He took a seat on a back pew. Drawn into the service by hymns and a solo, he opened his heart and drank in the pastor's message. When time for communion came, all believers were invited to take bread and juice. That included him.

God met with him in the confession of sin read aloud with the congregation. He repented and confessed his transgressions, though he did not promise to correct the one which now mattered the most—the lie about himself.

He intended to slip out unnoticed, but the pastor had a good eye for visitors. With a firm handshake, he projected a genuine interest. "Welcome, young man. You're here for the first time, aren't you?"

Henry's face heated. "Yes, sir. I happened by this morning and came inside. Hope you don't mind." He swept a hand over his sweater, regretting he had no suit and tie.

The minister, a pleasant fellow with silver-haired temples, kept his eyes on Henry's without looking down at his clothing. "You're always welcome. We hope to see you again."

The emotional effect on Henry of being greeted with such warmth made him tongue-tied. Words didn't come, so he nodded. He descended the steps into bright sun with gratitude for the unanticipated happy morning. It opened a door to heaven which had been closed far too long.

A middle-age couple came down with an adult, perhaps their daughter. Blonde and slender, in a yellow flowered dress with lace on the collar, she looked like an angel.

They proceeded to the parking lot and got into a car, which the gentleman drove away. As the vehicle turned right and passed out of sight, up a slight hill toward gracious homes, Henry realized he had been glued to one spot since seeing her.

The spell broke, leaving a yearning in its place. He made definite plans to return to this church next Sunday. Wearing a suit and tie.

CHAPTER TWENTY-THREE

March, 1945
Atlanta, Georgia

WOOLWORTH DID SELL suits, but Henry wanted something better. He may be the farm boy Henry, but he preferred to dress as well as Karl. He dug into his dwindling cash stash.

Americans knew how to celebrate Palm Sunday. The following week, the children's choir, frocked in white with red bows, waved fronds and sang their hallelujahs. The pipe organ swelled as the adult choir raised their praises. And a beautiful blonde called his attention away from the sermon by such simple acts as tossing her hair off her shoulders or looking sideways to the lady beside her.

By Easter, Henry had shaken hands with a number of church members, who accepted him like a regular. The sermon centered on the concept of grace, the unmerited favor of God. In his warm-up to the subject, the pastor commented on the use of the word as a woman's name, and gave a nod to the blonde with her parents.

She ducked her head, and Henry caught a blushing smile. He and others in the congregation lit with delight. So her name was Grace. He had to meet her.

He spotted her chatting with a couple holding a baby and cast about for the pastor or anyone—anyone at all—to introduce him. The few congregants he'd met talked with the pastor at the front door. The moment hung in the air. He had to do something.

Henry went upstream through people leaving, and she looked away from the baby toward him making his determined advance.

Forgetting the lady should offer her hand to be shaken first, he thrust his toward her with his best smile. "Good morning. I'm Henry Viertel. I take it your name is Grace."

Her tentative expression was pleasant enough, though she shook without removing her white gloves. "Yes, I'm Grace Shore and these are my friends, Mavis and Paul Rollins. Are you visiting church today? I don't believe I've seen you before." Her fixed smile contained a gram of I-shouldn't-be-speaking-to-a-stranger.

He greeted the Rollins couple and complimented their fat, happy baby. "I'm attending for the third time. I like this church."

"Haven't noticed you in the Bible class."

"Uh, well, I come out from the city on the bus. It takes a while to get here."

"Um-hmm." Her skeptical glance dipped to his suit and tie. "I'd better be going. My parents are waiting."

Paul shifted the diaper bag and Bibles he carried. "Are you single?"

"Single, unattached, and alone in the city." Henry nodded.

"You should come on Friday night. Our church hosts a gathering for single adults, especially veterans."

"I'm a veteran." Henry bounced once on his toes. "Friday night?"

"Yeah, like the church version of a USO canteen night."

Grace broke her departure to comment from several rows away. "The food's good. Starts at seven, or whenever people get here."

Food? That would pay for the bus ticket.

DOUBTS AND DARES clouded his intentions about attending Friday night. Stepping off the bus, he observed two girls enter a side door of the church. He followed them to wonderful fried chicken aromas in a large room set up with tables, hoping other men attended too. A half hour late, he almost turned around. But Paul said "whenever people get here." So American.

A middle age woman played informal music on the piano, where the others had grouped in USO style. Girls he hadn't met waved him over without missing a beat. A couple of guys sized him up as if he were competition.

Why had he bothered to ride a crowded bus for an hour after a hard day's work?

The singing stopped. They were invited to take a seat at the long table, and someone prayed before his metal folding chair had warmed up. Sitting on one end, he worked up enthusiasm for introductions and determined to be a grateful guest.

A parade of four women bearing serious supper came through a swinging door. The pastor's wife, the piano-playing lady, and...yes. Grace Shore, bringing a tray of mashed potatoes and gravy.

He sprung up to help her.

"Thank you, but I've got it. Just let us serve you."

Being the last seated became a huge advantage when the church ladies took the leftover places on the end. The older women, however, seemed more interested in him than Grace did. They flooded him with questions, which he answered with his memorized replies. Single, veteran, recently moved here from fighting in the war. Texas German family, sorry about the accent.

Grace didn't notice him.

"If your family is in Texas, why are you here?" The pastor's wife spoke with a melodious voice. "Are you staying with someone?"

"No, ma'am. Just got a job here. Thinking about going to college on the GI Bill."

Grace touched the paper napkin to her lips. His eyes followed the gesture, tracking on their own will. "Where do you work?"

"Woolworth, downtown."

"I see."

Henry ducked his head in embarrassment. She nodded without enthusiasm, unimpressed with his five-and-dime company. She'd think even less of him if she knew he was only a stock boy.

"Excuse me. I need to pick up dirty plates and pour ice tea." She stood and began busing the table.

Henry sprang up to help her, knocking his chair back with a bang. A few spaces away, the other two veterans jumped to their feet, their fists tight. If Henry caught what he thought he saw, one of them reached for his nonexistent side arm. With flared nostrils and eyes blazing, they braced for combat.

The women, startled by their reaction to the noise, stared with mouths open.

"Sorry, men. Just a chair." Henry set it right. "Don't worry. No one's shooting at you." He meant the joke to defuse the situation, but the former soldiers scowled.

They settled back in their seats, holding onto the angry glare.

Breaking eye contact first, Henry picked up his plate and stacked others on top.

"Thanks, Henry, but you don't have to do that. You're our guest, remember?" Grace lilted through the strained silence.

"A grateful guest doesn't let the hostess clean twenty plates and glasses." He continued gathering, and headed for the kitchen.

While others got out checkers and dominos, Henry and the women shared sinks of hot, sudsy water and cleaned the tables. With his cardigan off and sleeves rolled up, he went at the plates with more energy than he thought he had left.

The pastor's wife rinsed the dishes he washed. "Would you please explain to me what just happened?"

"Shell shock, ma'am. After combat, it takes much time for men to get over the threat of guns. They stay nervous."

"I see." She played hot water over the plates. "And why don't you have shell shock?"

He was sure Grace had noticed the long line from behind his ear and across his forehead, but no one had asked. He motioned to the scar now. "I don't remember anything about it. One of the blessings of amnesia."

Women's hands halted, paying attention to Henry's conversation.

Grace faced him and peered at his wound. "You don't remember anything?"

"Nothing before the injury. It's a blank."

Grace reached for a pile of wet utensils. "What did you do in the war?"

"I was an advance radio operator in Patton's Third Army. Wounded at the Siegfried Line. My memory starts in the hospital." Weaving the lives of the two Henrys, he continued to his rapt audience. "After that, I interrogated German POW's for information about their positions and equipment along our path from France."

The pastor's wife let a dish slip into the water with a clunk. "Wow. You were right in the thick of it."

Grace spread the utensils on the countertop, where she systematically separated and dried them. "How did you interrogate Germans? Did they speak English?"

"No, ma'am. I'm from an old settlement of Germans in Texas." Now he called upon everything he had read from libraries, newspapers, *National Geographic*, and *Saturday Evening Post*. He should get an "A" for his research. "Our group is there since before the Great War. I spoke German until grade school."

"You remember that far back?" Grace seemed skeptical, though not unkind.

"No, ma'am. I learned that from the letters of my family while I was in the field hospital."

One lady of about fifty, introduced earlier as an Emory English professor, regarded him with squinted eyes. "Wouldn't your accent be different after many years of separation?"

"Not so hard to understand German as Atlanta English." He laughed, and the women laughed with him.

By the time they had dried and stacked the clean items, they were first-name friends. That wouldn't have happened in less than five years in Germany.

And Grace smiled when she thanked him. He'd wash dishes every Friday evening for her favor.

Though the weather remained chilly, he walked about five miles to his apartment. It gave him time to think.

He needed the kind of work acceptable to a woman like Grace. He evaluated options. As Henry, starting college over seemed the only way to achieve a professional level of existence. He'd have to hold a job and go to school on the GI Bill. Money would be tight for years. Eventually he could pass the CPA exam. He didn't want that career, but it might be an entry to the financial world.

In truth, women in his previous life were impressed with his position and wealthy family. For sixty years, von Steubens perched on top of the social ladder. His father had cautioned him about dating the sort who cared too much for money.

He already suspected Grace had different values. He'd have to get her attention based on what he could do as Henry. The new definition of a man started here.

While the introspective mood remained, he wrote a letter to Lt. Bill, telling him he had a simple job and had met a fine Southern lady. He addressed the envelope with a dose of hope under the stamp. Fellows he knew usually weren't good at casual correspondence. Would he ever hear back?

GRACE HOPPED IN her parents' car with a step lighter than reasonable for having worked all day at the hospital before assisting with the unmarried adults' night at church. Shifting gears up the hill to their home, she made plans to return next week.

Lamps shined from the living room window. Mom had waited up for her. Did she have to move out to convince them she was an adult? Graduating nursing school and holding a good job for four years clearly wasn't enough.

She let herself in from the garage and passed by the living room to say goodnight. "Hi, Mom. You're still awake?"

Mom looked up from her *Ladies' Home Journal*. "Just reading the spring recipes and home decorations. How was the young people's group tonight?"

"Fine. About twenty came. It's growing."

[231]

Mom relaxed the magazine to her lap. "Any new young men?"

"Now, Mom, we're trying to offer hospitality, not be a match-makers."

"But the best place to meet a husband—"

"—is in the church. I know, but it isn't foolproof. Jenny met Ed at church, and look what a dud he turned out to be." She lowered herself onto the corner of Mom's footstool, making reference to her high school friend's marriage. "I'm afraid of getting locked into something like that. Now she's got two children, a mortgage, car loan, and a husband who can't—or won't—support them."

"Finding a man of quality certainly is important, but I'm sure that won't be difficult for you, dear." She leaned forward and placed her hand on Grace's for a moment. "Now tell me who was at the church tonight."

"Besides the usual ones, those two fellows who work for Coca-Cola came for the second time. And a new one, Henry something, who just moved here."

"What's he like?"

Grace took a few heartbeats to sum up her acquaintance. "He has very nice manners. He stands when a lady enters the room, and he helped us wash dishes while everyone else played dominos." She smiled as she told her mother of making light work of the kitchen cleanup.

"Is he tall enough?"

"Mom. Tall enough for me, you mean? You're still in the match-making mentality." At the same time she denied interest, a quiver of excitement scurried down her arms and legs. "Yes, he's tall enough, even for me. He has brown eyes and brown, sort-of-curly hair, cut military style. And an accent. Not much. Enough to be intriguing, you know. Different from the local fellows."

"What kind of accent?"

"German, but from Texas. He's American. Just got out of the Army."

"Would you like to invite him to dinner one night?"

"Not yet. Don't want to seem too eager." Grace checked her watch. "I'd better get to bed. I'm on at seven in the morning."

She stood and kissed her mother's cheek. "I do want to marry and have a family. But after Matthew, he would have to be very special. I'd rather be single than marry the wrong man. So many died..."

"Your husband is out there somewhere. Maybe your next patient, maybe the next soldier who comes home. You never know. Your dad and I are always praying for the right person for you to share your life with."

"Thanks, Mom. I love you."

Bone-tired, Grace lay awake begging God Almighty. Had Matthew been her one chance?

The gift of his love, though never consummated, remained a beautiful thing. She didn't deserve a second passionate relationship.

She wanted love again, more than she permitted anyone to know.

Pushing away the gathering clouds of depression, she willed herself from the edge of bitterness. This wasn't the life she intended, but she had to grab it by the reins anyway and ride hard.

CHAPTER TWENTY-FOUR

April, 1945
Atlanta, Georgia

HENRY GLARED AT his reflection in the chipped and fogged bathroom mirror while shaving. "You talked about yourself all evening. What do you know about her? Nothing. Quit pondering who you are and find out who she is."

Frustration netted him a bleeding razor nick, to which he stuck a tiny piece of toilet paper. He grabbed a bun from his one-corner kitchen, scalded his throat with instant coffee, and dashed to work. Sunday would come, with another chance to see Grace.

This week, he took an earlier bus which delivered him to church in time for Bible Class.

Grace entered the room, flashing joy from her bright, blue eyes. She glanced over the class, including Henry in the third row. With a nod in his direction, she sat beside Mavis and Paul Rollins. "How's the baby?"

Not his kind of conversation.

After the lesson, the teacher held Henry back, engaging him in a welcoming chat. By the time he got to the sanctuary, Grace was enclosed on all sides by her parents and others.

She granted him a few words after the service, which sufficed to keep him coming back.

He scoured the Sunday want ads for jobs and wandered through listings of used cars for sale. He needed a car to ask her out. He couldn't invite her to go to a movie on the bus.

Life would be so much easier if he returned to Germany and got only one of those gold bars he had hidden in the church south of Heilbronn. One bar could boost him from dime-store schmuck to a professional with a fine home, car, and family.

His aspirations became more vivid as the U.S. Army continued on its path through Germany, and Italy surrendered.

On a Sunday morning in mid-April, the radio said the Seventh Army liberated Buchenwald Prison Camp. Henry cried and walked for miles until he got lost and sat down on a bench in Piedmont Park. He missed church because he couldn't face people. He couldn't even face God.

Bent double with his head in his hands, his grief overwhelmed him.

"What could make a young man cry so hard on a beautiful spring day in the park?"

Startled by the gentle voice, looked up into the eyes of a grandmotherly woman whose face radiated peace.

"Buchenwald was liberated by the Americans yesterday." He wiped his face with his already-wet handkerchief.

She perched on the other end of his bench. "And why does that make you sad?"

"Because it didn't happen sooner." Hanging over his knees, he shook his head. "All those people. How can that...*animal* do the things he does?"

She touched his shoulder lightly. "He will receive his punishment from the Lord, son. Leave it to God."

Tears trailed down her cheeks. That she cared meant the world to him. He tried to explain his grief. "I didn't do enough. I was there, and I knew what was happening but couldn't stop it."

"You did what you were called to do, Karl. What matters now is what you do next."

Henry froze. She used his name. His real name. White spots swam in his sight as she stood and walked the garden path. And then she wasn't there.

What just happened? Did he even hear what he thought he heard? Was this a vision?

An unprecedented sense of calm descended from his fevered mind to his clenched hands. He thanked God for sending this message, sure he had received an unmerited gift of grace. He remained there for a while praying for guidance. When he left due to simple human hunger, he had no more answers than when he sat down. But somewhere deep in his soul, he was sure the answers would come when he needed them.

Hitler and his mistress, bride for a day, took their own lives the following week.

EAGER TO BE with Grace again, he arrived early on Friday evening. He went straight back to the kitchen where he found her stirring a big pot of chili to go over hot dogs.

"Henry, it's good to see you." She flashed him a welcome as warm as a hug. "We missed you last Sunday."

"I...wasn't well."

"There's a bad cold circulating. I hope you're better now."

"Just seeing your smile makes it better."

She blushed as the pastor flipped the swinging door wide and strode inside.

Henry helped with the serving of the meal, largely to maximize his time near Grace. He hoped kitchen duty didn't diminish his manliness in her eyes. She seemed glad to have the help, especially if anything heavy needed lifting.

Tonight they put all the food on a long table and let guests load and dress their own chili dogs. How American.

As he placed a second bowl of chili before one of the men, Johnny, the guy grumbled. "Yeah, gettin' served by a German." He pronounced the word more like "Churman," with obvious derision. "The pig knows his place."

The girl by his side gasped.

Grace halted at the table with a tray of hot dog buns, her face a mask of shock. "Johnny, I can't believe you—"

"What's your problem?" Henry spoke without anger, but waited for an answer. He had seen this attitude several times at work and on the street.

"Nothin'. I just don't like your accent is all."

"I'm not crazy about yours either."

Johnny put down his plate, inflated his chest, and planted his legs in a proud stance. "I served my time killin' Chermans. Shot ever'one I got my sights on. Didn't expect to find any when I came home."

"You didn't." The loaded table between them made an effective barrier. Choosing to swallow the acid rising in his throat, Henry maintained a calm expression. "I'm American. I served in the U.S. Army. If you had been in my unit, I might have kept you out of harm's way by intercepting enemy messages."

The pastor approached behind the angry Georgian and put a hand on his shoulder. "Now, men, you both served in the same army. Each of you owes much to the other. And here, in this house of the Lord, you are brothers."

Both the men said, "Yes, sir," and moved on.

After the others had been through the line, Henry took his plate to a table with the helpers. His mouth dry and appetite gone, he ate little, and with difficulty. The inconsequential chatter a nuisance to his thoughts, he retreated from the social setting.

Many men had said in his presence they had killed Germans. They would have killed him, as Karl, if he hadn't been reassigned as a translator of radio traffic. Jerked off the street and forced into the army made him the enemy. He knew for a certainty he would never have trained his rifle on an American, but he might have been killed by one. That knowledge chewed on his innards every day he pretended to be Henry Viertel.

He tried to shake off the mood and join the evening's activity. After the cleanup and board games, Henry found Grace gathering up supplies. "May I help you get these to the car?"

"Thanks. Mother will be here to pick me up in about fifteen minutes. We can close up and wait outside. It's lovely tonight."

Sitting on the steps to the parking lot, Henry turned words and phrases around, trying to come up with acceptable conversation. "You said you work at seven tomorrow. What do you do?"

"I'm a nurse at Emory Hospital, on the pediatric floor."

"Wow. That's wonderful." He almost said his mother was a nurse, but Henry's mother, as far as he knew, did whatever farm wives do. Pluck chickens and slop hogs?

"What do you do at Woolworth?"

He ducked his head. "Only a stock boy." He chuckled. "Nothing more than a strong back, at least for now. But I plan to get a degree in finance, maybe from Emory."

"Why not in Texas, where you have family to help? I'm sure Texas has good colleges."

"I'm not...I don't..." Standing on the precipice of repeating to her, in private, the story of his new identity, Henry felt queasy. He didn't want to lie, but found no way around it. He existed in America as Henry Viertel, plain and simple. "I don't remember the family in Texas. And I really like Atlanta."

The moon's glow on her face, upturned to him, showed her wrinkled brow and worried—or doubting—eyes.

"You were a radioman when you were wounded?"

"That's what they tell me. The dog tag identified me, and my lieutenant supplied the rest of the information when he came to the hospital."

"What about the interrogation of wounded German prisoners? When was that?"

"For a while, I couldn't speak. After I got well enough and started talking again, this other lieutenant found out I speak German, and he asked me to help him with a couple of cases. I was rather good at it. That became my new job until they shipped me to America."

Grace's mother pulled up. Their time together hadn't been long enough. Never would be long enough.

How had she received his story? Did she believe him? "Grace, will I see you again?"

"Of course. Sunday, right?" With a swish of her flowered skirt, she sashayed to the car.

Newspaper headlines blared the story. The American Seventh Army liberated Dachau prison camp. Henry scanned the front page before work. Acid burned his insides all day as he kept at bay the words he urgently wanted but feared to read.

Alone in his apartment, tired and edgy, he lay the paper full out on the scarred wood table. With nervous hands, he smoothed the newsprint and studied the paragraphs until he had memorized passages. He read the printed words and tried to read what was not said. So many questions remained. The pictures made him too ill to eat. After devouring the articles and sidebars, he ran down the three flights of stairs and walked for miles on the streets of the city.

Perhaps some of the notes he left from his last interrogations pointed the Americans to Dachau. He may be able to take peace now, knowing the remaining Dachau prisoners had been released. Would he sleep better without skeletal men in striped clothing calling out for rescue?

Sitting on a street bench in the dark, he beseeched the Comforter. "I did what I could, Father God. Was it enough?"

HENRY'S BOSS, A bald man with a chewed cigar, called him into the office on May first. "Betty says you've applied for the vacancy in our bookkeeping department. Do you have any experience?"

He did, hidden deep within the confines of his secret life. "I took accounting in high school." That was a lie. Henry did that. "My math marks were good." That was true. He handed over a copy of Henry's graduation diploma and course record, which he had requested sent to a post office box. "Actually, I have natural ability with numbers. Accounting's a job I do quite easily."

"Sorry, son. I need someone with experience."

Putting his best persuasion tactics in gear, he hung on. "Sir, perhaps I can convince you by working with the current bookkeeper until she retires. I'll prove myself worthy of your trust. The overlap of training time will benefit the company, rather than hiring someone from the outside."

The boss frowned at his desk and pushed papers over the cup circle left in its varnish. "Betty isn't easy to get along with. She likes everything done her way."

"She has had this job for—how many years?"

"Longer than I've been here." He cracked a smile. "Doesn't mind telling me, either."

Henry returned the smile. "I understand. I will learn her system and give her confidence the job will be done well."

The boss huffed hard enough to blow papers about. "Let's walk around to her office. I'll let Betty show you the ropes."

He got the new assignment, which provided just enough salary increase that he bought a used car from a family at church. They assured him it ran well. Essential, since Henry had never done the simplest of maintenance chores. It would never grow up to be a BMW or Mercedes, but it cranked and rolled. That would have to be enough for now.

On Tuesday evening, May eighth, he took his new toy for a pleasure ride. The car seemed to want to go toward the church, on a beam for Grace's neighborhood.

Fiddling with the radio, he caught the most marvelous news in the world. Victory had been declared in Europe. America had defeated Germany!

He turned the corner and spotted all the church lights on and the doors open. A crowd of people were laughing in the parking lot, and praise music rang from inside the sanctuary.

Grace recognized him as he parked. "Henry, you heard?"

As he emerged, she took his hand, made a circle with two other girls, and they danced a jig around and around. He laughed and hugged strangers, delirious with happiness.

And he hugged Grace, wrapping her in his arms, never wanting to let go. She backed away, smiling up at him, leaving his arms burning where he had touched her.

Fireworks popped and sparklers sizzled in the dark. The perfume of an enormous magnolia tree, especially fragrant at night, filled his head.

Tracing the path of a fireworks rocket to the sky, Henry never identified himself more strongly as American. He rested his hand on Grace's back. When he looked down again, her eyebrows lifted in question, the angle perfect for a kiss. He wanted with all his heart to taste her lips but didn't take the dare. No sense in triggering rejection. A relationship with a lady of her character had to be gently cultivated.

CHAPTER TWENTY-FIVE

May, 1945
Atlanta, Georgia

DELIGHTING IN THE freedom of his new-used car, Henry accelerated his courtship of Grace. His week anchored on Friday night "canteen" meetings and Sunday worship. Gradually gaining her confidence, he slipped and slid sloppily in love.

With little disposable income—and that spent on newspapers, finance periodicals, evening courses, and gasoline—he searched for opportunities to be together which didn't cost much. This woman deserved a professional husband, one who supported her with security. Henry dared dream of a time she'd resign from nursing to rear a family. His family. She might not wait four years for him to finish another college degree.

He shuddered at the thought. He hoped for an easier challenge by college the second time around, despite doing the courses in English and from the American viewpoint. As for the hours wasted in pseudo-academic discussions at the pubs of Munich, he'd be working days and studying nights. If only his rightful inheritance were available while concealing the source of the money. If he had enough to let go of this job and sail back to Germany... Again, would she wait?

Henry descended the wide, noisy stairs after Woolworth closed Tuesday night and found the wall-mounted pay phone in the women's toiletries department. He pulled out the scrap of church bulletin with Grace's home number and dropped a coin in the massive black frame.

When Grace answered, his jaw lost tension and a melting warmth poured over his head.

"I was wondering if you'd have time Sunday after church...if you'd like to take a walk with me in Piedmont Park."

"Oh, yes. Spring is passing me by, and all I do is work."

"I know what you mean. With the accounting job, I never get a Saturday off."

"Want to have a picnic?"

"Can't turn that down."

The enthusiasm in her voice charged his days and lifted his steps through the week.

She wore a sleeveless, flowered dress to church which took away his breath. He didn't hear a word of the sermon. They dropped by her house to grab the sandwich basket and drove to the park, windows down and her hair blowing in the breeze.

Despite crowds enjoying the afternoon, Grace led him to the perfect shady spot under a large oak tree. He spread the blanket he'd pulled off his bed. A chicken salad sandwich never tasted so good before.

She handed him a second one as a ragged man approached with bent posture.

"Pardon me, sir, ma'am, but could you spare a bite? I ain't eat nothin' since yesterday."

Henry quirked a frown and considered sending the skinny man away. The beggar's britches sagged on his frame, reminding Henry of the starving prisoners of Dachau. The waxed paper-wrapped sandwich crinkled in his hand. He looked back to Grace, and tried to read her reaction. "Do you mind?"

"Not at all." Her quiet reply assured him she would not be offended if he gave away the food she'd prepared.

He handed his lunch to the beggar, who heaped praises on them and left his blessings shimmering down upon their shoulders.

Alone again, he reached for her hand. "Grace. Unmerited gift of God. Your kindness…" At a loss for words, he kissed her fingers.

Blushing, she looked down. "It was nothing. Besides…" She turned to the picnic basket and held up a small, painted tin. "…I baked cookies."

The cool of twilight descended on the park before Henry could bear the thought of taking Grace home. Ambling toward the car, he glanced about and found no one near. He paused in the shadow of a pine tree and pulled her into a gentle embrace.

She slid her arms loosely around him then raised her face to his.

He brushed her lips with a kiss and went back for more. An electric thrill coursed his body. He wanted to shout. He wanted to dance. He wanted to tell her he loved her. "Grace, this has been the most wonderful afternoon."

The light in her eyes told him more than her words. "It was very special." She snuggled under his chin the briefest moment and then pushed away, blushing but smiling.

He hoped he hadn't caused her embarrassment. Absolutely nothing must hinder their growing relationship.

When Atlanta heat and humidity came to bear on their weekends, Henry remembered his twelfth summer with his Jewish grandparents. Papa had taken the family fishing and splashing at the Chattahoochee River. With Grace's unwitting assistance, he found the landing where he, Marta, and Mother had played with her parents.

Memories swirled in the currents. He stood at the bank, tossed a stick in the stream, and watched it float away. *I'm the only one left.*

Grace came to his side and placed her hand on his back. "What's the matter? You look worried."

He broke from his trance and kissed the top of her head. "Nothing's wrong. Just thinking."

"Tell me. What were you thinking?"

He couldn't tell her about the summer his family, minus Father, came to Atlanta. Or about the emotional upheaval when his grandparents learned he would not be having a bar mitzvah because he was Christian. Or that his mother and sister had been carted off unjustly. They may have been starved and tortured and then killed. So he made up something.

"Thinking about how time passes like a river and you can never get it back."

He must break his melancholy thoughts and focus on her. Spotting wild daisies growing on the grassy riverbank, he took out his pocket knife and cut a bouquet. Handing them to her he said, "Wildflowers in honor of your natural beauty, Grace. You bring such sweetness to my days."

His kiss lingered on her lips until she stepped back, blushing, and turned toward the river.

He slipped an arm about her shoulders and she held around his waist as the river flowed by.

"Did you send your application off to Emory for full time classes?"

He huffed, dropped his arm, and picked up a flat rock. "No. I can't go full time until I have some money saved to live on. With a six-day-a-week job, getting off at six in the afternoon, I can only do a course or two at night." He flipped the rock on its side three skips before it sank into the river.

"So what are you planning?"

Seeing her concern, he feared anything he said would cast doubt on his ability to be a good provider. What was he planning? He didn't have a plan. He had a wish. To return to Germany and come back with money.

Even that wouldn't work. His degree in finance belonged to a dead man.

Grace waited for his answer.

Henry stood squarely in front of her, his hands resting on her shoulders. Assuming a manner of confidence, he hoped to instill the same in her. "I'll work for a year, save everything I can, and then take as big a load as possible until the money runs out."

Henry proceeded to knock off a couple of freshman courses during the summer, which left precious little time with Grace. She seemed encouraged, though, and insisted she didn't want to date others. It would have broken his heart.

GRACE SWAM WITH Henry in the Chattahoochee, sometimes late on an evening as summer light lingered. They grabbed any opportunity to spend a few hours together. She relished the changing colors of the leaves until swimming became wading. Then wading turned to shivering on the bank.

War had caused such a shortage of doctors and nurses that she worked long shifts and enjoyed few days off. Many women put their husbands through school, but he hadn't asked her to and therefore she couldn't tell him she wanted to.

If Henry knew she had saved money for Matt's medical school, even while giving her parents a portion of her salary to live at home, he'd understand how fervently she hoped to help him finish college. She would wait for him as long as necessary if he asked her.

Christmas approached, and she wished for something more substantial to happen in their relationship. A blue slump overcame her mood.

Cleaning the kitchen, she sighed as she ran hot water over dinner dishes.

Her mother looked up from wiping off the table. "What's the matter, hon?"

"I wish he would say something."

"Henry?"

"Yes, ma'am. I know he likes me, and he treats me like a queen. Well, as much as he can on a budget. We have so much fun together." She dropped scraps into the garbage. "He likes me, but he never says…" Her words drifted off as a burn reached her cheeks.

"He loves you? It's hard for a man to admit that the first time."

"Yeah. I was hoping…Maybe Christmas…"

"What? For a ring?"

Grace pulled the plug, letting the gray, soapy water twist down the drain. "Or…that he *wants* to give me one. Even if he can't spend the money." A single tear dropped into the sink.

"You're tired, honey. You work all the time. Why don't you go to sleep a little early tonight?"

Grace never slept well when the blues settled on her mind. "Am I going to have to wait for him to get through college before he'll consider getting married?"

"That wouldn't be fair to you. You've already gotten your degree and your friends are having babies."

Grace's one tear threatened to become a waterfall. "And your friends are playing with grandchildren."

"You could date that other nice boy. What's his name?"

"It's not as if there's any huge pool of men, Mother. They died. Hundreds of thousands of them." Her sobs began in earnest. She blew her nose and tried to regain control. "Besides, I don't want to date anyone else. Henry is...he's the man I want to marry."

Speaking aloud her heart's desire brought some measure of calm. Not wanting to be cautioned, she avoided looking at her mother. She left the kitchen without wiping down the countertops.

HENRY STRUGGLED TO stay awake during the drive home from Emory. The world history test at his side, marked with an "A," glowed in the dark. A subject he knew well. He could get good marks, but feared a disadvantage on the English composition of answers. The professor had left many positive comments.

As a college graduate, he needn't be proud of a high grade on a freshman course.

The driver behind tapped his horn when the light changed. Henry jerked, shifted, and proceeded toward his apartment. He had to stay awake another ten minutes.

What to get Grace for Christmas? Something which didn't look bought on sale at Woolworth. He yearned to give her a diamond, the kind American brides expected, but if he had to complete college… The restlessness returned. He couldn't wait four years to marry her. But he had to finish his degree to be able to support her.

He parked at his building then climbed the stairs. He considered the peeling paint and rough facings. Grace deserved better. He slept at last, only to dream of diamond solitaires.

Approaching the final exam, Henry's impatience screamed. His few private hours were consumed plotting how to return to Germany for his father's fortune. With no identification or documentation in the name of Karl von Steuben, the banks of Switzerland and Germany would never transfer funds to the American Henry Viertel.

To his surprise, Lt. Hanson responded to his letter of several weeks before. Life in Germany relaxed compared to wartime, he said. Part of the population hated the soldiers, but a good portion received them well. Unspeakable war crimes came to light, and newspapers told of hauling German generals and officials into trials. The American forces couldn't learn the language fast enough to keep up with developments. Jobs were available in Germany.

Henry's mind stirred with possibilities. Had anyone found the bars of Jewish gold in the crypt? If he took only one of them, how could he convert it to useable funds? He would repay with money later, of course. He needed flexibility, a little wiggle room.

As much as he prayed for direction, he kept getting in the way of a solution. His lies, compounded daily, blocked his access to God Almighty. How could he expect guidance from a righteous God?

He stewed every waking minute, running on nervous energy, searching for a successful end to the maze he had created. Only in the presence of Grace did he find peace. No, he couldn't wait four years to make her his wife. Putting marriage on hold drove him crazy.

The December night closed in and choked Henry with a panic born of loneliness. He stopped at a pay phone on the way home from class. Just hearing her voice, setting a date for this weekend, would make another can of soup in his lonely apartment bearable.

He dropped the coin and dialed her number, on stage inside the street corner glass booth. One ring, two rings, three rings.

Her father answered, sounding none too pleased. Henry then checked his watch. Uh-oh. After ten o'clock.

"Rather late to be calling, don't you think, young man?"

"I apologize, sir. I didn't look at the time first. Would it be possible to speak to Grace?"

"She's already turned in. She has to be on duty early in the morning, you know. I suggest you call after supper tomorrow."

"Yes, sir." Henry replaced the receiver, burning with embarrassment.

Calling from Woolworth's main floor at the end of day, he heard her voice at last, visualized her perfect complexion and almost smelled the Jergen's lotion on her hands.

"Ahh, sweetheart, I've missed you so much since Sunday. I tried to call last night—"

"I know. Daddy told me."

An awkward silence threw him off track. "I am so sorry. I didn't realize—"

"Daddy was really angry. Henry, you've got to be more careful. Daddy doesn't...well, he's not too happy we're dating, you know."

"No, I was not aware... Why not?"

"Nothing really. Nothing I can put my finger on. Once he mentioned your accent. He thinks you sound too German."

"Do you think I have an accent?"

"Well, yes. Of course, I'm used to it. But one time—before you got the accounting job—I asked him if he would hire you in his store, and he thought you might not be received well by his customers."

"But I've spoken English all my life. Does he expect me to drawl like a Georgian?"

She laughed. "It wouldn't hurt. No, no, don't do that. I'm kidding."

"I'm American, Grace. Always have been. I served in the Army. Paid for the right to be here." Above mentioning his injury and scar, he let her draw her own conclusions.

"I know that, Henry."

"I've got to get to class. The final is tomorrow. Then we can relax and celebrate Christmas. Well, after the store closes on December twenty-four." He avoided the use of ordinal numbers, and couldn't master the pronunciation of "fourth" anyway. Not a good sentence in the present discussion.

"Good night, Henry. Be safe."

"WERE YOU TALKING to that German boy again?" Grace's father had put down his newspaper and waited with her mother in the kitchen for her to finish the call.

"He's not German, Daddy." She sang in a light voice to cover her irritation. "He fought in the war for you and me, while we lived safely here at home."

"He's descended from Germans. How do you know he doesn't have sympathies for those people?"

"Daddy, if you'd seen him the night we shot off fireworks and danced for joy in the church parking lot because the U.S. won the war in Europe… He had tears in his eyes. He was at least as happy as all the rest of us."

"There now, let's not get all riled up." Her mother twittered about, putting up the dishes Grace had washed. "I'm sure he's one hundred percent American."

Her father valued industrious traits, which Henry definitely had. "He's hard-working, and very intelligent—"

"Seems snooty to me."

"When have you ever talked to him? I introduced you at church, and you didn't even try to make conversation with him." Grace's voice rose in protest. "He's all alone in this city, and Christmas is coming—"

"Don't you think of inviting him here for Christmas, young lady," her father roared and pointed his finger at her, something he had reserved for breaking curfew in her teens. "Your sister-in-law wouldn't tolerate it."

"Daddy, that's not fair. He can't help his accent any more than I can mine." She dropped a bowl of beans on the table too hard and sloshed pot liquor on the cloth. "I live with Matt's death every day, just like she lives with her brother's death. War is war. People die."

Her father turned and strode from the room muttering. "He should go to Texas. Live with his own people."

AFTER THE CHRISTMAS ham, yams, and pecan pie were cleared, Grace slipped to the phone extension in her parents' bedroom. "I'll wait fifteen minutes and then walk down to the corner. See you soon, sweetheart." She ached to think of Henry alone on Christmas Day.

She took her heavy coat from the front closet without drawing attention from her brother's family at the fireplace.

Her mother blocked her passage through the kitchen to the side door. Grace noted her worried eyes and then the brown paper bag she held. "I put a little something aside for him."

HENRY LOWERED THE New York Times and turned the ignition when Grace hurried down the sidewalk against the frigid wind. Bounding out of the driver's side to greet her and open her door, he felt they were getting away with something.

Once inside, he kissed her, sure that neighbors peeked. "What's in the bag?"

"Mother packed some Christmas dinner for you." Her cheeks pinked and her eyes glossed with tears. He wondered if it were because of the cold.

"That's very kind of her." He accepted the fragrant offering, still warm.

"I'm so sorry, Henry."

"For what?"

"That they—Daddy—wouldn't invite you to dinner with the family. We had a terrible argument, and he wouldn't bend." She reached for his face, the soft leather of her glove tender against his skin.

He leaned in for another kiss. "Where shall we go?"

"Anywhere outside is too cold. The church is closed, and I don't want to visit at the hospital." On the verge of tears, she gave a small laugh instead.

Henry turned toward his part of town. "You've never seen my apartment. We could go there. It's humble but clean."

"I'm not sure. Mother and Daddy would—never mind. They didn't leave us much choice. Yes, let's go." Her voice quivered and her chin raised in a defiant angle.

"You have no concern. There will be no impropriety." His immense respect for Grace precluded gauche behavior.

Three flights of stairs was explanation enough for Henry's breathlessness as he unlocked his tiny apartment. He put his gift for her on the table and tried to gauge the room from her view. A single bed on one wall, the functional elements of a kitchen against the far side. A white-painted table and two chairs centered the space. A rickety chest of drawers held the folded clothes. Two suits and some slacks hung on a nail beside the closet of a bathroom.

"Oh. It's...nice. Everything you need is right here."

He closed the door and draped her coat on one of the chairs. He turned and opened his arms and she accepted the invitation. "Yes, now that you are here. I have everything I need."

Henry and Grace had never enjoyed total, certain privacy for a kiss before. A heady cloud of love swelled his heart and, for a moment, obscured reason. He pushed away and held Grace's shoulders at a distance as a flush rose to his head.

The intensity of her eyes revealed she felt the charge, too. "Ah...well... Let me put this food on a plate for you."

"I am not hungry now. I've already eaten."

"Christmas dinner?"

He gave a small shake of the head and smiled. "A can of soup."

She laughed, but her brow indicated something of pity. "Then let me heat you a plate in the oven. It'll only take a moment...but you don't have an oven, do you?"

"I will heat it in a lidded pan later, for supper. Right now, let's sit and talk." He pulled out a chair for her and they sat at the table. Handing her the present, he wished it were more. He wished it were an engagement diamond.

She drew a deep breath as she flipped the diaphanous silk scarf in the air. "It's beautiful." The pattern of blue irises complemented her complexion and eyes perfectly, just as he had imagined.

Then she took a small box from her purse and offered it to him. Inside he found a wrist watch, gold in color with a spring-link band. Eagerly, he unfastened his frayed leather band and put on the gift.

Her generosity touched him. Someday he would make her a very wealthy woman, but no manner existed to tell her now.

Thanking her graciously, he put aside Henry Viertel's watch, which he'd save forever.

"What can I do to convince your father I am not a threat? Have I offended him in some way?"

"How could you? You've hardly spoken to each other."

"If I were wealthy, would he consider me a better prospect for his only daughter?"

She bent her head. "It's terrible to say, but I think so. He wants me to marry a 'good provider.' Sometimes he even tries to match me up with men he meets in his business."

Like grit in his teeth, Henry abhorred the thought of losing her to another man. He took both her hands in his and locked eyes with his love. "Someday, Grace, I will be wealthy. I will be the son-in-law your father respects."

She drew a sudden breath.

His words were tantamount to a proposal of marriage.

He watched her recover from mild shock, and attempted to do the same. In truth, he had declared his intention.

She looked down with a blush. Then she leaned toward him and covered his hand. "Money isn't important to me. I love you. We'll make it fine. I'll work…"

"You won't have to, my sweet." In an echo from the past, he borrowed Father's words. "I have a plan."

Her smile opened her expression as if in wonder. Whatever her thoughts, pleasure ran through them.

He found courage to continue. "I don't know how long it will take, but I will not dally."

CHAPTER TWENTY-SIX

January, 1946
Atlanta, Georgia

HENRY'S EYES FROZE on the long, black Packard coming too fast, sliding sideways around the intersection on ice. A sudden throat-burn of terror rose from his stomach and his heart turned as stone cold as the Atlanta night. Nowhere to go, no possible defense. Every muscle and fiber tensed for the collision while on the radio Perry Como crooned "Far Away Places".

God, help me.

The crash, causing a cacophony louder than the artillery of war, slammed his car against another vehicle.

A drip on his hand. Something sticky. His head pounding. Windshield shattered, glass on the seat, in his lap.

Ear-roaring silence. Then —

Where did the people come from? They shouted at him against the window shards, words he did not recognize. He struggled to breathe against chest pain. Hunger for air surged through his very soul. It must not end like this. He wasn't ready.

A man in uniform shined a brilliant light in his face. They had found him. He couldn't hide. Couldn't escape.

But the guy wore a flattened hat with a shiny bill and golden badge. Not a military hat with insignia. What army was this?

Incoherent words hung around Henry until they clicked together like a puzzle and began to make sense.

"Got a man in this car. He's conscious. Let's get him out."

English. He had to remember to speak English. Don't say anything until you can open that section in your brain.

"Driver door's crushed. I'll go through the back and lift him over the seat."

Another man wearing the same uniform entered by the rear door. "My name's John, sir. How are you? Can you tell me your name?"

He cleared his throat. Inhaled deeper than seemed possible. His lungs begged for air. "Henry Viertel."

"Can you move your arms and legs?"

"Yes. All is good… Have trouble to get away my foot." He squirmed and pulled his left leg from the bent-in door. "There. It is loose already."

His helper crawled over the seat and checked Henry for injuries. "Just a little shock. Makes your fingers numb. And the cold. What a night. Were you out for a while?"

"Out?"

"Unconscious."

"Maybe. I think so. I just sit here at the red light, and that car came around the corner and hit me." Delayed anger at the injustice of being struck charged through his innards.

"Yes, sir. Lotta ice on the road. People in Atlanta don't know how to drive on this stuff. These accidents happen every time a cold blast passes through." His hands traveled the length of Henry's arms and legs, probing but gentle. "We're going to get you out. You relax and let us do the work. Do you think anything's broken?"

"Give me a minute to catch my breath, and I'll climb over by myself." He pulled against the steering wheel to scoot into a better position. "Everyting seems to work okay." Except my th's. Got to get back to the English.

Headlights of a long ambulance played on John's furrowed brow, and a police sedan flashed red lights nearby. "We're kind of in a hurry. That vehicle to your right has a fuel drip."

In smooth and practiced motions, they extracted him and laid his aching body on a stretcher.

Heavy wool blankets pressed upon him, more scratchy than warm. The back of the ambulance yawned open. They slipped him onto its padded floor.

Clipboard in hand, John leaned in and took his name, address, phone number, and birth date.

"Makes you about twenty-three. Next of kin?

"No one."

"Parents? Brothers or sisters?"

"No one." His throat caught on the words the second time. In a lonely life, he had never been lonelier. "A girlfriend. Grace." He gave her number, needing someone to know, someone to care whether he lived or died.

"So you live here? Thought I caught an accent."

"Used to have. Not much anymore. Texas German. Hill country, you know." He had learned in the past months few people in Georgia were aware Germans had settled in Texas.

The medic asked him to sit up to remove his coat for a blood pressure reading. His head whirled, but he didn't let on. *Ach! What a headache.*

Henry took in his surroundings. Nothing similar to that horrible ambulance ride—less than two years ago? Cold as fierce as a raging wolf, bodies of the dead and barely alive racked up left and right against dark walls. Vapor curled from their lips like ghosts taking leave.

He touched the sticky blood on his head. He recalled how it had dripped and flowed from the gash before, draining until the low temperature helped it stop. The natural foe saved his life. Just like the U.S. Army medics.

He clamped down the memory, shoved it back into its black corner. No one knew. No one must ever know.

Bright lights at the hospital, irrelevant questions. He could tell them anything he wanted to. Nothing mattered. It was all a lie.

He lied before God. He lied in church. He lied every day to Grace.

No. His life must not end this way. Grace. He wanted to marry Grace. He wanted her to know his name.

The hidden gold. No one would ever find it. He had to go back.

Father, forgive me. Let me live and correct my sins.

Blackness descended, and the pain floated away.

HENRY WOKE, THE plastic mattress cover crinkling under his restless limbs. Hospitals were the worst places to try to sleep. Chemical smells, machinery, hall noises, and nurses interrupted all night. The hours crept slowly, crammed with fitful visions of being chased by the enemy and burying himself in snow to avoid capture. He woke chilled, needing the comfort of a blanket.

"How're you doing, Henry?"

He focused on Grace as she rose from a chair in the corner.

An IV tube snaked from a pole to his arm. "Better than I thought, if I'm still alive."

Sunlight streamed from a space in the curtains behind her, haloing off her golden hair. A smile cracked his dry lips, but he couldn't *not* smile. He reached for her hand, and warmth coursed through his body.

She gave a little love-touch to the double dimples on his right cheek, and he tightened them a bit more. He liked that she liked his dimples.

"You lost consciousness last night. I was so worried."

"Sorry, *meine liebchen*." He rarely used the term of endearment, but German filled his head right now. He tried to recall what happened after the wreck. "I slept a lot. With many strange dreams."

"I guess so. Every time you stirred, you muttered in German."

Uh-oh. "What did I say?" That could be dangerous.

"Ha. I have no idea. The only foreign language I ever studied was high school Latin. They said doctors and nurses need it."

She teased his cheek with a finger as one does to a baby, making him smile. Then she leaned to brush his forehead with a kiss. "The new decorations look real nice alongside your old scar."

Henry wished his thick curls concealed the line, but his brown eyes and hair created even more contrast to the white streak.

"The doctor asked me how you got it, and I told him you're a real World War Two hero."

Henry heat rose onto his face. "I'm no hero."

"You probably are. You just don't remember. Anyway, you're my hero."

Tears stung Henry's eyes, and he looked away. At times like this, he wished he had concocted a good story to explain the white track that traveled from his neck, in front of his ear, across half his forehead, and into the hairline. But an amnesiac wouldn't remember how the battle injury happened. He left the explanation to anyone's imagination and got embarrassed when people assumed grandiose speculations.

Below the new bandage, her finger tickled the path of the old scar. "This makes at least twice God spared your life against the odds. He must have something very special for you to do."

He captured her hand and kissed her fingers. Did God have to try so hard to get his attention?

With the urge to kiss her came another awareness. "I need my toothbrush."

"We have some for patients. I'll bring you one."

"Could you please raise the head of the bed? I smell coffee. I hope with that racket in the hall they bring me breakfast."

"You're hungry?" She turned the crank while he shifted his weight to make her effort easier. "I'll go find your nurse and check what your chart says. With a concussion, food may cause nausea."

Henry watched her leave, taking his source of joy from the room. He patted his upper body and moved his legs to test whether everything worked. His chest ached with every breath.

Everyone dies someday. Death no longer frightened him. Not so much as life.

But before he faced God, he had to make things right. The wreck warned him how unexpectedly his life might be snuffed out. Time suddenly seemed short.

Grace returned with the toothbrush and a white-coated, sober gentleman wearing heavy, horn-rimmed glasses and brushy moustache. "Hello, young man. I'm Dr. Moore. How are you this morning?"

Henry braced on the metal bed railing and turned toward him, wincing with pain. "I'm very well, thank you. I'd like to be released today, if I may."

"Hmmm." The doctor consulted at a chart. "That might be dangerous. You have contusions, possible internal injuries, and two cracked ribs, head injuries, definitely a concussion. Think you'd better relax and enjoy our facilities for a few days."

"But I have a job." He ducked his head, ashamed that he didn't have a profession. "I cannot afford to stay."

The physician flipped another page. "You were in the Army?"

"Yes, sir. General Taylor's 101st, sir."

"I'm not your commanding officer. However, I'm advising you to stay with us until we've ascertained you're safe to go." He cranked the bed flat and lifted Henry's hospital gown.

Grace left quickly. She was a nurse at this hospital, but not *his* nurse.

Henry endured the punches and pokes, the personal questions. He framed every answer and reaction toward getting an early discharge. Dr. Moore couldn't be fooled. The examination ended with a truce, but Henry wasn't going anywhere yet.

The physician spun and left the room a few degrees colder.

Grace waltzed in with a breakfast tray of toast, red gelatin in a white ceramic bowl, and coffee. "Look what I found with your name on it." Her smile made everything better.

Steam rose from the heavy cup and delivered that heavenly scent. Real coffee. Would not be strong enough, but he welcomed it in any case.

She rolled a cumbersome, long-armed bed table over him and raised his head again.

Henry touched his breastbone and the cross wasn't there. The shoestring was not around his neck. After patting all over his chest, he twisted to see if someone had put it on the table. Pain stabbed his upper body. He groaned and lay back.

"What's the matter, Henry? Are you looking for something?" Grace's expression spoke of her tender concern.

"My gold cross. The one I always wear."

She opened the drawer of the metal table. "It's here with your watch and a V mail letter. Do you want it on?"

"Yes, please. I was afraid it got lost."

She lifted his head and slipped the frayed string down to his neck. "You could use a nice chain for this."

"It doesn't matter just to wear beneath my shirt. Thanks." He lay his hand over the ornate pendant, squinted his eyes closed, and calmed his breathing.

"I don't go on duty until four o'clock. Is there anything I can bring you?"

He almost declined, not wanting to be a bother. But he knew the tedium of hours in bed. Thoughts circled in his brain, fearsome and accusing worries. "Can you bring me something to read? A *Wall Street Journal*, books, maybe a *Life* or *Saturday Evening Post*. I have some money. My wallet is in my trouser pocket."

She laughed. "Why does a Texas farm boy think he has to read the *Wall Street Journal* every day?"

Henry couldn't invent an answer fast enough. He should have asked for *The Farmer's Almanac*.

She touched his hand with her soft fingers. "That's okay. I'll see what I can find. Meanwhile, last month's *Post* is in the visitor's nook."

[265]

He mattered to one person in the world. Had he made the request to prove she cared? Silly thought. Grace thrived on helping others. Bringing her hand to his lips, his vitality climbed a notch.

Grace leaned close, cupping his cheeks in her palms. "While you were unconscious, the police located your family in Texas. They've been informed about your accident."

"What? How did the police...?" If he hadn't been well awake before, this jolt would do it.

"I don't know. Your driver's license, maybe. The officer told me he called them." She removed her caress, a puzzled expression clouding her forehead. "That's alright, isn't it?"

"No, it isn't." He covered his clenched jaw then dropped his arm. Staring out the window, he huffed.

She lay a comforting hand on his shoulder. "Henry, the policeman said your mother was worried about you, but she didn't think they could make the trip. Your father's not doing well."

Henry took the cue. "My father isn't in good health. They shouldn't be bothered about my wreck."

"But they would want to know. She said your brother might try to come."

He must not. Grousing at Grace was useless. She didn't create this mess. The headache returned, pounding like an anvil.

"Please don't be upset. They were just trying to help." Tears welled in her eyes. "We didn't know how long you'd be out...or even if you'd live."

"I'm sorry. I didn't mean to be rude." He reached for her hand, limp by her side. "I don't remember my family. It makes me embarrassed. I never know what to say when they write."

"I understand. I mean, not really, but I can imagine." Her scolded child look melted him.

"You said the police called? Do they have a phone number?"

"Yes, don't you have it?"

"It's at my apartment somewhere. I haven't memorized it." He had never called the Viertels. After making the effort to get the number, he hid it among papers in a drawer to cover its accusing glares.

"That's okay. I wrote it down." She searched the pocket of her coat, hanging on a hook behind the door. "Here it is. Do you want me to call from the phone booth down the hall?"

He considered the options. What would Grace say? What would the Viertels tell her? "Leave me the number, and I'll call as soon as I can get up."

"Okay. I'll put it right here." She placed the torn scrap of paper on his tray table anchored by his gelatin bowl. "I've got to go on duty. It's almost four. I'll bring your magazines, and I'll peek in on you during my break. Don't try to stay awake. You need rest." She bent and kissed him lightly, transferring her gentle smile to his parched lips.

Henry twisted and rolled into every possible position on the hard hospital bed as the afternoon progressed. He stared at the *Post* pictures of Germany in recovery, but instead he saw Germany as it had been during the war.

The pages, spread across his chest, crackled as he stirred in the night. If Grace had returned, he had missed her visit. As he gave in to the cotton-mouth medication, the magazine rustled to the floor.

When morning's early light poked through his lids, he could tolerate the bed no longer. He braced sideways and let his legs slide off the edge. A muffled groan escaped his compressed lips. Standing on the cold linoleum tiles, he gained balance and took short, stiff steps to the window, pulling along his IV pole.

Ice coated the small, green leaves of a boxy hedge. The storm had passed, but the heavy gray sky spoke of more ice. Not as cold as Munich, though. Or the muddy roads where soldiers waged war in wet socks, worn boots, and a jacket unable to insulate men in ditches from bitter winter.

The door swished open to hall noises and a stern Dr. Moore. "What do you think you're doing, young man?"

Spinning around hurt his bruised chest. "Sir, looking outside, sir."

The doctor laughed, showing perfect teeth beneath his moustache. "Let me show you why you need to lie still." From an oversized envelope, he pulled x-rays and held them to the window's light, angling his way. He recognized the bones of a ribcage. "These faint lines here and here, and on the left side in the same area, show where you hit the steering wheel. Cracked ribs, still in place. Nevertheless, if one were to break, it could puncture the lung. Then we're talking about a serious injury."

Dr. Moore lowered the film and faced Henry. "You'll be wrapped in tape for a couple of weeks, but you need rest until they mend. Any kind of accident right now could cause…well, just don't have one."

Henry pondered his situation until after lunch and read again the V mail letter. Lt. Bill urged him to come back to Germany. They could work together like before.

He limped down the hall and called Western Union. The telegram to Texas bore words he had tumbled for hours, working out the best message to say, "Do not come to Atlanta."

"Hope Father is better (stop) I am well (stop) I return soon to Germany for translation job (stop)"

CHAPTER TWENTY-SEVEN

TWO WEEKS OUT of the hospital and everything still hurt. Henry stepped off the Atlanta midtown street car and ducked his head against the frigid wind. His jalopy had been hauled off for junk. Accident insurance gave him a miniscule bankroll. No need to find a replacement before he left. He could just take the money and run.

He hurried toward the corner diner a couple of blocks from Crawford Long Hospital. Even bending hurt his ribs, but hot coffee would feel so good going down. He hoped Grace got his note to meet him before her shift. He had a half hour to wait.

Sliding carefully into a booth, he signaled to the waitress for a cup. She didn't disappoint. He lifted the dark brew to his face and let the steam waft to his icy cheeks. The doc was right. This was too soon to be out, but he couldn't stand the hours, the cloud of memories. Had to keep moving.

He fingered the folded letter in his pocket. How would she take it? How much did it matter to her whether he went or stayed? The war had given him a statistical edge with so many men dead. How might one know if a girl just wanted to get married, or wanted to marry *him*?

He retrieved his New Testament from his coat pocket. Its compact weight, bound in brown leather, comforted his hands and radiated peace to his body. He wouldn't have been caught reading the Bible in a coffee shop in Germany, but he had some heavy decisions to make here and now. Besides, no one in the restaurant recognized him. He pulled the cloak of anonymity over his shoulders.

Opening to where he had left the burgundy satin ribbon, he read what he had well memorized, his lips moving over the verse in German. "My grace is sufficient for you, for my power is made perfect in weakness."

He smiled at the memory of the sermon when he went to church for the third time in Atlanta. The pastor preached on grace, and made a side comment toward Grace Shore, sitting with her parents in a middle row. Having no friend to introduce them, he simply walked up to her after church and did the job himself. First came the Friday night "canteen" meetings at the church. Then playing on her sympathies, he asked her to picnic in the park with him to celebrate Oktoberfest. Lonely, far from home, he promised bratwursts, not beer, and she accepted.

God's grace. Grace Shore. Maybe his Grace. The unmerited favor of God. He had experienced a lot of that, living through the war.

But this unjust wreck? How did that fit into such lofty thoughts?

The truth punched him squarely in his aching chest. The reality of the nearness of death forced him to reconsider the path he'd set himself upon, settling in America, finding a bare-sustenance job. He sensed God's orders to redirect his life, a part of which included returning to Germany.

Even that might not have been enough to change his self-defensive mind. But Father had left protected money somewhere, and now that the war was over, he had to at least try to find it.

The bell clanged again, and a waitress hollered, "Good morning." So American. But on the days he got only this much personal greeting, he welcomed it.

The new customer unwrapped her scarf from her hair and neck. She tossed her head, swirling her blonde curls, and looked around the diner, capturing the attention of any number of customers.

A sudden current flowed down Henry's spine, and he smiled for the first time today. *Grace.* He slipped out of the booth and raised a hand, and her sweet countenance blessed him alone.

Seated opposite each other, they leaned forward to share their words, the warm vapor of their coffees, and the barest touch of their hands. How could he give this up? How could he bear to leave her? Grace gave him a reason to live.

The page burned a hole in his pocket. Too late to change his mind. Would she still be here, still single, when he returned?

"I have to go to Germany, Grace." He studied her face for a reaction.

"Germany? Why?" Her eyes widened. "When?" Tears glistened.

"I've thought about it for a month already. Since before the wreck. The U.S. Government made me an offer working with my old lieutenant. It's a job, sweetheart. I get nowhere with the sort of work I've found." He took the dare, but couldn't look at her as he said the words. "I'd never be able to support a wife. Have children."

Her lips twisted, chin trembling. "What would you be doing?"

"Translations, something to do with the second round of the Nuremburg Trials of war criminals. I could help put away the monsters who…"

Thinking about what they did to his family made him furious. He leaned back in the booth and pushed on the edge of the table. The sudden change in mood hit his face with a flush. He tried to calm his reaction, and reached again for her hand.

"I'll research and translate for the trials. It would be a significant contribution to…to the whole process of justice. And a job with a decent salary."

She reached for a handkerchief and wiped her eyes with trembling fingers.

He had hurt her, and she had only ever been kind to him. He was good at hurting people. Like the Viertels in Texas. He had to leave before one of them came to find him.

After sipping the magic-strength potion, she held the heavy, white ceramic cup in front of her mouth.

He drank too, seeing in his mind a bridge crumbling between them, stones falling into a deep chasm. Trapped by his lies again, he left no return access to those autumn days full of laughter and heady infatuation.

She set her mug down with a clunk. "I thought you were going to use the GI Bill to go to Emory. So you could become an investment advisor."

"I was. But the GI Bill is just a small stipend. A hundred dollars barely covers tuition and books, and I don't make enough at Woolworth to save for living expenses." He turned his empty hands up on the Formica top. "I can't go to college with nothing, even if I live in a dorm and eat in the cafeteria."

Her fingers worried along the table's three rolls of chrome edging. She drank again, making a swallowing noise. "Mother

asked if you'd like to come to dinner, and I told her I thought so."
She looked down as she spoke.

Decisions hung in the air, dark thunderclouds churning. She knew he was shipping out, but still wanted him to have dinner with her parents? "Sure. That would be nice. If it's okay with you."

"Of course. But how soon are you going to leave?" Her eyes pleaded for time.

"I have a couple of weeks to get to New York City. The ship leaves February fourteenth."

"Ha. Valentine's Day." No laughter came with her words. She glanced at her standard nurse's watch. "Uh-oh. I've got to get to work. Saturday, then? About six?"

He agreed, wondering how he could wait three days, though soon to leave America for months, maybe years. "I'll walk you to the hospital."

He stood and lifted her coat from the rack by the front door. If they were alone, he might take the opportunity to reach around her for a little hug, but too many people were watching.

DAYS CREPT LIKE cold turtles until Saturday night. Trembling with anticipation more than temperature, Henry rapped the solid oak door. Grace swung it open, beaming a welcome. She must have been waiting nearby.

"Hello, Henry. I told Mother you'd be precisely on time." Her smile triggered warmth through his middle. She wore a fuzzy blue sweater he'd like to cuddle into.

Laughing, he stepped into the cozy living room. "It's my ancestry. I can't help it."

She hung his heavy wool coat on the hall tree and turned back to him with delight in her crystal blue eyes. He checked that they were alone. He closed the space between them and kissed her cheek. That little peck sharpened his desire.

The rattle of newspaper and a deep *ha-rump* preceded her father's advance.

She backed away, blushing, then swept her arm wide. "Daddy, you remember Henry Viertel."

In the months he had courted Grace, Henry never had a real conversation with her father. Until now, Mr. Shore had been the large shadow in the background. Henry offered a firm, masculine handshake, like his father had taught him.

"A pleasure to see you again, sir. Thank you for the invitation to your home." Henry noticed where Grace's high forehead came from. It gave an appearance of intelligence, which proved true for his nurse.

"Have a seat, Henry." She motioned toward the arrangement of sofa and chairs.

Henry bypassed the coffee table and chose the blue winged chair. Grace took another at his right, comforting his jangling nerves by her presence.

Her father eased onto the sofa and measured him with his gaze as if for a funeral suit. "Grace tells us you'll be leaving. I'm surprised you're returning to Germany so soon after the war."

Henry noticed the adjoining dining room, unlit and with the polished mahogany table unset. Fragrances of meat, vegetables, and something cinnamon tingled his dry tongue. He hadn't shown up on the wrong night.

He gave the question a couple of bounces before answering, then he remembered to face Mr. Shore. "I'm pleased to have meaningful work, sir. To help secure our position in Europe and right the wrongs done there is, eh, meaningful. Significant." He had dug himself into a verbal pit trying to project well as an adult. And his spacer-thought sound wasn't the southern *unh* or *ah*. He needed to come across more American.

"Your accent is German, Henry?" Rows of frown lines stacked Mr. Shore's forehead.

Henry maintained his poise against her father's pointed question. "Yes, sir. I'm Texas German, from the hill country. But my folks have been in Texas for generations. Even before the Great War."

"So that's your connection with the language. Did you speak it as a child?"

How much had Grace told her father about him? He had to be sure not to allow any discrepancies in the story. This man would catch him like a squirrel stealing from a bird feeder.

Henry dared to face Mr. Shore while reciting careful phrases. "Yes, sir. German was my first language, you know, the one my mother used to us children. I mean, that's what I've been told. Grace may have explained that I have retrograde amnesia. I don't remember anything before the injury that took me out of battle."

"She mentioned that, um-hum. Must be difficult. But you remember the language."

Her father didn't appear worried but not totally convinced either. "That's the way it usually works. The personal life is gone, but *you* would remember English if it happened to *you*. I remember both German and English."

"Yes, I suppose so."

Henry sprang from the chair as Mrs. Shore bustled in wearing an apron and steamy face.

"Mother, you've met Henry."

He advanced with a gentler handshake and greetings.

Mrs. Shore flushed again and smiled as if appreciating his courtesy. "We're so glad to have you visit, Henry. I hope you like pork roast. Grace said Germans eat pork. I wasn't sure."

"Oh, yes, ma'am. I'm American first, but even *German* Germans eat lots of pork. Sausages, ham, cold cuts, all that. A roast is very special."

"Then come ahead. Let's eat. Everything's ready." She led the way to an oval table at the near end of a long kitchen area.

Arranged with floral tablecloth and plates, cushions tied to the spindles of each chair, the setting invited Henry to the first family meal he had enjoyed in years. He seated Grace and took his place opposite. Her parents sat at the end positions and bowed their heads.

Realizing a second late that Mr. Shore would offer a blessing of the food, Henry jerked his head down.

"Heavenly Father," intoned Mr. Shore with somber voice, "we thank Thee for this fine meal and the ones who prepared it, and for our guest this evening to share with us Thy bounty."

Henry didn't hear the rest. Mr. Shore thanked God he ate with them? This was better than dinner in the finest restaurant. Better than vacation in Paris. And far, far better than a ham sandwich in his cold apartment.

"Amen." The family raised their heads. Henry blinked away moisture and reached for his napkin.

Mr. Shore passed Henry a healthy portion of roast and gravy. His fatherly smile, however, did not include his eyes.

Henry fought the habit of a soldier in a mess hall. He loaded his plate as bowls were passed and waited for each person to be served. His mouth watered as if he hadn't eaten in a week. He hadn't. Not like this.

When a platter of corn on the cob came around, he balked. He knew Americans ate corn, a food for farm animals in Germany. He had never chewed it off the cob, not even at the Army base. How to handle it? A large fork lay alongside. He speared the unwieldy object, which dropped onto his plate from two centimeters' height, splashing gravy onto the tablecloth.

Startled, he apologized. Mr. Shore chuckled.

Grace dashed to the kitchen area for a damp cloth. "It's just a couple of drops. Don't worry." She dabbed at the spots. If he had looked up at her, their faces might have touched. The thought, right in front of her parents, made him smile.

"Where did you get corn on the cob in the middle of winter, Mother?"

"Every summer I shuck a few ears and store them in the big freezer." She laughed with the confession. "Corn is the one thing I need to create a summer day during winter."

"I know what you mean." Henry talked through the awkwardness of his accident. "My mother made enough elderberry jam to last the winter." The memory caught him off guard. "She mentioned it in one of her letters."

Being the first one served created a quandary about how to pass food, how to use the utensils, even what to do with the left hand. The Shores kept theirs in their laps. Good manners here, but bad manners in Europe. He observed every detail while trying to maintain conversation.

Mr. Shore put down his knife. "How did your family fare during the war?"

The question sent Henry's mind scurrying. "They passed the war fairly well, sir. My parents were born in the United States, and I volunteered right after Pearl Harbor got bombed. That probably kept them out of the internment camp."

Mr. Shore exchanged glances with his wife then scooped a fork full of English peas. "That would have been for the Japanese, of course."

The tone of dismissal implied he didn't know what he was talking about. "Not only Japanese." He sipped his iced tea, thinking it a strange drink for a winter evening. "Families who descended from Germany were detained in seven different camps in Texas. Some of my parents' friends went to Crystal City, others to Kennedy and Fort Sam Houston. The same camps had Italians and Japanese who were also American citizens."

All three Shores stopped eating and stared at him.

"I had no idea." Mrs. Shore, wide-eyed, spoke first. "I knew about the Japanese hauled off to California, but…well, I guess I never thought about the others."

"Yes, ma'am. The irony is that the German detention started in 1941, after Pearl Harbor. America was not yet at war with Germany."

"What were the camps like?" Grace rested her fork and leaned on her forearm.

"My mother and sister wrote that they weren't too hard on their friends. The camps were villages inside the fence, with bath houses down the street. They had furniture, an ice box, electricity, and a company store. But back home, their farms would have died except for the kindness of other farmers. My father and some of the neighbors, even people with no German history, maintained their farms and cared for the animals."

That covered most of the information his family had written him in the French and English hospitals and what was printed in the newspapers. Henry needed to change the conversation. Weather? Politics? No, return the subject to the Shores. "How's your business, Mr. Shore? Dry goods, isn't it?"

"Right. I own a department store in East Point, not too far from Fort McPherson. Thinking about branching out closer to downtown." Then he rambled on about finding a piece of land and speculating on the coming economy.

Grace's countenance returned to her usual calm, and she ate quietly.

Henry watched the others butter the corn, lift it with both hands, and bite off the cob. He tried it himself. From the first succulent crunch, he knew he could get used to this. Why should pigs have all the fun? This was delicious.

He worked the kernels off his front teeth with his tongue and studied the ugly remains of the cob on his plate.

Mrs. Shore's reach with tongs surprised him. "Here, let's get these off our plates so we have more room." She stood and delivered the skeletons to the kitchen. "Would you like another, Henry?" She passed the plate again, cobs rolling precariously.

"No, thank you, ma'am. But I'll take another piece of bread, if you don't mind. I've never had better food in my life."

Chocolate cake with hot coffee stretched Henry to his limit of fine dinner. Mrs. Shore shooed him and Grace to the living room with a second cup.

They sat together on the sofa, the gas flames of a heater nearby toasting their shins. The family lulled Henry into happiness and satisfaction. He had seen a different side of Grace. If this demonstrated the kind of home she expected to create some day, he wanted to be a part of it. Strange to think of himself as a husband. And father. The thought brought an unusual twinge.

His thumb rubbed across the hairline chip of the flowered porcelain cup. Things. A home needed things, and he didn't have enough money. Before coming to America, he had always imagined his family in the Munich house with massive ceiling beams and carpets on the floor.

"So you're going to be a translator?" Grace broke into his thoughts. "What sort of translations will you do?"

He squinted at the flame, trying to imagine his assignment. "I don't know. Before, I only debriefed prisoners."

She smoothed the crocheted doily on the sofa arm. "Will you be enlisted for another four years?"

"No, I'll be a contract employee. I don't know exactly what comprises the work, but I'm happy to be attached to Lt. Hanson again."

She stared into the dancing orange flame. "I always wanted to travel. See Europe, taste foreign foods. I guess it won't be safe for years now."

"Oh, but it is." He put his empty cup on the coffee table, animated at the thought of being in Europe again. "With an American passport you can travel anywhere in Europe. *Ja*, you have to show it and keep the documents straight, but Americans have no difficulty."

"Even a woman?" Wonder played on her face.

"Women and children. Army families, even contractors who rebuild." Atlanta being so comfortable and safe, he hadn't thought Grace would consider moving to Europe. "American nurses work in the Army hospitals. You could get a job there."

Wild imagination colored her expression. "Really?" Then her countenance dropped. "But Mother and Daddy wouldn't let me go. They'd say I followed you, and it wouldn't be proper."

"What if we went together?" Henry took both her hands in his. "What if we…" He almost choked on the word. "…m-married and moved over together?"

CHAPTER TWENTY-EIGHT

A HUNDRED THOUGHTS clamored for attention in Henry's brain.

What are you thinking? How will you support a wife?

With the new job. Nothing to worry about.

Yes! Now.

Yes, but later…

Henry tried to keep his emotions in check while he waited to see if he had dropped a stink bomb in Grace's lap.

Her eyes went wide as if she were watching for him to pull a rabbit out of a top hat. Then she smiled. "Married? Now? Before you leave? But that's only two weeks."

He held Grace's hands in his as electric charges ran around and through them both. "I only know how much I love you. You are the person with whom I want to make my life." His heart seemed to beat louder than his words.

She hugged him tightly, her head on his chest. "There isn't time enough to plan a wedding. Besides, what would people think if we suddenly got married?" She pulled back, searching his face as though the answer lay somewhere between his eyes and his lips.

He laughed hard. "What do we care?"

Her expression clouded over like rain on a summer picnic. Not the effect he expected.

"I care. It matters. I don't want people to think" — she looked away and blushed — "that we *had* to get married."

"Well, no, but..." He hadn't thought about protecting her reputation. "Lots of folk do things differently during the wartime."

"Brides still have pretty weddings. With white dresses. Bridesmaids and three-layered cakes." Her voice wavered as tears welled in her eyes. "I've dreamed of the perfect wedding all my life."

Oh. The ceremony, the bride walks down a church aisle with flowers and organ music. The dress, white for purity. She deserved the very best. "I see. Don't cry. Please."

He took his handkerchief, shook out the folds, and touched it to her tears. Enveloping her in his arms, he nestled her face against his neck. Protectiveness swelled in his soul. Responsibility for a woman opened new rooms to life as an adult.

Anything she wanted suited him fine. Marriage to Grace embodied all his hope for a future. "We will marry later then. We will buy together a diamond ring before I leave."

She slipped out of his embrace and looked full into his eyes. "I don't need an engagement ring. It would cost too much. A simple wedding band will do."

Not for his wife. He had the car insurance money. And money never fell in his lap unless needed soon. If he kept just enough to get to New York and make it to his first government check in Germany, he could still buy a diamond she would wear with pride.

"You *must* have a ring to mark our promise until the wedding. Don't be concerned. This way, we'll have time to save money for our first home together. It will work out." He kissed her again, not caring if her father should walk in. They were engaged to be married.

With a clinch of nausea, he realized he needed to speak to Mr. Shore. They had a real conversation the first time tonight, and now he asks for her hand?

She studied his face. "What's wrong?"

"Can I wait until next week to talk with your father? I wouldn't blame him if he tossed me out. This is all quite soon."

She glanced toward the deeper areas of the house and twittered. "You're right. I'll talk to Mother first. She'll soften him up a bit."

Laughing, he took her in his arms again. "Do you want one of those round single stones, or a diamond in the center with the little ones on the side like your mother's? Those are pretty."

"Let's go pick one together. That would be so romantic."

He held his whole life in his embrace. Not the one given by birth, nor the one he had assumed. The life of his future. But under what name would they marry?

EXQUISITE AGONY FILLED his sleepless night. He didn't know how much he should tell her, and when. What if she never wanted to see him again? He'd rather tell her nothing and keep up the role forever. Her innocence would never be tainted by his guilt.

He considered the Viertels. They deserved answers. His unconscionable cruelty charred his conscience. If he went to Texas and told them, he might be arrested. Could no one even tell him if this was a crime?

At the least, he would be convicted as a spy.

And what about the gold? If it remained hidden, if he risked life, limb, and liberty to retrieve it, what should he do with it? He carried the heavy bag of guilt on his shoulders every day. A ponderous weight sat on his soul. Hundreds, maybe thousands of thin wedding bands, so many heirloom lockets melted into twenty blocks, fifteen kilos each. A fortune.

He roused from the lumpy single bed in his cold, one-room apartment. He fingered the delicate scrollwork, each flourish and curl of his mother's pendant which hung from a tattered shoestring. In his memory, it swung free from her neck when she bent over to him as a child. She had worn this treasure from his earliest recollection. Tonight the pendant served as evidence that she had died a horrible death of disease and starvation or the gas ovens. Her American citizenship had not saved her from her Jewish heritage.

If he slept at all, he dreamed of running his hands through the bags of gold jewelry. Every ring precious to a family somewhere, even if the owners lay in a mass grave or had been reduced to ash.

He had to go to Germany. No real choice existed. He survived the car wreck because he had a job to do. He would do it no matter the consequences.

GRACE INVITED HENRY to dinner with the family after church, hoping to impress her parents with his noble character and honorable intentions. Sunday fried chicken at a local restaurant would put them all in a good mood and give Henry more exposure to her mother and father.

Daddy seemed relaxed over his meal. He directed the conversation from the head of the table, aiming a smile at his guest with the piercing accuracy of hypodermic needle. "Henry, what are your plans? Do you have a college education?"

Henry finished chewing and sipped his ice tea. They should be impressed by his excellent table manners.

"I hope to go to college on the GI Bill, sir. Grace may have told you I'll be returning to Europe in ten days to serve as a translator for the Army."

"Yes, she did."

Daddy nodded to her, and she hoped he wasn't too glad Henry planned to leave.

Henry shuffled his feet and cleared his throat. "I'll make more as a contract employee than I did as an enlisted man. I can save for the return to college."

Maybe Henry would mention something about their plans for marriage. Her father wouldn't argue in an open restaurant like this, but he might seethe with anger until later.

"What career are you aiming for?" Daddy buttered a roll as if totally engrossed in the act.

"Business, sir. Finance." Henry spoke with determination and clarity.

Grace didn't understand what a job in finance meant, but it sounded like working with money. Other people's money? How could he get a job like that? But she had faith in his abilities.

Daddy paused while the waitress refilled their glasses from an icy pitcher. "Then you aren't going back to the family dairy farm?"

"No, sir. I have no interest to be a farmer, and my elder brother does. He and his wife live nearby and he works with my father. I plan to seek admission to Emory University and settle in Atlanta."

"A fine institution. Are you prepared to study the full four years?"

"Yes, sir. It may not take so long, if I work hard. And I will." He turned to Grace, his face shining with confidence.

She clung to his promise of their future together.

Henry rested his fork, glanced at her parents, and reached for her hand below the table. "Mr. and Mrs. Shore, Grace and I would like to be married."

His trembling, icy fingers laced with hers. Her mother coughed. Her father flushed red, something which rarely happened. This could be bad.

The waitress took up their empty plates, almost sloshing green bean juices on her father, who scooted back.

He resumed his position and sent a frown to Henry. "And when might that be?"

"Perhaps in a year, though if Grace came over and worked in the Army hospital, I'm sure—"

"Never. Grace is staying right here until she marries."

"Certainly, sir." He touched the napkin to his lips. "Then I could return to Atlanta for the wedding later and take her back to Europe with me."

Grace ignored Mother's sudden tears and leaned forward, unable to contain her excitement. "I could see the world, Daddy. It would be a wonderful way to start our marriage."

"Humph. We'll see. Don't make any travel plans yet."

Why was he being so unreasonable? She was a self-supporting adult with a respected profession. Maybe the time had come for her to move out. She willed her face to freeze in a pleasant mask, the same one she used when attending to messy tasks with her patients. In her mind, though, one rebellious thought presented itself—*elope*.

GRACE ENTERED THE reputable, mid-price jewelry store as if walking on marshmallows. Timid about arriving first, she admitted only to be "just looking" before drifting to the engagement rings. What if he didn't come?

The heavy-lidded, rotund salesman slid back the glass on the case. "May I show you something in particular?"

"No, thank you." She browsed toward the birthstones.

The bell over the door jangled and Henry rushed in on a cold draft, wearing his Sunday suit. She turned and their eyes met and held, saying everything she needed to hear.

"Have you found one you like?" He glanced at the gleaming display under bright lights.

"Oh, no. I just got here." This had to be a joint choice, the first big decision they would make together.

"Well, let's see what they have." He slipped his arm around her shoulder as they turned to the awesome array.

The salesman extended a small notepad and pen. "If the gentleman would please indicate a number, perhaps I can better assist in recommending something."

Grace pretended to be distracted by rings to the left.

The clerk's brow lifted, and a measure of pleasure lit his face. "Ah, yes, that opens the prospects quite a bit." He bent to retrieve a velvet-lined tray of larger diamonds, perhaps up to a whole carat.

Such opulence shook her focus. "Oh, Henry, those are too expensive."

"Not for you, sweetheart." His soft reply wasn't a brag to the salesman, but directed to her alone. "Your first diamond must indicate my intention to support you well."

First? A fortune in diamonds glittered against her impromptu tears. But modesty and caution first. He ought not to spend recklessly. "Henry, you're trying to save for—"

"Not today. I want you to be proud when you show your friends our engagement ring. Your father must know in what great esteem I hold his daughter."

She melted, and the clerk reached for tissues.

"What do you think of this one?" He lifted a ring with two diamonds on each side of the larger stone.

"It's lovely. But don't you think a solitaire is more…symbolic?" She wanted to say…*of our one, singular love.* But not in front of the salesman. The warmth of a blush rose at the thought.

Drawn to a certain stone of rare beauty, Henry surprised her by asking its cut, color, and clarity. She had forgotten to consider that even diamonds have measurements of quality. The salesman checked its tag and spoke a few initials that meant nothing to her, but seemed to satisfy her…her *fiancé*. Had he studied up on diamonds before shopping?

He put the solitaire on her finger and a beam ran up her arm to her heart.

Her beloved, soon her husband.

They agreed the size needed to be adjusted. Tomorrow he would pick up the ring and take her to dinner. She had a full day to dream that scene.

HE'D GIVE HIS next birthday for a spring night on a park bench right now, but a restaurant would have to do. After the waiter cleared their dinner plates, he pulled the black satin ring box from his pocket, opened the lid, and knelt before her.

The busboy halted gathering dishes at a nearby table. A middle-aged man smiled, nudged his wife, and nodded toward them.

Henry's eyes locked on hers, as blue as his mother's. "I love you, Grace. Will you marry me?"

"Yes, I will. I love you, Henry."

He caressed her left hand and slipped the diamond on her finger. "With all my heart, I pledge my love to you."

His pulse pounded with a pure passion. He stood, bent over his beloved, and kissed her with quivering lips. He tasted her tears and wanted to cry for joy.

He had a life now. He *was* someone again.

HENRY VIERTEL NEEDED a passport. He pulled out the Viertel birth certificate he had procured for admission to Emory and his honorable discharge papers. Combining these with a photo of the current Henry, he rushed through the request at the Atlanta passport office.

A whirlwind of sleepless days later, they held each other tight until the train conductor bellowed the final call. He sprang up the narrow steps at the last possible moment. The prolonged toot of the horn pierced his dizzy head, already hurting with the agony of leaving Grace. As the passenger car began to roll, she waved.

The diamond flashed in the morning sun. Only then did he smile, knowing she would wait for him. His Grace, by the grace of God.

CHAPTER TWENTY-NINE

14 February, 1946
Atlantic Crossing to Germany

HENRY WAS AMAZED at the extent to which his prayers had been answered. In a mere six weeks, he had given Grace a diamond, signed a contract with the U.S. Government as a translator, and soon would enter Germany at the port city of Bremerhaven.

Under the cover of Henry Viertel, American citizen, he could travel without fear. The prospect of using U.S. Army and Diplomatic Corps connections to find out what had happened to his father's investment company pleased him. Electricity surged with the expectation of crossing the border into Switzerland, changing at some point into the persona of Karl von Steuben, and presenting himself to his father's banker.

The Swiss had remained above the fray during the war, doing business with all sides. The numbered bank account would be safe. It had to be. Details got fuzzy after that.

Henry propped on the rail of the *USS Darby*, watching swirls of ocean water and the vast panorama of the sky. To the south, dark clouds pounded the sea with slanted gray lines of rain, but here sunshine beamed. Majesty, peace, and power controlled the waves.

Ten days on a liberty ship with men, military wives, children, and all manner of equipment. He didn't deal well with time on his hands. Too many hours to miss Grace and plan things over which he had no power.

Restless as a boxer waiting for the bell, he went below decks. Never one to play cards for money—and most soldiers couldn't see the point of playing without a little bet—he scanned the sparse library for anything worth reading. Something to take his mind off battle memories, the loss of his family, and self-recrimination for three twisted years.

The stuffy tin can of a room stocked a few biographies for children, classic literature he had read as a student, and books on the war that either angered or saddened him.

Angered because their slanted perspective regarded all things American as heroic and all things German as hated, stupid, cruel. Saddened because he loved his misguided, deceived fatherland. What a tragedy of cosmic proportions if Hitler had won the war. Caring more for himself than the millions of people who suffered and died for him, he took his life rather than face his failure.

Was there not one book in this dismal, dusty library about the German resistance fighters or the persecuted Jews?

The intercom clicked on, and its xylophone signaled dinner time. The notes triggered Henry's mouth to water. He followed the foot traffic to the dining hall for the evening meal, craning to spot anyone, anyone at all, who might be pleasant company.

Yet his nature had grown more guarded than a paranoid in a crowd. He sought the conversation of American passengers and avoided any man, woman, or child who spoke fluent German. Even on the ship, safety eluded him. He kept to himself, his only companion his memories.

24 February, 1946
Bremerhaven, Germany

HENRY'S EXCITEMENT AT arriving in Bremerhaven energized mind and body. Dressed in one of his two suits, he gripped the messenger's packet delivered to the ship for him. Inside, train tickets to Nürnberg and instructions in the handwriting of Bill Hanson, now Captain Hanson, outlined his itinerary.

The most essential rails had been repaired. That he could travel from Bremerhaven to Nürnberg without disruption surprised him, yet devastation ravaged the land. From the train windows, he observed the rubble of war and desolation of towns. His beautiful homeland suffered terrible retribution for following the Führer's greed and racism. Would its scarred hills and tumbled steeples ever heal?

By the time he reached Nürnberg, or Nuremberg as the Americans said, Henry felt deflated as a blimp caught on power lines. The hollow eyes and stunned expressions of other passengers showed they responded the same way to miles of destruction.

The Nuremberg depot swirled with people bundled in dark, frayed coats. He stepped on the platform with one suitcase and a duffle, everything he owned to wear and use. From the crowd he recognized a cheerful face and arm waving high.

The two friends met on the dock with much handshaking and back-slapping.

"How're you doing, man?" Capt. Hanson's smile stretched wide.

"Fine, sir, and how are you?"

"You're not in the Army anymore, Henry. I'm just Bill and you're on my team."

"Still my boss, sir."

Bill led him to a Jeep. From there they bumped and honked their way to a large hotel taken over by the U.S. Army, legal staff, and translators.

"We can't get enough support personnel to handle the job. The Nuremberg Trials are still in full process, and they're already starting investigations and indictments for subsequent trials of secondary criminals."

Henry glanced at Capt. Bill's U.S. Army print of the news in English. "I read the newspapers until the ship sailed, then picked up one in Bremerhaven. Sounded like a real tug of war just to set up the rules and definition of the crimes. Have the U.S. and England kept Russia from shooting everyone?"

"So far. Yeah, except for East Germany. Man. Not even war criminals deserve what the Russians are doing."

"Tell me, what do I translate?"

"Anything and everything. One of the reasons I wanted you here was because you always rolled with the punches. I mean, I could put you in a room with anyone. Downed pilots, village mayors, anybody. You could get information from clothes hanging out on a line."

"Any chance to get a job in the trials?"

"They've got professional translators. No offense, but certification helps." At the hotel, the captain requested Henry's room key, took his duffle, and led up three flights of stairs.

Karl might not have appreciated this hotel room with a bath on the hall, but Henry did. A good bed, desk, and drawers, and windowed doors opening to a tiny balcony which overlooked the street. He dropped his suitcase and splashed water on his face from the pan-sized sink. This would do fine.

"When do I start?"

"How about right now? I'll take you around to the offices where we work and introduce you to the team."

Henry opened his suitcase and pulled out a packet of letters to Grace. "What's the chance of getting these mailed to my girlfriend first?"

"Address them and leave them with the guy at the front desk." Capt. Bill grimaced. "They have to go through security, just like in the Army. Hope you don't mind."

"Not at all, if it doesn't take too long. We're planning a wedding as soon as possible."

"No kidding. Fantastic. I didn't know you were that serious."

A wide smile instantly pulled at Henry's face. "Yeah. Grace is...amazing. She's a nurse. Might want to get a job at the Army hospital. Any idea what the chances are?"

"Chances? Of an American nurse getting a job here? It's a certainty, and with good pay and benefits. Bring her over as soon as you can."

"Got to marry her first. Her father will not consider anything else." Bill didn't need to hear about the conflict with Mr. Shore.

Capt. Bill walked the block with him to an imposing office building taken over for postwar operations, including civil management. All this kind of work concentrated in the Palace of Justice area, where the Nuremberg Trials were held.

Henry's delight to be here, and to be assisting the United States in the process of convicting war criminals, was tempered by a fear of being recognized by former clients of his father. He trusted an American suit and haircut to be his disguise. His face had aged much more than three years since his comfortable life as the boss's son.

Father had dealt with the sharpest lawyers and businessmen. He wondered if any of them might be tried for crimes in Nuremberg.

In fact, would Father be indicted today for his control of Reich investments?

Shoving Karl back into his corner, Henry met his new team members with his best imitation of American-ness. The posture, handshake, everything he copied from life in the Army and in Atlanta. Contractions in speech had long evaded him as unnecessary complications, but he needed them now. *Slouch some and say "yeah" instead of so much formality. I can do this.*

The team seemed to accept Henry for who Bill said he was. Reporting directly to Bill were five men and a skinny, sickly-looking middle-aged woman, Ilsa. From her first sentence, he knew she was German and determined to avoid her as much as possible. She would recognize the slightest incongruity.

After assigning Tommy Land to get Henry started and be available for questions, Capt. Bill put them to work in a small room with a desk and a stack of documents. As the door closed, Henry let out a long breath. What had he gotten himself into?

He exerted more effort in mastering the Underwood typewriter than translation. Though he kept a three-kilo Cassell's German/English Dictionary at his right hand, the boring and repetitive vocabulary of the legal documents offered little resistance. Or entertainment.

By the end of the week, he obsessed on whether Grace had gotten his letters yet. When another passed, he wasted mental energy in the effort of waiting for her reply. Meanwhile, he wrote something every day, either a new letter or continuation of pages started previously. The more he flooded the system with correspondence, the greater probability a few of them got through to his beloved.

The business of the office pushed time along. Even on weekends, the team discussed documents with lawyers and searched for evidence and angles to be used in trials the following week.

Leaving work late on a Saturday, Henry realized he didn't need his overcoat. Spring was happening, and he was missing it. Hadn't Grace said that once?

Ilsa left the building at the same time, also walking to the hotel. They fell in step together, commenting on the weather, blooming fruit trees, and then the tedious translations.

"So, Bill says you have a girlfriend in the States."

"More than a girlfriend. We're engaged. I gave her a ring before I left." He yearned for Grace. Did she picnic in the park with someone else? Atlanta's spring evenings might beckon her to their special place on the Chattahoochee River.

"Serious, *nicht whar?*"

"Right." He ignored her German question tag and continued in English. Didn't want her guessing his Munich upbringing.

"Tell me something, Ilsa."

"What is that?"

"The U.S. has an absolute non-fraternization policy with Germans. How did you get this job?"

She kept walking, eyes straight ahead. "I'm Jewish. The American Fifth Army rescued me from Dachau on May fifth. No one can ever doubt my loyalty."

His steps faltered. She paused and turned to face him.

"Dachau." A profane and horrible name. "You were there?" His hoarse question scratched out of a secret pocket somewhere deep.

"My specialty in the department is translating prison camp documents." She quirked a sardonic smile as she resumed walking. "You wouldn't believe the records they kept. Every prisoner, every death, the disposition of each name. The human experiments." Her shoulders hunched up and she shook her head. "All in the records."

Awe-stricken, he whispered. "Perfect."

"You're Jewish too, aren't you?"

The question he had feared so long, no longer dangerous, still struck his pulse and set off white spots in his brain. He attempted to appear nonchalant. "Not as far as I'm aware. It's never been mentioned."

"Oh, yes, you're the guy with amnesia. Bill told us before you arrived." She didn't sound convinced.

Ilsa slowed a few meters from the hotel. She reached out for a lamp post and bent her head.

"Are you okay?"

"Happens all the time. Starvation…messes up things."

He waited, bracing her by the forearm in case she fainted. She had endured the worst. A heroine. Some day he wanted to ask her…when he could bear to hear.

Ilsa released the pole, straightened, and took deep breaths. With deliberate effort, she completed the block and mounted the hotel's front steps to the lobby.

Though she maintained a distance from Henry, he stayed close enough to catch her.

Inside, she bid him a pleasant weekend and turned left toward the women's wing on the ground floor.

Henry stopped at the reception desk attended by the usual fellow. "Letters?"

He shook his head and shrugged.

Another night alone, imagining why Grace hadn't written. He picked up the financial section of a newspaper left in the lobby. Before going to bed, he turned through his Bible, read a couple of passages, and threw a prayer toward the ceiling. Maybe he would find a church in the morning.

When he could no longer stand the absence of letters, Henry asked Capt. Bill to have dinner with him. Over a simple plate of roast chicken and potatoes, Henry poured out his heart to Bill about the need to communicate with Grace.

Capt. Bill propped an elbow on the table and massaged his five o'clock shadow. "How sure are you that she...wants to contact you?"

Henry leveled a firm gaze. "Positive. Security may be holding up the process, or perhaps Air Mail to the U.S. is inefficient. But she would at least tell me if she changed her mind. She accepted a ring. We made plans to marry." His words caused his face to warm.

Bill looked away first. "Okay, I want you to come to my office at, say, three o'clock tomorrow afternoon. She would be home at seven a.m. Eastern?"

"I think so. She wasn't working nights when I left."

"I'll arrange a transatlantic call. Be brief, and it's possible you won't be alone, you understand. Give me the number in the morning, and I'll work out the details."

Henry's smile pulled against dry lines of his face. "It's possible? That's wonderful. That's exactly what I need. Here. I'll write her number on this napkin." He babbled like an excited child at Christmas.

The anticipation of words with his precious Grace kept him awake that night.

GRACE STIRRED FROM sleep when the telephone sounded at six a.m. Mighty early for a phone call.

Three rings, and someone answered. Her mother. Then she realized it wasn't early in Germany. She sprang from the bed, grabbed a robe, and dashed to her parents' bedroom.

As she lifted a fist to knock, her mother opened the door. "The long distance operator says you're going to get a transatlantic phone call in one hour. She asked if you'll be home."

Grace jumped up and down, laughing. "Yes! Yes, I'll be here."

It was the longest hour of her life. She showered, dressed, powdered her face, drank coffee, and paced until her mother begged her to stop.

Her mother seemed pleased though, and twittered about the kitchen, sharing Grace's excitement.

Even her father smiled and took on a tolerant expression over his newspaper. "You can take the call on our extension. Don't talk long. It'll be expensive."

Grace sat on the side of their bed with her Bible, but didn't digest a word she read.

The ring shot adrenaline straight to her brain. "Hello?"

The operator confirmed her name and made the connection. A bit of static later, she heard the voice of her beloved.

"Grace? Sweetheart, it's Henry. How are you?"

She quelled a schoolgirl giggle. "Wonderful. I got your letters on Monday, and I sent you one right back."

"Oh, thank heaven. I was afraid…I hadn't heard anything from you. Look, I have only two minutes."

"Is it very expensive?"

"I'm sort of borrowing someone else's privileges. It isn't costing me anything, but yes, it's expensive. I only wanted to know you're okay, and you have my address, and…you hadn't changed your mind."

"Oh, darling, no. Never. I love you. It's been just awful without you." The sting of tears made her realize how close to the edge of emotional display she sat. "I mean, I can't wait until we can be together."

"I'm into the job, working hard six days a week. This is important, Grace. We're going to get the people who…never mind, I'll write all about it. Now that I know you're getting my letters."

"Yes, and I'll write you every day."

"Sweetheart, I can't come back for the wedding yet, but I want you to start planning. Find a dress you like, think about the guest list. All the details. When I get a date, I'll send you a wire. I love you."

The call terminated. Two minutes. Not long enough to tell him everything she wanted him to know. And suggest she call his Texas family about the engagement. She still had the number.

HENRY'S FEET DIDN'T touch the floor for hours. Letters on the way. No "Dear John." She still loved him. Better yet, she was still waiting.

Ilsa's drawn face brought him to earth with a clunk. She held pages and pages of handwritten lists of exterminated Auschwitz prisoners. "Do you want to see this?"

Did he? Was he ready to find their names in the tedious tables of a bookkeeper of death? He stared at the stack. He reached for it, took it from her without a word.

"You cannot leave this office or make copies. Better you do not mention you saw this." Ilsa's bone-white face and her shocky movements spoke volumes.

Nodding, Henry pulled out a chair at a side table and sat. Long past the dinner hour, bleary-eyed, he became aware of her presence.

"Who are you looking for?" Her raspy voice came like a rough whisper.

She knew.

"No one. No one in particular." He denied it.

"Give me a name. I'll keep an eye out."

With all fervor, he wanted to tell her, wanted to trust her. If he said "von Steuben" right now, he blew his cover. No one else in the whole world knew. No one must know. He shook his head.

She reached for the stack. "Everyone else has gone home. I need to lock up. These go back in the safe."

He rose with jerky movements, scraping the chair back.

She twisted the safe's dial and stood. "Give me a name."

"Just a friend of a friend. It's not important." He left the building and walked for kilometers. Two hours later, he sat on a bench staring at the Palace of Justice.

Vengeance is mine, sayeth the Lord.

Hatred could chew him up and spit him out. But he would do everything, *everything* in his power to legally convict these monsters.

[301]

CHAPTER THIRTY

June, 1946
Atlanta, Georgia

GRACE WALTZED INTO the hospital on a romantic high. First, she found her best friend peddling pills on the internal medicine floor. "Betty, he called me. All the way from Germany."

"Henry?"

"Of *course* I mean Henry. He wants me to start planning our wedding. You've got to help me pick out a dress and plan the flowers."

Betty set down the medication tray and gave Grace a giggling hug. "When are you getting married?"

"I have no idea. He said he can't come back yet. He'll send a telegram when he can, but you and I—and Mother, of course—we'll be working out the details. You will be my maid of honor, won't you?"

"I'd love to. Oh, this is so exciting. How many people are you going to invite?"

Grace had her first inkling of what it meant to plan a wedding. Guest lists, a reservation for the church, bridesmaids' dresses — pieces of every woman's dream.

"I haven't decided yet."

"How many bridesmaids will you have?" Betty bounced on her toes.

"Not as many as Constance. I think she invited every girl in her graduating class."

"No, only those who could afford nice gifts." Betty snickered. "Don't do pink. Everyone does pink. Pink dresses, pink flowers, pink punch at the reception."

"I can't even think about such details right now, because if the wedding's in autumn, or maybe even Christmas, all the decorations would change." Color schemes floated in Grace's mind.

"A Christmas wedding. How romantic."

Grace jerked around at the interruption of Betty's scowling head nurse with hands propped on her hips. Both girls scattered. On a day like this, was it too much to ask for a little joy?

June, 1946
Nuremberg, Germany

HENRY TAPPED ON Ilsa's office door. His associates shuffled behind him in the hall, draining down the stairs toward whatever quarters for the night.

She opened up.

He raised his brow in question. She knew why he had come.

She waved him in, the direction of her reach ending at the side desk where he spent most of his afternoons and many nights scouring the Auschwitz prison lists.

"Give me a name, Henry. I can help."

He shook his head and spoke to her, brown eyes to brown eyes. "You know I can't."

"A relative? Or a relative of a relative? I haven't seen any Viertels. I do check."

Unbidden moisture swam under his lids, and he bent away, toward the pages.

She pointed to a new sheaf. "Every few days we get more pages. Someone estimates wild numbers, like four million people were sent to Auschwitz. We think over a million were killed at that one facility."

An aching hole in his middle expanded deeper. So many souls.

"I left your place marker." A scrap of blue paper stuck out. "Even if you skim over all the Poles and gypsies... You do, don't you? You're looking for a German name?"

Giving her that much with a nod, he flipped the stack open. "You were at Dachau, right?"

"One of the satellite camps for women. The main camp was mostly men." Without concealing her shudder, she turned and picked up her bag. "Pull the door closed and turn out the light when you leave."

"Thank you for trusting me, Ilsa."

"I do. Trust you." She pulled her sweater on. "The prosecutor must not find out you are alone at night with all this evidence."

"And risk a mistrial? Never. These sadistic demons must pay."

"You know I want the same thing. Why won't you trust me?"

"I do. But why put you in a position of knowing something you might have to act on?"

She frowned, looked toward the door, and back at him. "Are you a spy, then?"

He chuffed a laugh. "No such thing. I just want personal information. A relative of a relative, like you said."

"Then why not—"

"Don't ask. Please."

Ilsa left. Muffled sounds of departing workers died. Accustomed to his habits, the janitor seemed to think nothing of his late hours.

Auschwitz prisoner extermination lists consumed Henry like a tyrant every hour he could spare. He poured over them until his eyes blurred. They might have spelled von Steuben wrong. He had seen a von Steuren. The pages went on and on, and Ilsa said this stack wasn't complete.

He rubbed his eyes and leaned back in the chair. What if they lived? His mind ran wild with the possibility of finding them. If they were carted there on trains, how would they be returned to Munich?

Or if they died of tuberculosis or dysentery? Would they be in the lists?

Too dazed to cry, he put the box of pages in the safe and gave the dial a whirl.

HENRY SPOTTED CAPT. BILL and Ilsa in a favorite *gasthouse* around the corner from the hotel. Hunched over their mugs like coworkers, not like a date, he waved and approached.

Bill returned the wave and invited him over. "How's it going? Had enough for tonight?"

Had she mentioned his scouring of the lists? "Yeah, thought I'd have a bite to eat and then get a few lines off to Grace. Say, Captain, I need to talk to you about something."

"Fire when ready." Bill glanced toward Ilsa.

"Not confidential. About the wedding. Grace's father won't let her come over until after we're married, so I can't send for her and have the wedding here. Besides, she wants the whole family and friends celebration, in her church and all."

Ilsa smiled, crinkling her network of face lines. "Every girl deserves to be princess for one day." The smile dropped as quickly as it appeared. She lifted her mug for a long swallow.

"The crossing takes about nine days each way, plus travel to Atlanta and back and having the wedding. What's the chance of getting enough time off to marry and return with my bride?"

Bill drew circles in the condensation on the table. For too long. He inhaled but didn't speak. Henry waited.

"Come by my office tomorrow, maybe about one. I'll check the calendar and see what we can work out."

HENRY PICKED UP another letter from reception. Filled with details of a wedding on hold for an unknown future date, Grace's messages drew more highs and lows than the postwar stock market. One day she ecstatically told of finding the perfect gown, the next she related disagreements among her best friends about their bridesmaids' dresses. Everyone wanted to be maid of honor. Henry reread the parts rhapsodizing of her devotion then tossed the stationary on the bed and went for a long walk in a light spring drizzle. He needed the exercise.

Entering Bill's open door at one o'clock sharp the following afternoon, he held his heart in his hand.

"Greetings, groom. I think I've got a plan."

A jolt of joy juice surged through his veins.

Bill held out a calendar scarred with appointments and notes. "If you can find passage pretty soon, maybe in July, I'll let you go before the secondary trials begin. It's a tiny window. No time for a honeymoon. Will that do?"

"Yes, sir." Henry slapped Bill on the back. They pumped handshakes and laughed.

Ilsa entered from the hall, a couple of other team members behind her. "What's up?"

"I'm getting married." He wanted to shout and jump around.

The coworkers joined in the merriment, and before the end of the day, "passageway radio" spread word through the building. People with whom he had the slightest acquaintance offered him ship and train schedules, a great deal on a small apartment, and essential information on sending telegrams. One of the lawyers even guaranteed a nursing job for Grace at the Army Hospital.

Henry passed around Grace's photo until wear began to show. Then he got down to planning the trip.

Would she go for a July wedding? Atlanta in stifling, blazing hot. That much he remembered from his visit as a twelve year old.

When would he tell her the name of the groom?

HENRY ARRANGED TRAVEL plans, and Bill set up another transatlantic telephone call.

Alone with the phone at the appointed hour, Henry's excited, shallow breaths puffed through the static. Men weren't supposed to be this nervous about getting married. But other men didn't have Grace for a bride.

"Grace, sweetheart, grab a calendar. I got good news."

"Mama, quick, please hand me the calendar." The voice of his darling, even though directed aside to her mother, came over his body like a warm, soothing bath. "Henry, it's wonderful to get your call and all the letters. Thank you for sending so many. They keep me alive. There are days when it seems our wedding is never going to happen and two years is too long. And then I come home and see that you've written."

"I love you, Grace. And you're right. Two years is too long. How about five weeks?"

She inhaled and then squealed.

He laughed and held the receiver away from his ear.

"Can you get the wedding together soon enough? I can book passage on July eighth, arrive in New York City on the seventeenth, be in Atlanta by train the next day. We could marry the same weekend and leave right away. Capt. Bill can't give me enough time for a real honeymoon, but we'll have a couple of days in New York before we sail to Germany. Will that work?"

"Mercy! Can we arrange—? Yes. Yes, we'll make it work. I'll reserve the church immediately, and call the lady who makes the cakes— Never mind. The bridesmaids' dresses may not be ready, but they can waltz down the aisle in their petticoats for all I care. You're on, mister. Let's have us a wedding."

"I understand that these things are important to you, sweetheart, but they don't matter to me—how do you say in Georgia, 'Not worth a hill of beans?' You have carte blanche to do anything you wish. All I want is to marry you and bring you back."

"Don't you think it's time for me to call your family, sweetheart? They'd want to be here."

As if thunder boomed in his brain, he recoiled. "No. I mean that, Grace. Don't call the Viertels. Don't write them. I'll call them when I'm ready."

He would never be ready.

7 July, 1946
Nuremberg, Germany

HENRY WOULD NEVER again board a passenger ship without a book to read. He stocked up on financial texts and a couple of histories of the Great War, written in English from the American perspective. He might learn something which would aid his understanding.

Jonathan, a lawyer with whom he had a speaking friendship, dropped by. "All your docs in order?"

"Think so. Anything I need to know before I go?"

"We like to have a will and basic life insurance on file for every married man. Drop by my office when you return. I'll help with your bride's paperwork."

"Thanks. That's kind of you. I do have one question."

"What's that?"

"For a wedding ceremony to be legal, does the preacher have to use my middle name? I don't like it, and would prefer he not say it out loud."

"No, he can marry you by your nickname and you'd be legally married. If you had one."

Henry chuckled. This might be easier than he had feared. "When my cousin married, the preacher could not pronounce 'Viertel.' He is still not sure they are man and wife."

"Doesn't matter. The man and woman standing there saying 'I do' are married, no matter what the preacher calls them."

"Ha. He will be glad to hear it. So will she and the children."

The lawyer laughed his way down the hall.

What a relief. With his office cleaned and orderly in case someone else used it during his absence, he hoisted his bag and thought a silent farewell.

Ilsa approached so quietly that he jumped. She entered and closed the door. "I could work on your search while you are gone if I knew what to look for."

Taking a three-and-a-half week break had its complications.

She leveled a calm gaze at him. Her soft voice communicated a shared concern. "Otherwise, hundreds of papers will pass through here which you'll never see."

Henry put down his satchel and rested a hand on her shoulder. Bill had told him she didn't like to be touched, but she didn't back away. "My mother was a Jewish American. She heard two of her relatives went to Auschwitz."

Ilsa nodded. And waited.

"Von Steuben. Anna and Marta."

"From what city?"

He paused, evaluating the risk.

Huge.

He told her anyway. "Munich."

SLEEP ELUDED HENRY. Excitement mounted for the trip, the wedding, their new life together. But fear clawed at his lungs. If a knock had come to his door, he might have climbed out the third story window. He couldn't leave town soon enough.

Capt. Bill took him to the train depot early the next morning and even walked with him to the tracks.

"I need a best man. Wish you were going with me."

"Thanks. Wish I could. Will your Texas family be there?"

Henry stalled. "No, my father isn't well. They couldn't come."

"Too bad. You're missing a great opportunity for a reunion."

"Yeah, but I don't think I'm ready yet."

Bill frowned but didn't push the subject.

The train whistle sounded, and Henry swung on. "Thanks for bringing me. See you in a few weeks."

"Hey, did you go by the paymaster?"

Henry nodded with a smile and patted his wallet. A three-month advance, to be repaid in six months, made for an easier and more generous trip. A small amount by the standards of his former life, but hard to pay back if he did not come into his inheritance.

18 July, 1946
Atlanta, Georgia

Grace paced at the Atlanta depot. When the train approached, her pulse raced so fast she feared she might faint.

Henry stepped off two cars away, and she rushed into his arms. "You're here. You're really here."

He loosened his embrace, looked into her face, and then kissed her, right there on the platform.

The exasperation of dealing with the flowers and friends, tiered cake and tired parents slipped into the background. She had saved herself for this man. Her heart swelled with love.

Reality returned in the form of a large, round clock mounted on the depot wall.

She took his hand and pulled. "Quick, let's get to the church. Rehearsal starts in an hour."

During the rehearsal, the pastor asked her father, "Who gives this woman in marriage?" He knew quite well to say, "I do." Instead, her father said, "Her mother does."

The cast laughed heartily, including Henry, but Grace felt like she had been slapped across the face.

Exhausted, Grace held up during the rehearsal dinner she had arranged for Henry to host, introductions to his groomsmen she had chosen, and many double-entendre toasts.

Henry had brought small gifts for his future parents-in-law, a gold brooch for her and a leather briefcase for him. When he presented them privately at the rehearsal dinner, her father shook his hand, but received the gift as if it were an insufficient bride price. Her mother cried again.

Driving Henry to her aunt's house for their last night apart, she crumbled. "I can't believe Daddy said that. He's been unreasonable." She had to park at the curb for a moment.

He pulled out a handkerchief and touched her tears. "Shhh, it's okay. He wants the very best for his only daughter. I would feel the same—will someday." He leaned in for a soft kiss. "Besides, he reserved the bridal suite for us at the Biltmore Hotel. Doesn't that prove something?"

"He assumed you couldn't afford a nice place and didn't want people to talk. When I started planning our wedding, he pushed me one more time to...well, to stiff-arm you and marry Johnny."

"Johnny? The guy who used to come to the church canteen nights? The rude one so proud of 'killin' Churmans?'"

She ducked her head, wishing she hadn't mentioned him. "Johnny was always his choice for a son-in-law."

Henry gripped his thighs. "How about you?"

She sniffed before the panic hit. Henry was asking if she wanted to back out. "I don't like him at all. Believe me, darling. You remember how he was such a smart aleck on Friday nights." She had to calm down. This didn't help either one. "Daddy keeps saying he'll make someone a 'good provider.' I've come to hate that phrase."

Grace drove the last two blocks to her aunt's home and cut the engine.

He took her face in both hands and kissed her as gently as the flutter of butterfly wings. "My sweet Grace, I don't deserve you."

She shook her head, but he maintained his tender touch.

"I don't deserve you *yet*, but I know…who I am…and what I'm capable of."

WHEN AT LAST she took her father's arm and stepped down the aisle to the "Wedding March", the congregation stood and beamed their love. Her eyes searched Henry's face and found certainty and devotion. She placed her hand in his and promised him her love and obedience without reservation.

Her parents gave her a magnificent wedding with the most gorgeous dress his professional contacts could arrange. Mother out-did all expectations on the flowers and thousands of details that make a wedding sensational.

And Henry. He was dashing in the rented tux her daddy had ordered. So handsome, flashing the double dimples in his right cheek. She hoped they showed up well in the photos. Grace and Henry shook hands in the reception line until she thought she would never be able to use her right hand again.

The last guest came through the line and the wedding director called them to cut the cake.

First, Henry turned to her parents with a serious, *terribly* sincere expression. "Mr. and Mrs. Shore, be assured that I cherish your daughter. I will take care of her and always respect her. In due time, she will be supported in the manner she deserves."

Her mother teared up and hugged him. Her father seemed unable to speak, but shook his hand, nodded, and patted him on the shoulder.

After the cake was cut, the flowers thrown, and rice tossed, a limousine carried them away to the Biltmore, all compliments of her father. Despite his grumbling and Mama's tears, it had been the wedding of her dreams.

Alone at last, Grace and Henry, frazzled but profoundly happy, kissed with abandon. Mrs. Viertel. She practiced pronouncing it like he did, starting with an "F" sound.

Henry released her to reach into his suitcase for a thin box wrapped in white satin with a red velvet ribbon. "A gift to commemorate this day, my love."

She opened the gift with shaky fingers and found a gold chain bearing a beautiful cross, embellished with delicate scrolls and swirls. On the back she read the engraved date of their wedding. "Oh, how beautiful, Henry." She turned for him to clasp it around her neck. "It's heavy."

"Purest gold, my love."

"I have a gift for you, too, and our minds ran in a similar direction."

Unwrapping his box, he discovered a substantial gold chain.

"It's for the cross you wear on a shoestring."

He unbuttoned the neck of his formal shirt and pulled up his pendant. Laughing, they took his cross off its worn string and placed it on the new chain.

"Yours has the names Anna and Dietrich. Are they your parents or grandparents?"

"When I woke up in the field hospital in France, the nurse said this cross was in my shoe. It has come to represent being rescued, and God giving me another chance."

"My dearest husband, I thank Him every day for you."

"Grace, my love, you are His unmerited favor toward me."

At eight o'clock the next morning, they caught the train north. With only one full day to tour New York City, they boarded the ship and sailed for Bremerhaven. Nine days with her husband (she loved saying the word) began her preparation for life with him in a new country.

CHAPTER THIRTY-ONE

End of July, 1946
Nuremberg, Germany

HENRY'S TEAMMATES GREETED him with handshakes and backslaps, offers of coffee and doughnuts, and a towering stack of pages to translate. As an office joke, the team had gathered folders, garbage papers, anything to make a pile ready to tip over.

Crowded in the tiny room, Capt. Bill raised his coffee cup in a mock toast, welcoming him back. "So you're married. Congratulations."

Showing his wedding ring as heat rose to his cheeks, Henry nodded. "Yeah, despite her father's intentions."

"Where is she now?"

"Applying to be a nurse at the American Hospital. We went over there yesterday, as soon as we put our bags down at the hotel.

She brought letters of recommendation with her. She's ready to start work." He controlled his smile enough to swallow some coffee. "Then she's going to check out a couple of apartments nearby. We want to consider the possibility."

"Good idea. Well, when you're ready to get started, come down to my office and I'll brief you on what's happening."

"Just a few minutes, then." Henry thanked his coworkers for stopping by, and stood around until they had left. The sense of family, though, did not leave. For all the seriousness of their job, the team worked as a tight unit. Memories returned of working at von Steuben Investments in Munich, which he squelched.

As he passed Ilsa's open office, she waved him in.

He nodded. "I've got to see the captain."

"Give me two minutes. Close the door."

He entered, hoping for good news.

"Anna and Marta von Steuben," she spoke above a whisper, "were prisoners at a tank assembly factory near Dachau in October, 1944. The prison roll of January, 1945, did not list them."

Henry reeled on his heels. His jaw went slack, and his ears rang.

Ilsa touched his upper arm in a grip meant either to comfort or catch him from falling. "I'm sorry. I hoped for something better. More definite."

"Thanks." He rubbed the back of his neck. "Doesn't look good."

She shook her head, sorrow and personal pain lined on her face beyond her years.

Henry drew a deep breath, straightened his posture, and left.

Capt. Bill bent over folders on his desk as Henry entered. "Really great to have you back. Work slowed a lot when we had to rely on people with textbook German. We all put too much pressure on Ilsa. I even talked up the organizational chart about having other Germans brought in, but you know how it is. We can't trust them to incriminate their own people."

"Ilsa can help us find fluent translators, especially Jewish former prisoners."

"She says most of those she would recommend were killed. The SS targeted highly educated Jews first."

Henry's ears rang. All the air had been sucked out of the room.

Bill, concentrating on the folders, didn't seem to notice. He selected a file and held it out to Henry. "This is your assignment. The Subsequent Nuremberg Trials are in the investigation phase, starting with the doctors and judges involved. Concentrate on Friedrich Flick and the 'Circle of Friends of Himmler.' Take a seat for a minute."

Henry sat and glanced at the first page.

"Himmler, the Nazi most responsible for creating the extermination camps, had his own cronies raising his financial support on the order of a million Marks per year. Wilhelm Keppler started the Circle in 1932."

Hanson's brief was old news to Henry, but he listened as if he'd never heard this before.

"Of course," Bill continued, "Himmler committed suicide the day after his capture, before we got any information out of him."

Henry's jaw tightened to the point of pain. He propped on an elbow and massaged his chin. "But we knew he commanded the SS and all the concentration camps, including the extermination camps."

"Right. We've already indicted Speer for slave labor in the armaments factories. Now we're going after the Circle, the industrialists and bankers who moved his machine. You seem interested in finance and economy. I thought this might be a piece you could bite off."

Henry snapped away from the page, fully on guard.

Bill had noticed his preference in reading material? And a few random conversations about the postwar economy?

Bill smiled. "Some guys read girlie magazines. You read about the European economy. I have no problem with that. I'd be bored to death reading the stuff you do. Think you can stomach financial documents in German?"

"Sure, Captain." In fact, those would be easier for him to digest than English financial documents. "Is the information already in house, ready to be translated? Or would you like me to dig through archives of periodicals?"

"Feel free to dig. How big a shovel do you need?"

The immense challenge pushed a charge through Henry which hit his brain like firecrackers. "I'll let you know."

If it weren't for Grace waiting for him back at the hotel, ready to show him apartments, he might have worked late over archived newspapers.

Pleased with the third apartment she had arranged for them to visit, he spoke with the realtor about appliances, utilities, and services. Grace stood to one side, unable to follow the German dialog.

Taking her hands in his, he relayed the information and tried to judge her reactions to each possible rental.

"This one I love." She stepped to the window light as a dancer, giving him a view of her slender frame against the aura of sunset. "The trees over the little park, the people on the street.... I think this is the one." She turned with a glow on her face. "I can walk to the hospital from here."

"Done, then. Our first home as a married couple."

With nothing to carry except their suitcases, they moved on August first. Bill arranged for an Army Jeep on Saturday and traded his help for sandwiches.

Long after the labor and lunch, brawn and brownies, Henry and Grace closed the door on their friend and turned to each other.

He held her close, aware of what a treasure he embraced. His to honor and cherish, to protect and keep.

If only she bore his name instead of that of a dead soldier from Texas.

"SAY, BOSS, WOULD it be okay for me to go to the Nuremberg Municipal Library during work hours? Their references could be useful." Henry paused as he met Bill in the translation wing.

"You think so?" He waved him into the office and closed the door.

Henry took note of the air of confidentiality. "A lot of the information we're looking for on Himmler's Circle of Friends was public knowledge before the war. The library is, at least temporarily, accepting books and papers returned by the Jewish Community of Nuremberg until their owners or heirs are found. Things confiscated by the government as far back as 1935. If you can get me permission to sift through them, we might find verified sources of public information, or at least leads for where to look."

"Sounds good. I'll type up something right away. Just check in with me every day or so. I need progress reports to justify what you're working on."

Passing the statue of some military hero on a horse, Henry inhaled the hallowed air enclosed by the library's massive stone walls. A few years ago, Jews were forbidden to enter any public library in Germany. Today he researched those vain villains who judged him unworthy to read their books. He pushed open the heavy door with pride and purpose.

Henry refined his search, ratcheting down leads through three days' digging. He uncovered further information in bits and snatches concerning Otto Steinbrinck, Wilhelm Keppler, and others in Friedrich Flick's Circle.

As his tension built, he found it necessary to leave the library and walk a mile or two. Sometimes he ran up and down the library's stairs until prepared to face the books and periodicals again.

How could they treat humans like animals, use them as slaves, and discard them when they died? This group of men plundered France and Poland and concealed funds to foster Himmler's personal advancement.

What Henry had not found was evidence of financial activity within Germany which amounted to robbery. That would not be in the library books or public periodicals during the time of extreme censorship. He needed to go to Munich, where the Circle of Friends of Himmler had been founded.

IN THE STILL of the night, when Grace's breathing slowed to a peaceful rhythm, Henry's mind ran down blind alleys and lurched into dark places. Had Father dealt with these men? Had Father known what they were doing? Worse yet, if Father were alive today, would he be under scrutiny?

Henry approached Capt. Bill on Monday morning. "Boss, I'm really onto something. I need to take this investigation to Munich."

"I don't know, Henry. I'm not sure we can do that. Another team may be researching from there." Bill slapped some forms against his palm. "Come on inside, and let's talk about what you've got."

Hanson sat at his desk and invited Henry to take a chair, but he danced and paced as he talked. Opening a large envelope, he pulled out notes, ideas, and leads, even a list of questions to research. Hanson remained silent, frowning, listening to details of the spontaneous presentation.

Henry ran out of ammo. "So now I know what I'm looking for. I've got hints at wrongdoing, but we need proof of indictable crimes. So much evidence is coming to light. Concealed funds, yes. Misappropriated funds, probably. Stolen funds—not yet. I need to get into the actual records of *Flick Kommanditgesellschaft. Flick KG.*"

"Huh?"

"The whole group of companies which Flick owned. Those records are in Munich."

Hanson exhaled. "Okay, I'll see what I can do."

Monday, 19 August, 1946

HENRY BID GRACE goodbye for a whole work week. He held her close one more time, dreading the train's departure whistle. "I never thought about this when you got a job. Well, at least you'll be busy while I'm gone."

She gave a sad little smile. "I might even ask for some extra hours. Everything we can save will make it easier later."

"Don't work too hard, sweetheart. I'll be back Friday night." One more kiss, and he left.

Resolve hardened as the hundred fifty kilometers passed by his window. He would go to the street where von Steuben Investments stood, and observe. Not the coffee shop in which he had been recognized before. Nor would he speak to anyone. He should have grown a beard. Hopefully, people would look past an American with his briefcase and new fedora.

A necessary risk. The rest of his life hinged on finding out what had happened to his father's firm. He checked into the Munich Army Hotel and left his suitcase in the room. With an almost empty briefcase, he took buses to Sonnenstrasse in the financial district.

Stepping off, he found damaged buildings and rubble still in the street. Von Steuben Investments, once a proud structure with sophisticated moldings at its entrance, had suffered more surface harm. The gaping bomb hole from before had been patched after a fashion, the broken back corner closed with plaster rather than good brick.

Few people moved about on the sidewalks. They ambled, heads down, as if looking for the community which used to be here. A quiver ran through Henry, upsetting his stomach and churning his innards. He scanned the shops, half of them closed, windows boarded over broken glass. A child walked by with a loaf of bread, triggering hunger though Henry had no interest in eating. He nursed the sense of being lean and ready for action.

At some distance came an old man, wearing an unkempt black suit. For all his rumpled appearance, he maintained perfect posture, a dark hat shadowing his wrinkled face.

Herr Olson? Could it be? Yes. His former mentor, his father's second in command. Herr Olson retrieved a key and jiggled the knob and handle as he worked to open the front door of von Steuben Investments.

Henry walked the neighborhood for fifteen minutes as if he had somewhere to go. Observing the firm from different angles, he witnessed no activity. He took a deep breath for bravado, approached, and tried the knob. The door swung open as if ready for clients.

He entered and closed the door. Dust swirled on the marble floor. Inside, he heard nothing. The musty air closed around him. He approached the stairs. The handrail had been used. He ascended, faking calm though his heart raced.

Tracks in the dust and leaf litter turned left, toward the senior partner offices. He followed the trail, fearing at any moment a guard might appear and shoot him down as an intruder. Approaching the open office, he found Herr Olson sitting at his desk.

The old man blinked and stared. He stood, and light from the front window created a halo of his white, un-barbered hair. "Karl? Is that you, my boy?" Tears filled his eyes. "I thought you were dead."

Henry noted that the desktop was clean except for a few papers. "Is anyone else here?"

"No, just myself. I'm the only one." Herr Olson straightened as if proud to be the lone sentinel of von Steuben Investments. "Some were arrested. Some…I don't know. No one is left but me."

"I need to talk to you, sir."

"Of course. You'll find everything in order." He waved an arm toward the other offices. "As your father would have wanted. Except…except what the SS took." Fear lit his eyes then, and worry lined his forehead. "I couldn't stop them. They shot the guard. Such a nice boy. He didn't deserve that."

Olson turned to the filing cabinet in the corner. "You'll want to examine the books, no doubt." He pulled the drawer open with difficulty and seemed surprised to find it empty. "Oh. They must have taken them, too."

Henry perceived this dear man to be addled, his thoughts scrambled. "It's all right, Herr Olson."

"Doesn't matter so much. We've lost all our clients." He raised a bushy eyebrow. "Some are in jail, like that snake, Speer." His glance flashed about, but there was no one to overhear. "Forgive me. I shouldn't have said that. Your father never allowed us to disparage clients."

He looked through the dust motes toward the big office. "But then, he's dead, as you are."

Henry didn't know how to react. Was Herr Olson out of his mind, or could he give the information required, urgently needed? "If we could talk, sir, there's much I need to know. I've been away so long."

"Please have a seat. Or would you like to go to your work space? No, I suppose you'll be taking charge now. You should be in the head office."

"This is fine. Sir, there are things the partners knew which never got committed to paper."

Olson nodded with all sobriety.

"Father managed enormous portfolios, investments of the Reich. What happened to those investments?"

"Everything belonging to the Reich passed to SS control the day they stormed in and rampaged the place. All the documentation, all the bank accounts, everything. The SS have them. They transferred to Himmel's control."

"I understand. I rather expected as much." One enormous weight lifted from Karl's mind. No further responsibility proceeded from that point for Reich funds. "Did they confiscate Father's personal and client accounts, too?"

Olson blinked. He stared wide-eyed and shook his head. "They couldn't have done so. They weren't here."

Henry nodded as if he understood, begging his breathing to quiet. "Then where are they?"

"Switzerland mostly, and some in Portugal. He only kept a working account in Munich."

"I've been to a bank in Zurich for Father. I remember where it is. Do you think they would honor my access to his accounts?"

With a huff, Olson spread his hands. "Naturally. Just give them the account numbers. They will not forget the only son of Herr Dietrich von Steuben."

"But I don't have the numbers." Henry tried to keep the pleading from his voice.

"Ah, well." Muttering, he seemed to be casting about for something. "That fatherless sergeant even took my gold pen." Opening his top drawer, he stared at the broken pencil leads and bent paper clips which collected in such spaces.

"A pen?" Henry flipped open his briefcase and withdrew pen and paper. Attempting smoothness, he endeavored not to do anything which would startle the old man.

"Um, yes. This one..." He drew a line of numbers, his gnarled hand barely up to the task. "...and the second...and the third. Then in Portugal we have these accounts in the bank, and our corresponding investment firm... Heavens, that number...I cannot..."

Squinting, covering his mouth with a boney hand, Herr Olson endured obvious stress. Henry wanted to tell him not to worry, but this might be his sole chance to get the information.

"Ah, yes! I remember now. The reversal of your mother's given names in numbers." He wrote the line from end to beginning, calling out the numbers as if they were letters. "One, fourteen, fourteen, one..."

"Anna." Henry touched the cross on his neck. His eyes stung for a moment.

"There. If you don't mind, I'd like to retire. My letter of resignation is on your father's desk with his mail."

"You've earned the right, my dear Herr Olson." Henry scanned the bare office, wishing he had a fine retirement gift for the faithful servant.

"Here is the front door key. It has been a pleasure serving von Steuben Investments, sir. I shall be at home if you need me."

They shook hands soberly, though Henry would have preferred to embrace his mentor. He accompanied Olson down the stairs.

"Herr Olson, may I please ask a favor?"

"Anything, sir."

"Do not mention to anyone that I was here. It's best for now."

Olson cracked a smile. "Whom should I tell? No one would believe me. Don't want people to think I'm crazy."

CHAPTER THIRTY-TWO

19 August, 1946
Munich, Germany

IN HIS FATHER'S office he found Herr Olson's dusty letter of resignation, written the week of the SS raid, and a leather-bound tray full of mail. So strange to be in this room without Father and the bustle of business on every board. He whipped his handkerchief across the royal chair, sat down, and pulled the letter box close.

Hours later, dazed, he had only begun to understand Father's responsibilities and methods of doing business. Skipping a meal left him hungry, thirsty, and light-headed. He needed food, but dared not eat in this neighborhood. Herr Olson recognized him in less than two seconds.

Did he trust the water in these pipes? Better not take a chance. Weighing the danger of being found with mail from the firm, he decided to leave it there instead. In the eerie near-dark of the August night, he caught a bus back to the Army hotel.

The urge to walk hit hard after a quick meal in its cafeteria-like restaurant. A run spent more nervous energy, but he thought better walking. The experience of finding Herr Olson and everything he learned today formed a thundercloud in his mind. Through the gathering wind of his mind, lightning struck. He had been so surprised and thrilled about a link to his inheritance that he didn't ask the questions of greatest importance. Was Father ever involved in the Circle of Friends of Himmler? Herr Olson mentioned Speer. Were Frick and Himmler clients of von Steuben Investments?

While he didn't think so, Father handled everything to do with the Reich funds and that whole tier of investors. If he had lived, he would not be touched by charges against Speer of slave labor and cruelty for armament production. But what of the money involved in such projects? The money generated to support the rise of Himmler? And where was that money today?

Worse yet, had Father co-mingled Axis funds with his own?

The most direct route to an answer lay with Herr Olson, if his mind could release those answers.

Henry looked with longing at the empty bed. The first night alone since their marriage. He hoped not to have many in the next fifty years.

After a miserable attempt at sleep, he had a light breakfast in a room of strangers. He borrowed a liter milk bottle, filled it with tap water, and wrapped bread and cheese in a napkin.

With brief confusion, he reached Herr Olson's home. The sturdy stone walls supported crisscrossed wood beams over plaster, much like his own house. Conformity ruled in Munich architecture. Ivy writhed upwards, cut away for the entrance. He knocked and waited, fighting the bubble in his throat.

An elderly butler opened the door and invited him into the front room.

Henry turned toward quick footsteps as Frau Olson bustled in.

"Karl. I can't believe it. Herr Olson told me you came to the firm, but it made no sense at all. Part of the time he seemed to think you were Karl's ghost." She gripped his shoulders, and tears pooled behind her bifocals.

He responded by embracing her, an action almost unheard of in this culture. "My dear lady, what a pleasure to see you again. Are you well?"

"As well as can be, considering the times we live in. Herr Olson, *ach*, he has his good days." She touched her head and then let her fingers butterfly away. "Ah, how I loved your mother and father. And you two children. Now only you are left."

"What did you hear of them, Frau Olson? Did you know for sure where they were taken?"

"The SS told us nothing. We thought they were taken to Auschwitz. So many...*people*...went there. But she was American, wasn't she? Could they take her prisoner?"

"I'm researching the matter now. Thus far I have no confirmation of her imprisonment or death at Auschwitz." He dared not mention the new information about Dachau, a mere fifteen kilometers from here.

"Might she be...?" She looked toward the window, eyebrows raised in speculation or maybe hope.

"Some people lived through the death camps. But if she and Marta were alive, I think they would have come to Herr Olson first. They would need support. Income to live on."

Herr Olson, straight-backed and fully dressed, joined the commotion. His clouded brow changed to an open expression of wonder.

Karl offered his hand, and Olson's expression warmed with the firm greeting. "Yesterday...I wasn't sure. But it really happened."

"Yes, sir. I'm not a ghost. I'm a man with a lot of questions."

"In that case, have a seat." He motioned to overstuffed chairs facing each other near the fireplace. They settled on opposite sides of a tea table which rested upon a thin, antique carpet.

"I'll let you men talk business." Frau Olson requested that the butler bring coffee, and she receded.

"What would you like to know?" The clarity in his blue eyes replaced the muddled expression of yesterday.

"My questions are personal, and I require unbiased answers." To ask for honesty would be an insult.

Herr Olson nodded. "Of course."

"Was my father or anyone at von Steuben Investments involved with the Circle of Friends of Himmler?"

The question slapped Olson's face back. "Never. Impossible."

The answer Karl passionately desired, but he needed substantiation. "How can this be proved if, for example, a legal charge were levied?"

"You cannot prove a negative, my son—pardon me, I should say 'Herr von Steuben.'"

A smile broke the tension of Karl's brow. "Herr Olson, to be called your son...that is the higher honorific." Karl wished for the sort of American relationship which allowed him to openly express his admiration.

Olson's color warmed and his eyes filled with liquid. "Be that as it may... It would not be too strong to say your father despised that weasely little Frick. You're aware he was author of the Nuremberg Race Laws?"

Karl nodded. Facts of history converged in his mind as personal life realities.

Olson's voice grew stronger with each point. "Himmel controlled the SS, which persecuted many nationalities as well as

[331]

the Jewish people. When your father refused to do even the expected interchanges with them or their peers, he came under close scrutiny. In retrospect, I've often thought Himmel ordered the...shall we say 'audit' of the firm, as a manner of discipline. Punishment of non-support."

"I understand." Karl mulled while the butler served coffee and a small cinnamon treat. He inhaled the fragrance as he lifted the gold-rimmed porcelain cup. "Umm. Real coffee. Delicious."

Olson smiled. "For special guests."

When they were alone again, Karl rested his saucer on the small table between them.

Olson cleared his throat. "On the same day your father had the heart attack and passed away, the SS raided the firm. No charges were brought and no arrests were made. Not even Himmel nor Speer found basis of wrong doing, in neither personal nor Reich accounts. Your father was impeccably honest."

"Then they found no mismanagement, no comingling of funds, nothing hinting of..." Karl dared to whisper, "...embezzlement."

Olson took a final swallow, rattling his cup on the saucer, and gave a tight smile. "I'm not in jail."

"What of the other employees? Are you still in contact with them?"

A squint and faraway look overtook Olson.

Karl waited.

"After a few days, they quit coming back. First the men, then the secretaries." Olson went silent, staring into the cold fireplace.

Karl did not want to lose him in the present. "Do you have their addresses, sir?"

Olson turned to him with eyes wide.

"Sir, do you have any way to contact the former employees?"

"They all left. Only I remained. I never left."

Clearly, the window to Olson's mind had closed. Karl made another couple of attempts at conversation to no avail.

The butler returned with the posture of a sentinel. Karl looked up at him and gave a slight shrug. The butler nodded, collected their cups, and left.

Karl stood when Frau Olson scurried in with a smile which did not reach her eyes. "*Ach du,* I'm afraid he's drifted off. It's time for his morning nap." She twittered a little laugh. "He pretends he's reading the paper, but one can't read with one's eyes closed."

"I must go. I hope I haven't caused a strain."

"Not at all, my dear. Please come back at any time." She walked Karl to the front door. "I'm so glad you're…alive. There's hope yet."

"Hope?"

"For the continuance of the firm. For…honest businessmen in the reconstruction."

"God in Heaven will always leave himself a remnant." He accepted his hat and satchel from the butler. "Good day, Frau Olson."

Stepping into brilliant sunlight, Karl decided to spend the rest of the morning at the firm. A few blocks away, he turned to the brick building, let himself in, and relocked the front door.

Dust rolled at his feet. His shoe prints led upstairs to the mail on Father's desk. Resuming his task, he opened requests of clients to withdraw funds and wondered if any action had been taken. The oldest envelopes lay on top of the stack, arranged in order of date. Curious. He would have expected the opposite.

Pulled back by his grumbling stomach, he ate his provisions and drank tepid water.

A couple of hours deeper, a letter from the municipal government came to light. He read with increased concern. A tax bill on the house, unpaid and overdue, left the city no recourse but to sell the property at auction.

Panicked, he noted the message had been sent over a month ago. The auction date—he pulled a calendar card from his briefcase—would be Friday. Three days to stop the sale of the home to four generations of von Steubens.

Anxiety pushed him from the desk. He paced to his own former work space, a cubicle in the back. Ceiling plaster trashed the room but the outside wall had sustained the bomb blast. From the window, he saw the rubble which remained of the building behind. He returned to the center of the hallway and mounted the stairs to the third floor.

The gaping corner hole evident on his visit to Munich as a German soldier had been walled off and patched by someone who knew nothing of roofs and ceilings. Water damage had caused wood to rot and plaster to crumble. While most of the trash had been cleared, birds' nests and rat pills occupied that end of the floor.

At the opposite end, though, filing cabinets and boxes slept under tarpaulins. Formed in rows with little space between, the stacks stood about head high. Karl assumed everything had been confiscated by the SS, and nothing had been returned. With a whole heart attack's worth of hope, curiosity, and fear, he approached the columns.

Testing a cabinet, he found it unlocked. Files in order recorded all utility payments and matters up to the time of the audit in October, 1944. These would have come from the office of the building and personnel manager. The next cabinet, though, contained files of a junior officer of the firm, a peer of Karl's. Next a box of stationary and supplies. He searched for the employee records. First, he needed light.

He'd never tried the switch. He had assumed... He twisted the round knob until it clicked, and was rewarded with electricity. So Herr Olson paid the bills. More to research about that later.

He raced downstairs to Olson's large mahogany file cabinet which matched his fine partner's desk. Locked, but small keys on the ring opened them. There, in perfect order, folders showed all operations performed since the audit. With this Germanic precision at hand, Karl had the information he needed. If he reached even a few of the former staff, he could organize this place, get it repaired, cleaned, and running again.

Think, Karl. You cannot go in all directions at the same time.

Three days to save the house. He had to have money. Though he did not know how much, funds waited for him a short train ride away.

He must go to Switzerland.

CHAPTER THIRTY-THREE

21 August, 1946
Zurich, Switzerland

HENRY STARED AT a book, hoping the other train passengers attributed the quiver of his hands to a night of binge drinking. Anything but the truth.

His phone call to Capt. Bill from the Army hotel reported he had found new documents, new information, and had made valuable personal contacts in the Munich financial world.

When asked for details, Henry expressed doubt of the Army phone line security and promised a written report at his return. He didn't mention this trip to Zurich. Today he was AWOL but not still in the Army. Was that a crime?

He touched his passport resting inside his suit pocket. Henry's details with his own photo and fingerprints. That was a crime.

In Switzerland as Henry, he had no identification as Karl. He brought with him the account numbers and a fervent hope to be remembered by the senior officer from over two years ago. If he still lived and worked there.

Switzerland. Such a reasonable country in which to do business. Passage through customs gave Henry confidence to proceed to the bank as Karl.

From his train window, he witnessed the difference from bombed-out, crumbled Germany to an untouched, pristine land. Stepping onto the street to catch a taxi was a magical experience. The city bustled with business. While the Swiss people had never been issued public smiles, they moved about with dignity and purpose unrelated to destruction.

Karl found the bank exactly where he left it, standing tall and reflecting sunlight from its white marble exterior. He paused and sent up a prayer in the space of time to check his tie. He removed his hat, corrected his posture, and entered with a nod to the guard.

He scanned the bank floor for Herr Kramer, attracting the attention of someone about his own age. Not having a business card, he had written the three account numbers and his name on a rectangle of good stationary, which he offered the man. "Is Herr Kramer still associated with the bank?"

"Indeed. Do you have an appointment?"

"I am afraid his contact information was misplaced during the war. I have come from Munich. Would it be possible to confer briefly with Herr Kramer today?"

"I shall ask. Please be seated." He motioned to a comfortable-looking lobby chair.

Karl pretended to relax. This was when the nice guard would come over and request that he accompany him without a struggle. Or the lock clunked together and alarms sounded. Karl imagined every possible complication within the ten minutes before the young man returned, inviting him through the heavy double doors and upstairs.

Breathing again, he was led to a grand office with a fine Persian carpet and burgundy velvet curtains.

Herr Kramer stood from his massive desk. His expression was inscrutable, but he bore the semblance of at least recognizing Karl. "Good day, Herr von Steuben. I admit to being surprised by your visit."

Karl shook his hand and accepted a chair. Herr Kramer joined him in its match in front of the desk.

"Perhaps you heard I was killed in the service of my country."

"Quite right. We sent letters to von Steuben Investments, and even had someone inquire independently about our clients. That was, in fact, the answer we received."

"Then you know Father died of a heart attack. I am still searching for my mother and sister. The word to date is not encouraging." Karl ran his fingers around his hat, hiding his emotions behind the moment's formality.

"I understand. What can we do for you today?"

"I would like to have a statement of the three accounts I know about with your bank, information on any other financial relationships, and then I would like to make a withdrawal and set up a secure process for future transfers."

Calm. Be calm. This was where it either worked or trouble began.

"Naturally. No doubt you will want access to your father's safety deposit box."

Karl swallowed. "I was not aware he had one at this bank."

"Your father was a wise and practical man. He gave me, as account manager, a copy of his will and instruction that any of the three who survived him would have equal and immediate rights to the accounts without delay of probate. Regrettably, I have appointments all day. May I give you a conference room and offer the services of Herr Schneider, the young man you have already met? He will be able to assist you with any arrangements you desire."

"Excellent. I appreciate the service of the bank, sir." He glanced at his American watch, the gift from Grace. He released Herr Kramer before eleven.

Seated in a small room with a cup of strong, real coffee, he spread the three statements. The amounts staggered him. Never before had a number been attached to Father's wealth. More waited somewhere in Portugal, a matter yet to be researched. He pushed away from the table and paced at the window, propping on its facing from time to time.

Schneider fidgeted with his gold pen, leaned over the table and then straightened. "Sir, what may I do to assist you?"

Karl stopped, legs braced apart, and faced him. "So many decisions. Here's what I'm thinking. I need to return with currency. Ten thousand U.S. dollars should be adequate."

Schneider scribbled a note and looked up as ready to please as an eager puppy.

"I wish to establish a written understanding, shall we say, that there will be future transfers to a German bank account in the name of a certain American, Henry Viertel. He has been most helpful through postwar difficulties, and I think he will agree to assist."

Schneider took down all the pertinent data, including Viertel's address in Nuremberg.

"Eventually, I shall set up a German account in my own name."

"Of course."

"Now let us take a look at the safety box."

[339]

Karl and Herr Schneider descended to the bank's catacombs. In the steel drawer, Karl found a copy of his father's will, various documents and deeds and several sentimental surprises. Grandfather's wire-rimmed glasses, his grandparents' wedding bands, and a delicate lidded porcelain dish about two centimeters across. Lifting the lid, he found baby teeth. His and Marta's? Father, the formidable bear, saved their baby teeth in a Swiss secure box. Karl chuckled even as his mouth twisted with emotion.

Wednesday, 21 August, 1946
Munich, Germany

RETURNING FROM ZURICH, Karl buried himself in the files, folders, and flotsam of the firm. Entirely too late that night, he visited the home of one of its respected officers, Walter Peters, whose address he had located in the third floor storage. An intelligent man in his forties, Peters had good managerial skills.

After going through the "I thought you were dead" conversation yet again, Karl asked him if he would be interested in helping to rejuvenate the firm.

The light of opportunity shone in his eyes. "Would I be willing to give up my dead-end accounting job for a small-minded, unappreciative boss and help you restart von Steuben Investments?"

Karl resisted the urge to push. He believed Peters' story that he had left the firm when the SS threatened the lives of his family. The scenario rang true to how the SS did business.

"Will I be paid?"

"Certainly. We will discuss your salary and that of the people you will hire. If you were not fully compensated for your service before, we will cover outstandings as well."

Peters laughed out loud. "Then I'm on. Give me a week to resign with honor, and I'm your man."

Karl outlined his general thoughts, beginning with the mundane repair of the building to his concept of business through the reconstruction period. Exchange and transatlantic commerce ideas came last.

Sometime after one a.m., Karl shared with Peters his interest in bringing to justice the Circle of Friends of Himmler, and specifically Frick. If Peters had been enthusiastic before, he now took on the fervor of searching for the Holy Grail. Karl had chosen his partner well.

Picking up the Army hotel phone the following morning, Karl returned to his Henry persona. Smiling to himself, he reasoned that he was not schizophrenic if he really was two people.

"Good morning, Captain. Here I find good *stoff* for you." *Get back into English.* "We have a treasure trove of information from one particular financial group. They maintained complete separation from the Circle due to their anti-Nazi position, and they are prepared now to point fingers and name names."

"Pouch it to me."

Henry had nothing to pouch. Most of this remained hearsay. "Give me more time to round up solid proof, sir. I can tell you where to look, but I do not have the authority to march into those buildings and confiscate the materials."

"Are you suggesting that you want to continue in Munich for a while longer?"

Henry's business in Munich pulled at his heart, which remained with Grace in Nuremberg. "No, sir. I prefer to come home and let investigators and lawyers take over. I have to be with Grace."

"I understand."

"GRACE, YOU HAVE a long distance phone call."

She excused herself from her patient and rushed to the nurses' desk. "Hello?" The line crackled.

"Grace, darling, it's wonderful to hear your voice."

"I've missed you so much. How could a few days be so long?"

"I cannot imagine how I did without you before. When I return Friday afternoon, we will be together all weekend."

"Do you have to go back?" Her voice went up a pitch.

"Not at this time. And perhaps you can come down with me when I do." Even as he spoke the words, Henry wondered if the plans of his alter-ego would countermand what he said to Grace now. He worked for control like a concert director trying to synchronize unruly strings and oboes.

"But I can't take off from the hospital."

"Let's watch for the next three day weekend. You would love Munich. Bavaria is much friendlier than the north. You're a Southern girl. You should relate to that."

"Darling, I just want you back home. I miss you so." To her embarrassment, she began to cry. What was wrong? She had been so blue and emotional this week.

They hung up, exchanging train schedule information and tender words of love. Chuckles came with thinly veiled suggestions for their weekend together.

HENRY APPROACHED A long counter in the tax office of the Munich City Hall with a folder of cash strapped under his shirt.

Speaking through a cut circle in the glass separating citizens from clerks, he attempted to pay the back taxes on his family home.

"You must show up at the auction tomorrow morning in the city auditorium." The attendant's cold rebuff bore total disinterest.

"But it's my ancestral home. My father died, my mother and sister were taken prisoners. No one existed to pay the taxes." The stronger he argued, the more recalcitrant the clerk appeared.

"I didn't make the law. The house will be sold tomorrow, and you will have the right to bid like everyone else." She turned from the counter and left the area.

Henry's breakfast burned in his stomach. He fought the urge to throw chairs, to break the window and crawl over the divider. Only the knowledge that an arrest would bring down his whole sham of a double life kept him on the side reserved for the powerless.

The Nuremberg Laws he fought against included taxation of Jews more than other German citizens. He would get his revenge legally, even if he had to buy back his own home.

Karl, masquerading again as Henry, tore out of the building in a fury. While Himmel and Hitler roasted in hell, he went after Frick, Speer, and all their rich and powerful cronies.

Knowing he would be recognized in the bank with which Father had always done business, he went instead to a shiny new American institution and established an account in the name of Henry and Grace Viertel. To this he instructed the Zurich bank to transfer immediately available funds. He visualized young Herr Schneider choking, blinking, and signing his approval. A von Steuben got the kind of service which the Henry Viertels of the world could only dream about.

Still angry, he locked himself in the firm until his eyes burned like hot lava rocks. After dinner time for Walter Peters' family, Karl picked through Walter's brain for facts, impressions, anything which might lead to hard evidence against Frick. He wanted the whole Circle indicted, given a fair trial, and hanged.

"Hire back anyone you trust completely, and no one else. For right now, do this in your own name. My existence must be a secret."

ANNA VON STEUBEN allowed the night air to blow in her face, mussing her hair. She lifted the bus window when lightning struck and released torrents as if a bowl of rain had been broken. Traveling overnight, they should arrive by eight-thirty, saving the expense of a hotel. "Remember the icy night we took this bus to Helga's?"

Marta nodded. "I was sure we were going to be arrested any minute."

"How strange to go back into Munich now."

"Crazy, you mean." She leaned close to her mother's ear. "We drugged a doctor and stole his car. We don't even know if he survived."

She patted Marta's hand. "We escaped from a prison camp. That's what it was, even if it was a hospital. That isn't illegal anymore."

"You believe what you read in the papers? For all we know, the newspaper's tax auction notice may have been printed to lure us back."

"I've prayed about this trip for weeks now. I feel led to go. You don't have to. You can return to Helga's. If I'm caught, you know I'd die before telling on you or Helga's family, God bless them."

"No. I'm not going to hide out on a farm for the rest of my life."

The bus groaned to a stop and maneuvered around a bomb crater, bumping, sometimes sliding in the mud over a worn path off the road. A baby cried in the back, and a gentleman stood to watch out the window.

When they were rolling again, Marta leaned close. "There's nothing in the house to sell. You saw how it had been looted. Besides, there isn't time enough to do anything to stop the sale. We should have come last week."

Anna gave the barest nod. But last week, she wasn't sure. This week, her mind had become infused with ideas, a conviction that she must go. God's answer to her plea for direction. Good enough for her, but not proof for Marta.

Awakened by the bus's lurch, she rocked against her daughter. The bus tipped to the right rear. Passengers stirred and called out. The driver's stream of curses caused her to fear the worst.

He left the bus, as did other men.

Marta went to the window and peered into the dark. "They've got a couple of flashlights. It's raining so. All I can see is a big hole. I think the back wheel dropped into it."

Anna's tears slipped from behind closed lids. She whispered a prayer. "Your will, not mine, be done."

ANNA AND MARTA reached the Munich bus station under a cloud of doom. Too late. They never had a chance.

Marta's stomach grumbled like an angry dog. "Didn't matter. We had no money anyway."

"I hoped… Maybe if we came and pleaded with the tax people. Your father's name used to be golden in this city. I just needed one favor."

They bought two crusty rolls with cheese and a bottle of milk and ate in the crowded station, watching dripping passengers rush about over the wet concrete floor.

Anna brushed crumbs into the paper wrapping. "Let's go to the tax office anyway. See what we can find out."

There a stone-faced clerk deigned to listen to her plea. "I came to inquire about my home. We traveled so far, but the bus…"

The woman shuffled some papers. "Hmm. The one on Rosenheimer Strasse. It was sold for back taxes this morning."

"But the house had been in my husband's family for four generations. Isn't there something—"

"*Ja*, I've heard that before." She turned to a scuffed desk behind her and picked up a folder. "Some American bought it. Henry Viertel. Talk to him."

"How would I reach him?"

Marta touched her hand on the ledge. "Mother, there's no point…"

"Well, here's his address. It's in Nuremberg. No phone number."

Anna controlled her desperation until they got outside. She and Marta clung together and cried in the drizzle, ignoring the staring passersby. Then they shuffled away with their cardboard suitcase to look for a cheap room for the night.

HENRY CALLED GRACE'S hospital again from a telephone office near the Munich Municipal Hall. "Sweetheart, I need you to come to Munich this weekend. How soon can you get off? Trains leave at two, four, and six—"

"Honey, wait a minute. I can't leave here until four. I'd have to go to our apartment and pack a bag. Aren't you coming home tonight?"

Henry took a deep breath. He pushed Grace and she didn't understand why. "Grace, sweetheart, I'll meet you at the Munich train station at any hour you name. I left a little money under the mattress. Finish the shift if you must. Tell your head nurse you're sick, but please come to Munich for the weekend. I'll explain everything when you get here."

Even as he said the words, he doubted their truth. Sooner or later, though, he would have to tell Grace whom she had married.

CHAPTER THIRTY-FOUR

23 August, 1946
Nuremberg, Germany

GRACE DIDN'T HAVE to fake being sick to get off early. Two days of general malaise condensed into an hour of throwing up at work this morning, and she thought she knew why. So much for postponing children until they saved enough money for Henry to go to college. If she couldn't work, how would they survive?

She placed a warming hand over her lower abdomen. Henry's baby. A thrill coursed through her middle, piercing the grip of nausea, and she smiled. She'd carry her secret to Munich on the six o'clock train. Two could play this game.

She stepped off the train into his embrace, and they held each other for a long, long time. Long enough to calm from the rush home, taxi to the station, and a two hour ride by train.

"I'm so glad you came. Thank you, darling. We'll have a weekend honeymoon in the most beautiful city in Germany."

"Being in your arms made the trip worthwhile." Here she belonged.

He kissed her in that public way that left her unsatisfied. Then he glanced both ways and gave her the kiss she needed.

She laughed and pushed away.

Picking up her suitcase, he walked with an arm at her waist to the taxi stand.

More expense, but she determined not to let worry about the costs spoil their getaway. They were both on a salary, at least for a while.

To her surprise, the taxi delivered them to a regal hotel lit brighter than the old Fox Theater in Atlanta. "Can we afford this?"

Her whisper of caution triggered a chuckle from Henry. They bypassed the registration desk, and he led her to a first floor suite.

"Darling, I've never seen a hotel room like this. Carpets, a sofa, why, there's even a fireplace. And velvet drapes." She went to the window. A fountain danced in a rose garden just a few yards away. "This is better than our bridal suite in Atlanta."

"Shall we go to dinner? We have reservations in fifteen minutes."

Grace had so many questions, but she knew he always timed everything down to the minute. "Is the government paying you that well?" He had told her his salary when they shared all their plans to save for the future, but maybe this assignment in Munich ranked above the translator job.

"No, they're not paying me this well." Henry chuckled again, seeming to enjoy her amazement. "But you have nothing to fear. Remember I told you long ago that I have a plan?"

Ice ran down her backbone. She had heard of bribes to government officials, kick-backs and smuggling on diplomatic passports. *Please, God, not Henry.* She would choose honorable poverty any day.

"What's the matter, sweetheart?"

"Is this legal? Is it honest?"

He sobered, wincing as if he took offense. He placed both hands on her shoulders. "Yes, Grace. It is honest, it is legal, and it is ours. Now let's get to dinner and I will explain later."

But he didn't. After an elegant candlelit meal, they crumbled together in the beautiful suite. He didn't tell her his secrets, and she didn't tell him hers.

GRACE DRESSED FOR breakfast and an outing, as Henry called it, for which comfortable shoes would be appropriate. While he enjoyed boiled eggs, thinly sliced meats and cheeses, she tried not to get sick eating a *brotchen* and jam. She didn't want to throw up on the white tablecloth and fine china. Nor tell him she was expecting in a room full of polite hotel guests. She fixated on his boyish grin with double dimples to get her mind off her own stomach.

In the taxi, he rattled off an address in German. She felt as if he were leading her blindfolded into a room. He would rip off the cloth and yell, "Surprise!" and then she would understand. But every time he pulled out his wallet and peeled off a few bills, she had a sinking sensation the surprise had a dark side.

The taxi arrived at a massive, old house, terribly Germanic with its stone base, white plaster top, and crisscrossed beams. Inside a low fence and gate at the sidewalk, weeds brushed her dress. Henry paid the driver and asked him to return in a half hour. He pushed open the gate and scraped a key into the door's heavy padlock.

Turning, he swooped her off her feet, triggering her shriek of surprise.

Henry laughed and stepped over the threshold. "Welcome to my ancestral home, sweetheart. I bought it yesterday." He allowed her to slip to the floor and stand in his arms. He lowered his lips to hers, but she broke off his kiss. "You what?"

He closed the front door and lit the electric chandeliers hanging from the ceiling two stories above. The enormous monstrosity of a house, barren but for a blanket of dust, sprawled from where they stood to the shadowy stairs and railed passageway on the next floor.

Running his fingers through his thick hair, in need of a cut badly enough to curl, he seemed to cast about looking for a place to start.

She prompted him. "Your ancestral home?"

He inhaled deeply. "I was…" He blew out the air and tried again. "My family lived here for four generations. I wish you had seen this place with all its furnishings, carpets—"

"Never mind the house, Henry. What are you saying?" Her voice bit with unusual harshness. This wasn't a cute game.

He took her hands in his, his expression urgent, almost pleading. "Darling, I am American, but I am also German. My name is not Henry Viertel."

Grace searched his face, hoping to see the smile of a breaking joke. The tension, communicated by both his eyes and his hands gripping hers, robbed her of any simple explanation. "What do you mean, you're not Henry Viertel?"

What she wanted to ask was, *If you're not Henry Viertel, then who am I?* One hand pulled away and dropped to that very warm place swelling with the new life of their child.

"I was reared in this home. In May, over two years ago, I was captured and forcibly conscripted into the Army. The German Army." He led her to the bottom landing of the stairs. "My father had a heart attack and died right here the day my mother and sister were taken to a death camp."

Numbed to the extent that she thought this couldn't be happening, she sank onto a step to keep from collapsing.

He sat beside her. "I made my way to the American Army, but was wounded. Eventually, I got to the United States and started life over again. You are all I have, Grace. The only family, the only thing that matters at all."

She leaned back to avoid his intended caress. *Not Henry? Married to a German? Our nights of passion... Now pregnant by this charlatan?*

"Come, sweetheart, I want to show you something upstairs." He bounded away.

Someone rapped on the door. They stood, him on the second floor and she half way, his upturned brow reflecting questions as well. She descended and opened the massive door a few inches.

"*Guten morgen—*" A woman with greying hair, wearing a thin smile and simple cotton dress, began to speak.

"Use your English, Mother." The younger woman at her side corrected her.

"Yes. Good morning. Are you Mrs. Viertel?" Unaccented, American diction.

The humble posture and polite voice dispelled fear, but in Grace's confusion she didn't know how to reply. Henry had just told her he wasn't Henry, so who was she? Nevertheless, she nodded and pulled the door wider.

Henry tapped down the stairs as the women gazed into the entrance.

They gasped. Henry stopped behind Grace, his sudden intake of breath setting off warnings. What startled him so?

"Mother!" He rushed forward, brushing past Grace. "Marta!" He threw his arms around the two women.

"My son, my son. I thought you were dead." The woman sobbed and held onto Henry. She sagged against his arms, and might have fallen if he had not supported her.

The three rocked and swayed together.

"Karl? I can't believe it. How did this happen?" The younger woman grasped his face and cried.

Grace backed away, horrified by her whole world spinning out of control. Her stomach roiled, reminding her of the baby she carried, and her hand went to her abdomen rather than her stomach. In desperation, she searched for a bathroom. Pushing open a door, she found the kitchen and rushed to its enormous sink. A few moments later she hung on its edge and ran water for her face. *Whose baby? My baby, and I will protect this child.*

Henry rushed to her side and put an arm around her. "Sweetheart, what's the matter? Are you sick?"

The women came behind him. "I'm a nurse. Can I help you?" The one he called his mother spoke in a comforting voice.

"She is, too. Mother, this is my wife, Grace. We've been married about seven weeks. Grace, please meet my mother, Anna von Steuben, and my sister, Marta."

CHAPTER THIRTY-FIVE

24 August, 1946
The von Steuben Home, Munich, Germany

ANNA? THE NAME engraved on the back of Henry's gold cross?

Grace mumbled some greeting, not offering her wet hand. Water dripped onto her silk blouse.

His mother offered Henry's handkerchief, though already dampened by tears. "This must be a terrible shock for you."

"Von what?"

"Darling, my name is Karl von Steuben. That's what I brought you here to tell you. I escaped from Germany as a wounded American soldier."

"Then the whole story about amnesia is a complete fabrication?" Anger rose, adding to the burn in her throat from the vomit. He lied to her, to her parents, and now she was pregnant by a German man she didn't know.

"Not exactly." He stammered and found nothing to do with his hands. "I experienced profound amnesia for several weeks. I didn't know I was *not* Henry Viertel. When my memory gradually returned, I had been rescued by the American Army and was already serving as a translator and interrogator."

"Then who is Henry Viertel?"

His mother and sister turned questioning brows to him also.

"A dead American soldier, a radioman at the Siegfried Line, where I crossed into American-occupied territory."

The von Steuben women looked to each other as if they were as puzzled as she. That expression dissolved as his mother touched the long scar high across his forehead. "Oh, my dear child. What have you been through?" She tip-toed and bent his head down to receive her kiss on the white line.

But Grace was both puzzled and angry. She had been deceived into marriage by a stranger. Even last night's passion had been under false pretenses.

THE TAXI'S HORN interrupted their confusion.

Karl had almost forgotten the driver had been instructed to return in a half hour. It seemed only a few minutes had passed. "There's so much more... Come, let me show you who I am." He ushered them to the car and gave the driver another address.

They pulled up in front of the three-story brick building with decorative scrolls, though its paint was peeling. Karl glowed inside with pride. Von Steuben Investments stood like a once-beautiful cake with gilt decorations, albeit with a back corner bitten off.

Karl ushered them inside, talking nonstop about his plans to re-enter the financial world of Europe and all the possibilities of currency exchange, investments, and portfolio management.

Grace looked dazed, and didn't seem to appreciate or even grasp what he showed her.

Upstairs, he told his mother and Marta about finding Herr Olson on duty at his desk. His mother smiled through yet another onslaught of tears, nodding at Herr Olson's faithfulness. "Beside your father, he was a pillar of the institution."

Karl recognized a light in Marta's eyes as they looked to the future of the firm.

"Marta, do you remember Walter Peters? I've hired him, starting next week, and he will help establish the company while I wrap up affairs elsewhere. And most importantly, use our connections in finance to garner evidence against Speer and Frick."

Grace wandered into his father's office.

Perhaps Karl had been talking too much about business. Grace didn't appear to understand what this meant to them as a couple.

He found her staring at the walls where the theft of diplomas and art left pale rectangles, and he took her hands in his. "I have already graduated college, my love, and was working as Father's junior officer during the war. I am fully accredited to do business in Europe, and plan to establish von Steuben Investments in America as well."

Rather than the relief he expected, she seemed near crying.

"You are a very wealthy woman, sweetheart. There is no longer any need for you to work."

"But…all my training. My career. I *enjoy* nursing."

"Yes, but when we have a family, you'll want to stay home with our children, won't you?"

Grace pulled away. "I'd like to go back to the hotel, please. I'm so tired."

"I am sure you can practice nursing in the Army hospital here. They certainly know about transfers."

"Please, not now. I can't think about that now."

"Of course, sweetheart. I understand." *How can she be that tired? I'm trying to show her our whole future opening up here. Guess that nausea is worse than I thought.*

Karl booked his mother and sister into a fine double room at their hotel, cautioning them to continue to use his alias for the present. "It will take a while to sort everything out."

When he arrived at their suite, Grace had closed the bedroom door. He assumed she was resting. Disappointed, he tried to read in their sitting room. Charged with fear, he paced and prayed instead, watching the afternoon dim with his hopes.

He heard her stirring about, so he knocked and entered.

She closed her suitcase. "I'm going back to Nuremberg. I've got a lot to figure out, like what my name is. I will not…share the bed of man who has lied to me about everything since we first met."

"Grace—no, please. I had no choice. It was the only way to escape. I thought the SS had killed Mother and Marta, and they would kill me, too." He embraced her. She stiffened against him but did not struggle.

"Mother was born and reared in America. She is from a Jewish family in Atlanta. But she is Christian. She had already converted before she met Father."

A new thought burst forth. The horrid, stupid prejudice. He bent to watch her expression. "Does it bother you that I descended from a Jewish mother?"

"What of your faith?" She flattened her hand against his breast bone. "What is in your heart, Henry? Or Karl, or whoever you are."

"I am Karl von Steuben. You are my beloved Grace von Steuben. I am Christian, as are my mother and sister, as was my father. German Lutheran, for generations."

[357]

"And what will I tell my father when I say we got the names wrong?"

Karl quirked a smile. "You can tell him I am a good provider."

"This isn't funny, K-Karl. I don't even know if we're legally married." She wailed this last and leaned into him with soul-rending sobs.

His fingers laced into her fine, blonde hair. She had always enjoyed that gentle cuddling, and he used it now. On the tightrope created by his duplicity, he employed every skill to maintain balance.

"Yes, my love, we are married. I checked with an American lawyer before I came back for the wedding. Shhh, Grace, please. I love you with all my heart."

"What about your job? Will you be arrested for impersonating an American soldier?" Her face twisted in agony. "You travel with a passport in his name. That can't be legal."

This had to be a hard a chasm for her to cross. "Step by step, sweetheart. I will proceed carefully. I have valuable information the government needs to indict war criminals. I think we can work something out."

She turned back to her suitcase. "Let me know when that happens. I'll be in Nuremberg. At least until I get passage to Atlanta." This last she finished weeping.

The blood drained to his feet. Spots flashed in his vision. He had to stall. He needed more time to explain. If she left, he ceased to exist. Surviving the war, reestablishing Father's firm, none of this was worth doing.

"Not tonight. You cannot leave tonight."

"And why not?"

Don't let her leave. Think of something! "There remains one more thing you must see. Tomorrow we will take a brief ride. I have hired a limousine and driver. Please, Grace, wait one more day."

"Give me a reason why I should go with you."

Her doubt stabbed his veins with ice. He had to convince her she had not made a terrible mistake by marrying him. He encircled her from behind and spoke against the softness of her bare neck. "Because you won't believe what I am going to show you if you don't see it with your own eyes."

She pushed away from him. "I won't sleep with you."

If he squeezed tighter, she would slip through his fingers like sand on the shore. He let her go.

"The bedroom is yours. I will sleep on the sitting room sofa."

KARL TELEPHONED HIS mother and Marta's room and asked them to meet him for dinner.

His mother paused so long he feared the line had dropped. "Karl, dear, we have nothing to wear in this hotel. We couldn't possibly eat in its restaurant."

"Careful, Mother," he replied. "*Henry* is going to come by and drop off enough to bankroll your new wardrobes." He hadn't needed as much cash as expected to buy back his home at auction. Not much more than the back taxes. Few families could support such a large house in this difficult postwar time. He split the cash from his pouch into three equal portions.

Responding to his knock, his mother pulled him in. "My son. I can hardly believe…"

He stepped into her hug and she held him close. When they backed apart, she again traced the white line of his scar with her eyes clouded by pain. They swiped away their tears.

Henry, clearing his throat and regaining restraint, offered her the cash. Surely enough to get his mother and sister into a fine clothing store.

Marta glanced from the money to his face and back again. "Are you sure you can spare this?"

A laugh escaped from its dungeon of more than three years. "It's your money, too. Yours and Mother's as much as mine."

He began to tell them about the trip to Zurich, then realized shops closed soon. "Go. Get a taxi. Buy things. I'll pick you up here for dinner at eight."

As the time drew near, he tapped on Grace's bedroom door.

"Yes?" Her muffled voice sounded as if he had waked her.

"Mother, Marta, and I are having dinner here at the hotel at eight. Would you like to eat with us?"

The rustle of linens, then her soft complaint. "No, I don't want anything."

With troubled heart, he crossed to his mother's room.

Mother's and Marta's new clothes had lifted their spirits. After more hugs—and Karl knew by now to bring extra handkerchiefs—they enjoyed a marvelous meal. He wished that Grace were with them.

"Let's take back something mild for Grace, like potato soup." Marta's care and common sense impressed Karl with her maturity. She had grown up in many ways during these awful years. Their time tonight convinced him of the need to become reacquainted with his sister.

They ordered a tray for Grace. Karl invited them back to his sitting room to continue talking.

Slipping in quietly, they didn't knock on Grace's door until room service came.

"Sweetheart, we have soup and toast for you. Won't you please join us out here?"

After a moment, she opened the door a crack. "I'm not up to getting dressed. Just hand me the soup."

His mother came near. "Do you have a housecoat? Don't get dressed, but won't you sit with us?"

Grace patted out, her feet bare and hair tumbled like a hunger-weakened waif. She tested the potato soup with care, either for its taste or her ability to keep it down. Gradually relaxing, she ate the warm, creamy food and a piece of toast.

Karl had directed the dinner discussion away from anything that might cause trouble if they were overheard. He could wait no longer to learn what his mother and sister had endured and how they had survived. "Mother, tell me what happened the day Father died."

His mother backed up her story to the day Karl left to find food. She recounted his father's heart attack, their imprisonment, transfer to work as nurses at the German hospital, and their escape to Helga's farm.

Hours later, physically and emotionally exhausted, they parted for sleep.

In the silence left behind, he turned to his wife. Without words, he came to her.

She allowed him an embrace. "I'm beginning to understand. A little. But there's so much... I'm still so...*angry*. I thought we knew each other. I believed we talked about *everything*. It was all lies. All of it."

He nodded without protest. "Please forgive me, Grace."

"I'm going back to bed now. We'll talk in the morning." She retreated into the bedroom. Alone.

CHAPTER THIRTY-SIX

Sunday morning
Munich, Germany

KARL SOMETIMES DOZED, but mostly he beat upon the gates of heaven. He confessed every sin of the past three years and he implored God to forgive him. As dawn broke, he stood at the window looking onto the rose garden whispering, "Grace. God in Heaven, please." *His Grace, God's grace. Nothing else matters. Your unmerited favor, Father God, and that of my precious wife, your undeserved gift.*

Taking his discrete turn in the bathroom, he shaved his haggard face and prepared for the ride.

ANNA ACHED FOR her son and his pretty, young wife. Their love had suffered a blow that many marriages could not survive.

She and Marta agreed last night after leaving Karl's suite that Grace was probably expecting. Besides the nausea and fatigue, she had the darker patch around her mouth which indicated that a woman was pregnant.

A grandchild. Might they be united as a family again?

Anna spotted Grace's suitcase in their sitting room when they gathered for the mysterious morning ride. Was there any way to influence her not to leave? Or should she remain silent and let them work it out? Being a mother-in-law gave her an unexpected role, one for which she was unprepared. One thing she knew to do, though, was pray.

Anna and Marta had kneeled in prayer for the couple late last night, on the deep carpet instead of prison concrete or farmhouse boards. In the cheerful light of morning, Anna continued her petitions in silence.

AFTER A PAINFULLY polite breakfast, the four von Steubens met their driver, waiting by the hired car in front of the hotel. The concierge had arranged a well-polished black Mercedes-Benz limousine. The proud, three-bladed hood ornament perched on its long, long engine cowling. A 1939 Pullman, it had been kept in good condition.

Karl gave instructions to the driver and they cruised west from Munich.

"I think it's time you tell us where we're going, Karl." Did Grace hit his name with intentional disdain?

Nodding, he slid the privacy screen to separate them from the driver's ears, and began the story with his forced inscription. He told how he had been charged with going to the various prison camps to collect gold. At the right point in the story, he pulled his mother's ornate cross from beneath his shirt.

She cried aloud and reached out.

"Grace gave me the chain as a wedding gift." He lifted the necklace off and passed it to his mother.

She held the treasure to her heart. "May I wear it?" She glanced from Karl to Grace.

"By all means. It's yours." Grace showed no hardness against his mother.

His story wound through the Bavarian hills as he recounted making the final trip with solid gold bricks to be delivered to the caves of Heilbronn. He answered volleys of questions, leaving the end of that adventure untold.

His tension mounted with every kilometer. His legs jiggled, crossed, and uncrossed with a will of their own. Would the gold bricks still be in the vault? Would Captain Bill come? What if the church were locked? But it was Sunday. He shook his head to throw off the fear of making a colossal error.

Grace turned toward him, brow upraised.

Karl extended his palm to her, both a question and a plea. She flipped a glance at his mother and Marta and then slipped hers in his. *Thank you, Jesus.*

During the last thirty kilometers, he told of riding a motorcycle to Aachen, crawling toward the Siegfried Line, changing uniforms with Henry Viertel, and receiving the head wound a few minutes after.

The autobahn to Heilbronn smoothed out while Karl summarized his life as an American soldier. This journey proved, he hoped, his loyalty to America and desire of justice for the persecuted Jews.

He opened the window to the driver. "We're almost there. Watch for a cemetery with a low stone wall, and then a small church. Quaint and beautiful. Really old."

The driver eased under a tree in the churchyard, shaded from the afternoon sun. A half-ton Army truck waited nearby.

Karl emerged with a wave to Capt. Bill and the "strong fellow you can trust" he had requested Bill to bring along.

"May I present my mother, Mrs. Anna von Steuben, and my sister, Marta."

Bill's eyebrows shot up.

Karl motioned to Bill. "Ladies, Captain Bill Hanson, my boss and closest friend."

Bill smiled and accepted their gentle handshakes. Then he introduced Gary, another fellow on their research team, to the ladies.

"Crowbars?" Bill had agreed to bring the tools without knowing their purpose.

He fetched three crowbars and three strong flashlights from the truck bed.

Karl led to the church and mounted the steps. The door opened. He called for the priest and checked in the vestry, but no one else was in the building.

The group ascended with him the three steps to the altar and then behind its table. They trespassed on holy ground. After removing a small carpet, he pulled up the trap door to the crypt.

The three men descended first. Grace, acting hesitant and weak, climbed down with all due care. Karl braced her by the waist and steadied her on the floor. Bill and Gary followed suit with his mother and Marta.

Karl noticed that the dust layer had been disturbed. "A new vault has been added." *How stupid not to come alone first.*

He turned, got his bearings, and led them to the vault in which his unit had left the treasure. "Over here."

Shining the light back and forth, he spotted scratches in the marble. A hard rock formed in his stomach. *New scratches, or were they made by my unit when we hid the bricks?*

Together the three men pried the lid and pushed sideways while the women held flashlights. When a golden gleam flashed back at Karl, he grinned and gave a sigh of relief. The dried and leathery priest had guarded the treasure well.

Bill's eyes popped at the sight. "Ahh."

"What the—?" Gary tripped forward on the carved base and caught himself on the vault rim.

His mother and Grace gasped. Marta inhaled and then choked and coughed. Whether they reacted to the cache or the cadaver he wasn't sure.

Karl lifted a golden brick. "Each one of these weighs fifteen kilos, over thirty pounds. There should be twenty of them."

Bill laughed. "Gonna be hard work getting these upstairs. Why didn't you request more men?"

"Too afraid the gold wouldn't be here. I would look such a fool."

Gary, flaunting his strength before the women, carried one in each hand. "So how much is a brick worth?"

Karl positioned gold blocks from the crypt to its top edge, keeping count and remembering the two tucked beneath the priest's robes. "Depending on the price of gold and exchange rate today, about twenty thousand dollars."

A murmur rose from the women, standing close together as the men began their task.

When all twenty bricks had been removed, Karl raised the priest's folded hands enough to work the pouch of gems from his prayerful vigilance and passed it to Grace.

"What's that?" As she closed her hand, the stones rolled about, making tiny rock sounds, begging to be released.

"Open and see." Karl waited for the moment of her discovery.

She loosened the string while Marta held the light. Both sucked in a breath as diamonds, emeralds, rubies—a fortune of precious gems tumbled into her palm.

Karl cupped his hands under hers. "Jewish gems, Grace. Stolen from thousands of people in the death camps. I fought the war for the Jewish people, too."

He looked to his mother then, not finding the words to express his love and understanding.

She nodded, leaving her chin a bit higher despite a flow of tears.

He was so proud of her. She and Marta had lived through rooms of hell he wasn't even ready to hear about yet.

The men toiled to the point of exhaustion carrying gold bricks to the truck. Later, removed from the others, Karl and Capt. Bill talked quietly while Gary chatted with the ladies and kept a watchful eye on Bill's truckload of gold and stones.

The time had come for Karl to level with the man he considered his best friend. Accepting whatever just punishment might result for his deceit, he organized his thoughts and controlled his voice timbre in an effort to prevent alarm. The message and manner were crucial. "Bill, do you remember the day, back at the field hospital, when I told you I didn't feel like my name was Henry?"

Bill squinted, his attention fully on Karl's face. He nodded.

"I was right. I'm not Henry Viertel. I'm a German-American, reared in Munich by a German father and an American mother of

Jewish descent." He waved to his mother and sister, standing out of earshot. "My name is Karl von Steuben. Until two days ago, I thought my mother and sister had been killed in Auschwitz."

Karl continued through the story outline. The uniform switch attempting to reach the American side, the battle injury, and amnesia. After years of increasing anguish, he relinquished the load.

Bill shoved his hands in his pockets and looked toward the women and Gary. "When did you know you weren't Henry Viertel?"

"The true amnesia lasted just a few weeks. By then I already interrogated prisoners and wanted to make my contribution as an American soldier. I had a purpose, don't you see? I thought my whole family was dead and my...shall we say *heritage*...destroyed. Nothing for which to go back."

Karl fought the bubble rising in his throat. "I almost confessed several times, even in England. But the chance to start over in the United States was such a prize. And I thought, well, that I had earned that right. Only...not as Henry. His family deserves my explanation and apology."

Bill listened so calmly that Karl wondered if he had suspicions before today. "I want you to sit down and write the whole thing out and pouch it to me. Do you have your passport with you?"

Karl fetched the false ID from the car and surrendered his identity as Henry Viertel, along with accumulated documents and notes pertinent to the Frick case. "Much more comes. I can do far greater for your investigation from here as Karl von Steuben than Henry Viertel could ever do."

Bill raised one eyebrow and nodded agreement. "Probably."

"I am dedicated to researching these criminals more than ever, and have personal resources and connections the U.S. Government can only dream about. I will continue, without pay, and will respond to your direction."

"Was Ilsa aware?"

"No. However, she won't be surprised. I'm sure she suspected something." Karl took care not to incriminate the one person who had cared during his lonely search for Mother and Marta.

Bill nodded toward the women. "And Grace?"

Heat washed Karl's cheeks, and he couldn't face Bill. "Not until this weekend. She had no idea."

"Well, you know how to reach me." Bill turned to go, then paused and looked back. "Don't come into the office. It would be considered a security breach."

"I understand."

"Since you're breaking contract, you'll have to pay for your passage over. Hers, too." He nodded toward Grace.

"Send me a bill. You'll have a check in dollars by return mail, or cash by Army pouch. Your choice. Oh, and Captain? Consider turning the valuables over to the Jewish National Fund. They help survivors resettle."

"Not up to me, but I'll pass along the information."

Grace approached from the hired limousine with her purse. Karl had a horrible premonition she intended to return with Bill and Gary to Nuremberg. She waivered, her indecision palpable as she looked from Karl to Bill to the Army truck.

In that moment, Bill shook hands with Karl, slapping his back in manly fashion. Neither man had dry eyes.

Bill turned to Grace. "Stay with this man. And take good care of him. You won't be sorry."

She flushed, bent her head, and allowed Karl to put an arm at her waist. Together they waved away Bill, Gary, and the whole U.S. Army.

KARL OBSERVED AT dinner how his mother and Marta reached out to Grace the way women do, pulling her into conversation and sometimes touching her arm. They asked about her family and her father's business, paying compliments at every opportunity. He appreciated their attempt to encircle her.

His mother's fondness for Atlanta and knowledge of the city brought out a discussion of its neighborhoods and wartime adjustments. "Do tell me the peach trees still flower along the avenue every spring." She discreetly signaled the waiter for more iced tea, which she had arranged especially for Grace.

"Oh, yes. They are as beautiful as ever. It wouldn't be Atlanta if Peachtree Street didn't bloom."

Ice cracked and popped as the waiter filled her glass. "The Chattahoochee ran high and wide last summer, didn't it, Hen—Karl?"

Their hours by its shores bloomed in his memory and brought a smile to his face. He touched her hand under the table. "We enjoyed a lot of cheap dates watching the river roll."

"Cheap dates? Since when were you a cheap date?" Marta teased her brother.

"Hey, I was a stock boy in the dime store, saving money to get another college degree. This lovely lady condescended to date me. What was I going to do?"

"Cheap dates?" Grace took back her fingers. "Was that what afternoons at the river meant to you?"

Karl squirmed, realizing his mistake. "The most beautiful days of my life, sweetheart. Money couldn't improve a picnic with you. Remember the daisies I cut for you? They were free, but precious."

She sipped her tea and offered no romantic response.

She's not eating much. This illness came at a bad time. Hoped she would be better today.

"Karl, would you help me telephone the hospital after dinner? I have to tell them I won't be at work tomorrow."

"Of course. We can call from the room."

"But won't that be more expen—never mind. I guess it doesn't matter anymore."

When they returned to their suite, Grace supplied the phone number, and he led her in the process of placing a long distance call. As the connection went through, he picked up a newspaper and pretended not to listen.

"I won't be at work tomorrow. I'm sick and, well, haven't been able to return from Munich." She hunched over the phone. He imagined how difficult it was for her to default in a responsibility.

"I'm not sure. There's a possibility...well, I might be moving... Yes, all very sudden. I had no idea when I left on Friday afternoon... I'll telephone again as soon as—" Grace stood and paced to the length of the cord. "I apologize. I'm sorry to disappoint you."

She replaced the receiver, crying too much to say *goodbye*.

"Grace, darling, I'm so sorry—" Karl followed her into the bedroom.

"Not now, Karl. I have a lot of big decisions to make. So much to figure out. We can talk in the morning."

Twenty bricks of gold hadn't redeemed him. Couldn't buy her forgiveness. "But sweetheart—"

She raised both hands in the unmistakable motion of *stop*.

Monday, 26 August, 1946
Munich, Germany

KARL STRAIGHTENED UP the sofa and sitting room, trying to make it look like he hadn't slept there again.

The room service waiter rolled in their tray and set up a fine breakfast over starched linen. He poured coffee from a silvered pot, accepted his tip, and retreated.

"Sweetheart, the food's here."

Grace came out, dressed for the day. He glanced behind her but didn't see her suitcase. She had made the bed as if the room had no maid service.

Since she took the separate upholstered chair, he sat across from her on the sofa, hoping it wouldn't be his bed again tonight.

She appeared more relaxed than in several days, sipping her coffee and nibbling at toast and jam. "Where are your mother and Marta?"

"They took breakfast early and wanted to ride through the old neighborhood. I would have gone with them, but you didn't seem up to it." He broke open a *brotchen* and slathered it with jam.

"I've spent a long time thinking about this, Karl. Praying, really." She didn't make eye contact with him.

He feared the worst.

"I want to take some time to get to know you—come to understand who you really are."

A tiny slice of hope pierced the heavy velvet curtains. "As long as you need, Grace. I will do anything you ask. Just please give our marriage a chance."

He fought to control his intense emotions, fearing that if she witnessed the passion in his heart and mind she would run and not look back. He must not frighten her now. *What can I say that will reassure her?* "I will never lie to you again. Ever."

"Everything I expected about our future has changed. Nothing but a blank slate stretches forward from this day." She sipped coffee with quivering lips. "Are we going to live here?"

His jaw tensed. *Complete honesty.* "In order to get the business functioning again and continue investigation for the Nuremberg Trials, I need to be in Munich. Do you agree?"

"Is this forever? Living in Germany, I mean?"

Pacing to the window and back, he lay out the dream. "I envision linking to a new branch in Atlanta or New York City someday. Father talked about such ideas for years. We could move to America if someone else managed the Munich base."

He squinted and studied her face. "We'll make those choices together. Equally. I do not want you to feel trapped."

"There's one thing I absolutely insist upon." Tears and shock were gone. This new side of Grace lay out the terms on which she might stay.

"What is that?"

"You have to tell the Viertels in Texas. They deserve to know."

"I've borne that guilt since learning the truth myself. I assume his body is buried in a German Army graveyard under my name. I'll find the plot and make sure he gets shipped home with full honors. Bill can help."

"Will you go to Texas and talk to the family? Tell them about their son?"

This would be the hardest feat imaginable, but his answer mattered more than all the other promises he made.

"I will go to Atlanta and level with your parents, and I will go to Texas and tell the Viertels of my duplicity. Furthermore, I suspect they have very little income without Henry. No doubt his father's heart disease is expensive. I will support his parents for the rest of their lives."

She nodded. "That's the kind of man I thought I'd married."

Karl took her hand. "Grace, my beloved, you are kind as forgiveness itself. I love you with all my being." His turn came for the sting of tears.

He bent, hoping for a kiss to seal their agreement. She raised her lips to him, but soon pulled away and curled her head low, supported in both hands.

"I'm concerned about your illness. Is this because of something you ate?"

"You really don't know?" A smile escaped her pale face. "We must get our names straight and have our marriage—legally registered or whatever. Frau von Steuben can't be having a Viertel baby. Or is it the other way around?"

"Baby? You're expecting?"

She met his eyes with a slow smile. "I'm married to you, whoever you are, and we're having a baby."

"But we always—"

"Except for once. Remember?"

His glance darted to the side as the memory burst with a sense of awe. "Once?"

"That's all it takes." She gave him a brow-shrug.

A baby. The possibility overwhelmed him. "Wow. Wonderful." His gaze dropped to her abdomen, but he saw nothing yet of the growing miracle. "Amazing."

He moved around the coffee table and went on one knee by her side. Hoping not to be rebuffed, he placed a palm over their developing child. "We don't have to wait for our family." His happiness bordered on being giddy. "Our honeymoon baby comes already."

He stretched up for her lips and surged with joy that she met him halfway. The kiss reminded him of the first time he dared, not so long ago in an Atlanta park. Not knowing what her response might be, fearing she wasn't ready to accept his love. Again today, she returned and even magnified his affection.

Karl stood and pulled her into his arms. For a long moment, he held Grace, his precious, undeserved gift.

She loosened her embrace and searched his face. "Would you marry me again, as Karl von Steuben? A simple wedding, but with the right names?" Her cheeks flushed with the proposal.

"Our child will be born rather soon after the wedding, won't he?" He teased her, aware of the importance to her of propriety.

"But he—or she—will be a legal von Steuben, and so will I."

He cupped her face in both hands, as if she were a tender rose. "And so will I."

Don't miss *Love Takes Flight* by Lee Carver, coming soon from Prism Book Group!

Volunteering in the Amazon to escape a broken heart, American R.N. Camille Ringold fears she has lost the chance to be married to a doctor and live well in suburbia. Serving two weeks with missionaries living out a sacred calling, she considers whether a more meaningful life might be hers.

When the Wings of Help plane is hijacked, she and missionary pilot Luke Strong escape into the jungle. Aided by a river village, they recover the plane, but she may be fired for returning to the U.S. late. Two weeks become four when she chooses to care for Luke through his malaria. Priorities change as experiences of faith mount. Where is the intersection of God's will and her selfish desires?

Here's a peek…

Morning broke bright and hot. When Luke came to haul a barrel of medicines to move the clinic to the next village, Camille approached him with a frown.

"I've been thinking all night about Pedro. I need to stay here. Any number of things could still go wrong with his leg."

"You can't stay if Dr. Flavio goes with us. You're only legal to practice medicine in Brazil as his assistant." Luke mopped his face with a worn bandana. Camille didn't seem to understand the laws they had to obey.

She planted her feet apart, hands on her hips. "I'm not practicing medicine. I just want to stay with Pedro long enough to make sure the artery holds and he doesn't contract a massive infection."

"That would still be illegal. Pedro looks good. He'll be okay."

Camille shook her head. "That pregnant woman, Josamil, had light contractions yesterday, and the baby is transverse. Dr. Flavio couldn't turn it. If labor doesn't push the head down, she could die screaming for help."

Luke tracked on a boy carrying a load down the bank to the plane. "You have to stay with the team. How are you going to get back if we leave you here?"

"Josamil's husband can deliver me to the next village by boat."

Luke snuffed a laugh. "It would take two weeks."

"I thought you said it was only fifteen minutes away."

"By air. It's on the other side of this finger of land. Going around by boat in dry season takes forever."

"Can't you stop back here on the way to Manaus?"

Luke could, but he didn't want to admit it. Leaving a volunteer—one who didn't speak the language—involved unnecessary risk.

The social worker, Angela, was team leader for this mission. He found her packing hygiene instruction posters. "We've got a problem. Camille wants to stay here by herself while we go on to the next village."

Camille followed him over, and he fell into a pattern of translating between her and Angela. As he explained the nurse's concerns, he watched Angela's resolve melt.

She waffled. "We can't take Pedro back to Manaus with us. There wouldn't be any way to return him for months."

"I'm not suggesting that. I just want to keep treating him here. The antibiotic doesn't prevent all the possible infections." Tenacious as a junkyard dog, Camille uncrossed her arms, hands up as if insisting that Luke see her reasoning. "He may need a different type. The wound will probably have to be debrided — trimmed and cleaned — or he may develop gangrene. And if he doesn't stay in bed, his artery stitches may not hold."

Angela rolled her big eyes.

Camille jumped back into the space. "And then there's Josemil."

Sensitive to the whole idea of motherhood, Luke winced. "But we don't know when she's due. It could be another week."

Camille shaded her eyes from the brilliant sun. "I don't think so. The baby had dropped before we arrived. If it doesn't move into the correct orientation, her labor will be rough. Maybe deadly."

"Doesn't the village have a midwife?" Luke looked to Angela for the answer.

"They do, but what they call a midwife out here is usually just someone who's been around for a few births. She's not necessarily trained, and wouldn't know about sanitation."

He translated that to Camille, beginning to see the danger.

"Lucas, you come back in two days?" Angela used two fingers and bits of English. "When we return to Manaus?"

He sighed, shoved his hands in his pockets, and glanced at kids playing with a small monkey.

Camille assumed victory without his confirmation. "I'd better pull out the medical supplies I'll need. And unpack my hammock."

"How are you going to communicate?" Surely she could see the impossibility of her proposal.

"I'll use the books I brought. I'm learning more words every day."

Maybe she had a gift for languages. Some people did. The pilots exercised final authority on every mission, but this decision didn't involve flying. If Alfredo agreed with Angela, he wouldn't argue.

Camille dashed a few yards away toward the pharmacy and equipment tent set up under a palm tree. "Jessica, wait a minute. I need some supplies."

Decisive and aggressive, that Camille. A Brazilian nurse would never do that. He went to find Alfredo.

Getting an executive decision from a bunch of Brazilians was harder than spearing fish in the stream. They were easy-going, non-confrontational people. He knew this well, reared more Brazilian than American himself.

Alfredo stopped loading while Luke explained the situation. He rubbed his knuckles against his cheek. "Josemil was the first convert in this village. We can't fly off and let her die in childbirth. It's a real pineapple." Spiny, hard to clean, a difficult job. "It would be disastrous for the start-up mission work here."

Luke left the loading to Alfredo and found Camille scrambling to put together a kit.

He advanced with caution into her whirlwind. "Are you sure about this?"

"Absolutely."

He tried to catch her eye, but she didn't slow down and look at him. "It isn't legal."

She never paused. "Who's to know?"

Setting aside medicines and resealing bags of pills, she gathered a small cache from their stock. "I can't let them die." She muttered under her breath.

"What about the patients in the next clinic?"

That stopped her for a moment. "I don't know them. But I know that brave little boy and the sweet mother with a baby riding sideways in her body. Sometimes I see the fear in their eyes and the

[379]

questions they don't ask—and I can't answer. I may not be able to save either of them, but they won't die due to indifference."

She tied a knot in her plastic bag of miracles. "Dr. Flavio can treat the next village."

Luke puffed his exasperation. "We'll be back on Saturday. There's no radio here, so be ready mid-afternoon."

He didn't like it. The other village couldn't be left out. People were dying there, too. Dying without Christ. They wouldn't be back for three months.

"Thanks, Luke. It'll be fine. I'll be ready on Saturday." Quite suddenly, she gave him a loose hug.

Brazilians gave air kisses barely touching cheeks, rather than a more personal embrace. Not resisting, he patted her on the back. Then she bent to her task again, leaving him with an armful of air and her warm touch on his shoulder. He stumbled backwards and turned, not looking to see who might have observed.

ABOUT THE AUTHOR

Lee has lived in six foreign countries and studied nine languages including German and French. She and her husband traveled extensively throughout Europe while living in Spain. A five-week World War II history tour covering the areas where her father-in-law fought created the stimulus for this book.

Lee taught biology and chemistry, served as a volunteer church musician, and in retirement was a missionary in the Brazilian Amazon. She is a member of ACFW and president of its ACFW-DFW "Ready Writers" Chapter, and is active in Stephen Ministry and Kid's Hope.

Learn more about Lee on her website at www.LeeCarverWriter.com.

Thank you for your Prism Book Group purchase! Visit our website to enjoy free reads, great deals, and entertaining, wholesome fiction!

www.ingramcontent.com/pod-product-compliance
Lightning Source LLC
Chambersburg PA
CBHW070619260626
47161CB00007B/2505